Praise for

EVENT

"The Roswell Incident—whether legend, fact, or some combination of both—has inspired countless novels and movies over the years, but David Lynn Golemon's *Event* peels back the layers of Roswell with refreshing originality. The action is spectacularly cinematic, the characters compelling, and the story is a flat-out adrenaline rush that pits real-world, cutting-edge military technology against a literally out-of-this-world threat. Even better, the Event Group itself is one of the best fictional agencies to arise in the literature of government conspiracies."

—*New York Times* bestselling authors
Judith and Garfield Reeves-Stevens

"Fans of UFO fiction will find this a great read, and fans of military fiction won't be disappointed either."

—SFSIGNAL.COM

"Golemon puts his military experience to good use in this promising debut sure to satisfy fans of *The X-Files*. . . . the plotting and hair's-breadth escapes evoke some of the early work of Preston and Child, and the author's premise offers a rich lode of material for the inevitable sequels."

—*Publishers Weekly*

"Imagine mixing in a blender a Tom Clancy novel with the movie *Predator* and the television series *The X-Files* . . . readers who enjoy nonstop action and lots of flying bullets will enjoy Golemon's first book in a projected series."

—*Library Journal*

EVENT

DAVID LYNN GOLEMON

St. Martin's Paperbacks

This is a work of fiction. All of the characters, organizations, and events portrayed in this novel are either products of the author's imagination or are used fictitiously.

EVENT

Copyright © 2006 by David Lynn Golemon.
Excerpt from *Legend* copyright © 2007 by David Lynn Golemon.

Library of Congress Catalog Card Number: 2006044417

ISBN: 0-312-37028-8
EAN: 978-0-312-37028-2

Printed in the United States of America

St. Martin's Press hardcover edition / September 2006
St. Martin's Paperbacks edition / April 2007

St. Martin's Paperbacks are published by St. Martin's Press, 175 Fifth Avenue, New York, NY 10010.

10 9 8 7 6 5 4 3 2 1

For Eunice and Valisa, Mom and Sis,
who are always in my thoughts.

My children,
Shaune, Brandon, and Katie, for just believing in me.

For Annemarie,
To put it frankly, the woman who saved my life.

And finally
for my father,
The only *real* hero I've ever known.
This one's for you, Pop!

ACKNOWLEDGMENTS

As any author will tell you, the process of listing all the kind and generous people who helped or assisted in some way to the actual foundation of any written story can be a daunting task. So it's always best to start at the top.

Heartfelt thanks go first and foremost to Thomas Dunne Books for taking a chance on a strange story from the desert. To Pete Wolverton (the best editor in the business), for guiding a novice novelist through the minefield of the written word. Pete's suggestions added heart to my soul and the end result was magical. To Katie, an assistant editor who patiently dealt with an out-of-control geek and answered every stupid question thrown her way (the publishing world will hear from Katie), and to every one of the editors at Thomas Dunne, who I'm sure thought about a career change right in the middle of editing *Event*. Now, for my agent, Bob Mecoy, the first believer in this little monster tale, here's to a long "E" Ticket ride, Bob!

I would like to thank a special man out in San Diego, Dr. Kenneth Vecchio of San Diego State University, for doing something for our boys overseas that not a lot of people think about; the special Abalone shell body armor mentioned in this book is real and on the wish list of this author to get it to the troops soonest! Along those same lines, kudos to Helicos BioSciences in Cambridge, Massachusetts, who are doing amazing things with their magical DNA sequencing machine, cutting precious time off a long and difficult process of sequencing.

With the exception of the M-2786 radio and the Cray Corporation's Europa XP series computer, all military hardware mentioned in this novel is real and either on the drawing board or in action. Also thanks go to the U.S. Department of Energy, who was very helpful in answering some very unnerving questions.

To the Mathies family of Babylon, New York, for treating a writer like a human being. It will never be forgotten.

For all those people in Roswell, New Mexico, who are tired of the notoriety. Someday it will all pay off, I promise.

And finally to all those people and friends I have failed (forgotten, let's be honest) to mention, thank you. Any mistakes or outright omissions are the author's responsibility.

AUTHOR'S NOTE

During the current times, it's easy for people to take for granted the men and women who are defending this country; right or wrong, opinion versus opinion, they are doing their jobs and doing things well in the most inhospitable conditions that can only be imagined by people who have been in war.

It is not the intention of this author or the publishers of this work to merely make the American military a mere prop in a fictional story. With the highest respect, we attempt to portray them in the highest regard possible. We would never disrespect their ability, their patriotism or their honor for the sake of realism.

But all those soldiers must admit, you would rather be fighting an enemy with a little more class than your current foe—after all, all monsters aren't bad.

PROLOGUE

Seventy-six miles northwest of Roswell, New Mexico
July 10, 1947

*T*he blowing sand stung like small buckshot striking his
face and exposed hands. The portly man held his hat
tight to his head as he ran from truck to truck shouting
at the drivers the best he could, repeating his commands
when the wind snatched his words away. He was becoming
hoarse with his repeated yelling over the sandstorm that had
arisen in the last fifteen minutes. The last truck driver in the
line of fifteen two-and-half-ton vehicles nodded, understanding that the convoy would wait on the side of rural
Highway 4 until this sudden show of desert fury subsided.

Dr. Kenneth Early, a metallurgist by profession, had been
placed in charge of arguably the most valuable pieces of
cargo in the history of the world, at least that's what he kept
telling himself. Garrison Lee had selected him personally to
make sure the crates they were transporting arrived safely in
Nevada. They would have flown to Las Vegas Army Airfield
but the dangers of an aerial mishap dictated they travel by
secure truck convoy, and Lee had provided ten of his best security people to guard this unusual cargo.

The doctor fought his way back to the lead truck and
waved at the driver inside, then proceeded to the green government Chevrolet at the head of the column. He opened the
rear door and was grateful for the shelter the car provided.

He removed his hat and shook it out, creating a small dust cloud and making his security driver cough.

"Sorry, it's really blowing out there," Early said as he threw his hat on the seat beside him, then took his thick glasses out of his coat. He placed them on his nose, then leaned forward, placing his elbows on the front seat. "Any luck with the radio yet?"

"Not a word, Doc, it's probably the storm; these army-surplus radios just aren't that good when it comes to weather."

"Damn, Lee will have my butt if we don't let him know we had to pull off, it screws up his time schedule," Early said trying to peer through the side window. "I don't much like sitting here out in the middle of nowhere."

"Me neither, Doc. To tell you the truth, knowing what's in those crates, hell, I can't seem to look at the world the same as I did yesterday." The driver swallowed and turned his head to look at Early. "There's some really bad scuttlebutt goin' round, Doc, really creepy stuff."

Early looked at the young army lieutenant, only attached to the group three months. "I know exactly what you mean, I'll feel better when we have it all safely at the new complex."

Early hadn't been bothered by the corpses as much as he had been downright afraid of that goddamn empty ten-foot-by-ten-foot container, or cage, as the rumors were saying. Lee had tried to keep the lid on all the talk going around, but what they were carrying to Nevada would haunt anyone who was there for many years to come. For Early, it was the image of that cage that kept slipping back into his thoughts like the flitting remembrance of a nightmare; he closed his eyes as he tried in vain to control a shiver.

"Who in the hell is this?" the lieutenant asked aloud.

Early opened his eyes and looked at the army officer. He watched as the man placed the radio handset down and pulled a Colt .45 automatic from the holster he carried on his belt.

Early looked up through the windshield and was shocked to see three men dressed in black. He narrowed his vision and adjusted the fit of his glasses in an attempt to peer through the sand that was washing across the side of the road.

"Are they wearing hoods and goggles?" he asked, but the lieutenant had already opened the door, allowing the howl of the wind to take the doctor's question and scatter it among the blowing sand.

"This is a United States government convoy. You men—"

That was as far as the young lieutenant got. As Early watched in horror, a black-clad man in the center of the three strangers raised what looked like a Thompson submachine gun and fired a burst of three rounds into the upper body of the army officer, slamming him first into the doorjamb and then to the roadway. The wind quickly took away the mist of blood that had exploded out of the lieutenant's back.

"My God!" Early screamed.

It suddenly dawned on him that the car was not the best place to be at that moment. He quickly slid across the seat and scrambled out into the wind and sand, slipping once and falling to one knee, then finally gaining his feet and using the rear quarter of the Chevy for a guide. He fought his way to cover, all thoughts of protecting the debris and bodies lost in his panic to escape. He hunched low and started to make his way to the first truck in line when five .45-caliber bullets slammed into him from behind. Early hit the windswept road and rolled into the side ditch. As his life's blood was soaking into the sand, he saw a tall man dressed in black combat gear standing over him. The man looked around, then slowly leaned over, going to one knee and placing a gloved hand on Early's quivering shoulder. The man spoke apologetically, as if he had done anything other than to brutally end Early's life.

"I'm sorry for this, Doctor, but your boss doesn't understand what it takes to make this country safe from our enemies," he said loud enough to be heard above the blowing wind. A confused Early could only look up at him.

"Controlled violence, planned well and executed, is a valuable tool, a new one to be sure, but one our new enemies understand." The man looked around a moment and shook *his head and leaned even closer to the doctor's ear. Gunfire had erupted up and down the line of trucks. "I'm just sorry it's you and these American boys that got in our way," the man said sadly, shaking his head. "A goddamn shame."*

The killer in black lowered his head as he watched Dr. Early take his last breath, then he stood and started shouting orders.

The rest of the convoy personnel met the same brutal fate. And together with their cargo gathered from a small desert air base in New Mexico, they would all disappear into legend, and a mystery was created that would haunt the country for over sixty years, creating the largest cover-up in American history.

Among the blowing desert sands, now mixed with the blood of the dead and lost, the Roswell Incident was born.

ONE

The USS *Carl Vinson* sailed smoothly through the calm waters of the Pacific. Her huge mass parted the sea 320 miles off the coast of South America, leaving a wake of incandescent colors and sea life that rolled and churned after her four massive bronze propellers.

The Nimitz-class supercarrier was on her way home after a cruise of six months in the south-central Pacific. Her home port was Bremerton, Washington, and that was where most of the crew's families would be waiting anxiously for their men and women to return from their long voyage. Her huge engines pushed her through the Pacific at twenty-six knots.

Flight operations on the *Vinson* were in preparation for the fighter and bomber air wings to lift off the following afternoon for their home bases of Miramar and Oakland. The only planes flying this morning were the carrier's combat air patrol, better known as CAP, and they now cruised at twenty thousand feet and were one hundred klicks out. The morning had been calm and without incident for the two old but formidable Grumman F-14 Super Tomcats when the first radio call was transmitted from the *Vinson,* call name Ponderosa.

"Range Rider flight, this is Ponderosa. Do you copy? Over."

Lieutenant Commander Scott "Derringer" Derry had his

visor down as he looked into the rising yellow disk of the morning sun, reminding him of the Persian Gulf and his many combat missions over Iraq. As he thumbed the transmit button on his joystick, he looked to his left and slightly behind, eyeing his wingman, satisfied he was still in position and no doubt hearing the *Carl Vinson* the same as himself. "Ponderosa, this is Range Rider lead, copy five by five, over."

"Range Rider One, we have an intermittent contact south at eight hundred miles and closing. Advise this information comes from Bootlegger and not Ponderosa. We have no contact at this time. Over."

Under the mask, Derry pursed his lips. *Bootlegger* was the call sign for the guided-missile cruiser riding shotgun for the *Carl Vinson*. The USS *Shiloh,* with her Aegis tracking and fire-control system, could supply better air intelligence than the huge carrier, so her information was always acted upon.

Derry once again took a quick glance over his shoulder at his wingman. His partner gave a small wag of the huge fighter's wings, indicating he had the gist of the call.

"Range Rider copies, Ponderosa. Inform lead of any target aspect changes, over."

"Roger flight lead, Ponderosa will advise. Stay alert to TAC 3, Bootlegger will monitor. Over," the *Vinson* answered.

Derry clicked his transmit button twice in acknowledgment. "Do you have anything yet, Pete?" he asked his radar intercept officer, or RIO, Pete Klipp.

"Negative, boss, I don't have a thing on scope at this time."

Derry raised the dark visor on his helmet and once again looked down and back at his wingman, Lieutenant J. G. Jason Ryan, call sign Vampire, who was flying smoothly as ever as he brought his F-14 level with his commander.

"Does your RIO have anything, Vampire?"

"Negative lead, we're clear," Ryan answered.

"Understood. Let's go see what we can see," Derry said.

The two navy fighters made a slow turn to the south and climbed.

• • •

The Combat Direction Center on the *Carl Vinson* was darkened to the point where the outlines of the operators were cast in a multicolored, luminous veil caused by the screens they monitored. On one of these screens was an air-search radar patch-through from the USS *Shiloh*.

"Still nothing?" Lieutenant Commander Isaac Harris asked.

The radar specialist adjusted the bandwidth on the monitor and looked over his shoulder at his commanding officer; a confused look crossed his features. "Comes and goes, sir, first solid, then nothing. Then on its next sweep it's there, big as a barn, and then vanishes."

"Diagnostics?" Harris asked.

"Clean, Commander, and *Shiloh* also reports their equipment is working fine, everything is up and to spec."

Harris rubbed his chin and straightened. "This is damn strange." He leaned forward and asked, "Heading change?"

"Negative, course still holding on a line to *Vincent*," the technician answered. By this time a few of the other radar, sonar, and communications operators were leaning back in their chairs and watching with mild concern. Harris squeezed the young man on his shoulder and turned to his station, a large red-vinyl-covered chair raised on a pedestal so he could see the entire floor of the CDC. He lifted the red bridge phone that was mounted on the chair's side and waited, looking hard at his operators until they all returned to their screens.

"Captain, this is Harris in CDC, we have a developing situation in our defensive perimeter." He waited a moment for the captain of the *Carl Vinson* to respond. "Yes, I recommend the Alert One aircraft to be launched and bring the battle group to battle stations."

Up on the massive flight deck, an announcement squawked: "Stand by to launch Alert One!" The message was repeated, and then came a call that brought everyone above and belowdecks to their feet running: "General quarters, general quarters, all hands man battle stations, all hands man battle stations, this is no drill, repeat, no drill." On catapult number one, with its locking gear removed, the pilot saluted the plane captain on deck who was in control of the launch. He placed his head and back firmly into the backrest of his ejection seat and held tightly to the sides of the Tomcat's canopy. The first of the two Grumman fighters screamed down the deck at full military power as the steam catapult literally threw it into the air. It was quickly followed by the second F-14 on full afterburner.

After the sneak attack on the USS *Cole,* on October 12, 2000, in the Persian Gulf, American warships had started taking security very seriously. It would be a terrorist's wet dream to strike at an American symbol like a Nimitz-class carrier.

Copy, Ponderosa, understand Alert One has been launched. Range Rider out." Derry turned his head slightly to the left after acknowledging the call from the *Carl Vinson.* "It's go time, Vampire." There was no verbal answer to the flight leader as just two clicks of Ryan's transmit button acknowledged his readiness. "Let's go see what's out there," Derry called out.

Both F-14 fighters lit their afterburners as a steady stream of JP-4 jet fuel exploded into the exhaust nozzle of the huge GE-400 turbofan engines, causing the nacelles in the exhaust bell to open wider to allow the expanding gases to escape, creating over fifty-four thousand pounds of thrust. At the computer's directive, the wings on the two Tomcats started to retract to align along the aluminum fuselage as they crept toward supersonic. With the wings tucked in, both Tomcats screamed through the air, their outer skins heating up with the friction of passing air.

"I've got it!" Ensign Henry "Dropout" Chavez, Ryan's backseater called. "Five hundred miles and closing."

"We have it now," Derringer reported over the secure link. Both aircraft knew their transmissions were being monitored by the *Carl Vinson* and every ship in Task Force 277.7.

"SOB, it's huge," Dropout said into his mask, and then: "Damn!"

"What's wrong?" Ryan asked.

"Bogey just went ghost on me, disappeared like it was never there."

"Derringer, did you copy that?"

"We have the same thing; last read was three-fifty and closing. Keep your eyes open."

"Roger."

All thoughts for Ryan became reflexive as he felt the thrust of the two massive engines pushing him back into his seat. His flight suit was filling with air around his legs and chest, forcing the blood to stay put in his brain.

"There it is again. Damn, this thing is big," Dropout repeated.

"Keep cool, I need closure rates, not comments."

"It's gone off the scope again, but last rate of closure was over three thousand miles per hour. She's really moving, altitude is the same, we should see target at any time, a little to the left and below us about two thousand feet."

Two thousand is a little close, Ryan thought. "Derringer, recommend we climb another three thousand, might be a better safety margin when we need it."

Derry shook his head. "Negative, Vampire, just follow my lead and put a cork in it, concentrate on finding the ghost, over."

Ryan shook his head, he *knew* they were too low. The possibilities of a head-on collision were too great to just ignore, but at the moment, he had no options but to obey his flight leader.

"I have a glimmer . . . *oh God, what is that?*" Derry's RIO asked, his voice becoming lower, almost a whisper to himself.

Ryan scanned the sea below and ahead of his Tomcat; he saw nothing. "You have it?" he asked.

"Vampire, hard left and climb!" Derry called loudly over the radio.

The voice coming through the headphones in Ryan's helmet was panicked. He had never heard his commander lose his composure, but it automatically made Ryan climb and turn hard without asking for details. His reactions were still the fastest in the squadron as his F-14 banked hard left as he applied flaps and power and the fighter jet shot higher.

"Ponderosa, Ponderosa, we have a bogey inbound your position," Derry said.

"Range Rider, this is Ponderosa, we have your flight on scope but no bogey, confirm again. Over."

Ryan came out of his turn a little later than he would have liked. When he regained his senses, after the extreme g-forces of his maneuver, he scanned the area and finally found his flight leader about ten miles ahead and slightly to his right. Derry's Tomcat was not the only craft in the sky. His eyes widened as the full impact of what he was seeing registered in his mind.

"Vampire, are you behind me?" Derry asked over the radio.

Ryan could hear the breathing of his RIO; it was one of those noises you grew so accustomed to that you never noticed it, but now it seemed amplified.

"Roger, Derringer, right here. Don't get too close to that thing," Ryan said as he looked at the most terrifying and wondrous object he had ever seen in his life.

"I've got to get a closer look at this thing, Vampire, stay back on my six," Derry ordered.

Jason Ryan, Lieutenant Junior Grade, United States Navy, knew that what his flight leader was attempting was dangerous, but all he could do was watch as Derry's Tomcat crept closer to the flying saucer.

The two Super Tomcats were about a mile behind the UFO. The shape was what they had always expected or thought they would have seen—if they ever saw one.

These images, along with many others, flickered in and out of the minds of the crews in the two fighters. The craft was round and looked like two plates that were sitting open face to open face. It was silver in color and had no discernible anticollision lights. Derry estimated it to be close to four hundred feet in diameter and at least fifty feet at its thickest point in the centerline mass. Then the words coming through his headphones finally registered and brought his attention back to the here and now.

"I've lost contact with the *Vincent*," his RIO was saying.

"Come on, you mean we lost 'em just like that?" Derry asked.

"Sir, we have nothing. The *Vinson* is either off the air or we're not transmitting."

"We get the same over here," Ryan said over the radio.

"Okay, we'll go standard. We try and contact. If nothing happens, a warning shot. We *cannot* let that thing break three hundred miles to Ponderosa, is that clear?"

"Roger," Ryan answered. For the past thirty seconds, the electrical tone in his headset had informed him that his Sidewinder missiles were locked on and were tracking the object. But even better, Ryan knew the gun cameras embedded in the belly and wing of his aircraft were filming this thing. As an added measure, and because of the size and unknown composition of the strange craft, Ryan made sure to also target a long-range Phoenix missile with its larger warhead and superior range.

Derry knew their strategy was flawed. He didn't know how far a weapon from this thing could reach, as its range and capabilities were a mystery. The assumption of a line three hundred miles out from the carrier was just a guess, as a line had been drawn in the sky instead of the sand. Had this been a normal aircraft, a hundred miles was the limit of any antiship missile outside the U.S. inventory. The French-made Exocet antiship missile made infamous in the Falklands war by its sinking of the HMS *Sheffield* was now the weapon of choice for most of the outlaw nations that threatened ships at sea. But this thing was not a normal air-breathing vehicle.

Derry cleared his throat. "Unidentified aircraft, we are United States Navy fighter planes to your rear. You are approaching a quarantine zone and you are hereby ordered to identify yourself and turn your aircraft immediately to a westerly heading, over."

Ryan heard the call repeated twice more by Derry and shook his head. He assumed this object wouldn't feel threatened by their two small aircraft. As he approached, a large and jagged hole was increasing in size at the rear of the saucer.

"Derringer, looks like this thing has had a hole punched in it."

"Vampire, stay in place with your finger on the trigger, we may have a . . . a . . . Well, something's in distress here. That's damage of some kind. I'm going to get a closer look."

Ryan watched as Derringer's F-14 started its advance toward the giant saucer. He nudged his throttles forward just a little; he knew his wingman would never notice. He watched his flight leader's Tomcat as it approached from the rear. The huge jet wobbled from wingtip to wingtip as it was caught in the saucer's vortex.

"Vampire, there's a situation on board that craft. It looks like they're venting something, you seeing it?"

Ryan saw what looked like some form of liquid as it streamed from several smaller holes in the craft's aft compartments.

"I'm seeing, just not believing," Ryan answered.

USS *Carl Vinson*, three hundred miles north

Men were speaking in quiet tones as they watched their screens. It seemed the temperature had risen ten degrees in the last few minutes as they waited for incoming information. Most of them had never felt this helpless.

"What have we got here, Derringer?" Harris asked. Static was the only answer he received.

Suddenly an enlisted man said loudly, "Captain on deck!"

Harris turned to see the captain of the *Vinson* leaving his marine escort outside as he entered the darkened Combat Direction Center. His stern expression told Harris that the captain was deeply concerned for the safety of *his* ship.

"At ease, continue with your work. What's Range Rider saying, Commander?"

"No answer yet, it may be interference or some sort of jamming, we're still evaluating. The Alert One aircraft should be in place in three minutes, Captain."

"I see. Keep trying to raise them," the captain ordered as he sat down in the chair normally reserved for Harris. The officer who drove one of the most powerful warships ever built watched his men performing their duties. He made no comment. The only indication of concern was the way he closed his eyes and listened to the calls to Range Rider that were going unanswered.

"Sir, Range Rider's radar signature has just gone intermittent. When the bogey goes, they go. Whatever electronic field that craft is emitting is now screening our own fighters." As Harris leaned over the man's shoulder again, he saw nothing on the green sweep of the radar. Then two small blips and one that measured at least four hundred feet or more in diameter appeared and then vanished on the next sweep.

"Two-eighty and closing," radar called out.

"Give me the status of the battle group," the captain asked, as he stood and started for the bridge, meaning he wanted the report now and while he was on the move. Overhead could be heard the roar of the steam catapult and thump of tires as another flight of F-14 fighters lifted skyward.

"All ships report in at battle ready, Captain. Air defenses are up and close-in weapons support is warmed and armed," Harris responded. He was referring to the Phalanx twenty-millimeter automatic cannons and Sea Sparrow missiles that were a major part of the carrier's close-in point protection. But their real defense was the Aegis cruiser *Shiloh* with her advanced missile defense system.

The captain heard the report as he paused at the hatch and then started for the bridge. Harris watched him go and rubbed his temple as he eased back into his chair. This close to home waters and the current threat board was clear. Of course, ships not much different from this one were sailing into home waters once when someone hit Pearl Harbor.

"Still no communication with Range Rider?" Harris asked.

"COM is clear."

"Sir, we have a second bogey inbound to Range Rider at four hundred miles behind the first bogey and closing at a high rate of speed. This contact is strong!"

Harris jumped from his seat and watched as the second contact closed on the first object and the trailing F-14s.

"Second contact closing at over Mach two point five," said a second, louder voice.

"What in the hell is happening here?" Harris said as he removed the bridge phone from its cradle.

Dropout, Ryan's RIO, caught another blip on his screen. "We have an inbound, mark it possible hostile, coming up our six and closing fast."

"Talk to me."

"Can't calculate distance and speed, it's moving too fast," Chavez said, close to panic.

"Damn, did you copy that, Derringer?" Ryan asked.

"Copy, Vampire, where in the hell are the alert aircraft?" Derry said, scanning the sky quickly for the two Tomcats that should be there any second.

Ryan didn't answer; at that moment his F-14 lurched in the sky, throwing him against his harness. His Tomcat quickly lost a hundred feet of altitude as something shot overhead in a blur of silver. The wings of his fighter wobbled uncontrollably for a moment and the nose dipped in a downward spasm. They were caught in the wake of a second saucer as it streaked toward the first. Several warning lights flashed on the Tomcat's control board. Ryan fought the stick, advancing his throttles to try to gain his original altitude. At that moment, a sick greenish light washed over their clear cockpit canopy, casting an eerie glow on themselves and the interior of the jet. The Tomcat's engines lost their whine and the engine-failure light came on. First engine one, then two, flashed their red warnings. A silence now filled the cockpit with the exception of a computerized voice warning of engine stall, and the eerie quiet outside was almost as loud as the engines it had replaced. He didn't panic as training kicked in and he went into automatic. He fought the stick, bringing it forward, then to the left; all the while a soft hum now filled his ears, seemingly coming from outside the aircraft.

"Flameout! Flameout! Range Rider Two is going tits up; repeat, we're a dead stick," Ryan called. *"Mayday, Mayday!"*

"Aw fuck!" Henry said almost too calmly from the backseat as he clenched his teeth together.

Ryan brought the stick all the way forward, at the same time lifting both feet from the pedals that controlled the Tomcat's rudder, allowing the ship to automatically control the spin they were in. This brought the Tomcat to a nose-down attitude, a straight position to gain speed, and now the huge aircraft hurtled toward the sea below like an arrow.

"Trying engine restart," Ryan said, keeping his voice under control.

The Tomcat was equipped with an air-powered generator used for emergencies like this. Rushing air caught vanes, and those turned a generator, and that in turn supplied the aircraft with enough power to restart her engines without the help of ground facilities. At least that was the way the engineers had designed her. This was one scenario you trained for but never actually did outside of a simulator. The high-pitched whine of the rushing stream of air outside the cockpit was close to unbearable.

Derry heard the distress call made by Vampire as his wingman plummeted to the sea. He thumbed the safety release for his Sidewinder missiles, but he couldn't get a lock. He was about to pull away from the craft to his front and try to eye the new assault coming up his back when his own Tomcat was thrown forward as if it were a toy. The tail section was pushed down and the nose went straight up. The twin vertical stabilizers were sheared away as if they were made of eggshell. In the split second before the cockpit was engulfed in flames, Derringer saw the second ship as it rammed him. The F-14 Tomcat disintegrated into a million pieces as the force of the impact, combined with its speed, pulled the plane apart. The wreckage scattered into the wind and pieces of debris fell smoking to a watery grave below.

Another strange light, this time bluish in color, shot forward from the second saucer and engulfed the first. The two ships were now encased in a giant silver-blue sphere.

USS *Carl Vinson*

W e've lost contact with the two bandits, sir."
Harris made no comment. He watched as the single blip of one of his fighters suddenly lit the screen. It was losing altitude fast.

"Sir, Range Rider Two has declared an emergency, both engines are out," the radio operator called, finally hearing the distress calls from Ryan.

"Where in the hell is Range Rider lead?" Harris asked.

"Only Rider Two is on the scope, sir. Our Alert One aircraft are almost to the intercept point."

"Nothing on the two targets?" Harris asked.

"No, sir. They have gone completely off the scope. *Shiloh* verifies also."

Silence filled the Combat Direction Center as Harris moved for the bridge phone, but placed it back in its cradle when he heard the announcement to launch rescue choppers. Harris stood in silence. His hand moved to his chin and he closed his eyes. "What in the hell just happened?"

• • •

T he Tomcat was falling too damn fast, Ryan thought. He
    had tried to ignite his engines twice with no luck. His
    panel was still brightly lit, but for reasons he couldn't un-
derstand, the big GE engines wouldn't fire. There was nothing left for the bird to do but fall from the sky.

"That's it, Henry, we gotta go, man, punch out now!"
Ryan flipped a switch and allowed juice from the onboard
generator to warm up his weapons system. *At least this
works.* He instantly selected the Phoenix on his control stick
and received an intermittent target lock. Ryan pulled the
trigger and was satisfied as the large Phoenix shot off the
Tomcat's centerline launch rail.

Henry Chavez grabbed for the yellow-striped handle over
his seat and swallowed hard. "Eject! Eject! Eject!" he cried
three times, and closed his eyes.

The canopy separated with a loud bang as Chavez pulled
the handle. The force of the ejection shot him out of the jet
at over a hundred miles an hour. The blast sheet that deployed when the handle was pulled down covered his helmet and head, so Ensign Chavez never saw the piece of
debris that killed him. A chunk of aluminum housing from
the destroyed Range Rider One stuck him in his visor-
covered face, the debris sinking straight to the back of his
skull.

Ryan's mind was spinning as his chute deployed and his
ejection seat separated. He was fiercely concentrating on his
own survival. He tried to turn and finally caught sight of the
Phoenix's contrail through the sky and watched as he saw
the long-range missile strike the second saucer, sending
pieces flying off its aft quarter. The saucer lost altitude but
quickly recovered, and it and the first saucer disappeared
into the clouds on a northeasterly heading.

Now as Ryan looked about, he knew Derry was gone.
Distant splashes in the water showed him where his commander's remains were striking the sea. The sky was now
clear except for the two chutes that settled lazily for the sea.
Ryan watched as Chavez's chute swung back and forth in

big hitching motions. Ryan looked closer and saw Chavez's arms hanging loosely at his sides. The lieutenant closed his eyes a moment, knowing in his heart what the uncontrolled chute meant.

TWO

Augustus Simpson Tilly had been on this desert since the end of the Korean War. Buck, his mule, had been with him for a third of that time, and they had both become something of a legend in these parts, along with the mountains he prospected. The locals referred to him as Crazy Gus or Old Nut Case, depending on their age. The old man knew they called him those things and didn't really care. He heard the whispers and the not-too-quiet laughter that followed him in the Broken Cactus Bar and Grill in Chato's Crawl, just down the road from Apache Junction. Julie Dawes, the owner of the bar, would shush them, then buy Gus a beer and tell him they didn't know any better. But Gus knew deep down they did. He knew how he looked to others: old, grizzled, dirty, and every year of his life chiseled onto a face that had seen the worst in others.

Gus had lived through the Chosin Reservoir in Korea, a long and forgotten valley that most history books try to skip over. It was one of those moments that would haunt the army and Marines forever. Gus had had to live through strapping the bodies of his best friends to the sides of tanks just to get them out of that frozen valley of death. He watched as men, *his* men, perished in the cold and snow. It had been a bloody, grim time, and after seeing what mankind was capable of doing to one another, he chose the company of Buck. And the reason way he now lived in the desert wasn't just for chasing the legend of a lost gold mine and all its riches. He was there just to be warm. He lamented the scorching heat to those that would listen, but inside it warmed him in places that he thought the sun could never reach again because of those freezing, desperate days in Korea. The desert had become his closest friend for the last fifty years, his shelter from a world he had found was better off without him.

He and Buck had been walking since sunup to get to the base of the mountains before midday. He wanted to start digging at a new site he had discovered the week before. He had told Buck the site showed some promise.

Without warning, the wind suddenly sprang up with a vengeance from the south. Sand pummeled the old man and his mule like a solid wall of speeding needles. The mule bucked and kicked; the braying of the animal was lost in the sudden fury of the wind and blowing sand. Gus quickly pulled his red bandanna up over his mouth and nose, then pulled at the leather reins, trying to steady the animal while holding his time-battered, brown fedora on his head with the other.

"Whoa there, Buck, settle down, it's only a little blow," he shouted, but the wind kidnapped his voice.

The mule's instincts were telling it this was anything but a natural windstorm, and deep down the old man knew it too. The temperature had dropped at least ten degrees and there hadn't been so much as a whisper of breeze just a moment before. Gus Tilly had lived by these mountains all of his adult life and this had never happened before, not like this. And besides, he knew Buck wasn't afraid of much, but this bizarre weather change was scaring the senses out of his friend.

The pots, pans, and other necessities of the old prospector rattled as Buck tried to shed himself of the weight of the loaded pack. As Gus desperately tried to calm him, a great roar filled the ears of both man and animal. The old man lowered himself to the ground as the very air above him ripped apart and something passed by with an ear-shattering roar. He was covered by condensed vapor brought down from the white clouds above, and then another roar, not unlike the first, tore the sky. As suddenly as it had begun, the wind died and the sand settled. The old man looked at the sky and then at the mule as Buck stepped uneasily as he looked around at the now quiet desert, sniffing the air. His ears flicked.

"Damnedest thing I ever saw, Buck boy. What d' you say?" he asked, pulling the dust-caked bandanna down from his face.

The mule just looked at his owner and then showed his teeth, all eight of them. But before he could comment further, a loud explosion roared across the desert, and at that moment the old-timer was suddenly thrown off his feet and onto his back, landing on small rocks and scrub, knocking the breath from his old body. He rolled over and placed his hands over his head. The rumble that followed took what little air remained in his lungs. Buck tried to spread his strong legs for better support, then suddenly lost his balance and collapsed. Going down first to its knees, the animal then rolled over, smashing the carefully loaded pack. The ground shook, rolled, and then settled, and finally all was still again.

The old man gasped for air and tried willing himself to breathe. He rolled over onto his aching back and peered up and saw the low foothills and then the mountains. They were the same as they had been the last half century of his life. Quiet and still. But he felt a strangeness within him that hadn't been there a few moments before. He swallowed and propped himself on his elbows, then rolled back over and gained his feet. He had never given the mountains a second thought, but now he was afraid to look at them too closely. As the old man looked on, several jackrabbits sprang from their holes and sprinted out into the desert, away from the mountains. A coyote then bounded across his vision, heading the same way as the rabbits, although it was not in pursuit. The coyote looked back at the rocky-faced mountains, then swung its head forward and sped along even faster, tongue lolling from its mouth.

The mule's reins were still clutched in Gus's strong hand, and he numbly watched as Buck first rolled to the right and then went to his knees, then to his feet, as items fell from the pack. The mule looked at the old man accusingly as if he were responsible for this embarrassing episode.

Gus shook his head to clear it. "Son of a bitch, things are gettin' a mite strange out here, and don't go lookin' at me, I didn't knock you off your feet."

But Buck wasn't listening; he pulled the reins free of the old man's grip, and like the rabbits and the coyote, he ran from the mountains as fast as his heavy load would allow. Gus could only watch in astonishment as the mule sped into the desert. He slowly turned and looked at the now quiet and, for a reason he didn't understand, menacing Superstition Mountains.

It had taken Gus over an hour to find Buck. He had followed the trail of pots, pans, and shovels until he came across his companion chewing some sagebrush down by an old washout. The mule casually munched away as if the blow that had happened upon them earlier was nothing but a distant memory. The tarp was hanging loose at the mule's side, and the old man's few possessions that hadn't fallen out during Buck's furious romp were dangling from the damaged pack. The old man cussed the mule as he tried to put everything back in and repack. The huge animal was outright ignoring Gus.

"Go ahead and act like it wasn't you running like a scared jackrabbit," he grumbled. He walked around and looked the mule in the eyes. "You could have broken your leg running across this hardpan like that!" Gus scratched his four-day-old growth of beard and softened his voice. "Well, that wind had me spooked a little myself, old boy, don't feel too bad." He stroked the animal's nose. Buck twitched his right eye and flicked his ears, but kept chewing.

"Okay, ignore me then, you old bastard. See if I talk to you any more today. Now let's get back up there and get to work." He grabbed the reins and started to tug. The mule, after some initial resistance, started forward, still chewing.

The old man adjusted the fedora he wore high on his head and wiped a line of sweat from the side of his face.

"But, Lord, it sure is gonna be a scorcher," he mumbled, looking at the sun. "Let's get movin', boy, gold's awaitin'," he said without much enthusiasm as he once again started his now reluctant trek to the mountain.

PART ONE
THE EVENT GROUP

Those who cannot remember the past are condemned to repeat it.

— GEORGE SANTAYANA

Welcome back, my friends to the show that never ends, so
glad you could attend, come inside, come inside . . .

— EMERSON, LAKE, & PALMER

THREE

Major Jack Collins walked into the Gold City Pawnshop at the appointed time. He placed his carryall on the floor and wiped the sweat from his forehead. The air-conditioned shop was a break from the relentless heat outside. With his last ten years in and out of deserts around the globe, heat was something the major was used to, but never really embraced.

Collins stood six foot two inches tall and his close-cropped hair was dark. His features were chiseled from thousands of hours in suns not unlike the Nevada one. He removed the sunglasses from his eyes and let his vision adjust to the dimness of the old shop. He glanced around at several of the items on display, sad treasures people had parted with in order to stay in Vegas, or to get the hell out, depending upon their disposition. Collins himself gambled with items a little more precious than money, usually the lives of men, including his own.

A man stood silent in the back room of the pawnshop. Six cameras arranged throughout the large shop area were motion-sensitive, capturing the new arrival in every detail, from the line of sweat that coursed down the man's temple to the expensive sunglasses he held in his right hand, the nice sport jacket and light blue shirt he wore. The observer

turned to a computer screen and cross-matched the image of
the stranger with one that had been programmed earlier. A
red chicken-wire laser charted the man's body, cutting his
head and body into reference points for the computer to
match. At the same time another invisible laser read the
small glass area that blended nicely with the antique thumb-
depression plate on the door handle he had used to enter the
shop. On another high-definition computer screen a large,
detailed print appeared; this one read the minute swirls and
valleys of his thumbprint. A print, perfect in every detail,
flashed onto the screen, then the computer broke the print
down to eighteen different points; lines indicating matches
went from the computer-stored print to the one just taken
from the door handle. Only seven points of match were used
to convict people in a court of law, but this print matchup
called for a minimum of ten. A name appeared in the lower
right-hand corner of the screen, followed seconds later by an
image of the man himself. In this picture he wore a green
beret and sat unsmiling for the camera. The scroll beneath
the picture read, *Major Jack Samuel Collins, United States
Army Special Operations. Last duty station Kuwait City, 5th
Special Forces Group, TDA this date to Department 5656.*
The man behind the door snickered to himself as he read the
screen. *Temporary duty assignment my ass,* the old man
thought, *not if the senator and Doc Compton have anything
to say about it.*

Collins looked around again and tapped one of the glass-
topped counters twice with the ring that was embossed with
the United States Military Academy logo. "Who's minding
the store?"

"You break that counter, friend, you're buying it," a voice
stated flatly from the back of the store.

The major looked into the gloom of the dingy, dusty
pawnshop. Back among the hanging musical instruments
and amplifiers, he saw a smallish man appear and lower his
bifocals down upon his nose from where they had been resting, propped on his forehead. He had cruelly cut gray hair
that showed his scalp.

"What can I do for you, sonny?" the old Hispanic man asked.

Collins left his bag sitting on the floor and walked to the back of the shop. He was aware of the items surrounding him on the walls and in the racks. As he passed by the boxes with old records and other boxes that held their technological replacements, the CD, he saw the old man's eyebrows rise.

"Maybe you can help me," Collins said, a smile lifting the corners of his mouth slightly. "I'm looking to sell a watch and was wondering what I could get for it."

"Depends on the quality, son."

"Well, it's an old railroad-retirement pocket watch, belonged to my father."

"Pocket watches are always nice, just can't get rid of 'em."

That was the answer Collins had been aiming for. He reached into his back pocket, drew his ID out, and placed it on the glass counter for the clerk to see. The man with the gray hair and bifocals looked down at the military identification, then back into the piercing blue eyes of the stranger. The passwords had been exchanged and accepted.

"Welcome to the Group, Major."

Collins looked the store over and grimaced. "I was told this would be different," he said as he looked back at the man before him.

"Don't laugh, Major, this store turns over a nice profit. You'll see the results in the Group's mess hall." The old man came from around the counter and walked to where Collins had left his bag. "I'm Gunnery Sergeant Lyle Campos of the great United States Marine Corps and security for this entrance. Gate Two is what she is," he said over his shoulder. "If you'll follow me, we'll get you started for the complex."

He picked up the major's bag and walked back around the counter, nodding his head for the younger man to follow. They went through two batwing doors into the back area of the pawnshop. Inside were two other men. The shorter of the two stepped forward and took the heavy bag from Campos. The other, more muscular and bald, walked up to Collins and looked him over. He placed the Beretta nine-millimeter automatic he held at his side into his pants at the small of his back.

"Welcome to the high desert, sir. I'm Staff Sergeant Will Mendenhall, U.S. Army. This is Lance Corporal Frakes, he's a jarhead marine." He gestured to the man now holding Collins's bag. "We'll be escorting you through the tunnel to Group, sir."

Collins was more wary than impressed. The two men wore civilian clothes; the marine corporal had on shorts, and the black sergeant wore an overly stated red Hawaiian shirt and Levi's. Jack just nodded his head and wondered to just what cluster-fuck job he had been assigned.

"Gunny, would you please put the closed sign on the door until we get back?" Mendenhall asked. The old man bobbed his head once and left the office area without further comment.

"You'll have to excuse the gunnery sergeant, Major, he's just a little miffed at recently being placed on the inactive field duty list. He wants to stay with the Group, but he's only allowed gate security, and I suspect even that may change soon enough."

"How old is he?" Collins inquired.

Mendenhall shook his head as he gestured for the major to follow. "No one's commenting on Gunny's age, sir, that's for self-preservation. He may be old, but he's a better man than most men half his age. If I asked him, I'm afraid he would break his foot off in my ass . . . uh, sir," he said, turning away as he realized he was talking to his new boss. He rolled his eyes at his own conduct.

The two men led Collins into a smaller room in back of the first. The worn-out wood paneling was cracked and peeling in places. A single, shabby desk occupied the space. A computer monitor sat atop it, looking entirely out of place on the ancient desk. A solitary man sat behind the computer and did not rise to greet the three men but gave an acknowledging nod in the major's direction. Collins would later learn that the computer monitor served only as window dressing. The real reason to have a desk and fake computer at all was for the Ingram submachine gun clipped to the underside of the desk, and the man's hidden hand had a finger placed firmly on its cold steel trigger. The computer monitor was equipped with a pressure trigger on the floor that the guard could reach, and if pushed, it would send the back of the monitor exploding outward along with three hundred disabling tranquilizer darts. This was a small gift from the CEO of Pfizer Pharmaceutical.

The three men stepped up to the far wall. A motion sensor activated a small panel that popped free of the chipped plaster. The sergeant punched in a six-digit code on the now exposed keypad, which allowed another doorway-sized panel to the right to slide up and into the wall. Inside was a small cubicle, the floor of which was covered in linoleum in the military's favorite color, puke green (the same found in any government building in the country). The three men stepped in and the sergeant placed his hand onto a clear glass panel as a bright flash lit the small room momentarily, causing Collins to blink.

"Voice print analysis, please state destination," a computerized female voice asked from a hidden speaker.

"Nellis shuttle," the sergeant said.

"Thank you, Sergeant Mendenhall," the voice answered after three seconds had passed for the handprint and voice analyzer to finish.

"The glass read my finger and palm prints and the computer analyzed the pitch and pronunciation of my voice, thus clearing us for Group entrance. It's a security device of biomechanical engineering," Mendenhall explained. "If *one thing* didn't come back as kosher, the computer with the sexy female auditory system would have rendered us senseless with a two-thousand-volt shock." He smiled as he said the last statement.

"Nice, so when do we meet Captain Kirk and Mr. Spock?" Collins asked, not returning the smile. He waited a moment, then turned to the sergeant. "Listen, uh, Sergeant Mendenhall, is it?"

"Yes, sir."

"I am well aware of the capabilities of the A2-6000 Kendall Encoded Bio Engineered Security System. It's a nice advantage to have, but I could have shorted the entire system out one minute after I walked into the pawnshop. The entire electrical hard line for the security gate is fed in from the Las Vegas power grid. Your backup generator is in plain sight in an unsecured cage just to the left of the back door, which I heard clearly kicking on and charging batteries just before I entered the building. Don't be too proud of something that isn't being utilized in a secure manner."

The door closed and the elevator moved quickly and silently down its hydraulically controlled shaft. Mendenhall was quiet, not knowing exactly how to take this man who obviously knew his security systems. As he looked the man over, he noticed small scars here and there on his exposed skin.

The elevator movement was whisper quiet, and the only way the major knew it was an elevator at all was because his stomach was still in the pawnshop. Collins mumbled something under his breath.

"What was that, sir?" Mendenhall asked, turning to face Collins.

"Awful lot of James Bond crap."

"Yes, sir, it is."

The elevator door slid open and the three men stepped out onto a concrete platform, and Collins was surprised to see it was a train tunnel. The track was different from any he had seen outside of Disneyland, as it only had one rail and that was made from what looked like concrete. It was a single track that ran down the tunnel and had only a metal strip on its left side.

"We usually bring people in through the Nellis gates and through our regular checkpoints, sir, just as if they were regular air force personnel, but we have those points under security renovation. Director Compton and the senator thought this would be easier."

"The senator?" Collins asked.

The two men said nothing.

"Please step back beyond the yellow line, your transport is arriving," the computer-generated voice said to them.

Mendenhall pulled lightly on the major's shirt as Collins looked down and saw he was an inch or two beyond a yellow stripe that had been painted about a foot from the edge of the platform. He stepped back. Suddenly, a swishing sound came from the darkened tunnel. The next thing Collins saw was a small tube, pointed at both ends and entirely enclosed in glass from waist level up, stop suddenly in front of them. There were no braking sounds at all, just the rush of air and a quick rise of his hair.

"Your transport has arrived," stated the computer.

"Damn, that was smooth," Collins said.

"It works on electromagnetism and pneumatics. Power, braking, everything," the sergeant volunteered, hoping he wouldn't be slammed again by the major's knowledge.

A door slid back and allowed the three passengers to enter. It looked like a smaller version of the monorail system Collins had seen at most major airports, the pointed nose being the only difference. As he took one of the plastic seats in the front of the transport, the door slid closed and the computer spoke again. "Welcome to the Nellis Transport System. There is no standing while the transport is in motion. The distance covered to the main platform will be eleven point four miles and time duration will be two minutes, thirty-three seconds."

Collins frowned at the thought of traveling that fast with no one at the controls.

The transport started humming and moved with ever-increasing forward momentum. The major could see the tunnel was dark beyond the glass with the exception of the blue strip lighting that lined the center of the track. The illumination zipped by until it was a solid line of light. There was a slight downward angle and he realized the tram was traveling deeper and deeper into the desert surrounding Las Vegas.

Two and a half minutes later Collins felt the transport decelerating. Then a lit platform came into view that was far wider than the one they had just left. This dock had people on it. They wore coveralls and moved about placing crates and boxes onto a lift. As they sped by, a few of them looked up. The personnel were a mix of different colored jumpsuits and sexes.

"Welcome to Group Platform One," the computer stated with enthusiasm. The door slid open with a hiss of air and the three men stood.

"You're not in Kansas anymore, Toto," Mendenhall quipped, then added, "sir," quickly, as they stepped forward into the underground domain of the Event Group.

M ajor Collins watched the men and women loading crated material onto a large lift. The huge elevator was capable of carrying no less than two tanks side by side, but at the moment the thirty-five or so personnel were loading only small crates and boxes onto the monstrous elevator.

"Please follow me, sir, we have another ride ahead of us," the sergeant said.

Collins allowed the corporal to once again lift his bag and he followed both security men to another set of doors. These doors only had a down indicator light set into the wall beside them. As they approached, the doors slid open without the usual rumble of a normal elevator, and they stepped in. Sergeant Mendenhall nodded his head at the other man, who waved good-bye with a halfhearted salute.

"I'll escort you down into the complex, Major. We don't like to leave Gunny too long without company. He has a tendency to gouge the legitimate customers we get in the shop." Mendenhall smiled as the doors slid closed.

Collins watched as the sergeant repeated the process he had used on the first elevator. Only this time, instead of his hand he had to place his right eye into a soft rubber piece that conformed to his orbital structure.

"Retinal scans complete, Sergeant Mendenhall. Will your guest please place his right thumb onto the pad to the right?" the computer asked.

Mendenhall gestured the major forward and indicated the glass plate to the right of the eyepiece he had just used. Collins placed his right thumb to the glass, watching as red laser-tracking lines appeared to wrap around his thumb. The light went off.

"Thank you, Major Collins, you may proceed."

"The computer weighed the elevator and knew that I wasn't alone in the car, thus knew I had a guest with me. This elevator is pneumatically operated. We'll be riding air down into the complex."

The elevator indicator to the left of the doors told Collins the only choices they had were down, and these read 1–150. He didn't comment on Mendenhall's explanation of the elevator as he didn't really care for the idea of riding air pressure anywhere.

"Where in the hell are we, Sergeant?" Collins asked.

The man smiled and said, "Well, sir, the men who will explain that to you are far above my pay grade, but I *can* tell you"—Mendenhall reached out and pressed a button indicating level 6—"we are on the most northern part of Nellis Air Force Base, below the old gunnery and target range. By the time these doors open, we'll be on the main level of the complex, five hundred and sixty-five feet below the surface of the desert."

"Jesus" was all the major could utter in response.

"Altogether there are one hundred and fifty levels, equaling four thousand and some change in feet. Yes, sir, quite a ways. The main levels below were excavated from a natural cave formation similar to Carlsbad, only these caves weren't discovered till 1906." The sergeant paused, then quoted from memory, " 'This is the second facility for the Group; the original was in Virginia. But this particular complex was built during the Second World War as part of the expansion under President Roosevelt.' " He smiled again. "I guess it was a little easier to hide the cost back then. It was designed by the same people who drew up the plans for the Pentagon."

"What does the Group do here?" Collins asked, eyeing the indicators.

"Again, sir, the most important questions you have will be answered by people other than me."

The elevator came to a soft halt with only a soft and minute bounce. Mendenhall retrieved the major's bag as the doors slid open. Collins stepped out into what appeared to be a quiet, well-appointed, and normal reception area.

"Major, enjoy your tour of the Group. And hearing of your reputation, I believe I'll like being a part of your team, sir," the black sergeant said as he placed the bag down. Then he leaned back into the elevator and the doors closed. Collins didn't even have time to say thank-you before he was left looking at the "up" arrow above the doors.

Collins surveyed the reception area. Three desks were arrayed at different corners of the plush, hunter-green-carpeted room. At two of the desks sat men, busily working at computers. At the center-most station, an older woman sat. Her desk was the largest of the three, and it was this woman who stood, smiled, and walked around her desk. She stepped forward and extended a hand.

"Major Collins, I presume?"

"Yes, ma'am," he answered, turning and taking the woman's small and elegant hand in his own. The woman was tiny and looked to be in her late fifties. Around her neck her bifocals hung from a thin, gold chain. She wore a long-skirted blue suit with a plain white blouse. Her graying-black hair was up in an old-fashioned bun with not a single hair out of place. She wore only minimal makeup, her only accessory a small American flag pin attached on her left lapel.

She smiled warmly. "Welcome to the Event Group, Major, otherwise known as Department 5656 of the federal government. I'm sure we will make your days here just as exciting as any you've had in your career."

Collins raised a brow in doubt and the woman caught the gesture. She just continued to smile and patted him on the hand, before releasing it.

Collins looked around the reception area once more. On one wall hung a massive portrait of Abraham Lincoln, a painting he had never seen before. The oil portrait depicted him sitting and reading a book, of which the title was obscured. On another wall, and a bit smaller, was a portrait of Theodore Roosevelt, complete in his hand-tailored Rough Rider uniform. Next to that was a picture of Teddy's fifth cousin, Franklin. Situated along the walls were glass-encased models of sailing vessels, ironclads, and other distinguished warships. Set back into the far wall were two huge wooden doors, each of which stood nearly fifteen feet in height, and the big brass handles gleamed in the office lights. Above the doors, in gold script engraved on a long oak plaque, was an inscription: *Those who cannot remember the past are condemned to repeat it.* Then below that, in smaller script: *In this labyrinth lay the truth of our world, our civilization, and our culture.*

"Good words, aren't they, Major?" the woman asked.

"Good, yes, a little ambiguous maybe," Collins answered, looking from the plaque to the small, smiling woman as he turned to face her.

"They will become a tad clearer to you before your duty is up here. My name is Alice Hamilton. I've been with the senator on an official basis since 1947 and now assist Director Niles Compton."

Collins was astounded. This woman, who looked no more than sixty at the extreme, would have had to come to work here when she was in her teens, and that would still make her somewhere in her late seventies. Talk about the years being kind to a person, Jack thought.

"Excuse me, ma'am, but you said 1947?"

"I did, Major; I came here when I was eighteen, after losing my husband during the war. It's been a nice stay, and being I was always afraid to miss too much, I refused to go away. The senator, who is now retired from the Group, is here as a special adviser to Dr. Compton, and, well, he always said he would keep me informed if I up and left, but I don't trust the old coot. I like being in the thick of it," she said, clenching her hands together.

She paused and gestured to a man who was typing away

at a keyboard at the desk nearest to them. "John, will you be so kind as to take the major's bag down to his new quarters on your way to take your break, please?"

The man stood, smiled, walked over, and took the major's bag. He straightened and said, "Welcome to the Group, Major, we saw you on C-SPAN last fall and admire you for standing your ground."

Surprised at the remark made about his appearance before Congress, Collins looked again at Alice. "I wouldn't think you would need the services of someone like me here. What is this, some sort of think tank?"

"Think tank?" The woman thought a second, knitting her brow as if contemplating this concept. "Why, yes, I guess we are. That and many other things, Major." She smiled that award-winning smile again and stepped toward the big doors. "The senator and Dr. Compton are waiting and they'll be happy to answer all your questions." Alice grasped both handles and the doors swung open easily, and she stepped aside to let the major enter and then followed.

The office was large; it had flat-screen television monitors mounted every foot around the circular walls, which were covered in rich wood paneling. Behind the mahogany desk hung another portrait of Lincoln—in this one he just sat facing the artist with a closed book in his lap. Next to that was a large portrait of Woodrow Wilson, poised with ink pen in hand.

A man was sitting on the edge of the giant desk, reading some papers he held at arm's length, when he noticed the two people enter the room. He straightened and stood with the aid of a cane, tossing the papers on the desk as he made his way toward Jack and Alice. A second, smaller man sitting in the large chair behind the desk also stood and quickly followed the first, eager to greet their new guest.

One of the most imposing men Collins had ever seen stood there before him. Jack stood six foot two and this man was looking down at him. He figured him to be at least six foot six and appeared to be in his mid- to late eighties. He wore a three-piece, black, pin-striped suit with a red bow tie;

his silver hair was swept back from his forehead and was in need of cutting. But by far his most outstanding feature was the black patch he wore over his right eye. A long, jagged scar ran from his jawline up through the patch and disappeared into the wavy hairline. The other man who joined them was quite a bit shorter. He wore glasses and was balding and had at least four ballpoint pens in his shirt pocket.

"Senator, Dr. Compton," Alice Hamilton began, "I would like to introduce the newest member of the Event Group, Major Jack Collins, United States Army. He's with us from the Fifth Special Forces Group, and his last duty station was in Kuwait City, attached to the Ninth Special Operations Team." She gently nudged Collins forward. "Jack, this is Senator Garrison Lee, retired, from the great state of Maine, and former brigadier general, U.S. Army intelligence, and one of the founding members of the Office of Strategic Services, and Dr. Niles Compton, the director of our department."

"We didn't need a history lesson on me, woman," Senator Lee said, looking at Alice, then over at the major. "Major Collins!" the man exuberantly greeted him, shifting the cane from his right to his left hand, holding the now free hand out to the major. Collins shook but didn't say anything in response. "Read a lot about you, son," the senator continued. "Glad you saw fit to join this band of fools." The man stepped aside to allow Jack to shake hands with Dr. Compton, who nodded his head and then pushed his glasses back on his nose.

The senator looked at Alice. "I take it he's signed his secrecy papers and disclosure forms?"

"Yes, that was taken care of at Fort Bragg," she answered with a frown, noticing the senator was a little unsteady on his feet as he greeted the new arrival.

"Thank you, Alice. Would you bring in a tray of coffee, please?"

Alice politely gestured with a roll of her elegant hand toward the credenza against the far wall, where sat a steaming silver service.

"When in the hell did you bring that in?" he stammered with eyebrows raised.

"As usual, you two were engrossed in one of your field reports," she quipped, winking at the major.

"Uh, thank you," Lee grumbled as if he were clearing his throat. "Now get the hell out of here." His one uncovered eye glared at her.

She gave the senator a mock salute, with palm facing out.

"That's a British salute, woman! When in hell are you going to learn?"

She ignored the remark, turned, and left the room, closing the huge doors gracefully behind her.

The senator, after glaring at the door a moment, gestured for Collins to take a seat in a rather large leather chair in front of Compton's even larger desk.

"Please, have a seat, Major; I'm sure you're more than just a little curious about our business." They walked toward the back of the room. "I know your papers say temporary duty, and I know you didn't exactly volunteer for this position." He smiled. "You see, we were owed a favor, and you, sir, are that favor."

Before the senator could continue, Niles Compton broke in, "Major, I'm afraid I must tend to an urgent matter. I'll be back momentarily. I apologize, but my duties since taking over as director require me to be in four places at once."

Jack watched Compton hurry out of the large office.

"Niles is probably the smartest person in the country, that's why the president chose him to be my successor, but he worries about small things too much, not that he micromanages his people, it's more his taking the time to see they have the tools they need to succeed. Have a seat, Major, and relax," Lee said.

Collins waited while Lee poured two cups of coffee, then sat in the overstuffed chair facing the desk. After the man had handed him his cup and saucer, he watched as the senator maneuvered with a limp back around the desk.

"Just what is it that you and the director expect me to do here, sir? I've been in the service twenty years and have never heard a whisper of this operation, and in the military, that's rare." Collins placed the coffee on the edge of the desk untouched, as if this move said he wasn't having anything to do with it until the man in front of him came clean.

Lee placed the cane along the edge of the desk, sipped at his own coffee, then placed the cup and saucer down and closed his good eye and leaned back as he started talking.

"Jack Collins, Major, United States Army, graduated West Point second in his class in 1988. First combat seen in Panama, first man in the conflict area so I understand." He held his hand up when he sensed Jack was going to say something. "After Panama you spent two years working on your master's from MIT. After that, to the army's displeasure, you rejoined Special Operations. Then a tour with the Aberdeen proving grounds with the top brass thinking you had finally come around to being one of the boys. Only it wasn't that. I think you were angry about Special Operations equipment and wanted answers to why things never worked the way they were supposed to, so you set them as straight as you could on the civilian and corporate side of things at Aberdeen." Lee opened his eye and looked at Jack. "Then again to the chagrin of the army higher-ups, you rejoin Special Operations, and then Jack Collins really went to war. You started in Desert Shield by infiltrating Kuwaiti and Iraqi territory on missions of a rather dark nature. You fought in Operation Desert Storm, winning the Congressional Medal of Honor. Then your tour in Operation Iraqi Freedom."

"You seem to have me at an extreme disadvantage, Senator," Collins said.

Lee smiled. "Previous to your tour in Iraq, you had set up a black OP in Afghanistan. Before you had a chance to deploy your outfit on a most dangerous mission, the army pulled you out, leaving your team with an inexperienced commander to lead them. When you arrived in theater in Iraq, you heard the entire team in Afghanistan was killed during the operation you had planned, because of a mistake that was made at the command level. We won't go into your testimony before Congress here. So, to make a long story short, the president of the United States, who didn't agree with the army's treatment of you after said visit to the Hill, saw fit to give you to us. I asked Niles to request you."

Collins sat silently. He thought back to the mission he had planned to a tee only to be pulled out at the last minute by military bureaucrats. He would never forget the pain and anger that had flared when he'd learned his team had been killed to a man in a rocky valley in the armpit of the world.

"Requested me for what?" he finally asked.

Both men looked up as Niles Compton returned to the office and nodded. He gestured for Lee to continue.

"Major, outside of certain aspects of the National Security Agency, you have entered the topmost-secret facility in our nation's government. We have been chartered in a roundabout way, since 1863." The old politician took a moment to let that sink in, then continued, "You've noticed the portraits of Lincoln and Wilson, I presume?"

"Yes, sir, they're pretty hard to miss," Collins answered, looking at the two large paintings behind the senator.

Lee smiled. "Well, Mr. Lincoln, although he didn't know it at the time, laid the foundation for the Event Group during the Civil War." Lee held Jack's stare. He liked that the major held his questions. "It's a foregone conclusion of historians that old Abe was far ahead of his time. Hell, most schoolchildren can tell you that, but, anyway, we are secret, because sometimes we uncover things that aren't very popular with the world, or even our own citizens. We roam the dark hallways of our government behind the auspices of the National Archives."

Collins listened to the old man before him and had the distinct feeling he was being set up. But for the life of him he didn't know in which direction it was coming.

Lee looked at Niles and the director nodded. He said each word slowly, thoughtfully, "Jack, the United States is most unique. Its citizens hail from every country on earth and they have a right to the truth of that history, and our job is to find it, process it, and to tell them facts that have led us to where we are, to give information to those that can use it to make better decisions for *them*. Information is *the* weapon of the future, and we will never, ever be caught off guard by not understanding the vital lessons of the past, for they have shaped and molded us into what we are. The world is shaped by pivotal *Events* throughout our past; they have steered us into making not just changes to survive, but civilization-altering changes. We here at the Group try and identify those moments in our current times, helping all to make the altering judgments that will lead us into our future. The current Events we identify will assist us into what we will become. Our job here is to find out the truth as history tells it, for our nation, for us, and maybe, just maybe, this world will begin to know and understand itself, and that can only bring about truth and understanding for all its peoples. The security of this nation is paramount. Oh, the CIA, the National Security Agency, and the FBI can physically gather intelligence, but it's left up to us to find it in the past, things the other agencies are not even capable of grasping. We here learn all there is to learn about everything."

"Yes, sir, I see."

Niles Compton smiled and shook his head. "No, Major, you don't see . . . yet."

"I know it's a lot to take in," Lee stated as he reached out to push a button on the right side of the desk. Then he flipped a switch and one of the many large flat-screen monitors flickered to life. "This is our computer center. If you know computers, Major, you will understand that the unit you see in the background there is a Cray Corporation prototype, generously given to us by . . . well, by one of our many friends in the private sector. It's the most powerful unit in the world used for processing raw data. We are 'hacked,' if you will—personally, I hate the term—into almost every university and major corporation in the world, and most governments also. The chairmen of several large software companies based in the Northwest and in Texas assist us in this endeavor. Oh, they fight with the government quite often, but most are very fond of what we do here and are large contributors to our fiscal budget. These chairmen are far more patriotic than they are given credit."

As Collins viewed the monitor's screen, he noted about fifty or so people all working in an elaborate, state-of-the-art computer-processing center.

"These men and women, who are specially trained and hold the highest of security clearances for the Group and the U.S. government, take information from archaeological digs, finds of any kind, reports of strange happenings, myths, legends, histories, new discoveries, and they feed it all into the Cray, where it is analyzed and referenced for historical or Paleolithic importance, and if need be, we send people into the field, either as part of another organization, or in the open as a part of our National Parks Service—even foreign nations recognize our parks system and hold it in high regard. The information gained is used to better understand where it is we came from, and sometimes more importantly, where it is we are going. Only the top chairmen or founding owners of the largest companies and presidents of universities have a hint of our existence, and even they are a marked few."

"And I fit in . . . ?" Collins inquired.

The senator pursed his lips. "Over the years, basically since just after the First World War, we have lost over a hundred personnel in field operations." Lee shook his head. "You see, Major, there are those that either don't want to share the information that's uncovered or deem it valuable enough to eliminate any who stand in their way of getting it and holding on to it. That is where you and your men come in, as field security for site operations and infiltration, and to put it bluntly, Major, I took advantage of your current predicament to get you here as you seem to be a hot potato no one wants to butter up right now."

Collins started to say something, then was stopped by a raised hand of the senator. He rose slowly from his high-backed chair and motioned for the major to follow him. He limped across to a screen that was much larger than the one that had just shown the image of the computer room. Collins, as he followed, noticed the senator looked a little bit older than he had originally thought.

"Your record in both Gulf conflicts warrants you being here, Major. The job you did in the first Iraq conflict, rescuing that downed A-6 Intruder crew, was amazing." The senator smiled. "You obviously have an affinity for dangerous situations." Lee watched Collins for a reaction, then held his gaze.

"And now the hard part. Even though you have been awarded three Silver Stars and a Medal of Honor, your career is all but over in the regular army. But as I said before, the president didn't hold any grudges, and because he knows you're a true soldier, he sent you to us. And with us you'll be able to stay in the service and continue on with a meaningful career."

Collins turned and looked at Lee. He knew of only a dozen people outside the White House who knew it had been his unit who had rescued the downed naval pilot. And no one really knew about his near court-martial after meeting with the president, Joint Chiefs, and the directors of the FBI and CIA. He was damned lucky after that to have a job at all. Whoever Lee and Compton were, they did have connections, and more than likely the strings on which to pull to get him here, wherever "here" was. So he knew this offer was for real, and Lee's eyes held no lies about how important he thought this was.

"It might be better to show you the fruits of our labors here at the Event Group, Major Collins, and then point out how expertise such as yours, and that of others, has helped us gather some of the wondrous things you are about to bear witness to." Lee paused a moment, then turned back to face Jack. He looked the professional soldier up and down, then looked him in the eyes. "Are you a religious man, Jack?"

"No, sir," Collins responded quickly as he held his gaze on the senator's lone eye. "Never found the time *or* the need."

The senator smiled, but the sadness of it made Collins wonder why he attempted it in the first place.

"It seems I'm looking at myself so many years ago." Lee lightly tapped the scar that ran under the patch covering his right eye. "I wasted a lot of time proving to myself that God didn't exist, when the question of God wasn't even the right thing to be asking. The right question is, what's the plan for us? The answer is maybe that plan is embedded in our past, now here we are, how did we get to this point, were we helped along, did elements just happen to combine and by fluke of nature we arrived here without us killing each other off?"

"Maybe we are just smart enough to realize how far we can push it. No divinity; maybe it's just as you say, a fluke," Collins countered.

The senator laughed out loud for the first time, then settled and looked at Collins once again. "It's like you read my thoughts of over sixty years ago, son," he said as he punched a button.

On the screen, a color picture flickered to life as the major looked on; the computer-controlled autofocus adjusted the view to fit the screen. When it cleared, it showed a panorama of an immense chamber. Buried into the walls of this chamber were what appeared to be rows of banklike steel vaults built into the solid bedrock.

"The only other person in the world who can tune in to this chamber is the president of the United States, our boss"—Lee hesitated—"and for better or worse, still your boss as well."

Collins nodded his head, viewing the screen with interest. Some of the vaults were enormous, some as tall as 150 feet, others as small as eight. The larger ones had stairs on either side; others had glass-viewing areas built into the sides of the massive steel doors. He saw numerous security cameras sweeping the entire long, curving corridor.

"The president is a frequent visitor here, as every president since Franklin Roosevelt has been. This facility, Jack, was their favorite place to be. And before that, the likes of Woodrow Wilson and Hoover frequented our very first facility in Virginia."

"Okay, Senator, you have my attention," Collins said.

"Good, Jack, good," Lee said as he punched another button on the control panel. A picture came up of what Collins assumed was the interior of one of the larger vaults. The camera shot was obscured for a moment as a man in a white lab coat walked by the lens on his way down a catwalk.

"Here at Group we have over a hundred computer technicians, thirty-five on-staff archaeologists, twenty-five top-notch chemists and biologists, two quantum theorists, four astrophysics people, five forensic specialists, one hundred field security men and women, consisting of army, navy, air force, and marine personnel, and twelve geologists." Lee took a much needed breath. "And this is not counting butchers, bakers, and candlestick makers." He smiled. "These are the best the country can offer, Jack. Their education is ongoing and continued by professors from MIT, Harvard, Jet Propulsion Lab, Cambridge, Princeton, and more, some with longer and far more expensive-sounding names. We spare nothing at the Event Group, Major Collins, and everyone from our cooks to field leaders have a right to furthering and deepening their minds. We don't want nor do we need puppets."

"Who pays for all this?"

Garrison Lee laughed. "There we have made some enemies, I'm afraid. As our budget comes out of the coffers of all the other agencies in the federal government and is hidden amongst their budgets and scattered to the winds, our front agency, the National Archives, takes a beating, but they live with it."

"I could see why that would cause concern with the other areas of government," Collins said.

"Our work is far more important." The senator waved his hand and again tapped the screen with his old wooden cane, drawing Jack's attention back to the largest of the vaults. The doors were closed and looked formidable in size and security.

"Now that looks like it belongs at NORAD, in Cheyenne Mountain," Collins said, looking at the screen.

Collins watched as the older man spoke, his one steely blue eye fixed on the screen, and when he started speaking, he never once turned to face Collins, as if he were concentrating on telling the story right, or he was trying to imagine or live it, so it could be told right. Jack knew this was the hook that was to be fed him. The senator's cane was still held on the large plastic-coated screen by his liver-spotted hand.

"I find myself drawn to this vault quite often," he said softly. "What you're seeing here, Major, was the first Event, what we here refer to as the Lincoln Raid." The senator paused and stared a long while at the screen. Lee's features didn't tell anything much about what the man was feeling. "It's a very well documented Event. Diaries and logbooks, all firsthand accounts, give an almost surreal telling of its discovery and acquisition."

He finally turned and looked at the major with a small smile lifting the corners of his mouth. "I guess it gives me a sense of peace, indescribable really, or maybe it's just my age." He chuckled to himself at this last remark.

Jack said nothing; he just looked the senator in his one good eye, looking for that flicker of untruth.

Suddenly, Garrison Lee deftly tapped the tip of the cane against another button on the control panel. Collins watched as another camera, from higher up in the vault, he assumed, came on and produced an image of an object that caught the major off guard. He didn't quite know what it was he was looking at, but it was enormous and undoubtedly ancient. Its raggedness gave the giant object a ghostly appearance. Without knowing he was doing it, Jack stepped closer to the large screen. A deeply buried, almost familiar memory started to burrow its way out of his mind. It was an unclear, distant thought, or was it a memory? Perhaps a memory of something he had seen as a child. But the harder he tried to remember, the more elusive it became; like the feeling of déjà vu, it came and left, leaving only a bare trace of its being there at all. Jack furrowed his brows and peered harder at the screen.

Lee stepped back to admire the view the vault camera gave them. Technicians were milling around it. Some were chipping away at it with instruments Collins had never before seen, others were writing on clear plastic clipboards, while still more manned huge diagnostic systems arrayed against one of the far walls. The giant object looked as if it had been made out of wooden beams of some kind, but had long ago petrified into near rock. The beams were curved and swept, high at one end and sloping down at a great angle toward its torn and sheared opposite end. As he watched, a three-man tech group was in the interior of the enormous object. They had a small chemical lab set up right there and were analyzing substances he wouldn't even guess at. He looked more closely at the exterior. There were massive holes in its side and on what Collins assumed was its sloping floor, or was it a deck? It now hit him that he was looking at part of a vessel of some kind. The petrified planks of what was once wood were laid out perfectly as a deck would be. It was long, at least three hundred feet from the view they had, and looked as if it was only half there as it ended in a jagged wreck. He was still struck by how ancient the object looked. But that feeling of *knowing* still struck him like a hammer inside his head. He couldn't help but get goose bumps when he gazed at the strange and mysterious object.

"What is it?" Collins asked of the hauntingly familiar shape.

"Don't you know, Jack?" the senator asked, still smiling at him. "Well, in all actuality neither do we. There are a lot of opinions, but one thing we do know, we can't tell the people of the world we have it, it would stir the souls of men, and we just can't predict how they would react."

Collins continued to study the image as the old man looked as if he was thoroughly enjoying the moment.

"The reason I am showing you this particular vault first, Major, is twofold. Number one, this was the very first Event. And number two, it shows the value of the military in our fieldwork. And believe me, Jack, fieldwork is even far more dangerous today than it was in Mr. Lincoln's time."

Collins's eyes never left the senator's lone one. He nodded in understanding, but said nothing.

"It started in 1863," Lee said, still looking at the major before letting his eye go back to the screen. "After the battle of Gettysburg, when the war had finally turned in the Union's favor, the president of the United States, Abraham Lincoln, was persuaded by a discredited Norwegian immigrant, a history professor from Harvard, to put together an expedition to what was then known as the Ottoman Empire." The senator paused and turned from the screen and limped the short distance to his high-backed chair beside Niles's desk.

"This meeting between the professor and the president brought forth an unusual truce between North and South the history books will never mention, and one you will find no documentation for in the National Archives, save for ours," Lee added. "A meeting was engineered through the office of the then U.S. secretary of state, William Seward, and the expedition was on. It would be mounted by six hundred Union soldiers and captured Confederate prisoners, and six American ships of war."

At this, Collins turned and looked at the man sitting behind that huge desk, then up at the portrait of Lincoln above the man's head.

"Their task," Lee continued, "as ordered by the president, was to search for, find, and bring back an object believed by some to be the greatest archaeological find of all time—not one that would fill the depleted U.S. treasury with riches for pockets already lined beyond measure." Lee had picked up a pen and was tapping it against his blotter. "The mission was to bring back the object you see there before you."

Collins looked at the screen, paused a moment, then glanced back at the senator. Then, slowly his eyes were drawn back to the large monitor.

"In short, Major, the president didn't really believe they would find anything of value. To his way of thinking, just the effort of two warring factions to come together would help in reuniting the North and the South after the war. There was one thing Mr. Lincoln overlooked, and that was the tenacity of the men involved. They brought back to this country, at the loss of three-quarters of the men and four warships, a relic that had sat atop a mountain in eastern Turkey for over ten thousand years. A lot of good American boys were left on that summit and in the slopes and valleys of that harsh and desolate place. And what they brought back, to what turned out to be for a murdered president and a country still divided, where hatred reigned unchecked, was the artifact you see before you. Some think it the Ark of the great flood, the ship that was supposedly built by Noah himself."

Collins saw it as soon as it was said out loud by the senator. All the pictures he had seen in Sunday school, the stories he was told as a child, the ridiculous tales and movies of his adulthood, they all rushed in as if a dam had burst inside his mind.

"You mean to say this . . . this thing is *Noah's Ark*?" he finally asked, his eyes glued to one spot on the viewing screen.

"As near as we can determine, the vessel is of pre-Sumerian origin, basically the cradle of civilization found between the Tigris and Euphrates river basins. The size, shape, and material of which it is made are a precise match to all biblical detail. Carbon-14 dating places it at some eleven thousand six hundred years in age, give or take a century," the senator said in a more technical tone. "We haven't any firm belief from science who built it; we have the legends of Gilgamesh and the Noah accounts, but that's not the approach we take here. Science says it's an ancient wooden vessel that's so old it petrified after it somehow landed on top of a mountain."

Collins turned and walked back to his chair in front of the senator and sat heavily.

The senator smiled over at Jack. Every time he had shown this for the first time, he had seen it in their faces: amazement, awe, and fear wrapped up into one thought.

The senator stood and limped to a cabinet next to the credenza with the coffee on it. He reached down, took out a glass, and poured the major a glass of water. He limped back and placed it in Collins's hand. Jack quickly drained it and was glad for the break in conversation. It had been a long time since he could remember being caught totally unaware. This was more than just a little unnerving, yet extraordinary at the same time. The senator started talking again while adjusting himself into his chair.

"Now, do we here at Group live in awe of this one artifact, or do we learn from it? We have gathered so much data
it's coming out of every file cabinet we have. The reason this
is so important to this country, Jack, is the mere fact that we
have learned that the dangers are there and are very real that
we could be hit by similar floods in the future. This report
has gone up the chain and plans have been made on how to
deal with a similar Event if it happens. Before I let you catch
your breath, Jack, I must tell you that the finding of the Ark,
or vessel, was the first file in the Event Group's long and
wondrous history. Altogether there are more than 106,200
files, from everything religion-oriented to possible werewolf
attacks in France during the time of the black death, from
possible sightings of electrically powered submarines during the American Civil War to a major conflict between
Viking clans in Minnesota involving Sioux Indians seven
hundred years before Columbus."

Collins held Lee's gaze without comment.

"But that's just history; we study, we learn, we file. But
sometimes there is that golden nugget that can alter our government's way of thinking; for instance, the report detailing
the history of the empire of Japan delivered from us to Roosevelt in 1933 by my predecessor warning of the historical
tendencies of the Japanese. It was all there to see for anyone
willing to dig a little deeper, dig like only the Event Group
can. Our Group informed the president six full years before
December of '41 that the United States was on a collision
course with Japan, and we also gave him options on how to
avoid a conflict. You see, we report, but in the end what the
president does with the information is learn from it." Lee
smiled at Collins. "Maybe he decided that what he learned
from our report was that Japan would indeed attack us, and
that would be enough to get us involved in a far more
dangerous game in Europe with the Nazis. What do you
think?"

"I believe I understand the need for secrecy; this information would unnerve a lot of people, and I believe I know why
you need me."

"No, Jack, you don't know just yet. We've lost a lot of people, good people, and we are sick and tired of it. The president has ordered Director Compton to take the gloves off. My killing days are far passed; I daresay I was almost as good as you at taking life for the right cause. But I'm an old man and my next big adventure is death. Niles here needs a man that is capable of defending the people he sends into the field, and so I started digging on his behalf and you are what I unearthed. I hope I have stated our case clearly."

"I believe you have," Collins answered.

"By that, I guess you see some of what we are about here and that you accept the task before you, that you are here to train and equip our security teams and make them a viable protective force. Niles and I are concerned over the recent escalation of deadly force against our people."

"We are being pushed around by outside elements, and to put it bluntly and more succinctly, Major, you're here to push back, and push back hard," Compton said, with the emphasis on the last four words.

"I believe I grasp the concept of the Group, but the times dictate how you react to certain situations. For reasons I've tried to explain, and have been banished from the troops I respect and care about for doing so, countries and people smell a weakness in the United States. To protect the people under you, Mr. Director, are you prepared to be offensive in nature?"

"Prepared? I'm ordering it, Major Collins."

"Then you're halfway to really giving your people a fighting chance. Our current world is one based on speed. Everything is moving faster, and to protect your own you have to move even faster than your enemies, and sometimes sadly to say, preemptively."

Niles nodded. "But there is something you must know, Major Collins. There are those here in our own country that believe as you, only they are taking matters to the extreme. It seems there may be a group of superpatriots with highly placed sources that are attacking others and us with impunity. You are right, it's a world of speed and we are lagging behind. Whoever they are, they are killing my people and taking our finds, and I must stress, Major Collins"—Compton clenched his fist—"that will be our undoing. Our knowledge is being stolen, by either outside sources for political gain, or factors from inside our borders for monetary or political reasons, and I want it stopped. The president says to start offensive operations to root these factions out. Get a light on them and bring them out into the open. And that is what you are here to do." Niles paced and continued, "When the senator brought you to my attention, I thought you might be just a thug, but reading your file and making a few calls of my own, I have found out you are quite intelligent and are constantly thinking outside of the box. MIT, UCLA, and numerous other institutions say you are worthy of being far more than you are. But I believe you were right where you wanted to be, protecting your men. That's why all the higher education—you learned so you could care for your people. I care about mine also, Major, but I can't do what you do." Niles turned and faced Collins. "Protect my people and I don't care how you do it."

Collins looked from Dr. Compton to the senator. He sensed their sincerity about how important they considered the job they had offered him. He felt their sorrow and anger at the loss of their people, but he knew that regardless of the intent, he was out of his element.

"I am a soldier," he started, looking from one man to the other, "one who is still a career officer, even if the army has no more use for me. I will still have to get used to that fact. It's a new position for me you see, being an embarrassment, being one they have to brush under the rug, it makes it hard to look in the mirror. So if you wouldn't mind, I would like to reserve my answer for any permanent assignment until I can evaluate my options. But it would be my duty to start training your Group as best I can while I do that, is that acceptable?"

Lee looked at the floor a moment. He knew this was where Jack Collins would remain. The Joint Chiefs would never allow him to return to active duty. But how do you get rid of a Medal of Honor recipient without CNN crucifying you in the press? You hide him in the darkest closet in the American house, the Event Group. In the end Lee decided to let Jack have the illusion his fate was still controlled by himself, because without the Event Group the major's military career was done.

"Then tentatively speaking, Jack, welcome to the Event Group," the senator said slowly, standing and limping around the desk with his hand extended. "Your second-in-command, Lieutenant Commander Everett, will shed some more light on your duties here. He's good, Jack, real good. He's Navy, a SEAL, and he's been there, and it was he who knew the entire system needed revamping."

The senator opened the twin doors and shook Jack's hand again.

"That wicked old woman will have someone show you to your quarters, and then you'll be taken on a small tour of our vault area. Niles and I have a meeting with Her Majesty's archivist in England and the British prime minister in ten minutes, and the president will be listening in. So I'll leave you in the Wicked Witch of the West's hands because, as I say, we have an argument ahead of us. It seems the Brits want a body returned to the soil of the Empire."

Collins released the senator's hand as he turned away to go back into his office. As the doors were closing behind him, he heard the old man say, "This body belongs to the world, not just the British, damn it!"

Collins was joined by Alice Hamilton, who placed her aged arm through his own and started walking him toward the elevator. Collins figured Alice was one of those people who actually ran things at the Group, the one you went to when you wanted to cut through the crap and get something done. He decided that he would want her ear in the coming weeks and months.

As he entered the elevator, Alice whispered as she kept the doors from closing, "Garrison is really up in arms because he and Niles don't want to give up one of our finds, but the burial site was found on an American naval base in Scotland, so they wanted to keep it a while longer. But as always, they will return it when it's been examined. The senator wants to keep it for good, but Dr. Compton is younger and calmer and knows the British deserve it, so the senator will defer to Niles." She smiled and looked at Jack. "It was one of the senator's pet projects here at Group, proving the existence of a fourth-century warlord named Artorius, in the Latin language, or better known as Arthur, in the English."

As Alice let the elevator doors slowly close, she had to smile, because the last thing she saw was Major Collins's face as he tried to stop the doors from closing. "You mean they found the body of King Arth—" But the doors closed, cutting off his amazed expression and question.

PART TWO
STORMS

They who dream by day are cognizant of many things
which escape those who dream only by night.

—EDGAR ALLAN POE
"ELEONORA," 1841

FOUR

Specialist Fifth Class Sarah McIntire closed her book and notepad at the end of class. Today's lecture had been on ancient burial pitfalls, traps made to prevent looting of various burial sites throughout the world that Event Group archaeologists had come across during the many excavations in places like the Valley of the Kings near Luxor, Egypt, and in the Peruvian Inca ruins excavated in 2004. Sarah taught geology and used the opportunity given her by the ancients to spice up an otherwise boring day of geological subject matter. She had been joined by a professor visiting her class thanks to a virtual video link from the University of Tennessee. He'd delivered a nice lecture on the use of hot springs and other natural elements as traps by ancient architects in their planning of tombs.

"Boy, was that dead or what?"

Sarah looked around to see her roommate, Signalman First Class Lisa Willing, USN, smiling and holding her books against her ample chest. The blue Group jumpsuit fit her a little too well, which helped in giving her part of her nickname, behind her back of course, of Willing Lisa. Sarah knew Lisa had to have heard it before, but her friend always said it was just better to ignore people. Sarah knew Lisa to be smart as a whip, and she was the best in her field of electronics and communications as well. And, as her roommate, Sarah knew her not to be *willing* to do much of anything other than study at night and, on rare occasions, catch a movie on the complex's cable television station. Though there was a certain someone in her life, it was secret, and sadly, nicknames like that lingered.

"Oh, thanks, so I'm boring?"

"Nah, just kidding, kiddo," Lisa said, smiling and nudging her friend with her shoulder.

"Well, just another week and I'll finish my graduate work and I'll have my master's from the Colorado School of Mines. That still won't guarantee a field assignment." Sarah looked at Lisa. "You've been there, haven't you?"

"Egypt? Yeah, last year we had that busted field operation when that French asshole blew the whistle on Dr. Fryman from NYU. We were this close"—Lisa held up her index finger and thumb about an inch apart—"to getting a good lead on some relics that may have escaped the destruction of the great library of Alexandria."

Sarah looked at her friend with envy. She longed for the day to participate in something other than simulations and attending classes. She would walk out of here with a master's degree in geology and an officer's commission, a second lieutenant's gold bar, but she wanted what everyone here at the Group wanted, and that was fieldwork. But the opportunity hadn't arisen in the two years she had been here. She was not like a lot of the scientists here at the Group. She was a soldier first and that was what was so damn frustrating for her. She had the training she needed to survive, she should be eligible for more than just geology and tunnel teams, and she should be placed on any roster where a soldier was required. She knew it had been just a fluke that her geology team hadn't had any fieldwork, but that didn't make it any less frustrating.

"I would have loved to have been there," Sarah said as they passed others on their way to class and the mess hall.

"You'll get your shot," the blond woman said. "Hey, you wanna grab a late lunch? I'm starving." Lisa had become quite adept at steering her roommate away from a very sore subject.

Sarah hunched her shoulders in a "whatever" gesture and started for the mess hall.

As they stepped into the main cafeteria, Sarah, concentrating on her thoughts, didn't see the large man with gold oak leaf bars on his collar. Luckily, he saw the collision coming before it happened. Moving quickly, he raised his tray full of roast beef and mashed potatoes at the last second above her small frame. Sarah raised her arms over her head, hoping if food fell, most of it would fall on her textbook and not her. As she was doing this, she inadvertently backed into another, only slightly smaller man. As she hit his tray, the man deftly backed up two paces and righted the plates before he lost his sandwich and green-tinted lime Jell-O.

"Boy, you're just a little pinball, aren't you?" asked the first, taller officer.

Sarah turned to the second man, who held his tray in one hand and was readjusting its contents.

"I'm so sorry," she said, embarrassed.

"You'll have to excuse my roommate, sir, she's daydreaming of caves and tunnels and all other kinds of nasty stuff," Lisa chimed in, letting her eyes linger a little too long at the taller of the two officers.

"Think nothing of it, ladies, just a minor traffic pileup, no harm done," said the man with the dark brown hair and wearing an army major's rank on his new coveralls.

Sarah backed away with her book held to her chest. Her eyes locked on the man's blue ones. His stare didn't waver; his smile was dazzling and his gaze almost hypnotic. She finally broke what was to her an awkward moment by turning and walking away quickly enough that Lisa had to run to catch up.

"Hey, slow down," Lisa called at Sarah's retreating form, looking back at the taller of the two men, the one with a navy lieutenant commander rank on his collar. He was returning her look, smiling as his companion commented on something, and then he had to finally turn away.

"Damn, that's the new head of security," Sarah said as she took a tray from the stack and placed it on the serving line.

"With you becoming an officer yourself soon, there could be something there," Lisa chided, nodding her head in the direction of the almost accident, but all they saw were people staring at them, waiting for the line to start moving again.

Sarah turned and looked at her friend. "Is it the entire navy that has dirty minds and reads nonexistent things into something as mundane as me almost getting a bunch of food knocked onto my head, or is it just you?"

Lisa smiled and batted her eyes. "Just me, I guess."

Lieutenant Commander Carl Everett stood six foot three inches, which was how he had maneuvered his tray over Sarah so easily. His blond hair was trimmed short. His arms were tanned and muscular in his short-sleeved jumpsuit. He set the tray with his lunch on it down and pulled out a chair. But he waited for his new boss to sit first and watched Lisa and her roommate, Sarah, the one he had almost run into, walk through the serving line. He waited for Lisa to look back again, but she was too busy talking with those around her, already joking with the cooks serving her. Giving up, he finally sat. He tried never to communicate with Lisa during duty hours because the secret they kept was a serious breach of military etiquette and a court-martial offense.

"Is the mess hall food always this good?" Jack asked.

"Yes, sir, they usually have three or four entrées, and since this is a government- and not a military-run outfit, it's officially called a cafeteria, whatever that is," Everett joked, then paused with a forkful of mashed potatoes halfway to his mouth. "But field RATS are still the same, MREs in quantity if not quality."

Collins smiled. In his time in the service he had eaten enough of the freeze-dried rations to feed Botswana.

"So, Commander, you like the duty?" he asked, then chewed.

"Enough so that I don't want to rotate out. They want to send me back to the SEALs with a promotion and a nice fat training stint, but I've officially requested another six years of detached service."

Collins's eyebrows rose.

"Yeah, I promised to re-up my enlistment if they cut my orders for another tour in the Group."

"Don't you miss SEAL duty?"

Everett thought a moment as he placed his fork down. He had learned in the past that while speaking to commanding officers he should take his time and give the answer he wanted to give and not the one they wanted to hear. "I miss my mates, but this is the duty I want. And to be blunt, sir, there is enough excitement here for three SEAL teams."

Everett looked up beyond the major's shoulder and saw Lisa and Sarah seated far across the vast dining complex. Lisa looked up briefly and gave Everett a trace of a smile. She leaned over and whispered something to her friend, then continued eating.

B y the way, I saw the way you and your Mr. Everett locked eyes just a minute ago," Sarah said without looking up from her lunch.

Lisa paused, her spoon halfway to her mouth, and looked at her roommate. "*My* Mr. Everett?"

Again Sarah never looked up. "You know, the more I think on it, you're probably better off with duties here at the Group and not aboard any ship. For a navy person you have a bad habit of talking in your sleep, and not only that, if I can notice these things, so can others."

"I do not talk in my sleep—or do I?" Lisa said, her thoughts turning inward.

"Yes, and remember, you're an enlisted-type person, and your Commander Everett is an officer and a gentleman, at least according to the Congress of the United States," Sarah said as she finally looked up from her salad.

"I've let it get a little too serious, and we *are* trying to cut back on our meetings. I just think about that big lug constantly," Lisa said, placing her spoon back into her bowl of soup and then rubbing her eyes with the palms of her hand. "So what about that new officer? Carl hasn't said anything at all. Have you heard anything?"

"He's supposed to be some sort of black-operations guru or something."

"From what I saw just a minute ago, he looked like an ordinary officer to me. But then again, you had a better look at him than me."

"You better start thinking about how to get yourself out of this thing with Commander America," Sarah admonished, raising her left eyebrow.

Lisa didn't answer; she just sat and stared at her soup without really seeing it.

The senator told me a few things, amazing stuff to be sure, but I'm not really sold as to the importance of all this."

Everett thought again before commenting and placed his knife and fork down as he slowly wiped his mouth with his napkin, then said, "Sir, you're no different than I or any other serving line officer that comes on board here. You wonder, are we here just to play games and babysit?"

Collins pushed his plate away and looked into Carl's eyes, then crossed his arms and listened.

"I can assure you, Major, we're not chasing fairy tales here, this is a very dangerous and, at times, deadly business."

"How so?" Collins asked, still looking intently into the younger man's eyes.

"Well, four years ago, it was maybe my sixth or seventh field assignment. The computer nerds upstairs stumbled onto a dig, an archaeological survey being conducted in Greece. The University of Texas and the Greek government sponsored it jointly. Their team consisted of Dr. Emily Harwell, a few Texas grad students, a couple of Greek professors, and of course myself and one other Event Group doctor, posing as part of their labor force." Again Everett paused and got a faraway look.

Collins watched him, and the way his second-in-command delivered the story, it was as if he were actually giving a field report.

"The good doc and her students came across a series of mathematical calculations that were buried in clay jars and sealed with beeswax. Now this was a no-name Greek alchemist that had buried them in the cellar of his villa. He wasn't famous for anything and was one of those people that history leaves anonymous for all his brilliant work, but the equations that were found were used to calculate the speed of light, three thousand years ago. The find was amazing and made a few jaws drop, I can tell you. It was a work on papyrus that would have made Einstein proud. How would he have done this? And most importantly, why would this no-name Greek mathematician do it in the first place?"

Jack was amazed. "I would like to see them."

"The account was taken by force," Everett said. "The Event Group, while unique in the world, does have foreign agencies we work and compete with in an offhanded way through our National Archives front. No one knows we exist, *officially*. Oh, Great Britain has a pretty good idea, but could never prove it. These other archival groups are basically in it for antiquities, whereas the United States has turned the world's history into a science. We actually change the present by looking into the past. Now, some of the more rogue nations and organizations don't play by the rules. The night in question, we lost the manuscript to a man named Henri Farbeaux. The French deny he works for them so he may just be a mercenary, but he is ruthless in gathering information when the situation dictates. He gets intelligence and equipment from someone, some organization, because his equipment is pure state-of-the-art stuff, right on par with our equipment, and we get the best."

"I've had operational run-ins with other special ops guys,

but I've never heard of this Farbeaux character, at least I've seen no intelligence dossier on him, French or otherwise," Collins said.

"Totally ruthless, Major. We suspect he hit us with a large strike team while we were in Greece, Men in Black we call them. Hit at night by the book and no one saw it coming. We lost twenty-two people, including one of our own, a lady doc from MIT. I liked her a lot. She was ugly as homemade soap, but the smartest woman I have ever known and flat out the funniest. She could tell the dirtiest jokes in the world." Everett smiled in remembrance. "I was held up in the hills surrounding Athens for three hours until a strike team of air force commandos from Aviano in Italy arrived and extracted me."

"Wounded?" asked Collins.

"Took one in the leg. I swear I'll get that bastard Farbeaux someday. He has a major hurt heading his way, and this swab's going to be the one to deliver it."

"So he took the documents and got away clean?"

Everett took a breath and leaned back in his chair. "Yes, sir, he did. And every time before and since, it's almost as if he knows our plans, knows where we'll be and what we're doing, thus the internal mole hunt we have going on at the moment." Everett closed his eyes in thought. "The Israelis almost had him three months ago, but missed just south of the Sudan. Fucker has a sixth sense about him. An hour before Mossad nails him to the wall, he skips, just like someone was tipping him. He's very good and travels with an international cast of assassins, and get this, a lot of them are known to be Americans, guys with training, like you and I."

"He has to have funding from someplace. With all this computing power around here, that information should be rather easy to come across. Does the FBI have anything?"

"All I know is that bastard has friends in high places and is always one step ahead of our Group. As for the Feds, all we know is that we're not the only ones this guy goes after, he's after technology also. It's said that he hits the big companies for new advances, that kind of thing, big-time industrial espionage."

Collins shook his head.

Everett reached in his back pocket and pulled out a handheld data-fact. He switched on the small portable computer and used the small aluminum pen device to find the information he wanted. Then he handed the computer to Collins.

"This is the list Alice, the senator, and Director Compton made up for security. He told me to show it to you as soon as I could."

Collins looked from the naval commander to the datafact. There on the liquid-crystal screen were listed fifteen names; most he noticed had computer sciences listed after their monikers and duties. He scanned the names, only recognizing the one at the top.

"Those are people of *interest* in our mole hunt, listed in the order of probability," Everett said as he looked around their table, then picked up his fork even though he had lost his appetite.

"This first name, are they kidding?"

Everett just looked at the major and then took a bite of his cold roast beef.

Jack glanced back at the name that headed the list of suspects. The other top six were the heads of all the investigative and intelligence agencies in the federal government, and the name at the head of the list was that of the president of the United States.

After lunch, Jack, Carl, and Niles Compton sat behind closed doors and discussed the security list Everett had shown Jack. Collins wasn't impressed with the way they went about screening names to place on the "watch" list. They assumed that their mole was high-ranking, but in Collins's experience it could be someone as low in security clearance as the night janitor. He knew this thing would have to be broken down and backgrounds checked more thoroughly. Home life checked. He had found that the easiest way for someone to be caught was in their home lifestyle. The IRS had used the same system for years; it was easy to catch someone living beyond his means. So that would be the first place the security department started, checking out how some of the Group's people lived at their off-base residences. Collins outlined to Everett and Niles how they would go about starting the next phase of the investigation, and that the first thing they should do is burn their current list of suspects and start fresh.

"Why, this is everybody with access to material that has been leaked," Niles said, incredulous.

"We have to start with a fresh outlook," Jack replied.

"And what is that?" Niles asked.

Collins smiled and stood when Alice walked into the room to begin their tour of the vault area. He looked down at Compton and Everett. "Everybody, Mr. Director, everyone in this complex is now suspect, from you to the last person to be recruited, and that's me."

Sarah McIntire saw the new major and Alice walking along the hallway. During her lunch with Lisa they had discussed field assignments and their upcoming commissionings, Sarah to second lieutenant, and Lisa to ensign, ranks that the new head of security would have to approve. She had wondered aloud what kind of man this officer was, and now she had a chance to at least get an opening impression. She spied a classmate of hers and asked her to take her books and drop them off at her room, then she hurried to catch up with Alice and Collins.

"Good morning, Alice, Major," she said from behind them.

Both turned at once and saw the army specialist standing there smiling.

"Hello, dear," Alice answered.

Collins looked at her and gave a slight nod of his head, recognizing her from the cafeteria and their near collision.

"May I walk with you?" Sarah asked Alice.

"I'm just taking the major on the Magical Mystery Tour," Alice answered, "but you're welcome to walk with us a ways."

"Major, have you met Sarah? She'll be a geological department head in just a few months and then she'll be drawing second lieutenant's pay."

"Yes, we met unofficially at lunch," Jack answered.

Sarah began to feel a little embarrassed and decided after looking into the major's eyes, this wasn't such a good idea. "If you're going to the vaults, it's probably important. I better . . ."

A speaker they were passing under drowned her out. It was Niles Compton: "Will Alice Hamilton and Dr. Pollock please report to photo intelligence? Alice Hamilton and Dr. Pollock to photo intelligence."

"I'm sorry, Major, it looks like I have to go."

"We can tour some other time, Alice," Collins said.

Sarah looked from the major to Alice and quickly volunteered, "I can take him down, I'm cleared for vault security."

Alice looked at the young woman and smiled. "That's an excellent idea. Major, would you mind?"

"That's up to the specialist. If she has the time and doesn't have to be anywhere . . ."

"Excellent, I'll see you later and we'll discuss the security drills you want to conduct. Thank you, Sarah, for volunteering your services, even though you're supposed to be deep in study for your engineering final."

"I helped Professor Jennings make up the test; besides, I think I'm a better tour guide than you, I'm not so clinical."

Alice laughed. "Perhaps so, and I will speak to our Mr. Jennings about having students, no matter how gifted, devise his tests for him." She turned to the major. "Jack, I'll see you later," she said, touching his arm and then walking quickly away. "And don't forget, Sarah, your final . . ."

"Wouldn't miss it for the world," she said as she strode confidently toward the three elevators aligned side by side against the wall. Collins watched her for just a moment, then followed.

"I guess you know we are situated on level seven?" she asked.

Collins didn't say anything, he just stood with his arms crossed. Finally the elevator doors opened with a soft ping and Collins caught the female voice of the computer announcing, "Level seven." Sarah stepped in, followed by Jack, who swiveled away from the door and stood straight-backed against the right side of the car.

"Level?" the canned voice asked.

"Seventy please," Sarah said, not really noticing she was being polite to a computer-controlled elevator.

Jack felt a slight movement and the hiss of air as the car started its long descent. He closed his eyes as he thought about the elevator riding on nothing but air. He thought he heard Sarah say something.

"Excuse me?" Jack asked.

"I said here we are," she repeated.

The elevator came to a halt. "Level seventy," the soft female voice stated.

Sarah stepped out and waited for Collins. The major looked at her, then down the long and high-ceiled corridor. The first thing Jack noticed was what looked like a normal bank of fluorescent lighting that wrapped around the entrance to the vault area. He knew what it was from his time at the proving grounds at Bell Labs and Aberdeen. He knew if you walked through that lighting without disarming the harmless-looking security system, lasers set inside would cut you to ribbons in seconds. This was what was known as a kill zone breach. They both stepped up to the portal leading into the vault area and presented their identification to a blue-overall-clad marine guard. He slid their IDs down an electronic reader one at a time and seemed satisfied when their information came up on the reader screen. The corporal handed their cards back without comment.

Collins followed Sarah inside after the laser defense was turned off. The vaults were made of thick-chromed steel, not unlike the variety you find in banks. They disappeared into the distance as they were set in a circular fashion into the

rock. Technicians roamed the wide corridors carrying clipboards and sample cases, not paying Sarah and the major
any attention other than to nod a greeting.

"As I'm sure you've been told, Major, some of the artifacts in these vaults will never see the light of day. Others
are being released one or two at a time for security reasons.
Our security mostly, as it wouldn't do at all to have this stuff
traced back to us."

Collins nodded his head in understanding and stepped
toward Sarah. "Is any of this worth people dying for?"

Sarah thought a moment. "Yes, sir, I believe most of it is."

Collins just looked down at her. Her eyes were honest and
he thought she really believed what she was saying.

She produced a card that she wore around her neck on a
chain and tucked into her coverall, then stepped to the nearest vault. She took the small card-key and swiped it down a
reader, which ordered the lock to disengage. There was an
audible click and the door slid silently inside the wall. An
overhead light came on automatically and the computer
said, "The vault requirements for file number 11732: all personnel are prohibited from making contact with the sealed
enclosure."

"We lost two people on this particular mission, a doctor
from the University of Chicago and a student from LSU.
They thought it was worth dying to bring it out."

Collins stepped past McIntire and into the small theater-
style room. Four spotlights shone down on a four-foot-wide-
by-eight-foot-long glass box, with latex hoses running into
its sides from the aluminum panel embedded in the wall.
The room was cool and smelled of wet stone. Inside the
glass box was a decomposed body lying on a slab of gray
granite. The tattered remains of khaki-style clothing hung
off the exposed bones, and the remains of short-topped
boots were visible through the glass. The blondish red hair
was short and still held a part just left of center of the head.
There was a nice clean bullet hole in the side of the skull.

Sarah stood motionless for a long time until finally placing her small hand over the glass as near as she could get

without contacting it and seemed to gaze forever at the figure inside.

"The Yakuza killed our people over her," she said in reverence, seeming to show deference to the dead.

"Come again?" Collins asked.

"Japanese organized crime."

"I know the Yakuza. Why did they kill a student and a doctor?"

"They thought it was important enough to kill for." She turned to face Collins. "The head of the Yakuza today is named Menoka Ozawa. He had a grandfather of not very high standing in the Japanese army in 1938." Sarah looked at the body through the glass again as she felt a kinship with it every time she was near it. "It was that man that was responsible for the bullet hole you see." She once again watched Collins for a reaction, and when none came, she continued, "This woman was executed on a small island in the Pacific for being an alleged spy, her and a man named Fred Noonan."

Jack looked closer at the skeletal remains. He smiled. It was the small gap in the cadaver's front teeth that clinched it for him.

"Amelia Earhart," Jack said, looking from the coffin to Sarah.

"How did you guess?"

"Believe it or not, I saw it on *Unsolved Mysteries*." He smiled. "So why not tell the public?"

"I can only assume, since the senator and director don't take me into their confidence."

"Assume away then," he said, sweeping his arm in a mock bow.

"She was on a stunt, that's all. That is until President Roosevelt and Naval Intelligence asked her to gather some information on Japanese movements and bases in the central Pacific, which she did. That was one of the unflattering things about Roosevelt." Once again Sarah looked at the major. "He played on her womanhood at being needed and accepted for his own ends. She had mechanical problems and her Electra aircraft went down. They found her and executed her without really knowing or caring who she was. A typical military response, if I may add. Anyway, this Yakuza fellow didn't want any bad taint to fall on his grandfather, who had left a detailed accounting of the incident in his personal journal. Thus he was willing to kill to keep the body right where it was found."

Sarah started for the door, pausing to look at the major as he was still taking in Earhart's body. He stood motionless for a moment, a sad look crossing his features.

"She was something, though, wasn't she?" he asked, still looking.

"In my opinion, one of the bravest women in history." Sarah thought a moment, then added, "Major, did you meet the old gunnery sergeant at Gate Two?"

"Campos, if I remember right."

"One of our people went on vacation ten or so years back and adjusted the thinking of this Yakuza person. They found him hanging in his rather expensive apartment one day. The person who vacationed in Japan that year was Gunny Campos."

Collins turned and looked at Sarah, wondering if viewing this particular vault had been a deliberate way of showing the worth of women, such as Earhart, or old people, such as the gunnery sergeant, or if it was just a fluke. He suspected Sarah was a person to watch.

"Well, anyway, her body is being flown back to Hawaii next month. We have arranged for Ms. Earhart to be found by a professor from Colorado State University and a University of Tokyo faculty member, both of whom had brilliantly proven this theory linking the Japanese and Earhart. So they deserve to find the body after we place it back." Sarah looked once more at the body. "Amelia deserves far better than this," she said as she gestured to the glass enclosure.

After Jack quietly left the vault, Sarah closed the door and it locked automatically. Then she turned and walked down a hundred feet before stopping at a larger, more heavily built door. She let Collins catch up before she turned and slid her access card into the slot. Instead of sliding up or into a wall, this one just clicked, and there was a gasp of air as it only opened an inch.

Sarah swung the large vault door open and stepped inside and the lights came on automatically.

Jack was amazed to see the metal ribs of a boat. It was long, about three hundred feet in length, he quickly deduced. The stern disappeared into the vastness of the vault. He made out hull plating that covered about a third of the vessel and the huge metal rivets that held them in place.

Sarah asked him to follow her up a large metal staircase that was permanently attached to the floor, allowing people to reach the top deck and travel the length of the find. As they reached the top, Collins saw what looked like more metal covering of what was once indeed a deck, which led to a tall structure that resembled a rusting conning tower of a submarine. Only this tower was rounded at the top with long diving planes attached to its sides. He could see large rusted-through holes that afforded a view of the interior, which was lit up by lighting that had been placed inside. He made out rust-encrusted gauges and levers.

"Resembles a submarine," he said.

Sarah didn't respond; she nodded her head and made her way along the catwalk. She stopped toward the stern and pointed down into a compartment that had been cut away.

"See those boxy-looking things lining the floor?"

Jack followed her finger and saw several hundred large, rusty boxlike rectangles. "Yes, what are they?"

"Batteries. This is an electrically powered submarine, Major."

"World War Two? But I've never seen a class of boats that had as strange a bow as this one. I don't think they had a spherical bow in the forties."

Sarah smiled. "No, they didn't. Our most advanced classes of submarines for most of World War Two were the Gato and Balao classes; they fought mostly in the Pacific campaign against the Japanese."

"So what are the dates on this craft?"

"Well, she was a little ahead of her time. Would you believe 1871?"

Jack looked at Sarah as if she had fallen off the deep end.

"This is what we know for sure. The boat was discovered off the coast of Newfoundland in 1967. She was totally buried in mud and she came up basically as you see her today. We have confirmed that she was electrically driven and, according to our engineers, had a top speed of twenty-six knots submerged, far faster than our boats in the war, and very comparable to our attack subs today. She had a crew complement of close to a hundred men and carried rudimentary torpedoes that ran on compressed air. For obvious reasons they are stored in a different vault. She had a ramming spike on her bow that has yet to be recovered, but we know it was there because the mounting for it is still bolted to the window frame. She had a glass nose made of quartz crystal for underwater viewing. She's just like the vessel described by Jules Verne in his novel *Twenty Thousand Leagues Under the Sea*."

"You have got to be joking."

"Major, all I can say is, there she is. You decide. Her electrical-powered engines are in some ways far more advanced than what we have today and far more efficient. We've had people from General Dynamics Electric Boat Division here who swear this thing was a model of efficiency."

"Don't tell me this is the *Nautilus*."

"No, I'm not telling you that because we know her real name. We discovered her commissioning plaque only five years ago encased in mud just aft of her control room. Her name was *Leviathan*. The senator suspects that Mr. Verne may have modeled his vision after a real craft. It's just speculation of course, but a sound theory."

"Her crew?" Jack asked.

"Went down with her. Carbon-14 dating places her right around 1871, but her demise could have been anytime within fifteen years of her commission. We know she was manufactured in 1871 because of the engravings on her gauges. That coupled with testing is tantamount to gospel."

She hesitated. "Only thirty-six of the crew remains were discovered inside the submarine. But we know her ship's roster was close to a hundred due to the berthing areas we found."

"Amazing," Collins said, looking at the rusted skeletal remains.

"We have all the data there is to collect. The Woods Hole Oceanographic Institute has been working on her for the past thirty years."

Collins acknowledged the name of the prestigious oceanographic institute. "Are they a part of the Group?"

"A few are consultants trusted with our existence. They owe us for"—she paused for dramatic effect—"*certain things we've sent their way.*"

Collins caught the innuendo. One thing he knew on the subject of the Woods Hole institute was that the oceanographer Dr. Robert Ballard was a part of the institute, and it was he who discovered the resting sight of RMS *Titanic*. He just shook his head.

Sarah was just turning to go on to the next Event vault she had in mind when they were interrupted.

"Attention, all department heads are to report to the main conference room immediately, all department heads to the main conference room. This is Code One Active. Major Collins, please contact 117, please call 117."

"Well, Major, I've never heard that call sign given since I have been here." Then she explained, "That's the director; code one active is an alert for an *Event, the big kind.* The phone is right there." She pointed to a wall line next to one of the vaults.

Jack removed the handset and punched in the number 117, then looked at Sarah, who was ashen. There was an audible click and then Alice picked up.

"Major, please meet Mr. Everett up on level seven. He'll show you how to get to the conference room, and step on it, Major, Director Compton is ready to bust about something," Alice spoke quickly, and hung up.

"Sorry, Sarah, I have to cut this short." He turned away toward the circular hallway and the elevators beyond.

"I understand. In the elevator hit the red EXPRESS button, that will ensure no stops between here and seven," she called after him.

She watched him vanish beyond the curve of vaults.

Code One Active. Sarah shivered at the thought of those three words. She had heard rumors of what those words represented. Code One Active—a possible Civilization Altering Event.

FIVE

The sound of a small engine perked Buck's ears up. Both sets of eyes were drawn to the desert to their right. The old man saw the small dust cloud and shook his head.

"That damn fool kid's gonna break his neck someday on that smelly thing," he said aloud as he started his trek toward the mountains again.

The noise grew louder and the old man finally spied the red, four-wheel ATV and its small rider. The all-terrain motorcycle was zooming through the old washouts and jumping clear to the opposite sides. Then the rider noticed Gus and Buck and turned their way, one hand in the air, wildly waving. As he approached, the kid didn't see a rather large dip of another wash. While his hand was raised in greeting, disaster was there to welcome the boy as the front wheels hit the dip and dug deeply into the sand. The only thing that Gus was able to see from his vantage point was the rear end of the small machine go flying up in a cloud of sand and dirt, obscuring the bone-breaking crash Gus knew to be happening.

"Son of a bitch, he did it! Went and kilt hisself!" he yelled as he dropped Buck's reins and ran to the scene of what he knew must surely be the boy's death. Pots, pans, and shovels clanged as the mule ran along noisily behind.

When he arrived, he saw the kid sitting on his butt, splay-legged and trying to remove the red helmet he wore. Besides being covered with dust and a little blood on his upper lip from a nosebleed, he looked alive. Gus jumped down into the small arroyo, carefully avoiding the still-turning front wheels of the ATV.

"Good goddamn, William! You took a good enough spill that time, boy." Gus placed his arms under the boy's and lifted him up.

"What happened?" Billy Dawes asked when he finally twisted the helmet off.

"What happened? You got throw'd is what happened, you young fool." Gus held him at arm's length to look him over.

"Damn," the boy exclaimed as he brushed the dust from his face and clothes.

Tilly released him and stepped back to take the boy in. Nothing looked broken. The small motorcycle-lookin' thing looked all right. Just to be sure, Buck, who had come down into the washout without being heard, nudged the boy with his nose, knocking him down across the ATV.

"Hey!" the boy cried out. "What ya do that for?" he asked the now innocent-looking mule.

Gus helped the eleven-year-old to his feet again and brushed him off. Billy just looked at Buck and shook his head. The mule just twitched his ears.

"Now you watch that mouth of yours, boy, your ma wouldn't appreciate your cussin' like old Gus none too much."

"No, she would probably take the soap and scrub my mouth some."

"Does your mama even know you're out here?" the old man asked, squinting his left eye and leaning toward Billy.

The kid wiped the blood from his nose and lip, then grinned at Gus. His silence was answer enough.

"Boy, you know this desert can kill you six ways from Sunday. What if you broke your legs and old Gus wasn't here to help ya?"

"Well, I didn't," young Billy protested. Then a look of deep thought suddenly crossed the boy's features. "You ain't gonna tell Mom I was out here, are you?"

Gus pretended to be thinking this over, then turned his back on the kid. "I don't know . . . that was a serious fall you took. You're blooded and everything."

"Aw, it's not bad, Gus, really, I never crash like that. You know I'm good at riding out here."

Gus tilted his head to let Billy think he was thinking this over. "All right then, you get back on that thing and scoot back to your ma." Gus pointed to the overturned ATV.

"Why can't I go with you and Buck for a while? It's Friday and you know what that's like at the bar. I'd just be in Mom's way."

Gus looked around and up at the noonday sun, half hearing Billy's plea. He removed the old fedora and wiped the sweat from his brow once again. Then he replaced the hat and looked toward the mountains ahead of him a good two miles distant. For some reason just the sight of them today made him a little edgy. He shook his head as if to clear it.

"Senility settin' in," he mumbled to himself.

"What, Gus?" the boy asked, pausing for a moment from brushing at his clothes to look at his old friend.

Gus turned and looked at Billy, then smiled, his false teeth gleaming in the sun. "It's nothin'. Well, wouldn't hurt none if you tag along for a bit, I guess. But I want you to head for the house when I say, deal?" He stuck out a gloved hand.

Billy took the handshake and smiled as wide as the Cheshire cat. They both righted the ATV and Gus got Buck moving. But his eyes were drawn to the mountains again. They mutely returned his stare, almost daring him to come.

"Did you hear that sonic boom earlier?"

"Yeah, I thought I heard something," Gus replied, not letting on that the something he spoke of had knocked him and Buck off their feet.

"It sure must have been a big jet that did that one, huh?"

"You scout up ahead and look for Injun sign, boy. If

you're going to hang with Gus, you gotta earn your keep and quit askin' questions," he said with a wink.

"Yes, sir!" Billy answered, giving a not-too-bad hand salute. Then he placed the helmet firmly on his head, snapped the strap on, and turned the key for the bike's ignition. He gunned the engine on the Honda and it shot forward, startling Buck and making him jump back a step.

Gus watched the boy go as he was silhouetted against the mountains with the sun gleaming off the chrome of his scooter. The old man shook with a sudden chill. He thought he would camp in the foothills tonight and head up in the morning. As the day had worn on, he had decided he wanted little or nothing to do with the mountain this night. As he looked at the range, he started to understand the ghost stories that were told about the place. And maybe the Lost Dutchman Mine was *lost* for good reason, maybe men weren't supposed to go there.

It was two hours later that the trio had stopped and Gus had passed around his old canteen. Gus used his hat to pour Buck a drink as Billy stroked the area between the mule's eyes and Buck nudged closer to the boy.

"You better stop your flirtin' with that mule and get your skinny butt home." Gus looked around the desert and up the white-tinged mountain above. "Don't want you to get caught out here tonight."

"How many people have been lost up there looking for that mine?" Billy asked, finishing with Buck and walking over to the small camp.

"Not as many as the Indians and tourism people in these parts would like folks to think, that's for sure," Gus said as he glanced around at the still desert.

"How many?" the boy persisted.

Gus finished laying his tarp down for his bedroll, then rubbed the whiskers on his chin and cheek. "Well, must be near to three hundred or so." The old man watched the boy's expression change from mere curiosity to apprehension. Inwardly, he smiled at his exaggeration. "Now you better get back on that scooter and skedaddle."

Billy Dawes took in the desert around him. The shadows were getting longer, and he did have to help his mom. "Yeah, I guess I better."

"And, boy?"

"Yes, sir?"

"Don't think I didn't notice that dust you knocked off your clothes back there," Gus said with one eye closed against the late-afternoon sun.

"What dust?" Billy said, knowing full well what Gus was talking about.

"Before you come lookin' for me, you were out ridin' that thing at Soda Flats, weren't ya?"

Gus had warned Billy about Soda Flats a million times. It was an ancient dry lake bed at the eastern end of the valley. The alkali deposit stretched for about two or three miles square and was as flat as a frying pan, which was perfect for riding at full speed on an ATV.

"I only skirted it, Gus, honest, I didn't cross it."

"Boy, that alkali will kill you eight ways from Sunday. It'll eat the skin right off'n you if you fall into it. Now, if you choose to ignore me, you can't come along with me no more, you got that?"

"I got it, Gus, I promise, no more."

"Alright, now I have your word, no more Soda Flats?"

Billy held up his right hand. "Promise," he said in all seriousness.

The old man watched the boy walk over to the mule and whisper something to him. Buck twitched his ears in agreement. Then Billy placed the red helmet on his head and started up the ATV; he revved the motor twice, then left for home.

Finished with his bedroll, the old prospector looked into his leather poke and pulled out a large bottle of bourbon, shaking his head at the way he was feeling and about the boy and his daredevil-may-care attitude about those damned alkali flats. He unscrewed the cap and took a long pull from the bottle, then looked at Buck, who was looking at him.

"What?"

The mule showed his teeth, then rotated his large ears.

"It's medicine tonight, old boy. I think I wanna sleep the night through." He looked at the mountain, then took another swig. "Too goddamn old to be afraid of the dark."

Buck snorted, seemingly agreeing with him.

"Snort all you want, buddy, but I feel like a kid that knows for a fact that the bogeyman is out there somewhere."

As he pulled on the bottle again, he looked at the mountains above him. For now, those mountains held a close-kept and dark secret that was about to be shared with the world. The bogeyman was starting to wake up.

The Event Group, Nellis AFB, Nevada

J ack found Everett waiting for him on level seven.

"Glad Alice sent you. No one told me where the main conference room is."

"The map is in your welcome packet, which you haven't received yet," Everett said as he gestured for Collins to go ahead.

"Now it sounds like the military," Collins said. They laughed as they walked down the carpeted and circular hall.

A s the two officers made their way up three floors to the conference room, another man rode a second elevator up to the thirty-third sublevel, to the Group's small club known affectionately as The Ark. He had just left early from his shift on the fortieth level, the level that housed the main computer networking systems. The man was tall and heavy, his red hair uncombed, and his white shirt prominently displaying an ink stain on the left breast pocket. He had left the computer center just minutes after the call went out to the Event Evaluation Team for them to meet in the main conference room, taking advantage of the rush of people leaving their departments.

Robert Reese had been chosen for his ability to write programs and network them to various illegal links with other systems throughout the world, but most important he was there for his knowledge of the one-of-a-kind Cray computer known as Europa XP-7.

Reese was performing a routine test on the Event Group's own KH-11 photo recon bird and was tying the systems into each other when he happened upon an incoming data stream that he hadn't been cleared to see. It was supposed to be Eyes Only for Dr. Compton and Computer Center director, Pete Golding. He quickly made a copy of the data as the stream was encoded and had just minutes to decipher the information and debug it. Only after viewing the coded data did he know he possessed the most amazing piece of information he had ever seen.

Reese had been recruited for the Event Group and hired away from a cushy job and a good career in Seattle working as a systems manager for Microsoft. But for Reese it had been the job offer after the Group's that interested him the most, and had come rather clandestinely, even more so than the Group's. But the job would only take effect *after* he had been hired into the Event Center. The offer came from people that paid well and asked little, with his only commitment to this new company being to forward items and information when requested, or if he happened to come across anything that he found interesting.

Thus far it had worked out beautifully. He dealt with some lowlifes in Vegas once in a while and was paid well for the secrets of the past he delivered to them. But he was ordered to watch for one specific item on the corporation's wish list, and that little item had come today through the recon bird.

The elevator doors opened and he stepped into the foyer across from The Ark and made his way inside the darkened club. Few people were there, mostly couples having a beer or mixed drink after duty. A rock-and-roll tune played from the jukebox, a song he didn't recognize because he never had time for anything as mundane as music. He walked over to a bank of three pay phones sitting side by side against the far wall near the restroom. He knew that inept security division that macho navy asshole was currently running monitored the phones at the Group, but he could take care of that easily enough. Reese didn't look around as he stepped up to the center phone. He knew what attracted attention and what didn't. The computer specialist slid his credit card into the slot and pulled down. The card was a special one that Reese himself had designed. It really was a Sprint credit line, but he was most proud of a few extra goodies built into it. As he slid the card in and swiped, the magnetic strip on the back of the card imprinted directly through to the Sprint Telecommunications computer, then on into a leased AT&T telephone line. The microcomputer chip in the card started a chain reaction that would continue to scramble the charge numbers at random. It was totally untraceable, and some guy or gal perhaps in Wisconsin would receive the charge for the call. If anyone checked, the call number would actually come up as two thousand different numbers, therefore no one would ever know who had been called. Not only that, the call would have a telephone prefix three thousand miles away from where the call had actually gone. Smiling, Reese then punched in the numbers and waited for the phone to ring in Las Vegas. While he waited, he gestured for the bartender and made a drinking gesture and mouthed the word *Budweiser*. The man nodded and went to get his beer. The phone began to ring on the other end of the unmonitored phone.

"Ivory Coast Lounge," a female voice answered.

"Yes, I would like to reserve a table for tonight please, the name is Reese. Bob Reese."

There was a moment's hesitation on the other end. "Yes, Mr. Reese, there should be no problem. At what time should we expect your party?"

Reese looked at his wristwatch and calculated. "Three hours."

"That will be fine, Mr. Reese."

"Thank you. Also, would you tell Simon the bartender to chill a bottle of champagne for me please?" Reese hung up.

He walked to the bar. He took slow pulls off the longneck bottle, made a face, and sat the beer down on the bar. Reese never thought of the things he did as treason. That was an ugly word, and a word that was lost on people like him because the only word that really mattered to Reese was a far simpler one, *profit*. And he knew this would be a highly profitable trip into town because in his many dealings with the Centaurus Corporation, he had never once given the code words he had just given to the Ivory Coast Lounge. *Chill a bottle of champagne* meant he was coming in with vital information from the number one item on their wish list, vital and expensive.

The bartender at The Ark, an off-duty marine lance corporal whose real job was in the security department, shook his head as Reese walked out of the club whistling. "Hey, Dr. Reese, that's three bucks you owe me."

But Reese just kept walking, off in a world of his own. The bartender looked at his watch and noted the time.

After Reese left The Ark, the bartender decided to make a report on the man who had appeared on the security list this morning. He walked over to the phone at the far end of the bar and looked up at those who were drinking and talking. When he saw none of them were paying him any mind, he picked up the phone and quickly punched in three numbers.

"Security Center, Staff Sergeant Mendenhall," the black sergeant said tiredly.

"Sarge, this is Wilkins. Is Commander Everett there, or the new major?"

"No, they're hanging with the senator and Dr. Compton at the moment. Something big is happening," Mendenhall said through a yawn.

"Well, would you note it in the security log that one of the people on our security watch list was in here about a half hour ago and made a call from the pay phones? It was the Comp Center assistant supervisor, that Reese guy. I only noticed because according to the Computer Center duty roster, he was still on shift when he came in here."

"Okay, that's a clear violation. I'll note it in the log and pass it along to the commander and the new boss, and then I'm sure they'll get Dr. Compton in on this, so Reese can probably expect a write-up or an ass-chewing in the morning."

SIX

Alice Hamilton met Collins and Everett at the large double doors to the main conference room. She stood with two briefing folders in her hand and made a "hurry up" gesture at the two men, fanning the folders toward the doors.

"Niles, the senator, and the others are waiting for you to start." She ushered them toward the conference room.

"What's up, Alice?" Everett asked in a whisper.

"Not now, Carl, get in there. You have some things to discuss before they call the president." She handed them the briefing folders, one each to Everett and Collins, on their way into the large room.

As they entered, Jack counted seven people seated around the huge oval conference table. The senator was at the opposite end, flipping through some papers in front of him on the polished table. He didn't notice either Collins or Everett as they seated themselves. Alice took her place to the senator's right, in between him and Niles Compton, who was sitting cross-legged reading a report and rubbing his forehead. He finally looked up.

"Ladies and gentlemen, thank you for coming on such short notice. But as you'll see, it's important that we put this thing in your hands as soon as possible." Niles paused and looked straight at Jack.

"First off, Major Collins, I'm sorry for having to throw you into the fire on your very first day, but you'll have to limp along the best you can."

"Yes, sir," replied Jack, looking at the faces around him.

"I assume the rest of you have seen the major's 201 file and know his capabilities and qualifications?"

There were nods around the room. Collins noticed he and Everett were the only two out of the ten in blue jumpsuits. Everyone else wore either a lab coat or casual clothes.

"Major, we'll save the introductions for later," Compton said.

Jack just nodded in response.

Niles placed his papers on the floor and took a laser pointer from his breast pocket.

"We had a situation occur this morning over the Pacific Ocean off the west coast of Panama. It seems on the surface we had an incident involving two naval jets. The aircraft, two F-14 Super Tomcats flying off the USS *Carl Vinson*, were lost at 0640 hours this morning."

The men and women around the table sat in silence at the news. Collins could see that they were accustomed to reports of field losses. He didn't know if that was a comforting thought or not.

"The navy at the moment is very tight-lipped about the incident, as they always are."

The senator interrupted, "Just to let you know, Major Collins, we don't normally investigate every naval incident that comes along."

"Uh, quite," Compton said, clearing his throat again. "We only know something was different because at the time of the incident, we were retasking Boris and Natasha."

Everett pulled his yellow notepad over and scribbled quickly, then slid it in Jack's direction. It read, *KH-11 satellite—we own it, code name is Boris and Natasha.*

Collins raised an eyebrow at this new information. For anyone other than the military, the CIA, or NSA, owning a KH-series spy satellite was amazing. He now knew the director and the senator had to have some kind of reach; they not only had access to military personnel, but their equipment also.

"The lucky thing is," Compton continued, "we left Boris's ears on and Natasha's eyes open. For the simple-minded among you, we left the damn thing running while we moved it, as we were recalibrating several of her systems. We were moving the satellite to observe an area of Brazilian rain forest that may be hiding some ruins we were interested in . . . so what we caught was by pure chance only." Now he looked at his paperwork and shuffled it. "Okay, here's what we know, people. The fighters were flying a standard combat air patrol, or CAP as the Navy terms it. They received a call about an intermittent contact closing on the carrier group position. We have that on tape for those of you who would like to hear it later. They were told the target kept blinking on and off the air-search radar of every ship in the group." Compton paused again. "Boris and Natasha could see with her cameras what the carrier could not with its radar." He removed the blank cover off the first picture on the easel.

"People, I want you to keep your cool about this and try to stay focused," Lee said calmly, not looking up. "We here at Group have dealt with the extreme in history, nature, and strange science, but none of you have ever dealt with anything like this before."

The gathered men and women exchanged questioning looks around the table. They had indeed had to deal with extreme Events, so what could be so shocking the senator had to put a disclaimer on it?

The first still picture was of the two navy Tomcats. Compton pointed them out with the laser pointer; the small red dot highlighted the aircraft. The picture showed them side by side, one slightly in front of the other, a good close-up shot. Then Compton removed the first picture to reveal the second high-definition shot.

"Here, we were checking the diagnostics on the satellite, and so we went to a more wide-angled shot to bring the optics to a nominal setting. It took us longer than I would have liked to wash these images through the computer afterward."

As everyone took in the second picture after Niles stepped aside, their eyes widened and not just a few hearts beat a little faster. Gasps and exclamations were voiced from around the table. Most leaned closer trying to take in what was clearly something most had never considered possible. The room suddenly became like a vacuum, and a few of the Group even leaned back and closed their eyes, then looked again as if that would change the image they were seeing.

"What in the *hell* is that?" Walter Dickinson, the head of the forensic sciences, asked, knowing full well what was depicted.

"I'll tell you what it looks like, Walter. It looks kind of like a flying saucer."

Collins looked from the picture, then back to Lee. Then he studied the photo again. It was definitely saucer-shaped, round and flat like a plate, with what looked to be a smaller dome on top.

"I've been staring at these pictures since early afternoon and I still can't believe what I see, but there it is, clear as hell. Those two fighters were chasing one damn big flying saucer."

Collins stood and walked to the easel for a closer look at the computer-enhanced picture. The others calmed their chatter and watched. Jack brought his right index finger up and traced a nearly invisible line from the back of the saucer to about two hundred feet behind the craft.

"Any idea what this might be, Dr. Compton?" Collins asked from in front of the easel.

"Only speculation at this point, it may be damage of some kind. We believe it was leaking fluid."

"Not caused by our fighters?" Jack asked, seeing the smaller Tomcats far behind the saucer.

"Not according to the chatter on the radio," Niles answered.

Jack returned to his seat.

"At about one and a half minutes into this Event, the fighters believed they had a second contact approaching at several thousand miles per hour." Compton let that sink in. "This speed estimate was confirmed by Boris and Natasha's

Doppler radar, and we have a printout of the actual speed of that second bogey."

"I take it the carrier battle group was aware of the situation by this time?" Virginia Pollock asked. She was in her early forties and had accepted Dr. Compton's offer to come from the General Dynamics Corporation and be assistant director. Now she was the department head of Nuclear Sciences.

"Negative, Virginia. All radio contact between the carrier and her aircraft were lost as they approached the object."

Compton reached up, then hesitated before removing the picture.

"Now, this is where we believe the attack occurred."

The room went deathly silent at the mention of the word *attack*. He took the picture of the two planes and the saucer down. The third picture showed the second Tomcat falling, really nose-diving, out of the frame. But there was something strange about it; this picture had a different color hue to it, a greenish color, possibly explained away by bad computer imaging.

"Right here the pilot of the second F-14, the wingman, called a Mayday. His engines had shut down, and before you ask, there's nothing wrong with the picture. That light is from a source other than the planes or the craft they were chasing."

"What source?" Everett asked, standing to see the image better.

"This one." Niles Compton removed the picture, revealing the new image beneath. Everyone now stood to get a better look.

"Damn," Everett said. A chorus of other exclamations followed. Jack could only clench his jaw muscles.

A second giant saucer was in the picture Niles had uncovered. The F-14s were far below it as the picture showed the second UFO closing in on the lead Tomcat. Without saying a word, Compton removed the picture and replaced it with another. Now several of the Group members sat hard into their high-backed chairs. Talking started all at once after the picture was digested.

The image showed in horrible detail the second saucer slamming into the lead navy fighter from the rear. In this still shot, the plane was already coming apart in flames. The image was so clear you could see either the pilot or his radio intercept officer falling free of the aircraft with his seat still attached.

The senator continued to write, having said virtually nothing to this point, but when he did stop writing notes and look up, he eyed Major Collins, who continued to study the picture. Lee tapped the tabletop with the knuckles of his right hand. It took three raps to finally get everyone's attention. The old man took a deep breath, and as he stood, he gestured Compton over to his side, speaking to him in a low tone. Then Compton went to his seat and lifted a large file to the table and then waited.

Lee started talking, looking toward the last picture that had been shown. "Major, this is exactly what Niles and I were trying to explain earlier about our Group. The few people in government who know we exist, and that's just the Joint Chiefs and the National Security Council, would say this isn't in our area of expertise, that it should be the military's problem, but this is what we call an *Event,* this could be life-altering on any level you care to look at. We have an advantage," he said, looking at all the faces around the table. "We have some experience with this sort of Event, or I should say, I do, in my younger days when I was director of this underground anthill."

Several people mumbled their surprise at what the retired senator had just said, but it quickly died down.

Alice slipped the senator two small pills and he quickly swallowed them with a sip of water, then he removed his cane from the edge of the table where he had hung it and stood and limped to the picture on the easel and tapped it with his index finger.

"President Truman first appointed me to this Group in 1945, and amazingly we had a similar craft follow the same trajectory as this current one two years later, on July the second of 1947. A little town in New Mexico was rocked by an explosion," Lee said, and paused for a moment. "I'm sure you know where I'm headed with this."

Collins watched Lee as the old man recalled the past. He was looking even older than he had this morning, and Collins wondered what medication he had taken just a moment before.

"The Roswell Incident," stated Celia Brown, an African-American professor of natural history from Cornell.

"Correct, the Roswell Incident." Lee then popped the picture again with his fist, rocking the easel. "Roswell, New Mexico. From the evidence collected back in '47, we had us a flying saucer crash, ladies and gentlemen. And at this moment I'm playing a hunch, just a spec of my old memory returning, if you'll so indulge me. If this guess of mine plays out, we have a very serious and dangerous problem on our hands. Just before Boris and Natasha lost contact with the two objects, indicating and confirming the facts we overheard on the carrier's radio frequency that the objects did have some sort of stealth capability, we got a possible track on their trajectory."

"You said that the satellite had lost their track, sir?" Everett asked.

The old man limped back to his chair, leaning on the cane even more. "Yes, after the targets went stealth, they vanished from radar and the imager on Natasha went out of range. But it was her track that we used to project the course. You see, it didn't gain altitude, maybe from the suspected damage, we don't know. So, if it continued to lose that altitude, it may just have come down somewhere."

Others around the huge conference table were looking from the pictures to one another, trying to absorb it all.

"The first craft not being in stealth mode I can understand, maybe damage, but why would the second craft not use the advantage of stealth? It doesn't make a whole lot of sense," Virginia Pollock said.

"We don't have any answers, just good questions like yours, Virginia," Lee said. "But it may very well be that the second craft didn't care if it was seen at that point or not, knowing it would not be tracked afterward. We just don't know and it's dangerous to speculate."

As if on cue, Compton opened the large file folder and then walked over to a fax machine. He entered his security code and started the pages through the machine.

When Lee was satisfied the fax was being sent, he turned to Alice. "Make the call now, please." Then he looked at Niles. "Dr. Compton, with your permission . . ."

Niles nodded and sat down after he had completed the faxing of the papers from the thick folder.

Alice pushed a small button on the tabletop and a lid popped up, and slowly, as if driven by small hydraulics, a red phone raised flush with the table. She then picked up the red handset and punched the only button on the instrument. She gestured to Compton, who went behind the camera and made a final adjustment, then went to the wall and pulled open a set of doors, revealing a hidden high-definition plasma television screen.

"Yes, sir, we're ready on this end," Alice said into the mouthpiece of the handset. Then she took it from her ear, placed it in a small cradle, and pushed it firmly down until it clicked into place.

"We set?" Lee asked.

"Yes, sir."

On the screen there was a flash of blue, and then it stabilized into a solid picture. An image flashed on: the seal of the president of the United States. Then another image appeared: a man this time, sitting on a sofa. He was wearing a denim work shirt and was leaning forward with his arms placed on his knees, his fingers intertwined in front of him.

"Mr. President," Niles said, standing and looking into the camera.

"Good evening, Dr. Compton, what have my favorite people got for me today?"

"Sir, may I first apologize for disturbing you at Camp David. We know you like privacy when you're away from your office."

"Nonsense, Doctor, actually you saved me from some

burnt hot dogs and underdone burgers." The president looked around conspiratorially. "My daughters are grilling." The people gathered in Nevada chuckled in politeness at the remark.

"Well, this may put off your appetite slightly, sir," Senator Lee interjected.

"Senator Lee, this is a pleasant surprise, how are you today?"

"I'm fine, sir, but we do have disturbing news to bring to you."

"I'm listening."

"Undoubtedly you've had the incident in the Pacific brought to your attention?" Lee asked.

"Yes, I have, a terrible tragedy."

"Has the navy provided you with details as of this time, Mr. President?"

"Not yet. The Navy Department said the preliminary results of their investigation will be forwarded by tomorrow morning," the president answered, leaning back on the sofa.

"The Event Group will send you some information the navy may not provide you, sir, not that they could. We came upon it purely by accident."

"What information is that, and why not forward the intelligence on through the NSA or the CIA? That shouldn't compromise the Group."

"We think this should be kept pretty close to the vest at this point, sir. Plus we have some conjecture we think is relevant that you may be interested in."

The president looked thoughtful for a moment, then looked into the camera. "You've got my attention, Mr. Lee, but I'm not comfortable with the fact you're not bringing the navy in on this. After all, we can say this information came through NSA to protect the source."

"I think you'll see why in a moment, sir." The old man hesitated briefly. "And we have made queries through and of the navy, sir, as Director Compton here can attest to, after having the door slammed on his ample nose."

"I'm used to handling territorial disputes, Senator."

"Mr. President, we . . . or I should say *I*, have a problem at the moment with the navy handling this situation."

The president looked down at his hands. "You know I give the Group a lot of leeway, Senator, but if the information you're sending me isn't compelling enough, I'm going to have to side with the navy on this issue. It was their aircraft and lost air crews. I see no reason why a sister agency of the navy should handle anything in this purely naval affair, outside of offering any intelligence they *may* have in their possession." The president was showing a little more color than he had just a moment before.

"Director Compton will get you up to speed on what we know, sir, then we can go into what we"—again Lee caught himself—"I suspect."

The president pursed his lips and gave a shake of his head. "As I said, the only things you are keeping me from are my daughters and their version of a barbecue. Continue, Dr. Compton, by all means."

Compton asked for Collins and Everett to help slide the easel to a position where the man at Camp David could get the best possible view.

Collins noticed that Lee walked over to a seat lining the wall where he could still see the presentation, but placed himself well out of the way. Alice sat in the chair next to him, and it looked as if she was admonishing him for something. He seemed to growl at her as she straightened and fell silent.

After Niles had finished briefing the president on the saucer incident, Collins looked at the screen as he sat in his seat. The others settled in their chairs and looked at the new folders that had been placed in front of each place by one of Niles's assistants.

As they looked at the screen, the president had disappeared.

"Maybe we scared him off," commented the senator, to break the silence in the room.

Everyone chuckled. Within a few seconds the president walked back into the frame. He sat down at the couch with his reading glasses perched on his nose. Without looking up he said, "Admiral Raleigh at CINCPAC headquarters concurs with your pictures. They have a survivor of one of the two Tomcats, and according to the admiral, he tells a pretty amazing story. A story that fits with the evidence you produced." The president looked up from the file he had just received from the Event Group via fax.

"What about the survivor, Mr. President? Does commander in chief Pacific plan on holding him?" Compton asked.

"He's being quarantined and flown to Miramar."

Niles Compton looked toward the camera and the large image of the president behind it. "Sir, we may want to interview that officer at the earliest possible time."

"That's impossible, at least at this time, Niles. I appreciate the Group's help in this matter, but it's their show. Do you understand?"

Once again, Lee stood and smiled disarmingly. "Mr. President, you know I wouldn't ask without good reason, and you also know I'm not a frivolous man. You have that file in your hand and you know we're going to amaze and astound you. And in the end you will bow to what the Group wants to do. Why? Because you know we won't screw it up, number one, and number two, you love the hell out of us."

The president of the United States shook his head and laughed out loud. He tossed the file that had been sent him on the coffee table beside where his feet were propped and sat back into the cushions of his couch. He looked at the screen over his bifocals.

"Goddamn it! I was afraid of this. You look like a stalking tiger. Well, this time I'm apt to say no, you old fool," the president said, trying to sound convincing. "Niles, I gave you the job as director to keep him away from me; you're not doing too well."

"He's my mouthpiece, Mr. President."

Lee just stared into the camera; he pursed his lips and leaned heavily on his cane.

The president of the United States looked indignant. *"Bastard,"* he jokingly hissed, "you know damn good and well I spoil you people too much."

The group around the table was settled and on the large screen the president of the United States was seated and ready. No one in the conference room, save for Niles and Alice, knew this would be Senator Garrison Lee's last actionable request to a sitting president; win or lose this last argument, he was done. The discoverer of numerous priceless historical treasures and rewriter of much of the world's history, Lee would end it all with a pitch to the president about going after a flying saucer.

"Mr. President, ladies and gentlemen, in front of you is a case file that doesn't show up on any computer and doesn't exist as far as the Event Group is concerned. None of you save Niles here has ever seen it."

The men and women around the room exchanged glances. The president just looked on.

"The much-denied yet well-known incident on July the third, 1947, happened. The Roswell Incident was real, and this is the order in which it occurred. On that date an unidentified flying object did go down in the rugged cattle country of Lincoln County, New Mexico, not far from the small town of Roswell. There were believed to be no survivors at that time. On that July third, at sunrise, a rancher by the name of Mac Brazel and a neighbor boy, seven-year-old Dee Proctor, investigated a loud boom they had heard the night before. On his property they found what was described as wreckage of an aircraft, and in Brazel's words, 'It must have been a bomber or something, 'cause it was strewn over hell and back.'" The senator paused; he looked at the man at Camp David and saw he was listening intently. As Lee spoke, eighteen flat-screen plasma monitors lit up around the circumference of the conference room. The file images of Mac Brazel and those of the Roswell crash site came into crystal clarity. The president saw the same images on his screen at Camp David on a split screen.

"After, Brazel collected a little of the wreckage and took it home and contacted the county sheriff, who in turn notified the U.S. Army Air Force at Roswell, the home of the 509th Bomb Group—the only base in the world known at the time to have atomic weapons on-site, I might add. The base's intelligence officer, a Major Jesse Marcel, was sent out with another man to investigate the report." At this point several of the monitors changed pictures and showed a smiling Army Air Corp officer out in the dusty crash site where he and several military police officers were standing in a large debris field.

"Upon returning to the base with strange material from the crash site, Marcel notified the base commander, and by this time radio station KSWS in Roswell begins to teletype information of the strange crash to the world, but the transmission was cut, presumably by the FBI. But it didn't end there." The senator poured a glass of water from a pitcher and took a sip. "On July eighth, a second lieutenant by the name of Walter Haut was ordered to issue a press release by the public relations officer for the 509th." They all saw the photostat of the famous newspaper headline. "Well, that angered quite a few people with stars on their shoulders, and if it weren't for President Truman's and the Event Group's intervention, certain elements inside the United States were prepared to act against its own citizens to protect the fact they had UFO wreckage in their possession."

"What do you mean when you say 'act against our citizens,' Senator?" the president asked.

"Just what that implies, sir, that the military and whoever was pulling the strings at that time, were ready to eliminate people to keep their secret. I know, I was there in Roswell when it happened," Lee said sadly.

"Where are the remains of the craft now?" Celia Brown asked the senator.

"We don't know. The convoy that was transporting the remains back to the Event Center disappeared in between New Mexico and Nevada. No remains were ever found, and that included ten of my best security personnel and a very good friend, a Dr. Kenneth Early."

"Was there any trace of the crash ever uncovered?" the president asked.

"The FBI investigation ordered by Mr. Truman got a lead that some of it may have shown up in Fort Worth, Texas, then Wright Air Force Base in Ohio. But by the time the FBI arrived the material had disappeared along with the people who reported the strange debris at each of the two bases."

There was a lot of whispered talk around the table now. Collins was looking at the president on the television screen, watching his commander in chief's expression changes. It wasn't every day you were told you'd had a flying saucer in your possession, only to hear that it had strangely vanished without a trace.

"Tell me you have some background, or at the very least a suspicion, on this?" the president asked.

"Yes, sir, but it's something that I would rather go into with you and my new security commander, Major Jack Collins. The FBI report was sealed by President Eisenhower in 1957."

"I think maybe the director of FBI should be in on that meeting, possibly the boys across the river also," the president said, referring to the CIA. His eyes had finally found Jack at his spot down the length of the conference table. He held the gaze for a moment, then looked at the others around the table.

"Yes, sir," Lee answered, then quickly saw he had to get the president back on track.

"Now, if you will open your folders, people. Mr. President, you have the same information in yours, which we faxed over. At this point I'll turn this over to Director Compton."

Niles stood once again. "From the records the senator turned over to me, we were able to compile a pretty accurate

record of the flight path the vehicle was on in July of 1947."
Niles pulled a sheet of paper out of his folder and held it up.

The others followed what he was pointing to on their own
copies. At the rear of the conference room a clear plastic
sheet that was ten feet in width and six feet in length came
down from a hidden recess in the ceiling, and the four
plasma monitors it covered were shut off. The new technology of holographic imagery, a new form of light-induced
liquid crystal sandwiched between two sheets of clear plastic, came to life with the diagram Niles held in his hand. One
of his assistants in the computer center had set up the program on a moment's notice from the comp center for this
briefing. The result was an image that was detailed enough
to show the movement of clouds and the blinking of lights in
the cities the map displayed.

"Venezuela, South America, approximately 2350 hours,
July second, 1947. The weather factors have been added by
computer from records kept by the National Weather Service. On that date, an unidentified airborne object was reported by a Panamanian airline crew on course for Panama
City to the west, and they stated to Venezuelan traffic control, 'It was round and moving at an incredible speed.' At exactly 2355 hours another report was intercepted by the
United States Army in Panama, eavesdropped from a British
battle cruiser off the coast of that country. It read as follows:

HMS Royal Fox, " 'A low-flying unidentified object
passed HMS ⁻causing burns to exposed personnel on deck.
This object was believed to be damaged, as Royal Navy sea-
men witnessing the craft sighted smoke exiting the strange
vehicle from the stern portion of the craft.'

"Now, we have it tracked to Panama at the very least, and
possibly, and I do mean possibly, damaged, just like the object this morning."

"Now we move north," Compton continued. "Witnesses
on the ground just north of Mexico City stated:

" 'At 2359 hours, a small aircraft was taking off from an
airfield when a roar filled the air to the south. As witnesses
turned, they saw a huge round shape fill the sky. It flew low

to the ground, so low it caused cars to rock and trees to sway so hard they cracked limbs. At that point a second disk-shaped craft dropped from the sky at an accelerated speed, enough so its wake parted and then sucked the darkened rain clouds down after its passing, and then the object slammed into a small Cessna that had just lifted off from the airfield, killing an entire family. This saucer then followed the track of the first object. Both craft swerved to the north and continued on.'

"Exactly twenty minutes later, the crash in New Mexico occurred during a rainstorm." As Compton said this, a small target blip on the hologram disappeared into moving clouds and a bright flash appeared on the screen inside the borders of New Mexico. "The senator is convinced the sightings in '47 were of the same type of saucer involved in the attack today on our naval pilots."

"It took years to piece this together by the way," the senator added. "But all witnesses to the Event said it was something they would never forget. The Royal Navy vessel had even entered it in the ship's logbook, much to the British Admiralty's displeasure."

The senator turned to address the president. "The gist of all this, Mr. President, is the fact that we have two incidents that occurred fifty-eight years apart, that are very similar in detail. The first object was attacked by a second, and we are under the assumption it was meant to bring the ship down."

"Yes, I see your point and the connections."

"The line of accounts is almost exact, the same route, two saucers, one damaged. The first saucer in '47 went down in the southwestern United States, and now we have the second Event, one on almost the exact same course as that of the first. And I believe it too may also have gone down in this country, in the same area."

"What is it you want, Senator?"

Garrison Lee walked back to his position at the head of the great conference table, his cane-aided limp now hardly noticeable. "Mr. President, I know the navy wants to keep a firm hold on this one, and under any other circumstance I would say yes, it's their bailiwick. But since this has possibly happened before, I believe it falls under the Event Group's jurisdiction according to our charter. Because of the nature of the incident in '47 we believe this episode was an *Event* of immeasurable proportions. Because of evidence we gathered many years ago, and I will expand on that with you and members of this group, I believe this incident today, like the one in 1947, was a deliberate action by an alien force to down that craft as an act of war."

There was mumbling around the table and the president blinked, but was quiet.

"What that brings to the table has been filed away since Roswell in 1947. I have sent a copy of our investigation of the incident fifty-eight years ago to you on a secure link, and you will be receiving it shortly, and I stress, it is highly confidential." Lee took a deep breath and paused for a moment, then let it out. "Niles and I want our people on it, Mr. President, as we don't believe in coincidence." Then he looked from the president to those faces around the table that he knew best, the ones he had groomed for Events this important. "With the same Events so closely related and what we know of the previous one, I believe we are witness to a deliberate act for reasons unknown to bring those craft down in this country. I believe the first act in '47 failed for reasons we learned that night in Roswell, which will be explained, and if this is a successful second occurrence of a similar act, we are in deep trouble."

This time the conference room was silent as the gathered group looked from Lee to the president, waiting, waiting for some explanation as to the senator's dire warning.

The president stood, making only his midsection visible in the frame, and walked away out of camera view. A moment later he returned. He slowly sat back down on the leather sofa with a bundle of papers in his hands.

"Okay, you damn well better keep me informed, is that clear?" He started looking through the pages that had just been faxed through to him from Nevada.

"Yes, sir," Lee answered. "And the *Carl Vinson* airman? We need that man here."

"I'll get on that after I've had my burnt hot dogs, is that good enough?" the president said, looking up from the papers.

"Yes, sir, and thank you, we'll be in touch. Enjoy your supper and—"

"Mr. Lee," said the president, cutting the senator off, "this may be just a little too big for just your agency to handle alone. I've got to bring some of the Joint Chiefs and Security Council in on it at the very least. Everyone across the river is already screaming bloody murder on what might very well be a military matter, regardless of what happened in 1947." The president looked into the camera with a frown as the screen faded to blue.

The senator walked over to his chair and seated himself, letting out a heavy sigh. Collins saw Alice pat his arm. He turned and smiled at his colleagues and nodded at Director Compton.

"Okay, people, an *Event* has been officially declared, the order will arrive shortly giving us the powers of an official presidential investigation. Now, how do we find that saucer?" Niles asked.

The room was momentarily quiet, and then the Group started making plans for what each of their departments could do to add to the search. Jack and Carl excused themselves. As for Garrison Lee, he sat heavily into his chair and rested both hands on his cane. Alice watched him but made no attempt at checking to see if he was alright. She knew he wasn't.

SEVEN

After the meeting broke up, Collins and Everett made their way to an early dinner.

"Well, that was different. Didn't like the way the old man looked though," Jack said.

Everett thought a moment, then stepped closer to the major. "I think the senator's not well. He shouldn't be this involved. Maybe he wants this to be his last hurrah, so to speak, but that's just my opinion, and I would die for that guy." Carl fell silent a moment. "There's scuttlebutt that says the president is thinking about fully retiring the senator, even taking away his advisory status, even though Doc Compton would kill to keep him on." Carl pursed his lips a moment. "Sure would hate to see that."

"If it does happen, what about all this?" Jack asked, gesturing at the complex around him.

"Dr. Compton has been calling the shots around here since 1993 or so, with Alice easing him into the position." Everett took the major by the elbow and steered him away from the others, walking slowly along the hallway. "As I mentioned earlier, there have been some serious leaks from somewhere. That goddamn Farbeaux and whomever he is working for have shown up at the oddest places and have done us, the Brits, Germans, and Israelis a lot of damage. A few of their intelligence agencies actually accused the U.S. of harboring this guy and whomever he works for. I'm glad you're here to take command and sort this mess out."

Jack knew he had a lot of hard work ahead of him.

Camp David, Maryland
1940 Hours, Eastern Daylight Time

The president of the United States sat for a moment after the view of the Event Center went dark. The president stood and walked over to the blinds and pulled them aside. He smiled and waved at his daughters with the red-bordered file and the pages that the Group had just sent over. The girls, along with the first lady, were playfully tossing the burning hot dogs into the air and letting them hit the grill, accompanied by laughter. He smiled and slowly turned away from the window in thought.

He had quickly scanned the pages the Group had sent over and felt numb. If what Lee thought was happening was indeed *really* happening, the president didn't know if they had the assets to stop it. He slowly walked over to his wall safe and opened it and placed the pages inside, then closed it and locked it with his key. He turned away and went to the side door of his office and opened it and waved the Secret Service agent in.

Roland Davis had been on the presidential detail for the past three years and knew when the president had a lot on his mind. When he wasn't smiling, that meant he was occupied with one problem or another.

"The staff just made a fresh batch of lemonade, Mr. President," Agent Davis said.

"Thank you, Roland," the president said as he turned and made his way for the door and his reunion with burnt hot dogs. "After I choke down dinner, I would like to speak with the chief of staff, and get General Hardesty on the horn, in"—he paused and looked at his watch and then outside to his smiling wife—"say an hour?"

"Yes, sir, one hour."

The president went through the door and into the nice evening.

Special Agent Roland Davis slowly slid the door closed, then pulled the blinds closed to offer the first family their privacy. The outdoor security teams were now responsible for the president's safety. Davis then went over and pushed a button on the coffee table in front of the large couch, sending the liquid-crystal plastic conference screen back into its nest in the ceiling, at the same moment he reached underneath and deftly removed a small device he had hastily placed there before the president's conference. He quickly clipped it to his radio on his belt, then turned and walked over to the swinging door that led to the small entranceway. He swung it partway open; sitting at a small desk was the Secret Service duty officer.

"Stan, I'm going off the air to make a personal call to my wife at work," he said, holding the door open with one hand. "The boss is outside with the family."

"You bet, just let me know when you're back on the air, and if the boss comes back in"—Stan tapped one of the six video monitors on the desk—"end the call real quick."

"Sure thing." Davis removed the earpiece from his left ear, and while the duty officer reached into his top drawer, Davis quickly reached down and shut off the radio on his belt, his hand moving so quickly he knew it went unnoticed.

"Here ya are," the officer said as he tossed Roland his personal cell phone.

Every agent on the president's security detail was required to turn in all personal equipment while on duty, including cell phones. Davis nodded his head in thanks and let the door swing closed. He walked back into the wood-paneled living room and stepped to the small window next to the bar and partially separated one of the hanging blinds. The president was now sitting in a lounge chair grimacing at the hot dog that was sitting in a plate on his lap. Roland let the panel drop back and then walked to the center of the room. He raised the cell phone and dialed a preprogrammed number. The connection was quickly made.

"Clausins Department Store," a female voice answered.

"Hi, can you connect me with accounting please, this is Roland Davis calling for his wife," he said, not giving in to the temptation to look around to see if anyone was eavesdropping. The cameras were still on and very much active even though the president was currently outside.

"One moment please," the voice said.

There was a series of clicks, and then just like any other holding signal, the gentle swell of a soft and melodic version of "Eleanor Rigby" came into his right ear. The Muzak was a nice touch, he had to admit that.

"I'm sorry, Mr. Davis, she's in a sales meeting at the moment. Would you like to leave a message?"

As he listened to the coded phrase, he quickly reached to his side under his jacket and switched on the miniature digital recorder that he had just attached to his voice-activated radio. The same one he had just removed from the bottom of the coffee table. Then he quickly placed the cell phone by his hip and counted to two; he left it there another four seconds just to be sure. In that short time, a burst transmission was sent three times through the cell phone that was completely silent, or if anyone was listening, such as the NSA, they may have caught the soft sound of hissing like any other cell call. The coded recording of the president's meeting with the Event Group would be heard by others in a matter of minutes.

He quickly placed the phone to his ear and said, "No thanks, I'll speak with her when she gets home." He closed the cell phone and smiled. He would be paid a nice amount for his treachery.

New York City
1948 Hours

The Genesis Group had been located on Seventh Avenue for the past sixty years and had passed that time as anonymously as any tree among many in the forest of buildings in one of the largest cities in the world. Few noticed that only a couple of people a day came and went from the nondescript sandstone building, but the ones that did were delivered to the address in limousines and wore clothing few outside of habitués of the largest boardrooms in the world could afford. The Sage Building was sixteen stories of boring turn-of-the-century architecture that drew absolutely no attention from anyone. The ornate interior decorations that occupied its dust-free corners had been purchased from all the best houses of Europe and Asia, but the most outstanding feature of the Sage Building was found five stories below the surface of the busy street.

The old man sat in a high-backed, electric wheelchair and looked into the glass enclosures before him. The three containers and the craft were there as they had always been. The information gained from them had long since been filed away, and the cabinets that held those files were being covered, he was sure, with thick layers of dust somewhere on the floor below him.

The largest display in the immense subbasement was to the right of the smaller enclosure containing the three aluminum bio-tanks. This viewing case was filled with the vehicle recovered from Roswell in 1947; its electronics and engines had long since been dismantled and analyzed many, many years ago at the then named Wright Field in Ohio. Little remained of the saucer after all the metallurgy that had been conducted on the debris. But what there was of it had been put back into some semblance of its original shape. The craft was almost unrecognizable as only the front and lower portions had been re-created. The upper dome was long gone, as the scientists and company engineers had had their way with it. He thought back through the years and remembered the excitement among his handpicked people as the technology had been retrieved.

The old man looked at the lower section, what the eggheads had confirmed had been the cargo hold of the vessel. This section was sparse in its reconstruction, but he could see the many metal containers that had been recovered and, once examined, placed back inside. The one in the center held his attention and had for the past sixty-odd years.

The large crate was sitting on the Plexiglas floor (that was a prop also, as the original floor had been used for testing as so much of the craft had). The contents, of course, had never been in his possession, but the mere thought of what it must have contained at one time was mind-boggling.

He closed his eyes as a small pain crossed from left to right across his chest. He knew it wasn't serious but he removed a small ornate Chinese case from his vest pocket nonetheless and quickly slipped a small white nitroglycerin tablet under his tongue. All the while his eyes never left the crate where spotlights illuminated it and it alone.

Again the old man reached out and this time removed a box from a small table beside his large wheelchair. He gently lifted the lid on the aluminum container and stared into the satin-lined interior. He lowered the box to his lap and used his index finger to touch the long and curved claw inside. It was fourteen inches in length and was serrated on both sides. The claw flared on the tip into what looked like two spoons that were arranged on either side just before the devastatingly sharp tip. The entire length curved like the prehistoric claws found in museums of animals long vanished from the surface of this world. He lovingly removed the claw from its box.

Whatever animal had used this weapon also used it as a digging instrument. The creature had obviously been a burrower of some sort, or so his expensive teams of scientists had said. The DNA recovered from the claw was so alien to our universe that the eggheads declared that the sample had to have been severely contaminated. Their analysis of the atomic structure of the sample told them it could never have survived anyplace with a gravitational field.

Bah! Sons of bitches don't know what they are talking about, the old man thought. *An impossibility, they said. Well, here it is right in my hand.* The claw proved that this animal had existed and he would have loved to have seen it. He had lied and cajoled the old boys in the Agency so long ago, fooled them into thinking there was nothing to it. Even the Majestic 12 council, President Truman's think tank, conceived after Roswell to discover the ramifications of life beyond this world, had no idea these artifacts still existed. Even the old hawks at the time, Curtis LeMay and Allen Dulles, were just as happy never to have to deal with anything from Roswell again outside of the technology they gleaned from it. As for the possibilities of the animal, out of sight, out of mind was their philosophy.

He placed the claw back into the box and closed the lid. It would go back into his safe upstairs where no one would ever lay hands on it. This was his only personal claim to the crash at Roswell, and no one would take it from him. He set the box on the small table and looked at the enclosure next to the saucer. They were lined up side by side. Glass viewing plates had been placed in the upper half of the lids for viewing the corpses inside.

Every once in a while he wondered if the evidence of that night should be shared with the powers that be, but then he would catch himself. He knew that it was he and his company, now his son's, that were the only ones that would be strong enough to lead the way in combating the enemy they had discovered in the scrub brush in New Mexico. Or, if it was handled just right, they might acquire a new weapon for their own country if the chance arose. After all, if it was good enough for use as a weapon outside this world, it would sure enough be good for America.

"You know, Dad, if you continue to come down here into this cold and dank basement, I'm going to leave orders for it to be locked up." The voice came from an open doorway at the top of the long theater-type aisle. "It can't be good for you."

The old man turned and faced the man who was backlit by the open door.

"It's all I have left, and now you threaten to deny me even that?" he responded, then turned back around.

The tall man let the door close behind him and made his way slowly down the descending aisle. The basement had been set up like a small theater, and the seats were strategically placed to view the craft. The old man's only son sat in the front row right behind the wheelchair his father had ordered placed on the small riser of a stage so he could see the artifacts better. He didn't say anything for a moment, just watched the old man and shook his head. He undid the waist button of his expensive suit jacket and waited. The younger man had jet-black hair that was combed straight back, and his features were just as his father's had been so long ago, aggressive and unyielding.

"I've received some information that may be of interest to you . . . and us," he said as he crossed his right leg over the other. He brushed a nonexistent piece of lint from the fabric of his pants.

The old man didn't say anything. His gaze never wavered from the exhibits in front of him.

"The president's been having some very interesting meetings with your old friend Garrison Lee and Director Compton."

At the mention of Lee's name he saw his father's shoulders twitch and his body tense.

"I take it I have your attention, for the moment at least?" The younger man enjoyed the advantage he momentarily had over the old man. He knew it upset his father no end that Garrison Lee still had people who depended upon him for advice, when his father had been cast aside by the ever-changing environment of a very different world, a world of science and manufacturing, not dreaming about monsters and invasions. Lee had outlasted him and he hated him for it. But the younger man decided to soften his approach. He still respected his father for his strength and foresight when America needed it the most.

"It's my understanding our distinguished president meets with the Event Group once a week, why should it concern me? It's you and our company that has a misguided interest in antiquities and mysteries from the past, not I," the old man replied without turning.

The current president and CEO of one of the largest defense contractors in the world, the son still tried to keep his father up-to-date on all that the corporation was doing, even their search for antiquities as investments.

"Even if it's something from the past that involved Roswell and Purple Sage?" the son said, letting the statement sink in for a moment. "The meeting was held in regards to a situation this morning involving an incident where two navy F-14s were downed."

"Purple Sage?" The old man went rigid in his chair.

"It's my understanding from what we received from our asset at Camp David that this incident involved two unidentified craft that closely resemble what you're looking at right now. We first learned of the incursion from our station at the pole. We even have infrared evidence of their arrival."

The old man didn't move for a moment. He just sat and absorbed the information his son had just delivered. The technology gained in Roswell had once again paid dividends. He blinked and he felt his body and mind kick into a gear he no longer thought he had.

"Purple Sage," he mumbled with a smile.

"The information has been confirmed by our Event Group asset who used the code name in his phone conversation." His father had given the Roswell Incident this code name years before.

"We must learn everything we can," the old man said as he finally used the electric motor and spun his chair to face his son. "If this is a new part of Operation Purple Sage, we must be in on it at every step, is that clear?"

The younger man stood and buttoned his coat. His father's manic demeanor where this subject was concerned was something he never liked. Purple Sage had been a godsend for the company and indeed it wouldn't even exist if it weren't for what had been found, but his father was overzealous.

"I understand how important this is, not only to you, but to the defense of our country. That's why we do what we do. But remember, it was you who drove the Genesis Group and aspects of our corporation so far underground that it was. hard for us to maneuver in the light of day. It was handled so badly your friends had to fake your death. Because of the way you and those two maniacs LeMay and Dulles handled things in '47, we're underground patriots. I won't allow such misplaced zeal to harm the corporation or this country again, is that clear . . . *Father?*"

The old man ignored the reference to his past and his official nonexistence. "You have someone competent to debrief the Event asset?"

The younger man never liked being too close to his father. It was as if he still had to look up slightly into those dark eyes, as if the old man had never been condemned to that damn wheelchair, and that unnerved him, and a man in his position never liked that loss of control.

"I'm going to contact the Frenchman's Black Team in L.A. He's not using them at the moment."

"What? Why not send the Frenchman himself?"

"The asset believes he's delivering information we don't have. I don't want Farbeaux anywhere near that man, he's a mercenary we cannot trust near Purple Sage, he would try and profit from it any way he could. You have shown too much trust in him in the past. If it weren't for the antiquities we pay him off in, he would have stabbed us in the back years ago. Now, with Purple Sage, he would have a reason to forgo his rewards."

"Do as you wish, but handle it carefully."

"I'm informing the Black Team to eliminate the Event asset as soon as they arrive in Las Vegas. We already have the information he's selling, and we simply don't want Reese and his treachery to lead anyone to us."

The old man reversed his wheelchair and stared at his son. "That's our main information source at the Event

Group! We can't just eliminate him. I taught you better than that! We need eyes next to Lee and that egghead Compton. We have to know everything they're doing, because if I understand Lee correctly, he'll see a danger to the country and that is all, not a possible resource."

"Hear me, Father. I don't order the deaths of anyone as casually as you did in your day, and you did teach me very well about dangerous people. This subject matter is far too hot to take a chance that Reese won't screw up somehow and lead the Group right to the doorstep of this company, or even, God forbid, the doorstep of this very building. We cannot have the Genesis history come spilling out, now can we? As a courtesy to you, and because I *respect* what you have done in the past, I will keep you up-to-date and as involved as I can. But know that if this is truly Purple Sage–related, I will not endanger either the group or the company. Reese is expendable, he's a traitor to his organization, which means, in a roundabout way, he's a traitor to his country, even if he is selling us the information."

"The thought of Lee being stabbed in the back by such a man, well, it has always made me sad." He looked at his son. "Just because I hate the bastard and because Lee's a Boy Scout doesn't mean he's not an American and a patriot in his own misguided way, he's just blind to the things that need to be done." The old man smiled when he saw the strange look on his son's face. "Does that shock you that I almost admire Lee after all these years?"

"No, but don't think for one minute that Lee has forgotten about his missing personnel back in '47. Everyone tells me, including yourself, that Lee has been waiting for years for some link as to what happened to his men. From his history, patriot or not, I understand *he's* the one who can really make people vanish. So, clearly stated, no one must be allowed to lead them to us. As of right now he isn't even thinking of you; after all, you're dead."

"Of course, you're right, but imagine what this country could do with a specimen such as that animal? Our soldiers wouldn't have to die fighting madmen around the globe. We must find out, we must." The old man reached out and took his son's hand.

His son exhaled and patted his father's hand. "We'll take care of it. If it's happening again and we can get anything out of it, more technology, or the animal, the country will be the better for it. As you say, maybe we can turn the situation, or the creature, to the benefit of the United States, to use against our enemies, either here, or out there," he said. Glancing upward, he patted the hand again.

The son released his father's hand and turned and left. The old man slowly sank into the plush cushion of his wheelchair. Then he lowered his aging head and turned the chair and faced the exhibits once again. His gaze centered on the containers holding the bodies of the three alien life-forms, and a sick smile slowly formed on his thin lips as he turned and looked at the cage that had once contained an animal that had specifically been brought here. A creature that might very well be back on this planet, and this time, it might just be alive.

He knew his son would want the secrets that came hand in hand with the animal. But it would all be wasted if Lee got there first. Everything they could have learned from such a magnificent species would be lost to that fucking Boy Scout.

He tapped the box containing the claw of the beast and smiled even more broadly.

"You better be careful, Senator Lee," he said. "If *they* are indeed back, and if they are successful *this* time, something may be out there that will explain to you in no uncertain terms why man has always been afraid of the dark."

Los Angeles, California
2140 Hours, Pacific Daylight Time

The man sat at the ornate czarist-Russian antique desk and studied the gold-encrusted cross that had just recently come into his possession. It weighed an astounding half kilo. With a jeweler's loupe he examined the green emeralds that adorned the cross down its center. Smiling, he removed the glass from his right eye and turned his large chair to face the huge glass wall that afforded him a view of Los Angeles as it sprawled westward toward the Pacific Ocean. The house on Mulholland Drive had been paid for in cash thanks to small trinkets such as the one he now held in his hand. His eyes roamed from the lights of the city below to the pool that wound its way around from the side of the house to a stop just below his window. He then held the gold cross up against the blue of the pool and admired the emeralds that sparkled.

"The Cross of Father Corinth," he said softly. The very cross the priest had made specifically to bless the Spanish soldiers that had helped loot and rape Peru in 1533. The late father Corinth had then been a part of the Francisco Pizarro expedition.

His reverie was interrupted by a soft knock on the study door. The man placed the cross on his desk and covered it with a satin cloth.

"Yes," he said, hating the interruption at what was supposed to be his quiet time.

The door opened and a big man with short-cropped hair stood there. He was well dressed in a black sport jacket and black nylon T-shirt underneath.

Henri Farbeaux, former colonel in the French Army and late of the French Antiquities Commission, looked the American over and then waved him in. The man walked toward the desk and sidestepped the huge lion skin that sat in front of the Frenchman's desk and held out a manila file.

Farbeaux looked at the file without moving. He then looked back at the cross and uncovered it and once again examined it. "What is that?" he asked, letting the man know his interruption wasn't appreciated.

"It's our Black Team's field report on our successful infiltration of the General Dynamics Pomona facility." The man patiently held the file out to the Frenchman.

"Ah, the Space Systems engineer," he said as he again laid the cross down and took the file.

"We can turn him, he's sloppy. It took us only three days to find his mistress. The initial approach has been completed by Hector, and our engineer friend would be quite amenable in assisting Centaurus in acquiring the blueprints for the TOIL system."

Farbeaux had been working in vain for over six months on his own to find something with which to blackmail the engineer in charge of TOIL, and then Hendrix had sent his Men in Black out to assist him and they had achieved results in only five days. The female agent code-named Hector was undoubtedly good at getting needed and well-hidden information out of highly placed sources.

Hector, he thought. Hendrix and his talent for naming his different Black Team members by ancient period names always made him smile. But regardless of their overly dramatic code names, they did get results. TOIL—Tactical Oxygen Iodine Laser, the new toy on the block that Centaurus had to have as their own. Where General Dynamics would have to face years of testing to achieve U.S. government certification, Hendrix would bypass all of that and have a working prototype in six to eight months and ready for government scrutiny. Another weapons system the company could call its own.

Farbeaux signed the report and handed the file back to Achilles, another stupid name.

"I suppose you will be taking your team out of here now?"

"It depends on the orders we receive from New York."

A near silent buzzing came from the man's jacket, and he removed a small radio while he looked at the Frenchman. Hendrix had warned him again and again about Farbeaux. He was not to be taken lightly. He was an opportunist and not an official member of the Centaurus family, therefore he was a man to be watched.

"Achilles."

"I have New York on the secure line in the office," the voice said.

Farbeaux acted as though he didn't overhear the man's counterpart downstairs and continued to examine the cross on his desk.

"I have the report signed. Inform New York it will be sent on the secure channel."

Farbeaux saw the man out of the corner of his eye tense up as the caller said something he couldn't overhear.

"Hendrix himself?" he mumbled into the small radio. "I'll be right down," he said quickly, and placed the radio back into his pocket.

"If you'll excuse me, I'll get this off to the New York office," Achilles said as he quickly turned with the file and hurriedly left.

Farbeaux finally looked up and watched as his door closed.

"Idiot," he mumbled, and slid the valuable cross across the desk and then leaned over and used a key to unlock his bottom right drawer.

The Black Team were guests in his home while they were here to assist in the Pomona operation. They had brought their own secure communications system and thought their software was invulnerable to tapping, which it very much was, but it wasn't the system that Henri was tapping into, it was the man himself.

He pulled a small box, a gift he had liberated from the French government while he had been employed with them, from the drawer and set it on his desk and opened the lid. Inside the opened lid were sixteen small six-inch monitors lined in three rows. He selected DOWNSTAIRS OFFICE, and the monitor came alive showing a clear color picture from an embedded camera in the heating duct on the ceiling. One of the Men in Black was pacing in front of the desk that had their secure phone system upon it. Farbeaux smiled as he reached down and found a small toggle switch and tested the camera angles. The picture easily moved toward the door and waited. Then he turned on the laser system that was mounted just below the camera and initiated the invisible beam. Then he turned on the small recording device and looked to make sure the small two-inch disc was turning.

Farbeaux saw Achilles enter the office and, ignoring his pacing counterpart, go straight for the scrambling device on the desk. Anyone hardwired into the system for spying purposes would only hear meaningless blips and beeps instead of words. But that didn't worry him as he watched Achilles pick up the phone receiver. He quickly adjusted the camera and pinpointed the laser on the man's ear as he sat in the chair behind the desk. Farbeaux adjusted the beam and moved it down an inch as the camera zoomed in. The laser was now exactly centered on the earpiece of the phone itself. Thus the conversation was being recorded after the voice on the other end had already been descrambled by the Centaurus system. *The cleverer you think you are, the easier the system is to beat in the simplest manner,* he thought. *Just eavesdrop, like putting a glass to the wall.* He set the system on AUTO-TRACK and the system imprinted on the receiving earpiece and kept tracking that spot.

"It's very rude to keep secrets from your host, Achilles," he said as he leaned back in his chair and waited.

The flashing light blinked several times when a few minutes later the call downstairs was terminated. Farbeaux then lightly punched a button that shut the system down as he watched Achilles leave the room. He smiled as he hit the playback button on the recorder and placed a set of headphones over his ears. He heard the chirps and whistles as the filter scrambled the call, making it come out the other end sounding like a slowed-down recording of Darth Vader. *Very dramatic,* he thought, smiling. Then he listened, it was indeed Mr. Hendrix calling his boys.

"Achilles," the man said downstairs.

"I have an assignment for your Black Team. The Frenchman is not to know anything," Hendrix said.

Farbeaux listened with his eyes closed, seemingly not even breathing.

"Yes, sir."

"This involves Purple Sage, so it is of the highest priority.

This is why the Black Group was first created. Do you understand that?"

"Perfectly," the man downstairs answered.

"There will be a man at the Ivory Coast Lounge in Las Vegas. He is our main asset at a think tank nearby. He is to be eliminated immediately, is that clear?"

"Yes, sir. Subject's name?"

"Reese, Robert Reese. He's expecting to sell information concerning our Purple Sage file. We don't need it and sadly we also don't need him any longer, as he has just undoubtedly and unknowingly compromised his position. We need him buried deeply. We believe he may even be aware of the Event personnel disappearances in '47. This we cannot have and cannot take a chance of Lee and Compton finding out about. Do you understand?"

"Yes, sir, I will gather my team and be in Las Vegas ASAP."

"Don't bother to explain your destination to Legion, the Frenchman can smell opportunity. His loyalty does not figure into our company's goals."

"Yes, sir, he is someone that can clearly be handled," Achilles said.

"Do not, I repeat, do not underestimate that man. He is resourceful, he knows the Group in the desert intimately. He is not one of your case files that you can scare into silence. Now, did he receive his payment for that detail work in Silicon Valley?"

"Yes, sir, he's admiring the cross as we speak."

"Good, that should keep the greedy bastard occupied while you're in Las Vegas."

"The field report on the success of the General Dynamics operation?" Achilles asked.

"No hurry, it's now a low priority. This Reese operation takes precedence, is that totally clear? Waste no time getting your Black Team out there."

"Yes, sir."

The connection was terminated.

Farbeaux removed his headphones and then placed his

magic box back in the drawer and locked it. *Purple Sage, Reese?* The only asset he was aware of in the Las Vegas area was the Event Group rat that worked for Compton and Lee. What was so valuable as to burn such a man as he? And this Purple Sage?

Farbeaux stood and retrieved the Cross of Father Corinth, wrapping it carefully in the black satin cloth, and returned it to his wall safe. He then went to his desk drawer and removed a walnut box and lifted the lid. He drew out a polished Glock nine-millimeter pistol. He also removed a small cylinder that was embedded beside the weapon and slipped the silencer into his jacket pocket and the Glock into a holster he had removed from the same drawer. The desk phone buzzed.

"Yes," Farbeaux said as he picked it up.

"My team has been ordered out of state for a day or so," Achilles said.

"Good, maybe I can do some research without interruption."

"Yes, sir."

He knew his corporate sponsor had been scared by something and knew that whatever Purple Sage was, it had been initiated by the Event Group. So, that's why this Reese had become a liability, that and information he had on Event personnel disappearing in 1947.

He would have to find out exactly what was at stake. He wasn't about to be left out of an Event that could well be beneficial to Henri Farbeaux. He looked at his watch as he slid his jacket on. It would take the Black Team a while to gather and then make the commercial flight to Vegas. He would have time to beat them if he hurried. He quickly called his pilot and ordered him to file a flight plan from LAX to McCarran Airport in Las Vegas. He would beat the Black Team to Vegas and find out why New York was in such a panic.

EIGHT

Superstition Mountains, Arizona
July 7, 2150 Hours

For those fortunate enough to take the time to really watch, the desert is a living, thriving place, and the magic is never more noticeable than at night. As the sun sets, the dance of life and death usually begins in all the violence and splendor that we humans can only imagine. It ensures the survival of those species indigenous to the desert, this delicate dance. Now the animals, confused and frightened, had all but vanished from the small valley, leaving it still and motionless and far different today than yesterday.

Gus had awakened twice to the sound of his mule wandering away from camp. It was as if Buck was attempting to sneak off, so after twice having his sleep disturbed by having to drag the beast back to camp, Gus finally placed the bit and reins back into the mule's mouth and tied him to an old deadfall. If he had enough rope to cut up, as much as he would have hated to, he would have hobbled him. As it was now, Buck was actually trying to pull the old fallen tree away from camp. The mule's rear legs dug into the sand as he tried to back away an inch or two at a time. He would jerk his head and move it back a foot, then he would gather strength and do it again.

Gus sat up and watched as the animal struggled. He finally stood and quickly began to roll up his sleeping bag, wrapping it securely with the tarp. He then started packing the rest of his gear.

"You're right, old boy, I don't want to be here any more'n you do," he said as he threw his things together.

He kicked out the smoldering embers of his campfire and tossed what coffee remained in the old, battered pot onto the coals. Buck seemed to understand what he was doing because the mule stopped his efforts to escape long enough for Gus to load him up. As he reached down to untie him from the fallen tree and undid the reins, a piercing scream filled the night. Gus clutched his hands to his ears, dropped the reins, and sank to his knees. Buck, sensing he was free, rose up on his hind legs and jumped over the old miner, the rear hooves and steel shoes missing the old man's head by mere inches.

Gus didn't feel the wind as the mule jumped over him, nor did he see him gallop away into the dark night. He was trying with all his strength to crush his hands hard enough into his ears to muffle the awful scream. He went from his knees to his back, rolling over sharp pebbles, thrashing around and kicking at the sand, rolling in pain. Unable to stand it any longer, he rolled onto his stomach, then risking further pain, he removed his hands from around his ears and used them to push into a standing position. He staggered a moment until he had his bearings. When he stuck his fingers in his ears, he realized the screaming wasn't coming from outside his head, but within it. He touched his fingers to his nose and felt the stickiness of blood. The old man couldn't know it, but the high-pitched screaming had opened pinprick-sized aneurysms in his outer brain. The flow of blood stopped as soon as the invasion of sound suddenly ceased.

As he looked around, the quiet was deafening. To Gus it was like being under fire by artillery during the war: once it stopped, you encountered the silence that anyone who has lived through it can attest to, a quiet that continues to roar. Now the only thing he could hear or feel was his own ragged breathing and a heart he thought was trying to escape his chest.

"What in the hell was that?" he asked himself out loud, his voice shaking. The uncaring desert absorbed his question, but didn't hold an answer.

He finally brought his ragged breathing under control and thought he heard Buck braying in the night some distance from camp. He looked around and finally noticed the mule was gone.

"Buck!" he called.

But the only answer he received was the return of his own voice from the mountain, and even it looked down with its unsympathetic, ancient face.

Eight hours after the craft slammed into the earth, the mountain clearing was still active with subtle and unnatural noises rising on the soft night breeze that swept gently through the valley. The wreckage was scattered among the rocks and large boulders of the mountain. Some pieces caught the light of the rising moon, while others were so dark in color they were invisible. The chunks of metal ranged in size from inches to pieces the size of pup tents. The ground was gouged into an ugly scar where the craft had hit the earth. Some of the debris had glowed for a time after coming apart in the impact, and even now some of the wreckage hissed softly with the pulsing of power. But now the site was dominated by one sound, an intermittent noise coming from a large boxlike structure that had survived the crash intact.

The container stood ten feet high and was about the same in width. The small canisters attached to the top were crushed and leaking a mist into the night. The hiss of the escaping gas seemed loud and out of place in the small valley.

There was movement inside the metallic box, slow at first. Then suddenly the huge object rocked onto its side, knocking what remained of the cylinders free. The cylinders rolled away and finally came to rest against a large rock. The liquid spread out as it covered the rock, and slowly the five-pound stone started to disintegrate, finally oozing into the sand with barely a trace left of it.

The metal box was still once again, then suddenly something from inside hit the container so hard that it bulged outward, wrinkling the metal like ripples in a calm lake.

The activity was being watched. Eyes as black as obsidian were opened wide in terror as the crate continued to rock. Gasps of breath escaped the hole the visitor had dug for itself under one of the larger boulders that sat on the edge of the debris field. It was hunched so low, every time it breathed it shot up tiny puffs of fine dirt. The small being knew it had to quiet all of its involuntary muscle spasms from its damaged body. The beast in the cage was capable of sensing the smallest movement through the ground, so the survivor pushed itself as far back into the depression as the rock would allow and waited, mentally ordering its battered body to shut down, save for the smallest of breaths.

Upon gaining consciousness, it had screamed and screamed for the others of its kind. When no answer came, it had crawled and stumbled around the wreckage until it came upon the metal container. Its eyes had widened as it had spied the damaged cylinders and the fractal acid that was leaking into the soil instead of being injected into the cage. It had panicked and crawled away as fast as possible to the safety of the big rock it now hid under. The fail-safe system, because of the damage, was unable to initiate the killing, and the Destroyer was awake, awake and wanting freedom from its enclosure.

Another bulge appeared, in the top of the cage this time. The animal was now testing the strength of its prison and was finding it sorely lacking. Suddenly, the entire side rippled as the creature inside pummeled the interior again and again.

The Visitor couldn't help it. It tried desperately not to scream and did well to keep most of it inside its head, unknowingly attracting the attention of an old prospector down the mountainside.

The container, weakened from damage, screeched as

three claws pierced through the metal walls of the box. They raked downward, then to the side, slicing through as if encountering nothing more than tinfoil. Once it had made the first hole, the prisoner started slicing and tearing at the enclosure until there was little left to block out the night sky. Then the remains of the cage were shaken free as easily as if it were nothing but paper.

As the moon passed behind the mountain, the Visitor saw nothing but the vague outline of the beast and closed its eyes to shut out what little it could see. Without warning, the roar of the animal filled the air and reverberated through the valley, bouncing off rock walls, then returning. The small being almost moved to cover its own ears, doing anything to drown out the horrible sound of the creature, but it caught itself before it could give away its position and lay as motionless as it could.

In a small alcove of granite, a survivor of the second craft watched. The debris field of this saucer was scattered on a higher level of the mountain, and most was buried upon impact. The wounds the crewman had suffered hadn't impaired its scramble to a high place when it heard the rumblings emanating from the metal cage. It had also seen the sudden panic in the eyes of the Green as it too heard the wakening of the beast. It had watched the terrified way in which it too had sought safety. The second visitor had momentarily been tempted to risk its own life by seeking a fast way to reach the Green and kill it. But it knew the beast would be free before it could drag its wounded body to the small one's hiding place. It would have to wait.

The being under the boulder wanted so badly to look around after silence once again filled the crash site, but it *knew* that the beast was still there. It had seen this animal in its natural environment and knew it to be the best hunter in the known universe. Its instincts for survival were unparalleled.

Suddenly the animal roared again, unfolding the layered armor-plated appendages from its neck and making them stand out from its body like a rooster before a fight. The horrible scream was directed at the setting moon of this new world. The animal shook its massive head violently at the falling, yellow orb. Then it calmed and surveyed the area around it. It was slowly regaining its senses from a long hibernation, and gaining strength as well. The creature hunched its muscled shoulders and lowered its giant body toward the debris-strewn ground as it started creating invisible waves of high-pitched sound from deep within its throat that hit the sand and rock surrounding its monstrous form. The sound was too high for any to hear, but it was strong enough that it changed the very dynamic of the strange soil on which the beast found itself. The floor of the small valley for a radius of fifteen feet surrounding the animal rippled like the surface of a lake, the base elements and molecular structure of the dirt and rock having been changed through that invisible sound wave. The beast sprang into the air, closing the armored headdress around its muscled neck, and dove into the liquefied ground. A fountain of earth erupted in a cloudlike geyser as the Destroyer swam deeply beneath the surface.

After an hour of running, Buck stopped and turned. His forelegs came up into the air and he brayed. The large mule kicked at the air, confused by the feeling of being stalked, then quickly turned and bolted once again into the desert. The pack strapped to his back made clanging noises as pots and pans, picks and shovels, were jumbled.

Ten minutes later Buck was still running away from the mountain when the ground suddenly and without warning opened up, and Buck ran right into an ever-widening crevasse. He almost made the jump across to the opposite end of the hole, but his hind legs came up just short, first gaining purchase, then sliding off the crumbling edge. As his large chest and belly hit, his legs furiously kicked at now empty space. The animal struggled and kicked up the side of the depression until he started to make headway. Buck had almost extricated himself when something sharp pierced his right hind leg just to the right of his swishing tail. The mule began screaming in shock and pain as the huge claws sank deeper, gaining a better purchase with more of the animal's flesh. Buck's eyes widened in panic as he screamed and brayed and desperately kicked out, tearing huge chunks of his flesh away for the effort. Another set of claws reached up from the desert and grabbed Buck's left shank, snapping it in two as the mule was dragged backward into the ever-widening hole until only the mule's forelegs and head were still above ground. It frantically clawed at the dirt and sand as it tried pulling itself from the hole. Buck fell heavily on his side with his forelegs still furiously scratching at the expanding sides of the hole. Then suddenly the mule vanished.

A long and powerful roar of animal triumph never before heard echoed against the nearby mountains; then another deep and horrendous bestial scream rent the night air. Then as suddenly as the night had been covered in terror, all was eerily quiet once again. Only the sound of collapsing sand and dirt could be heard as a large wave moved off into the desert.

G us held his ears again as a roar like that of a great animal rolled through the valley. After a minute the echoes of the scream died away, as silence swept the desert once again.

He turned away from the mountain and was about to call out to Buck when the roar was repeated. This time, before he had a chance to react to it, the sound stopped abruptly.

In the eerie silence that followed, he became aware of another sound, not like the first, the screaming, but softer. He shook his head in doubt because he thought it might be an after-echo from the horrible noise of a moment before. But this was distant, like someone, a child maybe, speaking in low tones.

The old man looked at the mountain and knew without thinking exactly where the crying was coming from, and then before he realized what he was doing, Gus Tilly started walking.

USS *Carl Vinson*, Four Hundred Miles off the Coast of Mexico
2155 Hours

Lieutenant JG Jason Ryan had been through hell the last few hours. After he had been checked out by the flight surgeon, he had been grilled by his wing commander, squadron CO, and the special board that had been convened to look into the "accident." The film from his gun cameras that were encased in a hunk of aluminum that used to be his Tomcat was sitting at the bottom of the Pacific. He had nothing to corroborate his fantastic story. The Alert One fighters that had arrived on the scene only in time to see the two chutes hit the water reported nothing in the skies around the area and had never at any time had any hostiles on their air-search radars.

As he walked down the companionway, sailors would step aside and allow him to pass, becoming silent on his approach. The word was out that somehow the hotdogging lieutenant had caused an accident. Oh, the board of inquiry hadn't come right out and said it, but Vampire knew his story was just too unbelievable, even with Commander Harris backing him in his report from his division that something out of the ordinary had indeed happened that morning.

Ryan was just about to enter his cabin when a signalman intercepted him.

"Sir, you have a message from CAG, he wants to see you ASAP in his office."

Ryan nodded and walked a hundred feet down the companionway. *This is it,* he thought, this was his grounding and the beginning of the end of his career. He paused a moment before knocking.

"It's open," the deep voice of his CAG boomed.

He quickly opened the door and stepped into the air group commander's office.

"Lieutenant Ryan reporting, sir," he said, standing straight as a board.

His commander was writing something and didn't bother to look up.

"Mr. Ryan, you have orders to report to NAS Miramar. Have your person and navy issue on board the COD at 1055 hours tonight. You are hereby summoned there on National Command Authority, that means the president of the United States, Lieutenant, clear?"

Ryan didn't miss a beat. "No, sir, I'm not clear on this. I'm now a Jonah on board my own ship. I would like to stay and get this cleared up." In his anger, he moved toward the commander's desk.

Finally the commander looked up. Ryan could see in his eyes he was still burning up about losing Derry.

"You are at attention, Mr. Ryan," he said, pointing his pen at a spot in front of the desk. "Evidently the powers that be, and they are the real power here, mister, want to hear your story, so someone pulled strings and had you transferred. But make no mistake, young Mr. Ryan, we will get to the bottom of this incident. Lieutenant Commander Derry was a close friend, he thought you were the best pilot in the squadron. Therefore, Mr. Ryan, I believe you when you say what you saw out there, but without evidence other than two lost aircraft and three dead men, there's not a whole lot I can do. Your shipmates will always judge you harsher than even yourself. Dismissed."

Ryan deflated. He caught himself and stood up straight and saluted, then turned and left the office.

Once the door was closed, he stood there in quiet and stunned shock. In fifteen minutes he was going to be catapulted off the *Vinson* in a C-2 Greyhound, or the COD, carrier onboard delivery, or in this instance, garbage jettison.

As Ryan started for his cabin to quickly pack, he knew his days aboard the USS *Carl Vinson* were at an end.

Las Vegas, Nevada
July 7, 2350 Hours

The Ivory Coast Lounge was a gentlemen's club in the loosest sense of the word. The interior was made up in a gaudy African motif, complete with cheap imitation ivory tusks and actual bamboo huts covering the darkened and filthy vinyl-covered booths, giving customers a false sense of anonymity. Ugly plaster ceremonial masks covered the walls, along with shadowy cutouts of native women in erotic poses.

The dancers plying their trade at this dive were there because they couldn't find work at one of the finer clubs on the Strip; they were either too old or too young for the legitimate establishments to hire. This was the kind of place that the city fathers were trying to ban from Las Vegas. If they'd known the small club dealt in more than just the exhibition of flesh, they would have moved to close it down even faster.

The Frenchman had been sitting in the basement of the club for the past twenty minutes. He had arrived at least two hours before the Black Team was due. Every once in a while he would look up from the newspaper he was reading and glance at the closed-circuit television monitor on the desk a few feet away. He was reading a nice little article on a new advance in the software field by Microsoft when the manager of this little piece of Americana cleared his throat, asking for attention.

"What is it?" he asked without looking up from his article.

"What should I say to this man? Do I pay him or what?" the club manager asked. "He's been waiting a long time and is real pissed."

Farbeaux slowly looked up, seemingly showing little interest. He carefully folded *The Los Angeles Times* he had been reading and placed it on the table. He watched the redhead on the monitor a moment and wondered what information he had that interested the big shot in New York or, more to the point, made him so nervous as to want to eliminate a most valuable contact as this man.

"So this is the man you dealt with before?" Farbeaux looked from the monitor to his host.

"Yeah, I'm positive; it's the same weasel that came in here couple a months ago."

The Frenchman watched the man on the monitor for a moment. So, this was the traitor that worked for Compton and Lee. Well, he thought, whatever information he'd given Hendrix, he would soon know. And if this Purple Sage really was worth something, so be it. Also he wanted to know about personnel eliminations in the forties; yes, he would know that too.

Farbeaux was growing bored with working for Centaurus and needed one final score to make his time with them worth his while. This might be just that nest egg he was waiting for. If Hendrix wanted him left out of the loop, there must be a reason why, and that reason smelled of opportunity.

"Send him a drink on the house and make sure one of your nicer whores delivers it."

"Yeah, I can do that," the man with the pompadoured hair answered.

"I'll be up in a moment," Farbeaux said, thinking as he again watched Reese on the monitor.

The club manager smiled, exposing his crooked and stained teeth. When he saw the Frenchman ignore him, he left to do his business.

Farbeaux turned as three men in black dress entered from the back entrance. Hendrix's men had shown up earlier than he would have liked.

Achilles, the tallest of the three men, stepped forward. "Why are you here, Mr. Farbeaux?"

"If you'll step outside I'll explain the change in plan I received from Hendrix." He stood and patted the taller man on the shoulder.

As he walked toward the rear door that led out into a

filthy alley, Farbeaux half turned. "Your target may have something more to offer than originally thought," he said as he opened the door. "I'm here to find out what that is."

"Is that what New York has requested we do, assist you?" Achilles asked.

The Frenchman fixed the man with an icy stare and his right eyebrow rose.

"It is what I request that should be paramount in your thinking," he answered with a soft growl.

The three men exchanged looks and then the tallest man in black nodded his head and followed Farbeaux out of the door.

He was taken totally unaware when Farbeaux suddenly turned and shot him in the head. Then he quickly fired two more times at the men behind him. The third actually had time enough to pull his own weapon before he was felled with a nine-millimeter round to the forehead.

"Getting old," the Frenchman mumbled.

The rented car the men had used was parked against a far wall next to the club. Farbeaux went to the prone body of Achilles and rummaged through his pockets until he found the car's keys, then he opened the trunk and carefully loaded the three bodies. Before closing the trunk, he shook his head. It was a shame, they had been good men and loyal to their company, but his action had committed him to a course that was now unchangeable.

Inside, Robert Reese watched the woman's swaying breasts as a new and much better looking topless waitress delivered him a drink. "Compliments of the Ivory Coast," she said with a broad smile, then slowly walked away, making sure he had a good view of the exaggerated way she swung her backside.

Reese followed the shapely figure of the waitress for a moment, then returned to his thoughts. It had never taken this long to receive his payment. Usually it was in and out and no words spoken.

Without Reese being aware of his approach, a man in a

well-tailored white sport jacket and blue silk tie, which stood out against his white shirt, was now standing next to his booth. He wore expensive Italian shoes and his hair was combed straight back. He looked to be about forty. He eyed one of the girls for a moment, then looked over at Reese.

"Hello, may I intrude?" he asked, gesturing at the other side of the booth.

Reese cleared his throat. "Actually, I'm just waiting on the owner to return."

The tall man smiled. "You mean the Elvis-looking character; I think we will leave him out of this for now."

Robert Reese watched as the man deftly slid into the seat opposite him. "My name is Tallman. Do you mind if I smoke? Mr. . . . ?"

"Reese. They're your lungs, not mine."

"Very witty, Mr. Reese, and, yes, they are, as you say, my lungs."

Reese noticed the smile didn't make it as far as the stranger's eyes. "What can I help you with . . . Mr. Tallman, is it?"

The man lit the cigarette and eyed his companion through the haze of smoke.

"It is not I that can help you, but you may be of great service to me . . . or so our friendly manager here tells me." The man smiled and took a drag off the cigarette and intentionally blew smoke into Reese's face. "You contacted the corporation and either gave them information or sent them information by another means. I need to confirm what was said in your communication," Farbeaux lied.

"Look, I don't know who you are. I was given orders to communicate any file that had to do with . . ." Reese caught himself. He wasn't going to give this guy anything for free.

"Continue," Farbeaux said, his eyes never leaving Reese's.

"This is top-drawer information and I'm uncomfortable with this, I don't know who you are."

"Obviously you believe the intelligence you have in your possession is worth something, or better still, you were told it was worth something, yes?" Farbeaux's eyes narrowed. "These people don't scratch an itch without me giving them permission; you are now dealing with me. Now, are you wasting my valuable time, Mr. Reese?"

Reese looked around and watched as a dancer threw her top into the small group of leering men who lined the stage. Then he swallowed and looked at the man across from him.

"It's a military incident involving an . . . an." He didn't know how to continue for a moment. He swallowed, then forged ahead. "An object, but you already know, I sent this to Centaurus already."

Farbeaux held his patience well as he blew smoke again at the redheaded computer supervisor. His eyebrows arched as he continued to stare at him with no comment.

"Two U.S. Navy planes were knocked out of the sky this morning."

Still the man said nothing.

Reese shrugged his shoulders and took a long swallow of his drink, not tasting any of it. "Now understand, whether you like the information or not, I still risked my job and freedom to bring it to the company's attention, and you people did leave me orders to report anything out of the ordinary, especially where this kind of incident is concerned."

"Why try to sell something to us that may already be on the evening news?" the man asked, snuffing out his cigarette in an ashtray that didn't have the name of this particular club on it, but that of another.

"The object that destroyed the two fighters probably came down, maybe in the Southwest somewhere, and believe me, the Event Group and the U.S. Navy are the only ones that know about it, there's no news on the wire, I checked."

"And I am to be interested in this because . . . ?" The Frenchman rolled his manicured fingers in a circular motion urging Reese to answer.

Reese felt this man was dangerous, far more dangerous than the hirelings that fronted this club.

"My contact at Centaurus said when I was recruited for

the Group that anything to do with a UFO attack or anything to do with 'Purple Sage' was of the highest priority, and that my payment would be substantial. Now, if you don't do what is expected here, then I'm walking out and you can answer to the company as to why you lost your number one contact at the Event Group."

The man suddenly but gracefully stood and slid into the other side of the booth, not too gently pushing Reese toward the center.

"Hey," Reese said in protest.

"Oh, *we* are interested my friend. I am also interested in finding out more about Purple Sage, and I suspect you have done a little investigating on your own on that subject where Centaurus is concerned." He placed his arm around Reese and squeezed his shoulder until he winced. "I need to know a few things about their interest and about possible Event staff disappearances." The man gestured toward the front of the club.

Farbeaux had done some investigating on his way to Vegas and found quite a bit of information available on the Internet about Operation Purple Sage. He had found out that the ambiguous title was the old code name for the Roswell Incident back in the forties and was popular with UFO nuts.

Reese felt his arms and legs go numb as he looked up just as three men arrived and were now standing beside the booth, appearing from seemingly nowhere. He saw that they were all rough-looking and recognized them as bouncers from the club, and Reese decided in an instant they had a definite air of harm about them.

The music was slowly but steadily turned up louder as the dancer onstage ripped her G-string off and placed a patron's face in her groin and was rotating to the beat as the men around the runway and stage gave a loud cheer for their lucky buddy, so not one of them noticed the big man in the white suit stand up, quickly followed by three others helping an angry and frightened man to his feet.

"Look, if you work for Centaurus or the Genesis Group,

you should know about it," Reese said as he looked at the three greasy-looking men holding him.

Farbeaux squeezed the shoulder harder. "Indulge me, Mr. Reese."

"Look," Reese said, then softened his voice, "it's rumored in certain circles that Centaurus ended up with the technology from the crash in '47, even killing other Americans to get at it, and they're queer for anything concerning UFOs and incidents like the one today."

Farbeaux removed his hand, looked at the three men, and nodded quickly toward Reese, and they quickly but quietly pulled him away from the booth. Farbeaux then sat back down and thought as they took Reese away.

Reese looked around hoping to see at least a few of the patrons seeing what was happening, but they were all hooting and shouting at the stripper, who had gone far beyond a mere tease, and as Reese watched, he saw the men by the stage all jump as she shot her G-string into the crowd.

Farbeaux was quickly calculating what this information would be worth outside of Centaurus. He decided he needed more information. He needed to know exactly what the corporation knew, and Reese, when persuaded, might be able to tell him.

If the Event Group and Centaurus wanted it, Farbeaux knew he had to have it first.

Nellis AFB, Nevada
July 7, 2355 Hours

The senator was lying on the couch in his office. Lee was under a doctor's care for his heart and had been warned time and again about stress, and after speaking to the president, even with his medication, he had felt depleted beyond his years. Niles paced by the huge desk and every other minute looked over at his mentor and friend and shook his head. Finally he slowly walked over to where the senator lay.

"You can't push yourself like this, Garrison, I mean that. I can't be here to make sure you stay down." Niles shook his head. "I've borrowed every damn recon bird we can get our hands on; we have depleted the inventory on unmanned drones and are scanning New Mexico like it's never been scanned before."

Lee raised a weak arm and put a hand up. "Shut up, Niles."

"Goddammit, I'm the director of this Group and all we need is for you to go and die on us while this thing is going on. Where would that leave you on proving your theory that this may be an attack?" Niles started to pace again, arms crossed and shaking his head.

The old man sat up. "I'm not going to prove anything. You are."

Niles stopped and turned as his normally red-tinged face was redder than ever. His glasses slipped down his nose and he made no attempt to push them back into place.

"The hell you say?" he said, nodding his head to look over his lowered glasses. Niles stepped up to the couch again and placed his hands on his knees and looked closely at the old man. "Look, Garrison, I need you, so don't you flake out on me."

Lee smiled as he looked at Compton. "I'll be here, but I want you to be aware you could be alone in this very soon. I'm very sick, if you hadn't noticed. Look, you're the most brilliant man I've ever worked with, Niles, you'll get it done."

Lee slowly laid a large file he had been holding weakly onto the coffee table in front of the couch. It was a secure file, red-bordered, and on its cover it read, "For Director's Eyes Only" and below that in bold, "Event #2120—Roswell."

Niles didn't pick up the file as he looked from it to Lee.

"I didn't tell you or the Group the whole story today about what was found at that crash site in 1947. I've wanted to show you this file for quite some time, since you were named director as a matter of fact. I didn't show the others because they don't need to know we may be at war."

Compton touched the red-bordered file and traced the red letters with his finger. And then he looked back at Lee's reclining form. He swallowed and picked up the thick file from the polished coffee table.

"You'll be better able to judge how important finding that crash site is after you've looked over the file. Share it with Virginia and Major Collins. Jack will be a real asset when it comes to getting advice from the military. If we're lucky, my theory is wrong and the damn thing didn't crash at all, but if I'm right and it did go down, for God's sake, find it and do it fast," Lee said slowly as he closed his eyes.

For the first time since Niles had been with the Event Group, he saw that Lee was not only deathly ill, but also scared. Jesus Christ, what was on that goddamn saucer that would scare a man who had seen the horrible things he had seen in his life?

NINE

Fort Platt was built in 1857 and served as a company-sized staging area for the U.S. Army cavalry patrols aimed at the raiding Apache bands led by Cochise and Geronimo.

The old fort was abandoned after a massacre in 1863 before the end of the Civil War when sixty-seven soldiers lost their lives in one of the Apaches' most daring and audacious strikes. The fort had been reduced to its present degraded state by the never-ending and relentless winds and sudden thunderstorms of the American Southwest. The eroded adobe walls whispered ghostly songs as these winds whipped through the low, broken foundations. The once manicured parade ground was now a dust bowl giving shelter to creatures such as Gila monsters and rattlesnakes.

Now, over a century later, the fort was occupied once again by modern nomads, visitors from Los Angeles.

A beer bottle barely missed Jessie's head. He had ducked at the last possible moment when he saw the gleam of the bottle in the light of the huge bonfire they had built. It hit the old adobe foundation and shattered, spraying beer and glass on the man it had narrowly missed.

"Hey, you son of a bitch!" he cried. "You nearly took my head off with that one."

"What are you doing over there, asshole? You too good to party with us or what?" a bearded giant of a man asked from where he was lying.

The others were around the fire leaning next to their bikes and drinking. The few girls they had on the trip were either on laps or lying beside them. Jessie wondered why he was on this trip in the first place. He didn't really like the guys he rode with on these long weekend trips, but found he just couldn't say no to that little bit of excitement that came into his life once a month. At the moment, what he called the biker wannabes were silhouetted, illuminated in a flickering light cast by the blazing fire.

Jessie walked over to the fire and knelt and held his hands out to the open flame and rubbed them together. "I was just thinking how weird this place is," he said, looking at the old adobe walls. "Man, think of it, the men that used to ride out of here after the Apaches must have been some bad motherfuckers."

The big man looked at Jesse as he twisted the cap off another beer. "Not as bad as this motherfucker right here," he boasted, tapping the fresh beer on his sleeveless Levi's jacket and sloshing beer all over himself and the man lying next to him.

Jesse just shook his head. Out of the fifteen people around the fire, he hated talking to Frank the most. Trying to exchange words with him about the history of anything was like convincing a dog not to be a dog. He felt the IQ points draining from his head every time he tried.

"I think I know what you mean, dude," one of the girls spoke up. She was one of the few chicks they had picked up in Phoenix. "I've lived in Arizona all my life and there's some pretty weird shit out here."

"Yeah, what would you know about weird?" Frank bellowed, kicking the girl's leg.

"I'm here with the likes of you, aren't I?" she said, slapping his large boot away. Then the young girl continued with her story. "I mean weird with the Indians and things like that. People say the desert's haunted. My dad said there were a lot of soldiers and settlers killed right here on this spot, and if you listen at night, when everything is quiet and still, you can hear them screaming." She lowered her voice in a conspiratorial tone. "And there's bodies buried right below us." She patted the ground. "So there!" she said as she turned toward Frank. "Besides, what would a bunch of jerks from L.A. know about it anyway?"

"Why do they say there are ghosts here?" Jessie asked, looking around into the darkness.

The girl was just grateful someone was paying attention to her, so she sat up and joined him in the heat thrown by the fire, squatting beside him. She looked the man over and liked what she saw.

"I mean, like this place we're camped in, the army used to have troops here, and my daddy said at night you can hear their horses cry and the men walking guard. While he was camped nearby one night in the seventies, he and his friends heard several horses with men whooping and hollering as they rode by, only according to my dad, there was no one there."

The man looked around him into the night again. "Really?"

"Uh-huh, that's what my daddy said."

"Did your daddy also tell you you're a fucking idiot?" asked Frank, standing up so quickly he let the girl who had been dozing with her head on his lap slide off and hit the ground.

"Knock it off, Frank, will ya?" whined the girl, rubbing her head.

"You're swallowing this shit, Jessie? Are any of you buyin' this crap?" Frank asked, walking away from the old adobe ruins while undoing his pants.

"I hope a ghost gets that asshole," the girl whispered.

"We couldn't be that lucky," Jessie mumbled, and they both laughed.

As Frank stumbled into the darkness, he looked up at the

stars, then at the ground. He was regretting this trip. It wasn't turning out the way it was supposed to. One more day and then it was back to that damn Chevy dealership in Pasadena. Back to oil changes, lube jobs, and blow jobs from that ugly-ass girlfriend of his. Bike runs were supposed to be full of hell-raisin' and chick-banging. Shit, all they had so far on this ride was six dumb whores from a bar in Phoenix, warm beer, and a lot of fucking boredom.

He stopped and finished unbuttoning his pants outside of the firelight. *Shit, you can't find anything exciting anymore in this country,* he thought. Frank was concentrating on not pissing on his new engineer's boots when in the moonlight he saw the ground thirty feet in front of him erupt into the still night air. The big man was startled, his heart pounded hard in his chest, then the ground settled and became still once again. He squinted into the night, stopped paying attention, and pissed on his new boots anyway.

"You guys quit fucking around," he shouted, "or I'll stomp your asses when you come back in," he called into the darkness.

He quickly pulled himself back into his pants and buttoned up. He started walking backward, first looking toward the camp, then at the area where the ground had just done that funny dance. He had to calm himself down before he returned to the fire so he took a deep breath.

The hard-packed sand and dirt did it again, but now it was about five feet closer. He froze with his eyes wider than a moment before. This time the sand and dirt didn't settle but rushed toward him like a bow wave when a boat slices through water. The dirt being tossed to the side was thrown ten and fifteen feet in the air. He could feel the tearing of the earth through his now entirely wet boots. He screamed, then turned and ran.

The dirt eruption then disappeared as fast as it had exploded.

He had almost made it back to the ring of firelight when the ground fell out from underneath his stomping feet. He frantically grabbed for the edge but missed, tearing most of his fingernails down to the quick. He hit bottom with a bone-crunching thump. He hissed in pain, then took a deep breath and started to shout for one of the others around the fire to help, but was suddenly grasped around the waist as two giant claws cut deep into his midsection, cutting off the scream before it could form. His brain continued to function even as he was squeezed like a tube of toothpaste and his entrails forced out upon the ground amid the sounds of snapping and breaking ribs.

T he men and women around the fire had ignored Frank's call for someone to knock it off and had gone on talking and making out.

"Anyway, the desert gives me the creeps most times, unless I'm with someone like you who'll protect me," the girl said, inching closer to Jessie.

Jessie was about to comment when a large object hit the bonfire and exploded, tossing flames, sparks, and burning embers into the star-filled night sky. The object hit with enough force to throw burning wood on those lying idly by their bikes, and shouts and screams filled the night air as people jumped up and started brushing burning embers from themselves and each other.

It was the girl speaking with Jessie who saw it first. The mass that had been thrown into the fire was the gutted torso of Frank. The beard and long hair had already sizzled down to nothing, and the eyes had exploded from their sockets and were hanging, one on the right side of his head, the other on his left cheek. The blond girl started screaming the screams only professionals made in the movies.

The ground around the old fort started to shake and shimmer in the remaining light cast by the now dying fire.

Faster than they were able to follow, dirt around the adobe walls started to part and cave in on itself. It was like a child drawing a large circle with a stick and was scratching faster and faster, digging a deeper trench with every rotation. It looked and felt as though the flying dirt and sand were encircling them. Finally they reacted and started running for their bikes.

Jessie pushed the girl away from the fire, trying to guide her toward the bikes, but she stumbled and fell, then rolled the wrong way. That was when her screams turned from terror to real agony as she rolled into what remained of the fire.

"God!" Jessie shouted. "Help me, somebody!" But the rest were busy running or getting on their bikes.

One biker had his Harley-Davidson quickly started and was moving toward a break in the adobe wall, but his front wheel caught in the depression caused by the swirling sand and he went flying over the handlebars.

Kneeling on hands and knees beside the girl, Jessie started to throw sand on her in an attempt to smother the fire. The others watched their companion who was thrown from his bike beyond the wall. The long-haired man was just starting to rise when the dirt parted about ten feet to his right and something unseen rushed toward him. The others screamed for him to run, but he was busy rubbing his knee and cursing. He was suddenly speared by something and pulled down. He was yanked so hard the others heard his back snap. His legs and arms were jolted into the air as his entire body disappeared into the earth. Then the terrifying tide of sand and soil rushed at those who had watched their friend's death in horror, exploding the lowest portion of the adobe wall upward as if dynamite had been placed under it.

Jessie had managed to put out the flames that had engulfed the girl, missing the horrible spectacle outside the adobe walls. She now lay on the ground moaning in shock and pain, burned the entire length of her once young body. Her long blond curls were burned away and she was left with what looked like burned and charred plastic against her scalp. He grimaced as she hissed and looked up at him. He mouthed the word *sorry,* then ran for his bike. He just wasn't brave enough to endure the horror that was exploding around him.

Without warning, the fire and the girl vanished. The only trace that there had been a fire was the line of smoke and a few floating embers rising out of a large rip in the earth. They were now, except for the setting moon, thrown into total darkness.

Jessie heard the other men and women screaming as they were pulled under the surface. What was happening? Caves? Mine shafts? That must be it, the ground was caving in. Jessie thought for a second about the ghosts of old, long-dead soldiers, but then the real cause of the terror of that night showed itself for the first time. It rose in front of him. Dirt, rocks, and desert grass slid from its armored back as it was framed perfectly in the yellowish glow of the low moon.

Jessie was sitting slack-jawed on his bike, his mind unable to comprehend what he had just seen. He didn't really feel the animal slice him in two. It did feel however as if he had been hit with a rather large pillow. But he did think just before dying that it was amazing, his hips and legs were still astride the bike as his torso was first lifted into the air, then plunged into the earth. His legs tipped over with the motorcycle, trapping one twitching leg under the heavy machine, and even those items were eventually claimed by the new master of the valley.

A few minutes later, the desert was still and quiet again. The old adobe fort once used by the U.S. Army to chase renegade Indians had again become a silent witness to another massacre in this forbidden piece of land, and a few more ghosts joined those already there.

PART THREE
DISCOVERY

When I look up to the skies, I see your eyes, a funny kind of yellow.
— "PICTURES OF MATCHSTICK MEN," STATUS QUO

TEN

Superstition Mountains, Arizona
July 8, 0530 Hours

Gus had walked in a dream state since the strange sounds
of the night before. He stopped and removed his sweat-
stained fedora and looked around him. He was on an old
trail he hadn't used since maybe '64 or so; he couldn't recall
the exact year because his mind was firing in all directions.
He imagined his brain as a distributor cap with its wiring
heading to all the wrong plugs. The incline was steep and the
rolling rocks of past avalanches had kept most prospectors
away, most of them afraid of being pinned or hit by boulders
larger than most houses.

The old man replaced his hat and wondered for a moment
just what he was up to. Where was Buck? The sun was starting to peek into the mountains and was stealing the cold
night air. He shook his head as he tried to convince himself
to get his old ass back down the mountain and find Buck so
he could at least get his morning coffee and maybe a biscuit
or two. He actually took two steps back down the mountain
when the sobbing came gently into his mind again. A child's
crying—that was when he remembered exactly why he was
climbing. He was doing so because some kid had been lost
up there and he had to at least try to find the child. It was up
to him to get the child out of whatever fix he or she was in.

The cries lasted at least a full three minutes this time before they ceased. The old prospector stopped again, more awake than he had been the previous times he had heard the strange sounds in his head. This time, unlike the others, he became aware of a feeling other than sadness. As he looked up the old trail, he became frightened, more frightened than he had ever been before in his life.

"What in the hell is wrong with you?" he asked out loud to himself, looking around him as if something were lurking, hiding behind one of the large granite boulders lining the old trail.

Suddenly he felt depression sinking in like a brick hitting him in the head, all at once feeling lost and terrified. Gus looked around the area where he was standing and nothing looked as it had before. The rocks had somehow become foreign to him; the dirt under his boots was somehow alien. His eyes widened as he desperately searched for something recognizable. He looked at the dark purple morning sky and the tip of the rising sun. This terrified him even more. Good God, what was wrong with him? It was as if these natural things were strange and foreign.

Gus turned and started back up. Whatever was wrong, he couldn't wait. He knew that. Something or someone was calling to him; he knew that beyond a doubt, and though he didn't understand why or how he knew, he was needed in the worst way. As he climbed, one strange sentence swirled through his mind that added to his confusion, repeating over and over, *The Destroyer is loose*.

He shook his head trying to clear it.

"Destroyer," Gus said aloud as he looked toward the sunrise, and it was never more welcome than it was this day, because that *one* word brought a sense of darkness to his soul.

Robert Reese was trying to hold his bladder in check. He had squeezed his eyes shut tight and was hissing between clenched teeth as it had been five long and agonizing minutes since he had begged and pleaded for them to let him urinate. The three men from the club whom Reese had seen on numerous occasions before this awful day had just looked at him and continued playing the same card game they had been playing all night. He had not seen the tall blond man in the eight hours he had been here.

"Come on, man, I have to piss, goddamn it!" he said, trying to keep his voice from having that whining tenor to it.

A heavyset man with a decidedly singular eyebrow looked over and spit his toothpick out, and it landed in Reese's lap. "You gotta piss, you gotta piss, whatya want me to do, hold it for ya?" he sneered.

Reese felt his bladder let go. He thought he could control it enough just to let the pressure off a little, but once he felt the warm trickle of urine soak his underwear and warm his leg and crotch, his bladder hadn't understood at all what the plan had been and it let loose in a flood.

"What the fuck is this?" the man asked, standing and sliding his chair back.

"Look, I just couldn't hold it," Reese said, feeling anger rise. *Goddamm it,* he thought to himself, *someone is making a big fucking mistake. They obviously have me confused with someone else. They wouldn't treat an asset as valuable as an Event Group supervisor like this!*

The man stood and started walking toward Reese.

Reese, through his embarrassment, fought with his restraints so he could get loose and strangle this son of a bitch. All he had wanted to do was to get paid for information the corporation had requested, and instead he found himself in some serious shit in a place that scared the hell out of him. Though his anger was blocking a lot of sensory input, he saw the man stop and look over his shoulder. He heard footsteps on the concrete floor, then someone patted his shoulder.

"Good morning, Mr. Reese," the same man he had spoken to last night in the club said in greeting. The brute quickly turned away and went back to the card table.

Reese looked up into that face again. The man had changed clothes, was now dressed in jeans and a blue, button-down shirt.

"You've had an accident I see. Well, those things will happen at times like this."

"Wh . . . what . . . do you want?" Reese desperately tried to sound as indignant as he could, but it came out as a pleading, mewling sound.

The man smiled and patted him on the shoulder again and pursed his lips, then smiled.

"Oh, Mr. Reese, I want so much from you. And you know what?"

Bob Reese just looked up at the man who had made his life into this nightmare.

"You're going to tell me whatever I want to know," the man said in answer to his own question. Then he grabbed one of the chairs near the table and swung it over and sat in it backward, his tanned arms resting on the top of the backrest. "It's going to be hard at first, because you will want to resist. You will think to yourself, 'I'm a man, I should be able to hold out for a while,' but then"—the man looked at the spreading stain of urine on his captive's trousers—"you will tell me all there is to know." Farbeaux reached into his pocket and pulled out a small notebook. He opened it and flipped through a few of the pages. "Now I wish to know the reason for the Group's interest in this most bizarre episode. It must be the technology, am I correct?"

"Look, there has to be a mistake, I have always given you the best information, your superiors will be very angry that I am being treated like this."

"To start with, Mr. Reese, let me introduce myself. My name is not Tallman, it's Colonel Henri Farbeaux. Does this name *ring a bell,* as you Americans say?"

The very moment the man mentioned his name, a slow, crawling coldness came to Reese and he literally felt the blood drain from his face.

The Frenchman smiled and patted Reese's right leg, then held his fingers up and rubbed them together, feeling the wetness. He smiled and gently rubbed them on his captive's shirt.

"To start the morning's festivities, Mr. Reese, tell me of this incident of yesterday in more detail than you did last night." Farbeaux paused a moment to light a cigarette, then blew the smoke toward the ceiling. "I understand from New York that Director Compton has declared an Event scenario. Would this have anything to do with his missing men back in '47, perhaps? But let's not get ahead of ourselves; let's start with this flying saucer, shall we?" Farbeaux asked, knowing that Hendrix had been alerted that the Black Team he had sent here was missing and had undoubtedly ordered another in. Farbeaux knew his time was short.

"Centaurus would never approve of you hurting me," Reese said hurriedly.

Farbeaux smiled. "Robert, I think we'll leave the company out of this one. I'm keeping the information you give me for selfish purposes. Besides, my friend, they have already ordered your termination by others; you're a danger to them now. Your only chance is to convince me of your value. Your reward will not be money, but your very existence. Surely worth the truth, is it not?"

Farbeaux once again patted Reese's leg, then reached out and brought up an unseen leather case and unzipped it. Inside, gleaming in the dim lighting, was a syringe. This he quickly and expertly plunged into a small vial, then he held the needle up and lightly pressed the plunger. A small, thin stream of amber liquid shot into the air.

"Let's begin, shall we?"

ELEVEN

Superstition Mountains, Arizona
0700 Hours

Gus was astounded at the scene before him. Scattered from one end of the high rocky valley to the other was what looked like the remains of a plane, a large plane. Material resembling tinfoil was spread in clumps and patterns that suggested it had hit pretty hard and dispersed over the wide area encompassing the valley. He slowly made his way down a small incline, over some large rocks, and entered the valley he had visited a hundred times before. He didn't notice it right off, but the feelings of being alone and afraid had ceased as soon as he'd gained a foothold on the rock- and debris-strewn soil. A slight breeze ruffled some of the metal and produced whispered whistles that seemed to penetrate to the core of the old man's being. The area reminded him of a ghost town, only this wasn't one made up of buildings and streets, but of wreckage on a mountain reputed to be haunted.

"Hello!" he called out into the valley.

Two pairs of eyes watched as Gus stood and waited for an answer. The large eyes of the small visitor were blinking rapidly in terror at the approach of the man. The other, smaller pair of eyes watched malevolently. They never left the man as he examined the wreckage. It growled deep in its throat. The small clear yellowish claws scraped the rock it leaned against.

Gus stepped farther into the debris field and carefully nudged a piece of the twisted metal with the toe of his boot. It was maybe five feet by four feet and seemed extremely light. He bent over and ran a finger over the surface of the bright silvery material. It was cool to the touch despite the rising sun's reflecting off it. As Gus curled his fingers around it and lifted, he expected one end to come up, but when the entire piece lifted off the ground, he was so surprised he dropped it again. It seemed to float down and landed softly on top of his right boot. He jerked his foot out from under with a small yelp escaping his lips. He then nervously looked at some of the other bright pieces of material around him, and that was when he noticed that hardly any of the objects had escaped the violent crash unscathed.

Toward the center of the crash area and strewn among the debris were several large container-like bins that looked somewhat intact. Most had small bottles on top of them that looked like oxygen cylinders. The old prospector walked to the nearest one for a closer inspection. The box or container or whatever it was stood a little over three feet in height and was oblong with a length of five feet or so. The front panel, or what Gus thought might be the front, was made of a clear material resembling Plexiglas. He peered through it as if he were looking through a window, holding his hand up to shield his eyes from the glare of the rising sun. When his hand came in contact with the clear panel, it warped and turned to a gel-like substance that first wobbled, then fell as water to the sands below. At the moment the substance fell, Gus felt a small electrical discharge strike his hand where it had touched the gel panel. He quickly stepped back, immediately disgusted with what he had touched. That was when he saw lying in the middle of the casing another viscous material that stank to holy heaven. It covered the entire bottom of the container and was murky and brownish. It was still bubbling around what looked like the remains of small bones and a little bit of fur floating on top. Gus looked from it to the small canister-like tanks on the top. There were three total, and one was still dripping a blue liquid into the mess that lined the floor. It looked as though whatever had been in there had been killed by the stuff in the small cylinders.

The old man shook his head, knowing he was guessing at things he knew nothing about. *What in the hell happened in this place?* The breeze picked up again, and along with cooling his skin, the wind brought the smell of something else as Gus sniffed and looked around. His eyes settled on a rather large piece of debris that was leaning against a huge boulder about thirty feet to his front. Stepping farther into the valley, a funny and almost scary thought crossed his mind and occurred over and over. There had to have been people piloting this . . . this whatever it was. If it wasn't automatically piloted, that meant a crew. If some had survived, just how in hell would he get them out of here and back down the mountain? Buck was missing, and even if he weren't, he was far too old to carry anyone all the way to town. He looked around at the scattered wreckage, doubly worried now.

He quickened his pace and walked right up to the piece of metal that was leaning against the rock. He hesitated a moment with his hand poised on the upper half of the panel. Gus figured he would check this out, then get the hell out of here and find Buck and go to the cabin and drink for about a week. He lightly touched the strange metal, running his fingers over what looked like hieroglyphs etched on the surface. The memory was vague, but he had seen something like them once in the museum up in Denver. He had taken a whole paycheck one month, splurged, and caught some culture for the first time in years. He went to the movies, saw a film about wars in space or something (stupid was what he thought), then he went to see the Egyptian exhibition over at the Museum of Natural History. While there, the tour guide had explained that the name of the writing that had been found on things in Egypt was called hieroglyphs. He believed that was what he was looking at right now. They were a metallic pink and violet in color and were engraved deeply into the metal about a quarter of an inch. He ran a finger over the engravings and received a strange electrical charge through his entire hand to his elbow. The feeling was familiar and somehow comforting.

Suddenly, the metal fell over toward him and he had to step back quickly to keep from getting hit by the sharp edges on the piece of wreckage. When what was on the other side was revealed, his eyes widened in shock. Still strapped into some sort of reclining seat was what looked like a person, but from what he could see, it was small and skeleton-thin. Gus swallowed and looked closer. The body looked half-crushed and had been gashed all over. He realized it was without clothes. It was light green with darker, grayish green highlights, and it was possibly bloated in death. The old man realized he wasn't looking at anything that would pilot an airplane that *he* knew of. He swallowed and stepped backward, his eyes never leaving the small body that had died strapped to its seat.

While in Korea, his squad had come across an American F-84 Sabre jet that had crashed not far from their position. They had assumed the pilot had escaped, parachuting to safety. But when they investigated what was left of the aircraft, they saw what appeared to be the body of the pilot still strapped tightly to his seat. He had been as mangled and crushed as the being Gus was now staring at.

One side of its face had been caved in on impact, so Gus couldn't get a good idea of what the person, or thing, looked like. He did see that the being was without one strand of hair on its head. The small hands had three long fingers and a thumb. The thumb was almost as long as the digits it was curled up beside. There were no visible fingernails. Its one visible eye was large and the pupil was black as coal. Gus had to turn away as he saw his own aged reflection in the dust-covered eye.

He swallowed and was just starting to turn away when his foot slipped into a hole in the ground. He dropped down, catching himself at the last moment, desperately clawing at the sides of a large boulder to keep from falling into the gaping hole. Gus quickly scrabbled away and gained his balance. When he looked back into the hole that had nearly swallowed him, the old man saw a gaping maw that resembled a mouth. As he watched, rocks and dirt were still trickling into the hole from his close call. As his breathing finally calmed, he noticed the edges of the dark pit were smooth all around, as if the sides had been carefully excavated and not torn. It was as if a plug had been pulled from the compacted earth. Gus reached down and ran his fingers around its opening. It was not only smooth to the touch but was coated with a shiny substance that was still somewhat damp. He quickly pulled his hand away from the strangeness of the hole and rubbed his fingers together, finding them sticky. It also gave off a sweet odor, like a just-peeled banana.

The old prospector was close to panic. He found himself backing away, and then he remembered what was waiting behind him. The mangled body would be lying there strapped into its seat. He stopped and stood as straight as he could, then he took first one step, then two, then suddenly found himself walking faster.

Gus was almost to the spot where he had entered the valley when he fell to his knees holding his head. The immense and overwhelming feeling of fear and confusion were sounding again; this time jabbering accompanied the feelings. It was even more desperate than it had been before. Suddenly the old man realized something as he removed his hands from his head. The sound wasn't coming from his own head as it had been earlier; no blood was trickling from either his nose or his ears. The sound was coming from somewhere behind him in the valley. As he listened, the confusing sounds echoed off the rock walls and bounced around. What was more confusing, Gus had the horrible feeling that the sounds would attract something he didn't want to see.

Gus turned and crept slowly in the direction of the cries. He carefully stepped around some of the metal debris as he crept closer to the noise. He bent over, shakily placing his hands on his knees to get a closer look at the bottom of a huge rock. He at first thought the sound might have been coming from inside the piece of granite, then realized this was ridiculous. That was when he saw it was coming from beneath the huge boulder. He noticed movement at the base of the rock as the soft jabbering suddenly stopped. He went to one knee as he felt something akin to relief mixed with horror flash into his mind.

Gus tilted his head and looked farther into the hole, trying desperately to penetrate the blackness. He moved his head closer, fear filling his mind. *God, this thing must be terrified even more than me!* A feeling of dread washed over him like a small wave, making him hesitant, and he tensed a little, but the feeling lasted only a second. Inside, he still sensed danger and pure animal terror, just as a deer might feel at the sight of a pair of headlights. As he looked into the coal blackness of the hole, he thought he saw two small pools of darkened water. Then they disappeared. Confusion clogged his mind as he tried to figure out what he was seeing in the dark. Then it struck him with the suddenness of a lightning bolt, as the twin pools reappeared: he was looking into the eyes of something that had come down with this thing, and its eyes had just blinked at him.

"Hey," he said softly, "I'm not gonna hurt ya."

The thing blinked and continued to talk in the strange jabber Gus didn't understand.

"You hurt?"

As soon as he asked, he knew without a doubt, that, yes, the thing in the hole was indeed injured.

"You wanna get the hell out of there?" he asked, not really knowing what to call it, or even if he was being understood. "Hope ya understand my lingo, boy."

Gus suddenly straightened and looked around him. His eyes settled on the hole at the other end of the valley, the one he had almost stumbled into. Now it wasn't confusion, but terror that struck his mind. The dark void of that hole that was coming toward him, freezing him with the horror he sensed was there. Then his eyes quickly traveled to the rocks above him. He felt as if he was being watched. He had had that feeling a hundred times on a hundred different nights in Korea, and this was no different. He thought that whatever eyes watched him meant him harm. Again his eyes roamed to the large hole. That was a different fear from what he was now feeling. The hairs on the back of his neck were still at attention, so he shook his head to try to dislodge the confusion he felt because of the hole in the ground and whatever was up in the rocks.

He turned back to the creature still cowering underneath the boulder.

"Well, come on, let's getcha outta there," he said nervously, looking back at the hole a distance away, half expecting something to come charging out of it. When he turned back, his eyes widened in shock. There, with long fingers shaking and extended outward, was a hand. The slender fingers were light green, like the first mangled being he had found in the wreckage. A darker smear of liquid was on one of the extended fingers, and as Gus watched, a small drop of fluid fell from the digit and hit the sandy dirt around the hole and soaked in. Then his eyes went back to the hand, and without realizing it, he reached out and grasped it. He felt the shivering of the owner and relaxed his grip. He reached deep into the hole with his free hand and found what he hoped was purchase under the unseen being's other arm. Gus pulled gently at first, then harder as he realized the little body was wedged under the boulder like a cork in a bottle. As he pulled, he felt the creature shift and start to help. A long minute later he was done. As the strange being came to rest after Gus had released it, it immediately started looking around at its surroundings, its large eyes blinking rapidly in the brighter world outside the shade of the boulder. The old man sat hard on his butt and stared in amazement and wonder at what he had pulled from the rock.

The creature, after surveying the crash site, slowly lay down on its back and began gazing up at the blue sky with eyes the color of obsidian. The almond-shaped orbs again blinked, and the eyelids, to Gus's amazement, slid not down from the top but from the outer sides of the eyes. Then the small creature looked over at its rescuer, clearly in pain. The head was big, shaped like a lightbulb. Not a hair was to be found on its light green skin. Dark green blood was covering most of the boy-sized body. Some had dried, and more was still flowing, albeit slowly from several small wounds. The creature slowly moved its hand away from its body and held it out toward the sky. The small, long fingers reached almost longingly toward the heavens, before falling back into the dirt at its side.

Gus looked up at the sky and then down at the slowly closing deepness of the being's eyes. The strange eyelids closed from the sides again, enveloping the eyes from the temples toward its small nose.

"I don't think I can get ya back to Mars or nothin' like that. Hell, boy, couldn't even get you to Phoenix, but maybe I can fix you up a little and get you to someone who knows just what to do with ya. And if you have a friend up there in them rocks, I don't believe I care to meet him."

As Gus looked on, the eyes opened and the small mouth and thin lips tightened in either pain or anger, the old man couldn't tell. Then the large eyes roamed to the rocks above them for a moment as if it knew what Gus had said before. Then it turned back to Gus, and the thing's right hand came up and clenched around Gus's blue denim collar and squeezed, the eyes closing with pain at the effort. Then the grip loosened and the hand fell away. The eyes half closed and the small being shuddered.

The prospector reached down and took the small, broken body of the survivor in his arms. It weighed almost nothing as he lifted its small frame against his chest. The head rocked back with pain, then lay against the old man's dirty shirt. He only hoped his wildly beating heart didn't pound the poor thing to death.

Gus knew the injured being had passed out because the small body had lost its tenseness. He looked down into the now serene face. The features were soft, the mouth relaxed.

He saw the small nose, no more than a bump with two little holes he thought were its nostrils. They were moving, so he assumed the creature was still breathing.

Gus shook his head and started toward the far end of the valley where he had entered. He steered a wide path around the large, ominous hole in the ground he had almost fallen into earlier. As he passed it, he didn't notice the small thing in his arms clench its fist in an unconscious gesture of fear. But the man did feel the terror engulf his own mind as he struggled out of the valley, leaving the mysteries of the crash site behind. But the image of that large hole and the feeling of being watched from the rocks remained, and the two memories pushed Gus forward as if Satan himself were on his tail.

The larger Gray watched the rescue of the keeper, the slave of its home world, and this time it let the growl escape its lips. Again it turned and watched as the man started his long struggle down the mountainside. The yellow eyes narrowed as it followed the retreating form. Again the nails scraped against the rock and left long scratches.

The Gray stood and limped toward the small opening in the mountain valley. It started tracking not only one, but two enemies of its kind.

TWELVE

Event Center, Nellis AFB, Nevada
July 8, 0850 Hours

Jack had been up since 0400 this morning going over his security staff files. His new department wasn't in as bad a shape as he'd originally thought. He had some real good men on assignment here. Sergeant Mendenhall had top scores in all his field evaluations. Jack figured with his record, the young man should be targeted for officer candidate school. He closed the file on Mendenhall and took a swallow of coffee. The cafeteria was just now filling up with personnel from all of the departments. He watched as a familiar face walked in yawning. As their eyes met, Sarah McIntire smiled and gave Collins a small wave of her hand. Jack nodded and went back to his files.

He placed Mendenhall's file aside in a group that included that of Everett and five others who would eventually compose his initial discovery team if the crash site was found. Across from that file was another larger grouping of paperwork that included lists of the equipment they would need to receive from logistics. He had been most impressed with the equipment the Group had buried deep beneath the sands, such as weapons and night-vision gear. His predecessor had been serious enough to at least know what was needed for field operations. Right now Collins was only guessing at what would be needed for this mission. But he did know that this site would have to be secured first at all costs. He took another sip of coffee and watched as Sarah McIntire turned to him as she took her coffee toward the door. He looked away quickly when she noticed him and smiled again.

Collins walked into the computer center cleaned and in a fresh blue jumpsuit after his post-breakfast mile in the athletic center. Alice had called and left a message for him to meet her there.

He stood and watched the buzz of activity. The whole time he had been studying his personnel files, his mind had been here, wondering how the search for the saucer was progressing. Technicians in white, static-free coats were at consoles, and others were walking around with printouts. Large flat-paneled screens lined the walls, while smaller ones were mounted at every workstation. The largest high-definition screen was located in the middle of the white plastic wall and was filled with a color map of the western United States, and as he watched, a computer-generated line started sectioning the various points into a grid. A small dotted line ran up from Panama through Mexico and then split off into several lines as it crossed the border into New Mexico. The major noticed that where the dotted lines entered the state, they had been changed to small question marks instead of dashes by some imaginative technician. On other screens he saw raw data and real-time images of desert locations that were obviously bouncing via satellites to ground stations. Niles was sitting at one of the technician desks and staring at the large screen as if he were hypnotized.

"Jesus, Dr. Compton had to pull a lot of strings and dish out favors from now until next century to get that many KH-11s on this," Everett said, coming in after Collins.

"He did. The NSA is screaming bloody murder at the use of their bird," Pete Golding, the Computer Center director, said. He was standing nearby, tapping at a set of computer keys.

Collins looked from Golding to the wall projections. "Nothing on the crash site?"

"No." Golding seemed irritated as he looked back at the two military men and then removed his glasses and rubbed his eyes. "Damn thing isn't where we thought it would be according to the track we initially calculated."

"Maybe it didn't go down at all," Carl said.

Golding just gave the navy man a sour look, then abruptly turned and walked away.

"Forgive Pete, he and Niles are a little tired and on edge this morning," Alice said.

"You look chipper," Collins said.

"Old people don't require the sleep you young ones do."

"It looks like Dr. Compton and Mr. Golding need to take five and get some shut-eye," Everett remarked.

Alice tilted her head for a moment watching Niles, knowing he had been shocked by the file the senator had given him to read. She turned and eyed the two men standing next to her. "He needs to be right here. You gentlemen better get used to the idea that we're basically on a war footing here. Never before has the center been placed on total lockdown and all departments deployed for one specific Event. Our need to find that crash site is paramount, absolutely paramount."

"Where is the senator this morning?" Collins asked.

She smiled. "He's sleeping, personal assistant ordered rest." She winked at the men, then walked over toward the middle of the room and looked closer at one of the satellite images for a moment, then shook her head and stepped back. "He may bellow and bark at the rest of us, but at least he still knows who is smarter. But I'm afraid both he and the president are taking tremendous heat from the Joint Chiefs about this incident. Everyone who's aware of our existence thinks we're way over our heads, and I'm afraid all the old agency enemies are coming out of the woodwork on this one."

They stood there for a moment, not knowing what else to say, then Niles started raising his voice about something.

"This is why I called you both," she said as Niles took a printout from one of the techs. "This doesn't look good."

Niles was calming when he noticed Alice, Jack, and Carl on the walkway above the desk area, and he hurriedly moved up the stairs to the three carrying the printout and handed it to Alice.

"See what you can do with this, will you?" He saw the blank expressions on Everett's and Collins's faces and tried to quickly explain while Alice read his findings. "That son of a bitch Reese was on the new system yesterday and observed the saucer attack in real time. Europa, our newest and most powerful computing system, says he made a damn copy of it!" Niles grimaced and snatched his glasses off, then looked at the faces before him. "Reese is missing! He didn't report for work this morning. Jack, he has to be found and found fast, there's no telling what he's up to." Then Niles abruptly turned and placed his glasses back on and irately called out to one of the computer team about scanning a search area too fast, then he turned back to face Collins. "I mean it, Jack, this is no good. It's against all our rules here in the computer center," he called out as he turned away and went back to the main floor to continue his search for the saucer.

Alice watched him go and shook her head. Then she again scanned the paper she held. She removed her glasses and looked at the two men in front of her, thinking for a moment.

She quickly walked to an empty workstation and seated herself in the large swivel chair, then opened a drawer, rummaged through it for a moment, then closed it. She repeated this with the other drawers until she found what she was looking for. The two officers exchanged a questioning glance as they watched.

Finally she looked up and smiled. "Reese may be working for a very dangerous enemy."

"He's on the senator's watch list, along with almost everyone with a clearance to the computer center," Everett said.

"I take it it's unusual for him to miss work like this?" Jack asked.

Alice thought a moment while staring at the darkened computer monitor on the missing man's desk. "Not in and of itself, no, but like everyone here, he does have his quarters inside the complex. The computer system would have notified him of an Event alert, so he hasn't checked his messages if he's off base, as per his orders." She wheeled around in her chair. "He's gone bad. Niles is right. He has to be found."

"What can we do?" Jack asked.

Alice turned back to the blank computer screen and tapped a few commands into the keyboard and the monitor lit up. At the same time she reached behind her chair without looking, offering to Collins the paper that Compton had given her earlier.

Collins took the offered printout. It was columns of military times and what looked like computer commands.

"That is a printout of the last few commands that were asked of this station. SOP for someone who doesn't show up for work, then signed off base and didn't return. We automatically check their computer for what its last commands had been."

Collins handed the paper to Everett, and he too looked it over.

"There," Alice said, straightening up. "All phone lines are monitored and recorded in this facility. It seems Mr. Reese used his security clearance and his position in the computer center to shut down the monitoring devices for a bank of phones in The Ark. He tried to cover his tracks, but doing that with someone like Niles and Pete Golding is a foolish thing. It took both of them all of three minutes to get through the firewall Reese had set up on this hard drive. Now, according to this"—she gestured at the screen—"there were only two calls made from the complex at the time the bartender noticed him inside the club. One was to a home inside Las Vegas City limits that we checked on already, made by a sergeant to a woman he met at Lake Mead. The other call went to a home in Vidalia, California." Alice picked up the phone and punched a few numbers and then waited. "Send the sergeant in, please," she said, and hung up. "I had Staff Sergeant Bateman in the security center run a few things for me using your network into the Europa XP-7, the new Cray system Niles was just speaking of."

As they waited, the comp center doors slid open with a hiss and the sergeant was allowed in. He saw Alice and walked up to the small group. He stood at attention when he came to a stop and noticed Everett and Collins.

"Normally I would have gone through you of course, Jack, but as I said, you don't even know your department's capabilities yet, and this was rather important and urgent. I believe the sergeant and Europa have given you a starting point in your search for Reese, but listen to how it was found in case you find a flaw in the pattern."

Collins just nodded, and then looked from Alice to the sergeant.

"This is what we have so far, ma'am," the sergeant said, holding a file out to Alice.

"Just give us a verbal report. If I look at one more scrap of paper this morning . . ."

The sergeant nodded and looked at Jack. "What we did was run the two numbers through NSA. They were both dead ends as no calls were actually made to those phones from Nevada. This was confirmed by AT&T, Sprint, and the actual residents of those homes. Thus we were left with a dead end. Our friend had managed somehow to scramble the hard lines leading out of the club and the transmission to the phone company's Comsat. We were stuck until we examined the security monitors from The Ark." The sergeant handed the major a cased computer disc. "We came up with this thanks to Dr. Cummings in Photo-Recon."

Jack took the disc and handed it to Alice, who inserted it into the hard drive at Reese's station. Alice used the touch feature the system was set up with, and her finger touched the header *Sur.Ark.Reese.*, meaning surveillance at The Ark on Robert Reese. Immediately a video started that showed Reese walking to one of the pay phones. They watched as he slid a card into the side of the black instrument, then dialed a series of numbers. He then hung up and walked out of the bar. It even framed the bartender inquiring something of him as he exited.

"What in the hell did we just see?" Carl asked.

The sergeant just nodded his head at the video. "The doc fixed this up for us."

On the screen the same video started, then suddenly stopped. The screen started flashing the frames forward one frame at a time, at the same instant the picture was computer-enhanced to zoom in on the keypad on the face of the pay telephone as Reese's fingers jerked over the metal numbers.

"We washed this through Europa and asked the computer what numbers Reese could have been dialing." The sergeant pointed to the screen as a full-framed picture of Robert Reese appeared as he just stepped up to the phone. The frame froze and a computer-generated tracking grid covered the man's entire body. "Now here, Europa started her measurements. We at first thought the new system had misunderstood the command, but we were in for a surprise, at least I was."

As they watched, green numbers started appearing in rapid succession along Reese's body and changed as he moved and leaned forward into the small kiosk that the phones were tucked away in. The grid stayed fluid and conformed to his body as he moved, changing the computer's calculated measurements. As he started dialing, another grid, this one red, appeared over the keypad his fingers had just started to touch. More numbers appeared, small arrows going this way and that across the numbered pad and Reese's fingers.

"Doc Cummings explained what was happening. He said that Europa started by taking the video measurements of Reese himself, height, estimated arm length, and so on. Then it measured the height of the phone kiosk from blueprints of the complex, and the height of the keypad in relevant terms to Reese's measurements. As he punched numbers, the computer really went to work, running the constant figures his movements caused in minute increments."

Again they watched as the numbers were now changing at a rapid pace, so fast they couldn't keep up with the calculations. When Reese stopped punching numbers, the calculations stopped. Then a window opened and on the display over a hundred phone numbers appeared. Some had the same area codes, but most looked as if they were random.

"Europa narrowed the phone numbers Reese could have called down to a hundred and fourteen just through the measurements taken of his movements in relative distance to the phone height and distance from his body and the minute distance his fingers moved over the numbered buttons on the phone's keypad."

"That's still a lot of numbers, Sergeant," Everett said. He looked at Jack and saw he was smiling. The major must have known what was coming.

"What did Europa use to cross-reference these numbers?" Jack asked.

"That's good, Major. Yes, she did cross-reference."

As they watched the screen, the monitor tinted green. They could see the tape as it played again and Reese once more stood before the phone. This time the computer enhanced the keypad in the green light that engulfed the scene and expanded the picture to where only the keypad and Reese's fingers were visible. When Reese was done, several of the metal numbers were glowing a light red. As the three watched, the computer-enhanced glow started to fade, but not before a series of six phone numbers popped into another window that had opened on the monitor's screen.

"The computer picked up the oil smudges from Reese's finger on the pads," the sergeant said. "The light in the club provided the difference in the sheen off the metal, some after they were just punched, leaving a different shine on the numeric pads from the oil. Thus the oil on the pads was not dried like the others, so they produced a different reflection in the club's lighting, and the computer deduced it had been these numbers just depressed."

"But there are too many numbers for an actual phone number," Everett stated.

"That was the easy part. Europa took the first set of one hundred and fourteen phone numbers from the measurements and cross-referenced them with the second set of six from the optical scan, and she boiled it down to two phone possibilities. Then she noted that some numbers may have been pushed twice, and maybe even three times. Thus you see too many numbers for actual private numbers. Then she boiled the numbers down to two by processing the remaining numbers as some were eliminated as not being actual, according to the national database of phone books, and now we have two, and they are both local. The first was Kindercare, a small preschool out on Flamingo Boulevard, in Vegas. The other is a strip club called the Ivory Coast Lounge. I think you know which one my bet would be on," the sergeant said.

"Amazing," Jack said, looking from the screen to the young sergeant. "That's good work. Thank you, Sergeant."

Everett just looked at the young enlisted man and smiled as the sergeant turned and left the computer center. He turned to look at Jack, but he was watching Alice as she started for the door herself.

Alice waited for the men to catch up in the long circular hallway.

"Okay, we need to know first his condition, then find out if Reese passed along anything about the Event," Jack said.

Alice looked Jack over closely. "We take it very seriously when our people come up missing. We take it extremely seriously when it's on the heels of what happened yesterday. I don't like the look of this, and neither does Niles."

"Yes, ma'am."

"I took the liberty of alerting Gate Two. If you would go see Gunny Campos, he'll have your identification and sidearms. Go get Reese and bring him back to us. And fast."

THIRTEEN

It was close to ten in the morning when Collins and Everett hurriedly stepped from the elevator into the pawnshop. Jack looked around and thought how the world had changed for him since he'd stepped into this very shop yesterday. It seemed it had been months and not just a single revolution of the clock since he had been in this dingy and dusty store.

They were met as the doors of the elevator closed behind them. Campos was there with Staff Sergeant Mendenhall and two other men. All were dressed in civilian clothing and Mendenhall was smiling.

"What is it, Sergeant?" asked the major.

"After your arrival at the center, we were laying bets on what security personnel would be reassigned. I'm just glad to have a job this morning, sir."

"The morning's still young," Collins replied, letting his eyes linger for a moment on the staff sergeant. He turned and asked the older marine, "You have something for us, Gunny?"

The old man nodded in affirmation and produced two large manila envelopes. He gave one each to Collins and Everett. They opened them, and inside were two forms of ID and a badge in a leather wallet and a holstered nine-millimeter Browning automatic with two extra clips of ammunition. Collins raised his eyebrows.

"Better to have too much than not enough," Everett said, sliding the two magazines into his back pocket.

Collins did the same and clipped the holstered nine-millimeter into the waistband of his jeans under his Windbreaker and toward the small of his back. Then he looked at the badge he held in his hand. It was a star inscribed with DEPUTY UNITED STATES MARSHAL. Collins slid the leather-encased shield into his waistband, allowing the badge to dangle there.

"What in the hell do we do if we just happen to bump into real marshals?" the major asked.

"We go to jail for impersonating a federal officer and pray that Niles can get our asses out," the naval officer answered, grinning.

"Great. Well, who's coming?" Collins asked.

Mendenhall introduced the other two men as marine PFCs, O'Connell and Gianelli. PFC O'Connell had a decidedly Southern drawl, and there was no doubt at all Gianelli hailed from New York.

"Gunny here wants permission to come along with us. He doesn't really expect to be used in any real capacity, maybe watch the car. Mrs. Hamilton said it was totally up to you," Mendenhall said in a lowered voice. "Spec 5 Meyers up front will mind the store, if you concur, sir."

Collins looked the old man over. He wasn't real comfortable with the idea, but the man was still a marine, thus had earned respect long ago. "Getting some air with us today, Gunny Campos?"

"About goddamn time too. I'm damn tired of babysitting these boys and bickering with the tourists. I can still run rings around most of these men, and the day I let someone from the army beat me, I'll just . . ." He saw the major looking at him. "I . . . uh . . . yes, sir, very ready to get out of here. I know the town and I know exactly where you need to go. Present company excluded on the army comment, Major."

"Quit while you're ahead, Gunny. You're welcome to

come along, but don't get used to it. You know the area here, so let's roll."

"Yes, sir."

Staff Sergeant Mendenhall drove while Everett rode shotgun with O'Connell in the middle. The other three, including Collins, rode in the back. In less than five minutes they were in the area of the old Strip that housed all the famous and older casinos.

"Gunny, see if they have a back door to this place and stake it out," Collins said as he left the car. "You stay with him, Gianelli."

"Yes, sir."

Collins watched them head toward the back of the building. Then he, Everett, Mendenhall, and O'Connell walked around to the front of the club. Once there they didn't hesitate. A bored-looking woman sitting behind an old desk didn't even glance up from her *People* magazine as they passed, merely blew a bubble with her gum and let it snap before sucking it back in and starting over. They went up a long flight of stairs toward the smell and noise of the Ivory Coast Lounge.

The room was dark and much larger on the inside than it looked from the outside. Music was playing, but no one was onstage. A waitress with rather large and sagging breasts was leaning down and speaking with a man in a black suit who sat in a palm-covered booth. He looked up at the newcomers and slid out of the booth, ducking his head under the fake elephant tusks and palm fronds. He whispered something to the topless woman and then walked away, disappearing into the back of the club. The waitress watched him leave, then placed her tray down on the table and hurried away through a curtained doorway to the left. She glanced back at Collins and Everett as she pulled the drapes closed.

Through the strains of the Moody Blues singing "Nights in White Satin," a man with a swooping seventies Elvis haircut stepped through the same curtained doorway after a few minutes and up to the four men, eyeing them closely.

"Can I help you, gentlemen?" he asked loudly over the music, smiling with stained teeth exposed and moving his shoulders as if he were warming up for something.

Everett sized up the tall, unbearably thin man and decided he wasn't much of a threat.

"Looking for someone," Collins said, leaning forward a little, noticing the slight bulge the man had under his own jacket. He was definitely armed.

"Have a name, cop?" the man asked, pegging them immediately as some sort of law enforcement.

Collins said nothing; he just looked at the club's proprietor. After a moment he produced a small wallet-sized photo that Mendenhall had given him earlier in the car. It was Reese, the picture having been taken last year for his Event Group ID.

"His name is Reese, he may have been here last night or earlier this morning," Collins stated.

Elvis hunched his shoulders, then popped a toothpick into his sneering mouth.

"Man, you know how many people come in here a day?" he asked, eyeing the other three men on either side of Collins.

The major looked around the empty club and smiled as the Moody Blues' haunting melody was still playing to an empty house. "It must be a bitch with all these people here to notice one man."

The Elvis wannabe just smiled and looked at the floor, not saying anything.

"You mind if we have a look around?" Everett asked.

"Not without a warrant, my friend," Elvis said, looking up, the smile now gone.

"Ah, we paid the cover," Everett said, smiling, "can't we take an itsy-bitsy look around, pretty please?" He held his right index finger and thumb about an inch apart.

"Fuck off, cop."

The four soldiers exchanged amused looks. The man saw this and became a little unsettled. Collins brushed by him before Elvis knew what was happening and walked farther into the club.

"Hey, *fuckhead*," the man started to protest, then felt a hand slip quickly under his jacket and deftly remove the gun from the hidden holster. "Hey! I have a permit for that!"

Everett effortlessly punched the release button and ejected the ammunition clip, then pulled the slide back and allowed the chambered round to fall to the floor.

"I'm sure you do, I just don't feel comfortable with Elvis and firearms, call it silly," Carl said.

Collins was walking toward the stage, looking around at the cheap décor of the club. He fingered some dust off the platform of the stage, then suddenly the darkened room filled with the bright flashes and sharp reports of gunfire. Collins threw himself to the floor, crawling around the base of the stage. He pulled his sidearm and was pointing it to where he thought the shots had come from. The noise was deafening in the empty lounge. Two more loud explosions rang out, and this time he saw the muzzle flash. It came from the same curtain the woman had disappeared into earlier. Collins rolled but knew the shots hadn't been aimed at him.

"Anyone hit?" he shouted to his men, with his gun pointed and his eyes still on the curtain.

"We're alright, but Elvis took one in the head," Everett called out.

"Shit! The curtain, there's gotta be a door. That's where the shots came from."

"You lead, we'll cover," Everett shouted, coming to a knee with his own weapon already drawn and aimed at the shoddy curtain.

Mendenhall was already duckwalking toward the major, using the booths for cover. Everett and O'Connell stood as one and ran toward the side of the curtain with guns held up in the air. Everett nodded and Collins ran for the curtain, coming to his knees. At that moment three quick shots rang out and echoed from what seemed like considerable distance. The two men looked at each other and Collins pointed his finger at the door, then pointed down.

Everett mouthed the word *basement* to O'Connell.

The music on the jukebox went suddenly silent. They looked over at the black army sergeant; he was just dropping the cord he had yanked from the wall. He stood there with his gun pointed toward the curtain in an area in the center between the two officers.

Other distant shots sounded, echoing until they faded away, erupted again and then stopped.

Farbeaux was furious. The fool he had sent up the stairs from the basement to check on their visitors had obviously panicked and opened fire. He didn't like admitting it, but he had become used to the professional way the company's Black Teams operated, not like these goons the club had on staff. Now he calmly waited for the man to reappear so he could shoot the incompetent fool. He quickly turned to the other two who were standing by the card table and put two rounds into them, just as the closest one turned and fired. The round missed the Frenchman by two feet, but caught the unfortunate Reese in the head.

"My apologies, Mr. Reese, I'm afraid circumstances have prevented me from keeping my promise," he said as he quickly turned for the door that led to the alley behind the club.

As the door opened, he saw several things at once. First was an older man who was coming toward him while reaching for something behind him, probably a weapon. The second was, Farbeaux assumed, the old man's younger companion, who was turned and looking at three men in black who were approaching from the lot. They had already drawn their weapons and opened up, making the younger man hit the asphalt and roll under a car. Then they turned their weapons toward the old man himself. That man had turned at the sound of gunfire behind him, then suddenly flailed his arms and fell as Farbeaux opened fire with his silenced weapon, making the old man's assailants all dive for cover. Farbeaux made his way for the fallen man and saw he had been hit in the upper chest. He grimaced and fired twice more toward the three men in black as he used his own cover fire to sprint from the rear lot.

Gianelli had regained his composure and started firing toward the men who had taken cover behind the parked cars. They returned fire and broke for the alley toward the running man Gianelli had seen exit the club, then the marine noticed that Gunny was down.

L et's go," Collins said.

He burst through the curtain first, followed by the taller Everett. They were at the top of a stairwell that descended into what had to be a basement. The paint on the walls was peeling and the stairwell looked as if it was seldom used. Collins, Everett, and O'Connell started down. Mendenhall placed himself at the top of the stairs with his nine-millimeter pointed outward into the club.

One minute later, a *very* long one minute of creaking wooden stairs, Collins stepped onto a concrete floor. The only door was five feet in front of him. He knew he was a sitting duck to anyone who wanted to plug a couple of rounds into the door from the other side, but he felt the urgency of what was happening. He glanced back at Everett. They both started forward and placed themselves on either side of the door. The major motioned with his finger, pointing upward for Everett to go high, then used the same finger pointing down, indicating he would go low. It was a classic police maneuver he had learned in terrorist training at Fort Bragg. The lieutenant would kick the door in, then Collins would dive and quickly roll, bringing his gun to bear on anything in front of him. Then Everett would come in high, and in theory the odds of both of them getting hit were low, and that was why policemen and military people used it all over the world.

What Collins saw after finishing his roll was bizarre to say the least. The topless girl from upstairs was now dead. She was propped up against a man that lay against a far wall with a perfect round hole between her eyes. As she had tried to follow Farbeaux outside, a stray round had ended her flight. A small trickle of blood had run down between her sagging breasts.

"Jesus, Major, what the fuck happened here?" Everett whispered.

Collins said nothing; he just looked at the body of Robert Reese, still seated in the swivel chair in which he had died. One of his white shirtsleeves was rolled up, indicating he had probably been drugged.

"Jesus," said Mendenhall as he stepped around Everett and into the room.

Collins made a shushing gesture with his finger to his lips and looked around at the two men lying by the card table. He could see they had been dispatched at close range. Then Jack saw the notebook lying on the blood-covered floor and quickly realized that it was filled with notes about the Event yesterday, penned in a neat hand that hadn't been hurried to say the least. Jack frowned when he saw notations on Operation Purple Sage. Then question marks after it.

Suddenly, the doorway was filled with a form and Jack raised his pistol.

"Major!" a familiar voice called out, hollowly echoing off the basement walls.

"O'Connell?" Everett called, the handgun now pointing toward the doorway.

"Yes, sir," the marine answered. The others watched as O'Connell, holding up a severely wounded Gianelli, stumbled in through the doorway. Everett and Mendenhall lowered their guns and helped with Gianelli, and Collins covered their movement.

"What the hell . . . ?" Collins hissed.

"Sir, he told me Gunny's hit bad," O'Connell said as his teeth clenched in the effort to hold the other man upright. "I found him when I went back out the front toward the gun-fire."

Collins moved his head, indicating Everett and Mendenhall should get outside and check out what was going on.

"Report, Gianelli. What are we up against?" Collins asked, bending down to come eye to eye with the injured man.

"One . . . man ran . . . from the building," Gianelli said, getting his breath, "Then others ambushed him and . . . us. Some . . . guys bushwhacked . . . us from behind. They hit Gunny, but they were gunning for the guy who ran . . . out of the club."

Collins looked around and saw the video monitors. One of them had a view of the back, and as he was staring at the black-and-white image, he saw Everett break into the sun-light and head off camera, followed quickly by the sergeant.

"Come on, son, let's get the hell out of here," Collins said, helping to lift the young marine.

He supported most of the wounded man's weight as the three made their way outside. When they exited the back door, Mendenhall was on his knees, bending over Gunny, pushing down steadily on his chest. He was trying to stop the life's blood from draining from the old marine. The gunnery sergeant's gun was still wedged between his belt and his tucked-in shirt. Everett knelt beside him.

"Hang in there, Gunny, we'll get you some help."

Gunny took a deep breath as sirens started to sound a dis-tance away.

"Get in there and get Reese, we're not leaving anyone be-hind," Collins ordered O'Connell.

Mendenhall looked from Collins to the gasping gunnery sergeant. Blood was now bubbling at the corners of the old man's lips. Mendenhall was stunned and quickly swiped a tear of frustration away.

"Grab that videotape out of the recorder on the desk," Collins shouted at the retreating O'Connell. The private didn't turn but just raised his right hand in acknowledgment as he ran for the rear door.

Everett stood. "He wants you, Major," he said, still looking at the gunnery sergeant. Then he reached for the wounded man.

Collins placed Gianelli gently into the arms of Everett. "Get him to the car, Commander."

"Yes, sir," Everett replied.

Collins bent over the still form of Gunnery Sergeant Lyle Campos.

"Sorry, Major," the old man whispered. "Caught me with my drawers down."

"It happens to the best of us, Gunny."

Mendenhall turned away.

The marine shook his head. "No excuse . . . too damn old to play soldier.

"Major," Gunny said, barely whispering as his eyes started wandering off over the major's right shoulder into the blue sky, "the men that killed me, I think they were shooting at the . . . the French . . ."

Collins leaned closer. "Frenchman?"

"Fa . . . Farbeaux . . . fit . . . his description." Campos coughed, blood spilling onto the front of his shirt. His eyes focused for a moment. "Sorry for letting him get away. He fired on the fucks . . . that . . . killed me," Campos whispered, then died, his eyes still looking at the cloudless sky.

Jack closed Gunny's eyes. Flashbacks of operations gone bad snapped to the forefront of Jack's memory. After he had just told the senator he would never be a part of hurried planning again, here he was, holding another dead soldier in his arms. He shook his head to clear it.

He heard O'Connell exit the club and Sergeant Mendenhall go to help him with Reese. Collins now stood and looked at the young private who had carried the dead computer tech. Reese's blood was soaking into the marine's yellow Hawaiian shirt and onto the black videocassette he held. Mendenhall had the body in the backseat and Everett was already getting the car started.

"We better boogie, sir, it sounds like the entire Vegas police force is charging this place."

Collins said nothing as he reached down and pulled the

gunnery sergeant up and carried him like a child in his arms to the car.

Now Jack Collins knew why the Event Group had needed someone like him. The people whom the Group was butting heads with were not mere mercenaries; these people were trained and had assets. Henri Farbeaux might not be working for the French government, but one thing was for sure: to have a setup like this in one of the most secure cities in the world, he wasn't working alone, and whoever that employer was, it wanted that saucer as much as the Event Group.

The platform was crowded with personnel as word had spread that a field team was coming in with casualties. As the sleek monorail transport pulled next to the loading area, Collins still held the lifeless body of Gunnery Sergeant Campos.

Everett stood first and handled Private Gianelli with gentle and agile movement. Waiting EMTs started working on the boy as soon as he was laid on the stretcher. Private O'Connell walked alongside talking softly to his friend as they moved him to the elevator.

Others on the platform moved aside as Collins lifted the body of the old marine out into waiting arms. There was a surreal silence at that moment as the major looked into faces of men and women he didn't know. He bent over and with the help of Everett lifted up the lifeless body of Reese. They handed him over to the EMTs, then stood and stepped out of the transport. All the while Collins felt the wetness of the blood of both Reese and Campos soaking through his nylon jacket. He smelled the coppery odor he had smelled a hundred times before this terrible day, in fields and towns around the globe, but never here in the streets of his country.

He looked at Everett, who was now speaking in low tones to a woman whom he recognized as Signalman Willing. Next to her was Sarah McIntire, whose eyes followed the body of the gunnery sergeant as it too was laid on a gurney next to the one in which they had laid Robert Reese. Then both bodies were covered with red sheets and wheeled away.

Sarah looked back at Collins, hesitated a moment, and then, gathering courage, walked toward him. She was dressed in the standard blue jumpsuit, and her hair was under a red baseball cap all the geology team wore. She had books under one arm.

"Are you all right, Major?" she asked, seeing all the blood that covered him.

Collins looked at Sarah, then beyond her for a moment, then met her eyes. "I've been better, Specialist."

She looked back at Lisa, who had finished talking with Everett and was looking at her curiously. Even Carl raised an eyebrow in their direction.

"You weren't hit or anything? I mean, you are absolutely covered in blood."

Collins continued to look at her and then down at his jacket and pants. "No, it's not mine. Why is everyone here?"

Sarah looked around and then back into the army officer's troubled face. "Word spread pretty quickly, and before you think it, we're not morbid, it's just that we all knew Gunny and liked him very much. He was a fixture here for a long time. This is a pretty small and very tight organization. Everyone knows everyone."

Collins looked at her a moment, sadness etching his hard features, then he turned and left.

Sarah watched him leave as she brought her books to her chest and breathed deeply. Everett and Lisa joined her.

"How's the major doing?" Lisa asked.

Sarah just shook her head and then looked at Carl. "Does he have any idea he's just a man, Commander, and not immune to feeling for his men?"

Everett watched the elevator doors slide closed.

"No, Sarah, he knows he's a man, but he's also a soldier that's seen too much shit and wants people under his command to go home at night."

Sarah turned and looked into the blood-smeared transport for a long time before she turned away and followed Carl and Lisa, waiting for the next elevator to take them down into the complex.

Jack had cleaned up and changed into a fresh jumpsuit. He had tossed the civilian clothes he had been wearing into the garbage can next to his desk and stuffed an entire newspaper over them. He wanted rid of the clothing that was still damp with the blood of Gunny Campos. He looked at himself in the mirror and rubbed a hand through his short hair. He was numb inside. He felt the inevitable guilt he always felt at not being the one who didn't return alive. A knock at his door interrupted his thoughts.

"Yes," he said a little louder than he wanted to.

"Major, it's Niles, you have a minute?"

Jack again ran a hand through his dark hair and walked the few paces to the door as if it were ten city blocks away and opened it.

"What is it, Doctor?"

"Major, you need to come with me; the senator wants you to hear this yourself."

Jack saw that Niles was in a far worse state than he had been this morning.

"You find the crash site?" he asked.

Niles looked around behind him; after seeing no one in the dormitory hallway, he looked back at Jack. "No, not yet, but now I know the reasons behind why it's so important we find it, and that's what the senator wants to explain. He wants me to sit in, even though I have already read the file. It may explain to you the reason why lives were lost over this. Hell, maybe you should have known from the beginning, but as you'll see, Jack, this is a first and there are no rules written for this kind of thing."

"What file?"

"The file containing reports on what really happened that night in Roswell. Major, please, hurry." Compton turned and left. Ten paces from Jack's door, he turned and looked at Collins again. "*Hurry,* Major."

F ive minutes later, Collins was in the director's spacious office with Niles, Alice, and the senator.

"Thank you for coming. I'll make sure to tell you this as fast as I can," the senator said. "Before you go after the Frenchman and his employers using Europa, Jack, I think it's time you know what we may be up against. I didn't tell the Group the whole story of what happened that night in '47, but you need to know now, because it's looking more and more like the worst-case scenario I have always feared is happening. And the extreme violence that occurred against your team this morning tells me the situation has turned for the worse."

Jack looked from the old man to Niles, then took a chair as the senator started speaking.

FOURTEEN

The former OSS general watched the silver-haired president as he stood just aft of where the dragon's-head prow used to be attached to the ancient hull. He placed a hand where the ancient carving used to sit it and drawled, "I just can't believe they sailed this thing across the Atlantic Ocean all the way up the Mississippi River! Damn it, that's amazin'!"

Garrison Lee removed his brown fedora and stepped up to the edge of the gunwale. The scaffolding that surrounded the vessel was a little shaky, and with only one eye he had to be more careful than most.

"We believe the voyage may have been made as early as AD 856, Mr. President. We have a team in Norway now, researching some information we came across last year that indicates it was an entire village uprooted by civil war that came across and tried to settle in the New World over six hundred years before Columbus. We should know more this time next month. Right now we believe this is the largest longship ever to be constructed, and that there may have actually been six on this voyage. According to some rune stones discovered nearby, each carried close to a hundred souls and their supplies."

Truman looked over at Lee and just shook his head. "Son,

your people have done one hell of a job here, one hell of a job! This is absolutely magnificent!" He ran his fingers along the jagged edge where the headpiece had once been attached. "To think about the voyage they must have endured and the spirit they had to have shown to make it. Goddamn, they weren't Vikings, son, they were just as American as you or I with the spirit of adventure they'd shown."

Garrison Lee smiled at the simple way Truman put it. It may not have been the spirit of adventure, but perhaps desperation that drove them from their homeland, but he didn't correct the president. He then watched as Truman grinned at the technicians looking up at him from the scaffolding surrounding the ancient ship. The visiting president had drawn a large crowd at three in the morning.

"Didn't think you would be doin' this back in '41, did you, Lee? Just like I didn't think I'd be president, but I guess we both got our hides nailed to the barn wall with jobs that sometimes go beyond the ability for a man to believe." Truman looked at the men and women around and above him as he spoke. "This man"—he gestured with his hat outstretched at the much taller Lee and looking at Lee's Event Group—"had a record with the OSS that read like a damn adventure novel, one of them serials they have at the by-God movies. I met the young Mr. Lee when he was just out of law school, knew he was going to be something different from the bloodsuckers that usually hold to that particular profession." A sad look clouded the man from Missouri's features and he looked down for a moment. "Then the war came, and off he went."

Lee touched the eye patch and the scar that ran under it. *Yes,* he thought, *off I went.*

"I just wanna tell you all that this is one hell of a piece of work." Truman patted the ancient and stone-hardened wood again. "It's nice to see that the entire federal government isn't made up of people that fear the future and scoff at the past. I can see you people here are trying to make it better for us all, and it's appreciated, I assure you."

His predecessor had warned Garrison that it would take

something like this to get a president to come around and support this hidden branch of government. If that was true, then he should receive funding for at least the next four years. Lee smiled as he looked at Harry Truman.

"Mr. President, this wasn't only a ship of exploration, it was also a warship, one of the most technologically advanced and swiftest afloat at the time. And as I'm sure you know, the United States has the right of salvage to her, and thus she can be renamed. Which is not an uncommon occurrence in a situation such as this."

Truman stood there silently with his hands on his hips, the gray suit now a little muddy from his crawling around the interior of the great longship.

"I wasn't aware of that, no, sir. Right of salvage, huh?"

"That's the truth, sir. Even if it weren't, it's ours, an American vessel on American soil."

A smattering of applause came from the people observing the president and *his* first Event.

"Well, sir, it's our honor to present to you the longship USS *Margaret Truman*."

The president let his hands fall to his sides and he looked astounded. He watched as a white cloth was pulled from the vault's rear wall. The name of the ship was inscribed in gold on carved wood with a dragon's head fronting the words. The president looked at the plaque a moment, then slapped his hat against his thigh and broke out clapping with the rest of the men and women. He shook his head and stepped deftly to the scaffold and took Lee's hand in his own in a powerful grip.

"Goddammit, son, I'm proud of you and your people. And this"—he gestured to the nameplate—"is a real honor that I can only say is thrilling to me and would be to my wife and daughter, if I could just tell them about it." He winked and laughed as they shook hands.

Lee's young new assistant, Alice Hamilton, walked up and gave the grinning Lee a Teletype message. The woman had come to work at the Event Group because Lee felt he owed her something. Her husband had been with him in

South America after the end of the war, and he was still there, buried in an unmarked grave.

Lee read the message she had given him, trying not to be thrown off-balance by the president's overzealous handshake and trying to keep the Teletype in focus as he was jostled. When he was done, he leaned over and whispered in the president's ear. Truman's face wrinkled into a puzzled look, and he took the yellow paper. He too read it, then asked a question, to which Lee nodded his head in response. Then they both hurriedly left the top of the scaffolding and used the stairs to reach the bottom of the newly installed vault.

The men and women, all security or technicians of the Event Group, watched in curiosity as their boss and the president of the United States left with looks on their faces that told them something wasn't right in the world.

Garrison Lee saw the president to a secure area lining the new level of vaults so he could call the Pentagon situation room.

The president hung up the phone and joined Lee in the corridor outside the secure communications room.

"Mr. Lee, I'm very pleased with what I've seen here today." He paused long enough to place the now crumpled fedora on his head, and Lee helped the older man into his coat. He noticed that the president had a distant look on his face. "After the things you've shown me, I think I can guarantee your current budget and maybe a little more, although I know for a fact that the brass-hat sons of bitches are going to scream that I'm stealing from them. To hell with them, I say. What's a couple of overpriced bombers when it comes to doin' good for the American people?" Truman walked toward the main elevator. "After all, who am I but a country boy just following in the footsteps of great men? Tell your people, Lee." He turned and shook the senator's hand again. "I'll talk to you soon."

Garrison Lee took President Truman's hand and firmly shook it, pleased by the minimal promise of the Group's current budget. But he had to risk the next question, which was burning him up inside.

"Mr. President, I believe the Event Group may be better equipped to handle the situation in New Mexico, if you would allow us."

A Secret Service agent cleared for the Event Center held the elevator doors for Truman. The president turned and gave a quick shake of his head.

"Sorry, Lee, I have to stick with the boys who won the war on this one. I have to assume they know what they're doing." The last words were almost cut off by the closing doors.

Lee stood at those same doors for a moment and watched the green indicator light glow. He felt as if he was being left out of the biggest event since the coming of Jesus Christ, and there was nothing he could do about it.

Garrison Lee hadn't heard from the president of the United States for almost five days and was assessing field assignments when Alice stepped into his office. She quickly opened the right bottom drawer of his desk and removed a bulky red phone. There was a small handle on the top that she practically punched with the palm of her hand, instantly freeing the device from its security holder. She lifted the receiver and held it out to Lee.

"It's the president and he doesn't sound happy," she said quickly.

"Mr. President, this is Lee."

"Mr. Lee, I want you to get your ass with your best security team and science people and get control of that goddamn situation in Roswell."

"What do I need to know, Mr. President?"

"Know? Know, Lee? Haven't you read the goddamn papers?"

"Been busy here, sir."

"Well, damn, man, the Army Air Corps just released a press statement that they have a flyin' damn disk in their possession. I had General LeMay, General Ramey, and Allen

Dulles on the phone and all they gave me was the runaround! Sons of bitches don't know who they're dealin' with!"

"LeMay and Dulles will do that, Mr. President, if they think you're treading on their turf." Lee knew Allen Dulles and knew the man always had ulterior motives for everything he did. Every move was calculated for what good it would do him and whatever group he was working with.

"Let me tell you something, *M i s t e r* Lee"—Truman spread the word *mister* out for a month—"it's all my goddamn turf, you get me, son?"

"Yes, sir, I hear you and agree, Mr. President, it's your backyard."

"Damn right, mine and the people of this nation who pay our salaries. I think sometimes the damn generals and spooks need to be put in their place, no offense, Lee. I take it you have an aircraft available to you?"

"We have twelve, four converted C-41 Dakotas, three P-51 Mustangs, and several scout craft, sir."

"P-51s! Who in the hell gave you those? Ah, never mind. As I was saying, you and a team of scientists or whatever eggheads you need get there and get control of that crap in the desert, now!"

"Yes, sir."

"And, Lee?" The president sounded as if he was grinding his teeth. "I've sent you a letter with my signature on it, authorizing you to do what you think is right, and I'll back you one hundred percent. If you have to hang someone, I'll supply the rope!"

"I'm on my way, Mr. President, and thank you, sir."

"Thank you nothin', get there and find out what's going on. You tell them if I have to come down there and fire some butts, I will."

"I'll pass along the message, Mr. President," Lee replied, but found that the call had already been terminated.

Alice handed over a sealed envelope. "This was just wired over from the White House," she said.

Lee opened it and scanned the words. It did indeed authorize him to do anything just this side of murder to gain the cooperation of the air corps and army.

"What's going on, Garrison?"

"Well, Alice, I guess that's what I'm flying to New Mexico to find out."

FIFTEEN

Roswell, New Mexico
July 8, 1947, 2000 Hours

The four converted C-41 war-surplus Dakotas touched down on the runway at Roswell Army Airfield at eight that night. They passed row upon row of Boeing B-29 bombers lining the runway and taxied to a small hangar, all the time under the watchful eyes of air police, who escorted them in four jeeps. Lee wasn't concerned with their presence. As he looked out his window, he saw the giant Boeing bombers and noticed how the aging birds still looked lethal. The 509th Composite Bomb Group was world famous for a plane that was once listed among its ranks, named the *Enola Gay*.

The bomber-group intelligence officer, Colonel William Blanchard, stood at the bottom of the staircase after it was rolled into place by the base ground crew. The high wind was flapping the bottom of the officer's trousers, and he held on to his hat as he waited for Lee to descend.

"General Lee, I had heard you were a private citizen after your service during the war." The colonel extended his hand. The offered handshake was ignored by Lee. He was followed down the staircase by men who carried bags and boxes full of equipment. The second, third, and fourth Dakotas were unloading larger pieces of equipment, and the Event Group's security teams exited through the rolling side door used for cargo. Garrison wasn't at all surprised the base's intelligence officer knew of him and whom he used to work for.

Lee looked at the base roster sheet he had studied on the plane ride over. "You must be Colonel Blanchard?"

"Yes, sir."

"Colonel, where is your commanding officer?"

"The base com—"

"I don't need the base commander, Colonel, I mean the man that's in charge of"—Lee once again looked at his clipboard and flipped a few of the pages that had been wired from Washington—"Operation Purple Sage."

Blanchard seemed taken aback by this. "I don't think you know the way army intelligence works any longer, sir."

Lee smiled and tilted his hat back, fully exposing his eye patch. "Colonel, two years ago I was still a brigadier general on active duty in the OSS. I now hold a civil rank equivalent to that of a four-star general, so don't you dare pretend to tell me how the army or its intelligence apparatus operate. Johnson! Bridewell!" he called over his shoulder.

Two men broke away from the Group's security team and ran to where Lee and the colonel were standing. They wore army fatigues and were carrying sidearms.

"If the Colonel says anything other than 'Yes, sir' and doesn't lead us to where they either have the wreckage, or to the gentleman in charge of this investigation, arrest him on charges of disobeying a direct order from the president of the United States and obstructing an official presidential inquiry."

The two men moved to either side of Colonel Blanchard and stood at parade rest.

"Very well, if the president wants amateurs running this show, it's his funeral," the colonel said into the rising wind, then abruptly turned and started for the hangar entrance.

They followed Blanchard as if they were in a parade. Garrison had assembled the largest field team since the Lincoln Raid on Ararat in 1863. He had metallurgists, language experts, paleontologists, atomic and medical-research scientists, quantum theorists, structural engineers, machining experts, and sixty security personnel. The quantum theorists were on loan from his friend at Princeton, Albert Einstein. They had been flown from New Jersey into the dirt runway at Las Vegas by his P-51s and weren't at all happy about it. He knew Albert would charge him a huge favor in the near future for the loan.

Blanchard walked over to one of the huge hangars that held sway over Roswell Army Airfield. It was large enough to house two B-29s side by side. Military police had surrounded the building, and they all carried M1 carbines or Thompson submachine guns. The colonel glanced over his shoulder at Lee and gave him a sour look as he saw the Group's security personnel advance on the MPs and give them new orders. He scowled and then opened a small door just to the left side of the large hangar doors. Lee followed him into a spacious office with several people in the smoke-filled room. Colonel Blanchard walked over to a surprised man in a white shirt and whispered something to him.

Lee scanned the faces in the room as his security team followed him into the office. They closed the door behind them, shutting out the noise of the blowing wind, and totally surrounded the men in the office.

The men standing around in mild shock were the intelligence types Lee had come to know well during his hitch in the Office of Strategic Services. But it was the one man who was seated all alone at a table that caught Lee's immediate attention, as he definitely looked as if he didn't belong there. He was sweating profusely because of the huge light they had trained on him. The disheveled man looked at Lee with a dull gaze, then quickly looked away. Garrison spied an officer standing against the far wall. He recognized this man from the roster and briefing material, which included his photograph. Major Jesse Marcel. He held Lee's gaze, then slowly shook his head.

"Can I help you . . . General Lee, is it?" asked the man

with whom Blanchard had spoken. He stepped forward and held out his hand and said, "I'm Charles Hendrix, Army Intelligence, and special adviser to General LeMay."

Lee continued to look at the man in dungarees and sweaty denim work shirt sitting with head lowered at the table. He handed the letter from the president over to Hendrix instead of shaking his hand, not sparing the man a glance while doing so.

Hendrix read the letter, first frowning, then with a shrug of his shoulders. "The president shouldn't be too concerned with what we have here."

Lee knew the type of man who faced him. He had run into a few during the war. Their favorite saying, "For the good of the country," was a phrase this man would use to justify everything from torture to murder.

"Would you like to tell President Truman he shouldn't be concerned, personally, Mr. Hendrix? And if you're looking for a title to use in connection with me, try *The Man in Charge*."

"The point I'm trying to make is, I think the president has little understanding of what has happened here," Hendrix said, taking a Camel cigarette out of the pack in his shirt.

Lee smiled. "You may be surprised by what he understands, and if he has little understanding of this situation, it's because someone is not passing on the adequate amount of intelligence. Don't ever play word games with me again." Lee pulled out a chair next to the man sitting at the table and slowly sat down. He removed his hat and placed it on the table. He gave the man what he hoped was a comforting smile to try to relax him, knowing at the same time his scar might have just the opposite effect.

"This man is being detained for questioning," Hendrix said calmly as he paused with the match held an inch from his cigarette.

Garrison turned and looked at the man from Army Intelligence, then back at the scared gentleman with his head lowered at the table.

"Sergeant Thompson, remove this light, please."

One of the security men in the detail walked to the wall and pulled a plug. The area of table where it had been shining darkened to a more comfortable setting from the soft fluorescent lighting from the ceiling.

"Don't know about you, but bright light hurts my eye."

The man at the table didn't respond; he just raised a shaking hand up to his face and touched a bruised spot on his cheek.

"Who are you, sir?" Lee asked.

"Br . . . Br . . . Brazel," he answered.

Lee searched the notes he had taken from a Teletype he had received from Washington. The name was familiar. "You work a ranch about . . . what, seventy miles from here, don't you?"

The thin man looked at the senator and then looked quickly at Hendrix standing behind Lee, who was calmly looking down at him. Lee caught the movement of the man's eyes and thought, *This man is scared to death.*

"Mr. Brazel, make no mistake, I'm the boss man here. I speak on behalf of the president of the United States." Lee placed a hand on the man's knee and patted it softly.

Suddenly the man's right arm went up and he pointed to Hendrix. "That's what he said, said the president wanted me to say it was a lie what I found." Brazel lowered his eyes. "What I found was real," he mumbled in a barely audible whisper.

Lee looked at Hendrix, who arrogantly returned the stare.

"That was a lie itself, Mr. Brazel. The president wouldn't ask that. He may ask that you stay quiet about this, but not to lie."

"No?" was all the man asked. He was looking deeply into Lee's eye, trying to see if there was truth there.

"No, Mr. Brazel. *This* man said that, not President Truman."

"He said something bad could happen to me and mine, said we would never be found."

Lee closed his eye and tried not to turn to face Hendrix. Instead, he patted the man on the leg again. "No one is going to harm you or your family, Mr. Brazel, I promise you that." He leaned forward and looked into the man's face.

"Now, you found some wreckage from something that crashed out on your ranch, correct?"

"Yes, sir, that and the three small green fellas I found the day after."

Lee was stunned. "You found bodies?" He turned to look at Hendrix. "That wasn't in the reports to Washington."

Hendrix stomped his foot and walked away and whispered something to Colonel Blanchard, who in turn started for the side exit.

Lee snapped his fingers and a Colt .45 appeared in Staff Sergeant Johnson's right hand. He pointed it straight at Colonel Blanchard. The man came to a halt and raised his hands slightly, as if he were embarrassed and didn't know how to proceed.

"Are you going to shoot an officer in the United States Air Corps, Lee?" Hendrix asked.

"You bet. You weren't hesitating to threaten Mr. Brazel here." Lee nodded toward the rancher. "What makes you any better than the very people you are sworn to protect?"

Hendrix took this all in with a calm that only experience could teach. But Garrison could also see the muscles in the man's jaw working in slow clenching movements. He definitely wasn't used to having his orders countermanded.

"You found three crewmen in the wreckage?" Lee asked, still looking at Hendrix.

"Yes, sir, I saw one thingamajig knock down the other, leastways that's what I thought I saw. Then the one . . . air-a-plane or whatever smashed into the ground. Next day I found the three green fellas in the wreckage, only they wasn't people like you and me, and one of the little guys was hurt real bad. The other two were as dead as doornails and it looked like coyotes had a go at 'em."

"You mean you witnessed a collision of some sort between craft?"

"Wasn't no collision, 'cause the other thing in the sky just took off. It was like one car running the other off the road.

He wanted me to lie about that too," Brazel said, nodding toward Hendrix.

Lee stood and pointed to six security men standing just inside the door. "You men, place Mr. Hendrix under arrest."

"You don't know what you're doing, Lee, General LeMay gave me orders to—"

Lee cut him off. "Curtis LeMay takes his orders from the president, just like every man in this room!" Garrison's voice echoed in the huge hangar. Lee stood and with a strong arm gently assisted the rancher to his feet. "Mr. Brazel, please accept the apology of the U.S. Army for their decidedly unprofessional behavior. This . . . this episode hasn't brought out the best in people. They're scared." Lee grasped the man's limp hand and shook it. "Rest assured, sir, we don't eliminate American citizens." *Or very seldom do,* he thought.

Brazel let his hand be shaken. He was still sweating.

"But I would ask a personal favor of you, sir, if I could?" Mac Brazel just looked at Lee.

"Don't say anything about this to anyone unless you hear from me that it's all right to do so, fair?"

"Fair enough, not a word," Brazel said with a slow deliberateness that told Lee this man would keep his word. Then Lee noticed a slow curl of Brazel's upper lip; it was the first smile he had seen on the man's face.

"Sir, on behalf of President Truman, I wish to thank you. Mr. Elliott here will escort you home." Lee gestured for his meteorologist, who stepped forward and shook hands with the rancher. "He has some questions he would like to ask about the weather that night in and around your ranch. Give him a full description of both craft, everything you can remember."

"Yes, sir, I will. But one thing I know, that weren't any accident. One of those things hit the other on purpose."

Lee just nodded, thinking about the man's bizarre statement.

"Where do I get transportation, sir?" Elliott turned and asked Lee.

"Steal it," Lee said. "I don't think the 509th Bomb Group will miss a jeep for a few hours."

"Yes, sir," Elliott said, gesturing for Brazel to follow. He was stopped by a lieutenant in Lee's security force and given a Colt .45 automatic.

"Just in case someone outside of our group has any ideas about tagging along behind you, I'll have two more jeeps with our men in them escorting you. But if you're approached by anyone other than our people, don't be afraid to use that." Then the lieutenant turned to Lee. "Senator, I recommend we station a couple of our people with Mr. Brazel." He said it loud enough to make sure others heard it.

"Thank you. Elliott, get everything you can about this collision that knocked this second disk out of the sky. Mr. Brazel, again, thank you, sir."

Garrison watched and waited until the two men had stepped out into the night's windy darkness. When the door was open, the loud engine noise of a B-29 bomber was heard.

"The rest of my team is already inside." Lee turned to the dark-haired major who had stood silently through the bizarre scene of a moment before. "Major Marcel, isn't it?"

The man stepped forward and gave a quick nod of his head. "Yes, sir, and your team is already coordinating with our base investigators."

"Excellent. Was that your idea, Major Marcel?"

"Yes, sir, I was hoping someone would show up with a little common sense, so I left orders to cooperate in advance."

Lee turned to face Hendrix and was silent as he watched the man light another cigarette.

"For Mr. Brazel and anyone else you may have on this base, Mr. Hendrix, you could be brought up on charges for kidnapping and, most probably from the looks of your guest, assault. And did you expect to hide the fact you had a survivor, or that there was evidence of another craft in the same area as the first?"

Hendrix tossed the burnt match away. "I know you, Lee. I was also briefed. You were with that old dinosaur, 'Wild Bill' Donovan and those OSS boys, so let me tell you a little secret: things have changed."

Lee just glared at Hendrix as if he were some strange bug.

"If you were one of the best and the brightest, you should know how we work, Lee, how the job gets done," Hendrix continued, even though Garrison had heard enough and turned and walked away. "We have a unique situation here and you can't be allowed to foul it up," he called out loudly. "A few of the new guard have a saying that you may want to embrace for the hard years ahead. It's called *controlled violence,* and it means the gloves come off and anything and everything goes, just like our little Red friends in Russia."

Lee slowed but didn't stop walking toward the door.

"And another thing, the controlling of information is paramount in today's world, keeping it from the public, who have always been too adolescent to understand the real world. We'll play like the rest of the bullies on the block now, no more Pearl Harbors."

Lee stopped and almost turned around to answer Hendrix, but he just took a breath and continued on. He knew that man was more than likely the future of intelligence, and he also knew it wouldn't be the last time he would run into him, or another hundred just like him.

"The world will be a place you won't recognize in ten years; it's going to become very cold and hard."

Garrison knew Hendrix might be right, but today, all he could do was *control* his small corner of this changing world. Lee ignored Hendrix, just shook his head sadly, then stepped into the brightly lit hangar to face the Event that would change the world forever.

The hangar looked even larger from the inside than it did from out. Extra lighting had been installed in the last twenty-four hours to give added illumination. Pratt & Whitney, Rolls-Royce, and other engine brands waiting to be installed in aircraft or under repair lined the walls as they had hastily been pushed aside so the area could hold the remains of a very different kind of aircraft.

Lee studied the wreckage that littered the expanse of oil-stained floor. It seemed there was enough to account for ten B-29s. The wreckage had the color of unpainted aluminum, bright and shining. Some of the pieces of debris were of brightly colored violets and reds. Some of it was large, others small as confetti. Some were box-shaped, others in strange pentangle and quadrangle configurations.

As Garrison watched his people moving from one piece to another, he noticed an area in the back of the old wooden hangar that had been sectioned off by what appeared to be large plastic sheets. Outside of the semitransparent area there was a mixture of the base's air police contingent and the Event Group's own marine and army security personnel. Lee could see strange and ghostly shadows of men walking inside due to the brighter lighting installed there.

As the director started to walk in that direction, Ken Early, the team's metallurgist, stopped him.

"Sir, I think we have something here you should see right off." Ken was holding out a piece of the strange metal for Lee's scrutiny. It was small, about the size of a regular postal envelope. Around the edges were what looked like dots and dashes. Interspersed with these were symbols such as lines through circles and smaller circles inside pyramids and other octagon-shaped glyphs.

"Are the linguists working on this writing or whatever it is?" Lee asked.

Early looked from the metal in his hand to his boss, then swung around to look at the others in his team. His white lab coat was already dirty. "Uh, yes, sir, I think they are already on it." He shrugged, letting his thick-lensed glasses slide down his nose.

The answer was lost on Lee as a sound the like of which he had never encountered issued from beyond the plastic in the back.

"Look," Early said at his elbow, aware of the noises but choosing to block them out.

Without consciously knowing it, Lee had started toward the rear of the building. Only the metallurgist's voice brought him to a stop.

Early held the piece of metal in his right hand; he slowly closed his stubby fingers around it and crushed it. The sound reminded Lee of saltines being crushed. As the director watched, Early opened his hand, and amazingly the strange metal slowly reverted into its original flat shape.

"Well, I'll be damned," Lee said softly.

"It's like nothing we know of, almost as if each fiber"—Early hesitated, then corrected himself—"like its genetic makeup and shape has been programmed into each . . . each . . ." He looked lost for a moment, searching for the correct term. "Hell, sir, it remembers what its shape is supposed to be, as if programmed in design. I mean, there are a few polymers that companies like 3M are working with that have tendencies toward healing themselves, but that technology is fifty or sixty years away and is all so much theory right now."

"That *is* something, Doctor, but if that is the case, what happened to all this other material, why didn't it return to its original shape?"

Early looked around him at some of the twisted wreckage with a look of bewilderment on his face.

"We won't figure this out in one day, Ken. We have to do what we can and start documenting. I don't know how long we'll be able to keep this to ourselves. The military can usually talk presidents into anything, and eventually they'll get their way."

"Yes, sir," Early said, moving quickly back to his materials team.

Lee started for the rear of the building again. The cries had lessened somewhat to small whimpers. As he walked, his personnel were combing through debris and writing and snapping pictures. Except for a few, who glanced up from their work every so often to look toward the sealed-off area, most were busy doing their jobs and seemed totally willing to ignore the scary noises filtering throughout the entire hangar.

Lee walked the final paces to the closed-off tent area and spoke to the two Event guards.

"Bring Mr. Hendrix here," he ordered.

Lee stepped through the flap. The tent smelled of strong antiseptic. Major Marcel had arrived inside ahead of him, and he quickly stepped up to meet him and take him to the doctor.

Lee turned and watched as Hendrix was led into the clean area. Garrison immediately saw three gurneys. Two were covered with white sheets and obviously had something under them; he could see where a dark liquid had soaked through the white cloth of one. A medical team surrounded the third table; these doctors were his people from the Group mixed with base personnel. Dr. Peter Leslie, Captain, U.S. Navy, formerly of Walter Reed Medical Center, was in charge. He was a surgeon handpicked by Lee to lead the medical teams on field finds. He hoped Leslie could handle something like this. The doctor looked up as Lee and his group entered. He gestured for one of the nurses.

"We're trying to keep this area as sterile as we can, please put on those masks."

Lee accepted a gauze mask from the nurse and tied it around his mouth.

"These are appalling conditions. The base surgeon tells me he was kept from treating the survivor at the base clinic."

"Well, Doctor, there hasn't been a hell of a lot of clear thinking going on out here. Now what have we got?" Lee asked.

"Those two there, I understand they were found already dead. The base surgeon reports that the bodies have indications of massive head trauma, more than likely impact-related, and they also show signs of postmortem predator activity." Dr. Leslie pulled back the sheet on the first one. The body had been short, about four feet and thin, the skin was pale green and it had a large, hairless head that had been ripped open. One of its large eyes looked as if it had been torn out, and a huge gash ran along the left side of its head from the temple area. The wound looked deep. The remaining eye was partially open, and Lee could see the black orb beyond the thin eyelid. He noticed the black pupil itself was large and had a tint of red in its dilated state. The mouth was small, almost the size of the opening of a beer bottle, and no teeth were visible. Lee looked at the thin frame and the small, rounded belly. The smooth skin was featureless and unlined; veins were coursing through just beneath the grayish-green skin.

Leslie gestured for the director to step forward and view the second figure. "This one died also of crash trauma and was dead when they brought it in."

Lee looked at the doctor and nodded, then walked over to the third gurney. The doctors and nurses made room and moved away. As he looked down, the small, thin lips of the creature trembled, then the small body tensed and went into spasms and it cried out. The sound was piercing and it brought to mind the cries of an injured child.

"Can you do something for its pain?" Lee asked, removing his hat and holding it tightly.

"I'm absolutely terrified of killing it with any assistance I give it. We don't know its metabolism or nervous system. For all we know our pain-reducing drugs could kill it. I hate seeing it like this, but the consensus of everyone here is that it's just too dangerous."

"Can you save it, Doctor?" Lee asked.

Leslie looked at his shoes, then glanced at his colleagues. "With the right facilities and—"

"Is it going to live?" Lee demanded.

"No. It has massive internal bleeding from wounds that we just can't close up. It's so delicate our sutures tear right through its flesh."

"Then use your best guess and ease its pain, Doctor, on my responsibility."

"You can't do that, Lee!" Hendrix yelled, shaking off his guards once again.

Lee saw the small being tense for a moment when the shouted words disturbed it.

"Take that man outside and put him into submission."

"We need the creature awake and answering questions, not spending its last minutes pain-free, goddammit!" Hendrix was screaming as he was pulled from the enclosure. "You better listen to me, Lee, the first saucer was intentionally brought down by that second ship . . . goddammit, Lee, you have to listen!"

Lee clenched his teeth and gestured for the doctor to do as he had been ordered, and the voice of Hendrix finally faded away.

"Did Hendrix question this being?" Lee asked Marcel.

The major stepped forward and looked around, making sure to keep his voice low. "Hendrix had more than a few minutes alone with the . . . crewman. I think he got information from it."

Lee shook his head, then gestured for the doctor to get to work.

Leslie quickly grabbed a stainless-steel syringe and a small bottle and pulled an amber liquid into it. "I'm going to treat it as I would a child with similar injuries," he said. "If you're a praying man, Mr. Director, now would be a good time. I don't know what this morphine will do to it."

Lee watched as the doctor easily slid the needle into the small creature's arm. He watched being winced as the syringe penetrated its thin skin.

"With the exception of my group, will you ladies and gentlemen excuse us, please?"

The Roswell base nurses and two doctors left without comment.

Lee turned back in time to see the being's body relax and its pain-filled features grow slack. He was afraid it had died right before his eyes when the small mouth opened and then closed. Leslie carefully lifted its right eyelid and quickly stepped back when the black pupil rolled and looked at him. As Lee watched the startled expression of Leslie, he looked down and saw both eyelids flutter open. The large head rolled and the next thing Lee saw was the small being looking directly at him.

Lee had hoped for something better to come out of his mouth, but when he said, "I'm sorry," he didn't know why.

The creature continued looking at Lee. As Leslie moved

back toward the gurney, it moved its head slowly and looked at him. He quickly lifted a thin piece of gauze from its chest and replaced the greenish soaked bandage with another, which the doctor laid as gently as he could on the large puncture wound. He repeated the process with the head wound, and again with an injury on the throat that was deep and more than likely beyond his surgical prowess to repair with any equipment. The small being blinked and took a sharp intake of breath. Its eyes closed and it hissed again. Leslie closed his eyes, knowing it had caused the small thing pain in removing the bandage. Slowly the eyes opened, and to Leslie's and Lee's astonishment, it smiled and blinked its eyes once again.

"I think it may understand you're here to help it, Doctor," Lee ventured.

Leslie nodded, thankful that his intentions had been understood.

The alien slowly rolled its head to the left and took in Lee once again. They watched as its arm rose from its side and slowly pointed at Lee's face. Garrison raised his own hand and felt; then he understood. The small finger was pointing at his patch, or possibly the long scar that marked the right side of his face.

"I was wounded in the war," he said. Then he smiled. "I hope you have no understanding of that."

The creature again looked away. It saw Leslie and its eyes moved to the small chrome table beside the gurney. It again pointed, but this time it was indicating the syringe that had been used to ease its pain.

"No, I don't think we can give you any more, my little friend," Leslie said as softly as he could.

The being again attempted the smile and turned its head back to the left and pointed at Lee, again indicating the scar or eye patch.

"Amazing, I think it believes you are injured and he wants you to have the same shot I gave it," Leslie said.

Lee smiled and slowly reached out and with his fingers gently touched the being's fingertip. The alien again smiled.

"I'm afraid this wound is an old one," he said, using his other hand to touch the eye patch.

Lee was watching the small being and leaned closer. "Doctor, could this injury to its neck cause it to lose vocalization?"

"Right now we can't be sure if it talks at all. The wound by itself wouldn't be life-threatening, at least I wouldn't think. But is it keeping it from speaking? I really don't know."

The creature seemed to be listening to their exchange and reached for the gauze-covered wound at its neck. It swallowed and removed the hand and looked at Lee and reached for the scar again. He leaned over so the being could touch. It lightly ran its long, thin finger along the pinkish scar tissue, then lightly touched the patch. Its eyes were slowly opening and closing. The mouth was moving. Still looking at Lee, it swallowed and again reached for its throat.

"*W . . . arrrr,*" it said barely above a whisper.

Lee was astounded. He looked at Leslie, who nodded that he too had heard the word. Lee turned his attention back to the little creature and jumped when it slowly and painfully sat up with difficulty. It was shaking badly and was obviously in much pain as it attempted to move. Lee and Leslie both tried to gently push the being back onto the white sheets of the gurney. The small alien resisted and looked at Lee with eyes that pleaded for help. Garrison relented and removed his hands. He nodded once at the doctor, and he too stepped away and allowed the visitor to sit up. It turned over on its belly and slowly slid from the gurney, almost falling. Leslie quickly disconnected the IV from its bottle and rolled up the tube.

The alien made first one step, then another tentative and smaller step. Lee and Leslie adjusted to allow for the motion. The small creature stopped after four steps and shook extremely hard, closing its large eyes in pain. Leslie reached out with a fresh square of gauze and dabbed at its chest wound, but the alien wasn't paying him any mind as it reached out and tentatively took Lee's large hand and then took Leslie's. The little hands held on tightly to both men as they slowly made their way from the plastic-lined area of the hangar. As Garrison reached out and parted the curtain that separated the hospital from the rest of the huge hangar, they felt the eyes of the Group on them. People were stunned at the sight of their boss leading the injured alien from the secured area at the back. Hendrix, with his hands now cuffed in front of him, stared wide-eyed at the strange trio as they moved. The alien stopped and watched as the Group security men, their mouths ajar, moved Hendrix back away from its path.

"Major Marcel, quickly remove everyone from the hangar with the exception of my departmental supervisors. All other personnel, including my technicians, are to evacuate the hangar, *now*," Lee said quietly in rapid-fire orders. He stepped to the front of the small alien to block the view from the interior of the hangar as Marcel started barking orders.

"What did it say, Lee? Tell me!" Hendrix said loudly, startling the small being and forcing it to take a step back. "Tell me, goddammit!"

The small alien narrowed its eyes as it took in the handcuffed Hendrix. The large head first moved left, then right, as if it were sizing up the intelligence man in its mind. The eyes, still narrowed, blinked, and then it moved on, dismissing Hendrix outright.

Lee waited until the last of the technicians were out of the hangar, then he stepped aside and allowed the alien's progress into the hangar's interior to continue.

The supervisory men and women of the Event Group were standing and watching the most amazing happening in history; one by one their activity stopped as the small alien with Lee's and Leslie's assistance gingerly stepped through the debris of the crashed saucer. Its thin legs suddenly became wobbly and it almost collapsed. Lee placed his other arm in the small of its back, helping to support it more firmly. That was when it gently removed its hand from first Lee, then Leslie. It stumbled and fell; both men reached down for it, but it stood quickly and started moving faster through the piles of debris. Event personnel moved out of its way. A couple of the women and at least one of the doctors let out a cry as the alien came a little too close to them as it walked, then stumbled and fell in front of a huge container. Again the body was racked with shudders as it stared up at the enclosure. Leslie grimaced as he could see it was bleeding quite freely from the wound in its chest.

It touched the side of the container and seemed to relax again. Then it lowered its eyes and closed them, and without looking, it pounded softly on the side with its tiny fist, producing a hollow sound that echoed slightly in the large hangar. Then the alien looked up and saw Lee standing over it.

"*Destroyer . . . dead,*" it whispered.

Lee leaned down. "I don't understand you."

"*The Beast . . .*" It swallowed, making a face as if its speaking caused great pain. "*Dead,*" it repeated, then suddenly slid to the floor.

The remaining few people inside the hangar gasped as it fell over. Lee and Leslie immediately reached for it. But Lee was quicker and lifted the small alien into his arms and nodded for Leslie to take the lead. There was loud talking among the group now as they made their way back to the hospital.

"Alright, what you saw is top secret. Now get your teams back in here, let's move, people," Lee said over his shoulder.

The small creature opened its eyes and watched as Lee carried it back to its bed. "*No, w . . . ar. War,*" it said, and swallowed gingerly. "*No ex—tinct man.*" It reached up and touched Garrison's face. "*Man is . . . safe . . . for now. No extinct by Destroyer.*" It smiled far broader than it ever had, then it weakly tapped its chest. "*Kill Des . . . troyer.*"

Lee quickly returned the small being to its bed and Leslie went to work, applying pressure to get the bleeding to slow.

The alien was looking at Lee, its eyes drooping and its small breaths coming in short gasps. *"We use . . . animal . . . to assist . . . our master race, to, to . . . clear . . . new worlds . . . for . . . Gray Masters. . . . Destroyer . . . not . . . meant for . . . here, but uninhabited planet. . . . Some Gray . . . want to . . . clear . . . your world . . . for their . . . need. I . . . kill Destroyer, animal . . . is dead . . . No . . . war . . . this time . . . but . . . my masters . . . try . . . again maybe . . . kill your . . . world."*

Lee watched as the being's gaze went beyond him to nothing. He saw the large pupils dilate, then fix. Leslie checked its small chest for some kind of movement but found nothing. Its greenish skin immediately started to turn a grayish white. It had died as if content; it went with a small smile that was now frozen in death.

Lee sat with a distraught Dr. Leslie for ten minutes, then headed toward the exit of the hangar thinking about monsters and war. His head pathologist, Gerald Hildebrand, approached him. "Sir, I'm afraid I have something you must see." The young professor stepped back when he saw the greenish blood that soaked the director's clothing. Lee's eye patch was almost off. Hildebrand reached out and pulled the patch back into place.

Lee absently nodded his head in thanks and placed his fedora on his head.

"You have to see this," Hildebrand said again.

Garrison followed the doctor to a rather large piece of debris. It was at least ten feet high and the same width and also had small canisters attached to its top. Lee remembered it was the same container the small alien had insisted on seeing and touching. He came out of his thoughts as he realized that the animal the small being had called the Destroyer had been in this *cage*. It now made sense why the alien had to confirm to itself that the creature was dead.

"It's here, sir," Hildebrand said, still looking at Lee with concern.

He followed him to the front of the enclosure. The professor leaned down and pointed to a large brown, jellylike mound on the floor of what Lee now knew was a live-animal cargo container. A disgusting smell emanated from it.

Lee suddenly turned away. "Jesus, that's bad."

"Yes, sir, it is. It looks like whatever it *was* had been completely covered by something that ate it down to this." Hildebrand removed a fountain pen from his lab coat and slowly slid it into a liquid that had gathered on the floor around the gelatinous mound of material. As he lifted the pen, it slowly began to melt, first bubbling, then turning to liquid as the doctor threw it to the floor. "We tested all three containers separately and received no reaction, but once the chemicals are mixed, it turns corrosive, more so than anything I've ever seen."

Lee listened but didn't comment.

"There are other containers like this one, some small, some large, but none as big as this one, but they all have the same kind of substances in them. It may be genetic material that's been reduced to that," Hildebrand said, pointing to the fluid substance at the floor of the cage.

"Get samples and be careful," Lee said, suddenly tired.

"We did find this in the large container, or what I now believe may have been a cage, sir. It was embedded deep in the metal." He walked over to a nearby table and brought back something for Lee to see. The object was some sort of appendage, large and curved. Its tip was like a shovel, sharp and seemingly serrated at its leading edges. It had to measure a good fifteen inches in length. Some kind of scaly flesh clung to its base.

"If I didn't know any better, I would say that is one hell of a big claw, sir," the doctor said in awe.

Lee nodded, his thoughts turning to what the small being had said about the Destroyer. The director turned and walked away. His mind was traveling a hundred miles an hour. *"The Destroyer,"* he mumbled to himself as he entered the hangar's office once again. Could Brazel be right, could one of the saucers have brought the other down? Could this have been a . . . God, could this have been some freakish act of war?

The room was empty and he walked to the phone and dialed fifteen numbers. He waited for the clicks and the chirps to stop and for the phone on the other end to ring.

"Yes."

"Mr. President, Garrison Lee reporting, sir," he said into the black handset. He rubbed the bridge of his nose with his left forefinger and thumb.

"What's goin' on down there, Lee?" Truman asked.

He hesitated a moment as he gathered his thoughts.

"It seems, sir, our flying saucer may have been downed by a second, similar craft, and I believe it was brought down here, on Earth, on purpose."

"Downed! Downed by whom?" Truman asked in confusion.

Lee waited until the famous "Give 'em hell, Harry" temper subsided a little.

"It's all pretty speculative right now, but the craft may have been some type of *container* or cargo ship . . . and . . ." He hesitated. "Hell, sir, I think you better sit down for this one."

Present Day

Compton hadn't moved from his chair throughout the whole of the senator's story; he stared at his shoes, just listening. No questions had been asked by Jack or Niles, and the old man had finished uninterrupted. The senator had added more to the story than he had included in his written report those many years ago. After all, he had had years and years to theorize and piece things together to update his file. The theories fit. Throughout all of the recorded abduction reports made by citizens throughout the world, there had been two factions. One, the Gray beings that were encountered were aggressive and hostile, and two, the Green creatures were kind, gentle, and always benign. Therefore, Lee deduced there were two separate groups involved, one group aggressive and bent on invasion, the other passive and helpful, intent on stopping the Gray whenever they could. The theory fit the facts, and Lee embraced it.

Jack stood and slowly walked to the credenza and poured a glass of water from the pitcher, then walked back and placed it before Lee, repeating the scenario from the day before, only in reverse. The senator lifted his tired eyes toward the major and accepted the water in silence.

"Now you think the same thing has happened, another premeditated attack?" Jack asked.

"Yes, I'm not a believer in coincidence," Lee answered. "We don't have much time if that creature survived the crash; I just wish we knew what it was and its capabilities."

Compton took a deep breath and stood. "Speaking of which, I'm not getting anything accomplished sitting in here." He started to turn away, then stopped and looked at Collins. "I'm relieved the weight of this thing is not only on our shoulders now." Then he left the conference room.

"This Event has haunted me for almost sixty years," Lee said to the remaining two people in the room. "Now another saucer is here again and we can't find it. I guess we need a break and hope God favors the lucky."

"So what it boils down to is that we have to find the remains of this . . . *Destroyer* . . . and verify that it was killed by its present keeper or in the crash itself," Collins said. "If it has indeed followed the same pattern as the incident in '47, that would clearly explain the aggression of that second saucer yesterday and its attempt to keep our naval fighters out of the way."

"There are so many variables to consider, Jack. For instance, the master-slave relationship as told by the being in Roswell. What if this time the animal's keeper isn't as benign as the last?"

There was silence for a moment and then Jack looked at

the senator. "We have very little information to go on without the testing that needed to be done in '47 on the animal's remains. Someone out there, whoever stole the debris and murdered the Event personnel, has vital information that may help in saving this planet if it comes down to that. What about this Hendrix? Where did he vanish to?"

Lee shook his head. "He was killed in an air force plane crash two weeks after Roswell. And, yes, before you ask, I know it was that son of a bitch that hijacked the debris and bodies from Roswell. After I turned in my final report, Mr. Truman, as I suspected he would, bowed to the pressure from the Pentagon and their intelligence communities. Then Eisenhower, completely paranoid about anything he didn't fully grasp, buried it and we were out totally. The Event Group had essentially been pushed aside by the triumvirate of LeMay, Dulles, and Hendrix, and men like them, who ended up having the last say in the matter after all."

A knock sounded at the door, stopping the question in Jack's head. Alice stood and walked to the huge double doors and pulled them open. Outside stood Carl Everett and a man in a green flight suit. Alice beckoned them in.

"Commander Everett," she said, smiling, "and you must be Lieutenant Ryan?" She stepped aside as the two men entered the room. "I hope you had a nice rest, Mr. Ryan?"

"Yes, thank you," Ryan said.

The senator stood and, using his cane this time for support, walked to greet the newcomer.

"Senator Garrison Lee, this is Lieutenant Junior Grade Jason Ryan, of the USS *Carl Vinson*," Alice said as the two men grasped hands.

"I understand you have had a trying experience, Mr. Ryan," Lee said sadly.

Ryan was looking around the huge conference room while he shook the old man's hand. "Somewhat, but I'll live. Senator?"

"I suspect you will live, son, and, yes, former senator," Lee said, letting the man's hand go.

Ryan watched him turn and head back to the long conference table. Everett made the other introductions while Lee sat.

"I must admit, I've never seen the back room of a pawnshop before, but this is a little much," Ryan said while still looking around him. Then he smiled as he took in Major Collins.

"I'm going to be blunt with you, Lieutenant," Lee began. "Your flying for the navy? Those days are over. We need information from you and we're also short on personnel. You are now a part of our group, so consider yourself on detached service and your new commander is this man." Lee gestured toward Collins.

Jack nodded at Ryan, looking the naval pilot over, and accepted his 201 file from him.

"Is your incident report in here, Mr. Ryan?" Jack asked.

"Yes, sir."

"I'll debrief Lieutenant Ryan," Lee said. "I want you and Mr. Everett to see what you can do to give Niles a hand in the Computer Center. We just received word the NSA's pulling their photo-recon satellite, so that's going to leave Boris and Natasha and the National Weather Service as our only eyes out there. That's only two KH-11s to play with and five remote drones, and we need that ship found quickly," Lee said, almost pleading. "Jack, find out who's been piggybacking us since '47; you'll have full access to the Europa XP-7, and the best backdoor technician we have. Find out all you can, discover who's been on our back for sixty years, and then get the Cray back to Niles. God knows he's going to need it."

Jack and Everett nodded, then turned to leave.

"I'll have to excuse myself, as well," Alice said. "We're having a very small memorial for Gunnery Sergeant Campos. You two have work to do, so you're excused. I'll make your apologies." She too headed for the door.

Lee called after Collins, "Jack, you have a moment?"

Jack stopped short and turned to Lee.

"We have an extensive file on the activities of Mr. Farbeaux. Somewhere there's a link to whom he is working for.

If you can't find anything, study him; learn his tactics, because I expect him to show his face right when we don't need him to. That notebook you found tells me he's interested, either for himself or whomever he's working for. As you know, you and Commander Everett will lead the discovery team when the saucer is found. Niles has already ordered all of our security personnel off field duty and we're bringing them home. If the worst happens, we'll need everyone, so plan for it. And you had best start considering what we do if"—Lee looked at Ryan, then back at Collins—"if the animal is loose."

"Yes, sir," Collins said.

Lee turned to the young navy flier. "We have a lot to discuss, and I'm feeling a little tired. May I just say, welcome to the Event Group, Lieutenant?"

"Will I fly here, Senator?"

"I think we can accommodate that, yes, Lieutenant."

Ryan took the senator's hand again and gave it a brisk shake. "My days were numbered in Tomcats anyway," he said, just now realizing his naval aviation days were all but over. "If you're offering me a job, I'll take it, sir. Now, what in the hell is the Event Group?"

PART FOUR
THE STORM BREAKS

Run you fathers and pick up your sons, for the night of the Destroyer soon comes.

—ANCIENT HEBREW TEXT

SIXTEEN

The Arizona State trooper glanced over at his partner, then slowly removed his sunglasses and scanned the area. The heat of the day was settling down as was the sun in the west, its glare still blinding off the mountains. The trooper's right hand went to his service automatic as he stepped over the low wall that outlined the foundation of the old cavalry post. The feel of the steel hand-grip comforted him as he viewed the utter chaos in front of him, and that view made him slowly pull the nine millimeter from its holster. There were at least six motorcycles in different positions, some on their sides and others lying broken against the adobe walls. Their owners were nowhere to be seen.

The state trooper jumped when the crackle of his cruiser's radio broke the eerie silence that had settled into the old fort. He looked back at the open door of the patrol car, then at his partner, and let out the breath he hadn't noticed he had been holding. He had been by this location a hundred times before today, and the most he had ever had to do was chase kids away on their dirt bikes or have a maintenance crew come out and remove beer bottles and other garbage.

Tom Dills, his partner, had taken his hat off and was kneeling by one of the overturned bikes. He shook his head in wonder at the scratches in the fuel tank of the big Harley-Davidson. The gouges were long and ragged and penetrated the double-walled tank.

"What in the hell happened here, George?" he asked his sergeant.

Trooper George Milner looked from one of the bikes lying on its side to one that was upright, the kickstand still holding it in place.

"Damn strange," he answered.

They were both startled by a dust devil that sprang up from the middle of the old foundation; Dills quickly pulled his weapon from its holster. Both men watched as it twirled against a low wall and then broke apart, only to reform on the other sight and move off into the desert. Milner tilted his Stetson back on his head and wondered if his partner was going to try to shoot the dust devil. He noticed another strange sight in a mess full of strangeness and stepped closer to a dirt mound that circled a large hole. It looked as if it had recently been dug. The earth looked freshly turned over, and as he kicked at it, he found only the top few inches had been dried by the desert sun.

"Think they had trouble with another group of bikers?" Dills asked, standing and holstering his automatic.

"No other tracks but theirs leading in, Tom." Milner continued to look down. "Come and look here."

Dills walked over and looked down at the hole. Something wet had dried on the dirt mound and had hardened.

"What is that, oil?" he asked, looking around nervously.

"Or blood." Milner holstered his weapon and leaned down on one knee. He reached out and felt the clump of drying sand. He rubbed his fingers together and they produced a bright red smear. "Damn." He stood, absentmindedly rubbing his fingers together harder to rid himself of the blood. "Look around, it's all over the place." He pointed to other areas where blood had been spilled and then left to dry in the sun. "We better call this in." He started to move toward the cruiser.

"There goes the damn weekend," Dills said with all the

bravado he could muster, but he wanted more men out here also.

Dills looked at a license plate on the rear fender of one of the bikes. "Goddamn people are from California, Sarge, they may have been just stupid enough to walk off into the desert." He grinned, but sobered when he saw his sergeant wasn't in the mood for California jokes, which was just as well because Dills had only said it to keep up the brave front that he surely wasn't feeling at the moment.

"Notice something else?" Milner asked, coming to a stop just inside the weatherworn adobe walls.

"What?" Dills looked around nervously.

"I haven't seen or heard any animal life out here at all, not even the damn crickets."

The younger trooper spit his toothpick out onto the sand. "Okay, you've succeeded in giving me the creeps here, Sarge. I could have gone all damn day without you pointing out that little matter."

Both state troopers watched the desert for any kind of movement. Not hearing or seeing any intensified their already hardworking imaginations. They had both heard the stories about this place from that old geezer Gus Tilly down at the Broken Cactus and had laughed with the rest of the bar's regulars when he'd talked about the ghosts that haunted the old fort, laughed to his face even to the point of being hit with a wet dish towel by Julie, the owner. But looking around at the remains of the old adobe fort at this moment in broad daylight, you were able to believe just about anything, including ghosts.

"Well, we better call this thing . . . whatever it is, in."

Milner stepped over the low wall and was ten feet from the cruiser when the dirt and sand erupted in front of him and then sped off in the direction of Dills. He turned quickly and followed the spewing earth until it disappeared beneath the adobe wall, actually exploding a six-foot section of mud brick into the air.

"Watch it, Tom!" he shouted in fear, his right hand reaching for his gun and pulling it free.

Dills had his back turned to the patrol car when the ground and old wall behind him flew skyward. He turned quickly, and both troopers watched in stunned silence as dirt, sand, and rock were thrown high into the air, obscuring their view of each other. Milner heard his partner yell something he couldn't understand, and when the sand and dust settled, Trooper Tom Dills had vanished. Only his hat was rolling away from where he had been standing.

Milner still had his automatic aimed in the direction he had last seen his partner and quickly started to run to where Tom had been just a moment before. He had gone three or four feet when he realized that he needed to call this in fast because no one knew they were out here. He turned and ran for the car, trying to find purchase in the thick sand as his cowboy boots fought for traction.

The earth exploded into the air again right where Tom had vanished. This time whatever it was moved faster than it had before. The wave crashed into the low wall of broken foundation, again spewing the old mud brick in all directions. Milner screamed and tried to move faster, running for his life while dodging the airborne adobe. He glanced back, then took quick aim and desperately fired two shots over his shoulder into the dirt wave as it drew nearer. He saw the bullets strike, but the wave actually accelerated. He turned just in time to avoid crashing into the hood of the cruiser. The driver's side door was open and he half closed it to get around. He threw his large frame into the front seat and reached for the radio, almost shooting himself in the head with his own weapon in his rush. Loud crashing noises came from above as adobe landed on the hood and roof of the cruiser.

"This is Unit Thirty, Unit Thirty, goddammit!" he screamed into the microphone, but there was nothing but static in return. He was about to repeat his frantic call for help when more sand and dirt were thrown onto the hood and windshield of the cruiser.

Outside the car, dirt was being thrown up around the vehicle in an ever-accelerating circle. First it was three feet in diameter from the car, then five, then six. The area around the large cruiser was obscured by swirling dust as Milner tried in vain to see what was happening. The car shook from side to side, lifting and then dropping back on its springs. The microphone fell from his hand as he tried to steady himself, grabbing at the seat belt and dashboard simultaneously. He heard a sudden wrenching noise as the cruiser dropped down into the ground. As he looked out the side window, he saw through the swirls of dirt and flying rocks that the patrol car had sunk about four feet into the earth. He screamed again and fumbled for the car radio, finally grabbing the microphone, trying desperately to hit the transmit button. Suddenly he and the cruiser were tossed to the right violently. The driver's-side door slammed shut hard enough to send a crack cascading through the glass. The closed door cut off most of the noise from outside. As the dust settled in the car, he felt the cruiser sink even farther into the ground. Soon the dirt and rocks covered the windows and he knew he had been buried alive. Again he tried to transmit, but again the microphone was knocked from his trembling fingers. In his haste to grab the elusive mike, he hit the overhead red-and-blues and they came on.

Darkness filled the interior of the patrol car as a final crashing movement bounced him deeper into his seat, then suddenly shot him straight up, smashing his head against the roof of the car. Blood flowed from the crown of his scalp and lower lip as the vehicle finally settled. He fumbled for the dome light, and finally his shaking fingers found the switch. He pulled and turned on the headlights, then twisted the knob to the right and the interior was filled with light. He raised a hand to his head and it came away red with blood. Then he looked around himself and took stock of his injuries. That's when he noticed he could see something outside the car. The headlights were cutting through the darkness and bouncing back at him through the swirling dust. The strobe effect of the overheads flashing against rock and dirt made the whole seem as if it were some strange light show. The swirling dust still obscured the light from the holes opening far above him.

He realized he wasn't buried, but had fallen through into some kind of shaft or tunnel, maybe a cave of some sort. He reached for the heavy-duty flashlight that was clipped under the dashboard and brought it up and clicked it on. He aimed both the light and revolver outside the front window. The dust still eddied and swirled as the light cut a swath through the semidarkness.

"What the hell happened?" he asked himself, his voice sounding distant and muffled in the stuffiness of the car. He jumped and voiced a yelp when rocks and dirt thumped down on the roof of the car from above.

He knew he couldn't have fallen that far, or there would be more damage to him and the cruiser, so maybe he could stand on the roof and pull himself up to the surface. He glanced up through the window at the fading sunlight shining in through the thirty-five-foot sinkhole he had fallen into.

"Doesn't look that far," he mumbled.

He shone the light against the wall nearest him. From what he could tell, it looked smooth, almost as if some giant bit had drilled it out, or as if it were made of black concrete that had been trowel-smoothed to a shiny finish. He saw the old roots of long-dead trees and bushes buried into the semi-gleaming surface, reaching through like ancient skeletal arms and hands. Milner was just getting ready to crack his door when a shadow fell between the light and the wall.

His eyes tried to adjust to the sudden movement and darkness beyond and see what had caused the distinct change that had come into the strange tunnel. Then he screamed as something crashed into the dirt-covered windshield, sending a spiderweb of cracks through the safety glass. He screamed again, the yell bouncing off the glass and reverberating through the car.

Dills's body lay torn and bloody and looked as if something had taken out a huge bite between his head and left breast, as the light fell on the man's glazed, dirt-filled eyes.

Milner screamed again while he retrieved his gun and forced the door open and started to scramble from the car.

The beast rose from the cool earth under the patrol car

fending off of advances by the miners and construction workers who found their way into the Broken Cactus. She was still pretty at age thirty-eight.

She gave him a wink as he walked back behind the bar and started cutting limes and lemons for tonight's run.

She walked up behind him, lightly throwing the bar towel over her shoulder. "Why don't you go riding for a while before it gets too dark, baby? I'll do that."

Billy cut the lime on the cutting board into four wedges and sighed.

"Gus is in the mountains," he answered, hoping she didn't see the worry on his face as he didn't want to answer any questions about how he was feeling about the desert.

Julie raised her left eyebrow. "That's never stopped you before. I thought you liked it out there."

Billy set the knife down and looked through the large plate-glass window again. He wiped the acidic juice from the fruit on the apron he had tied around his waist, then brushed back some of his brown hair as it fell across his forehead.

"I don't want to go out there today." He hesitated. "I . . . I think I'll wait until Gus gets back."

Julie didn't really like Billy's only having one friend. And that friend being Gus Tilly, who was old enough to be his great-grandfather, made it worse. Oh, she liked the old man well enough, but she thought it couldn't be too healthy for Billy to be around Gus only. For that very reason she was thinking of selling the Broken Cactus and moving back to the Phoenix area. The boy needed kids his own age.

"What's wrong with you, kiddo?" she asked.

Billy turned and faced his mother, then glanced at the two tourists who had driven up in one of those battleship-sized Winnebagos. They were busy looking at a map, arguing about whether they wanted to drive to the San Carlos Reservation or move on to New Mexico and Carlsbad Caverns, and weren't listening, but he lowered his voice anyway.

"Something . . . I don't know, Mom." He looked at his tennis shoes. "It's weird out there since yesterday and I don't know why."

Julie looked out the window a moment, then patted his head. "Why don't you go upstairs and watch TV for a while and I'll bring you a couple of cheeseburgers, okay?"

Billy acted out the best smile he could muster and nodded his head. "Yeah, that'll be great."

Julie Dawes watched her son as he sadly climbed the stairs. Then she turned to the window and the street beyond. She didn't know what her son was talking about, but for some unknown reason, she wished more people would arrive a little earlier tonight just for the added company. Then Tony, the town's lonely drunk, tapped his glass.

"I'll take one more beer, then tha's all," the drunk slurred, raising his head.

Julie turned and shook her head. "I think you'll not. You go and lay down in your truck until later, and then we'll see about another."

He raised his head and squinted at Julie. "I have a truck?" he asked, swaying.

Julie watched him stumble off the stool and out the door. Then she looked out the window at the desert beyond and pondered what Billy had said about something being wrong in the valley.

EIGHTEEN

Gus sat at the rickety kitchen table in his one-room shack and sipped the now cold coffee from an old, chipped mug. The chair creaked as he leaned forward to eye his guest, who was almost totally covered by the old green army blanket he had laid over its battered body. There was no movement other than the occasional shiver or spasm. As he watched, the feeling of helplessness had once again seeped into his mind.

Gus now understood that, for reasons he would never quite understand, he had been feeling this little guy's thoughts. Those snippets of thought had guided the old man in how and where he'd bandaged the strange visitor, placing an old Ace bandage around its middle, taking the pressure off of what he hoped was just a couple of broken or cracked ribs. As soon as he had rubbed the area down with alcohol and put the stretch bandage on, the small creature seemed to breathe better.

The head wound was a little easier. He sprayed Bactine into it, then applied some iodine, making the little thing in the bed wince in pain. He used gauze out of his bathroom medicine cabinet to wrap the bulbous head.

Tilly shook his head as he set the coffee mug on the old kitchen table, which had clearly seen better days, then stood up. He stretched and yawned. As he did, he saw the blanket, and above that were the large eyes looking at him.

"You awake there, little guy?" he asked, taking a tentative step toward the bed.

Gus had carried him the whole seven miles back to his small house, calling out for his mule, Buck, most of the way. He was bone tired.

The old man took another hesitant step toward the old army-surplus metal cot. He placed his gnarled hand to his unshaven cheek and scratched.

"Ya feelin' any better?" he asked, tilting his head to the side, looking for the smallest of movements.

Slowly, the top of the blanket slid down. The fingers that gripped the rough material of the green blanket were long and thin. The hands were still dirty because Gus had let the small creature sleep instead of waking it with water and a washcloth. He saw the huge almond-shaped eyes blink and winced as he saw the lids disappear into the side of the thing's head. That would take some getting used to, he thought. Then his visitor slowly raised his head.

"Well, 'bout time you woke, I was getting worried 'bout you," Gus said with the biggest smile he could muster under the circumstances.

He took a step back when he heard a mewling noise escape the creature.

"Come on now, son," Gus said as he held up his hands. "I brought you back from the mountain, fixed ya up. Trust is the thing you gotta learn first, boy." He turned his head and looked over at his old electric hot plate where a pot sat with warmed-up chicken soup. "Got some hot Campbell's soup ya can eat." He had laced the soup with three Tylenol in the hope the small green stranger would eat.

He walked over to the small hot plate and picked up the steaming pot. He tested it with his index finger for warmth. Satisfied, he wiped the soup off on his dirty jeans and poured a small mug full of the steaming liquid. He took a spoon from one of the kitchen drawers and walked back into what he always joked to Billy was the living room/bedroom/dining room/drawing room/library. He took the old chair he had been sitting in and carried both items to the bunk. The thing still lay under the blanket, not moving an inch. Its eyes were still watching Gus, and another whimpering sound issued from its small mouth.

"Come on now, you gotta eat somethin', or I'm gonna have to take you to the doc up in town—if the old bastard's sober, that is." Gus placed the chair next to the bed and waited.

Slowly the hand gently pulled down the blanket. The black eyes stared at Gus, then as the black pools traveled down to what he held in his hand, the eyes blinked. Then a small line furrowed the soft green forehead.

What a forehead, Gus thought. He didn't move, just looked at the creature as he tried to smile.

The small hand let go of the blanket and went to its head. It rubbed the spot and looked at Gus. It felt the gauze the old man had wrapped around its injury and fingered it, winced, and then looked at Gus as if its injuries were his fault. The eyes narrowed even farther.

Gus still didn't move, he just concentrated on keeping the silly grin on his face.

The small being then brought its hand back up to the wound on its head and grunted. Lowering its hand, it looked at Gus for a moment. The head tilted to the right and then its eyes roamed around the small cabin. They lingered a moment on an old Charles Russell print of a cattle drive. The copy of the famous painting showed horsemen and cattle in a long procession on the prairie. The big eyes lingered there a moment, then they returned to Gus. It blinked and then returned to the picture. Below that Gus had an old porcelain chicken he had found in the desert some time ago. He thought it used to be a child's bank, but was never sure.

Then its gaze went to a stack of books that were lined up neatly on a shelf, and then they fell on another picture. It was one of those corny things with all the different breeds of dogs playing poker and smoking cigars around a green-felt-covered card table. The small alien's eyes widened, then its little mouth formed an *O* as it looked at the strange picture.

Gus followed its gaze, then he turned and shrugged his shoulders.

"Little Billy Dawes gave me that for Christmas. I got a kick out of it the first thousand times I looked at it," he said, his mouth etching a sad smile.

The creature's eyes left the picture. Then went back to it, then found another. This one was an old black-and-white photo of Gus in his army uniform. It had been taken in San Pedro, California, just before he had boarded a transport ship for Korea. He was young and every bit of his youth showed. He was cocky and ready to take on the world back then. Gus looked at the picture and saw what had been a young and foolish kid who didn't know the first thing about the world or life in general. He had been taught since then that most of the time the whole damn planet made no sense at all.

The alien looked closely at the picture, then at Gus. It slowly raised a hand and pointed at the picture and then toward Gus.

"Yeah, I know, and you don't have to go pointin' it out. I was a pup then." He lowered his eyes. "Things make you feel older than you ought to feel."

The little being tilted its head. The small nostrils flared, then relaxed, then flared again. The large eyes settled on the mug of soup Tilly held in his hand.

"Hungry?"

Gus lifted the spoon and dipped it into the mug. He brought it out and blew lightly on it. The creature watched him, forming another *O* with its mouth. It leaned forward, sniffing again.

"Chicken soup." He pointed to the chipped porcelain chicken on the chest of drawers. "Like that there chicken."

"Shitinnsooop."

The voice caught Gus off guard. It was as if the words were being said through wet cotton. It had startled him so much he found he had spilled some of the soup onto his hand because of the shakes, but he still managed a forced smile.

"No, not shitin' soup, chicken soup," he said again, pronouncing the word as clearly as he could.

The eyes blinked. Then they went from Gus to the mug, then back to Gus. *"Chiiiiicken soooop."*

"That's it, boy, chicken soup." He smiled, then laughed out loud, not really feeling the joviality of the situation.

The creature looked at him and tilted its head again. It grunted in its throat until it saw the laughter wasn't a hostile gesture on Gus's part.

Gus slowly lifted the spoon toward the small being's mouth. It sat there, a look of near panic filling its large eyes, then reached out slowly and lightly touched the tip of the spoon with its strange, elongated finger, tilting the utensil until the soup spilled onto the bed. The eyes widened as the yellowish soup struck the army blanket and soaked in.

Gus smiled and dipped the spoon into the soup again, then quickly had the spoon back up and into its small mouth. The big black eyes widened for a moment, then relaxed and swallowed. Gus tried to pull the spoon away, but the alien had a clamp on it and he had to tug.

"The spoon doesn't go with the soup," he said as the spoon was finally freed. "Now, how was that?"

It looked from the spoon to Gus.

"You have a name?" he said, leaning forward and placing his elbows on his knees.

Again it began the tilting of the head. Then it started duck-walking toward the old man, until it was only two feet away. It stopped and looked at the mug, then lightly rubbed the bandage around its rib cage, and then looked Gus over again. Then, tentatively, it reached out and curled its long fingers through the handle of the porcelain mug and duck-walked backward until its green back was against the far wall.

Gus slapped his chest with his fist. "Gus," he said. "The mighty," he joked. The being was startled and stopped the soup halfway to its mouth and looked.

"Gus," the old man repeated, slapping his chest again.

The creature didn't respond as it slowly brought the soup to its mouth. The eyes closed, then suddenly opened, and it took a larger swallow, then another, gulping the soup quickly until it had the mug tilted bottom side up.

"Gus." He hit his chest again.

"*Gussss,*" it said simply and quickly, not knowing or caring about the soup that dribbled from its mouth.

"That's right, son, Gus," he said, grateful it spoke and didn't use that mind-talking that made his head hurt something awful. Then he pointed at his visitor, index finger safely two feet from its green chest. "You?"

The eyes went around in a small circle, and then the mouth pursed into a small, thin line and the visitor shook its head, looked at Gus, and relaxed. Gus saw a stray noodle poking out from the left side of its mouth.

"*Mahjtic.*" The word was spoken aloud in that strange, wavering, cotton-filled voice.

Gus's eyes narrowed. "Well, I'll be damned."

The being turned the mug upside down and shook it, then when he saw there was no more, just looked from Gus to the pan on the counter.

"Want more?"

Although the creature didn't have eyebrows, the area where they should have been furrowed.

"Is that your name, Matchstick?"

The large almond-shaped eyes with their round pupils locked on the old man and his sad ones. Then a long, thin finger went to its green chest, lightly touching the bandage. "*Mahjtic.*"

"Matchstick?"

The creature shook its head. "*Mahjtic.*"

"Matchstick, I got it. And that's about right, you're about as skinny as one. I'm glad you're talkin' with your mouth." He pointed at his own and moved his jaw up and down. "It seems when you were cryin' in my head in the mountains, every word you said was like a punch in the nose to me, *and* my brain too, I think."

Another look of confusion filled the alien's soft features.

"Well, Matchstick boy, what say I get you some more chicken soup, and you can tell me how come you gone and crashed your spaceship right about where I was gonna dig for my gold?"

But the visitor wasn't listening. It had turned away and discovered the filthy window and the semidarkness beyond. Its small brow creased in several thin lines, and as Gus watched, it pointed out the window at the desert beyond and started shaking. The large head and arms were in the throes of small spasms of what Gus was guessing was some sort of shock, or maybe it was fear.

The old man went over and pulled the yellowed blind closed over the window and turned to face his visitor. "Something's out there, ain't it?" he said, remembering the hole at the crash site and the raw fear he'd felt when looking into its depths.

Mahjtic didn't respond as it slowly slid down onto the bed. It turned and looked at Gus and blinked.

"I'm gonna get you some more soup and me some coffee, and then I think you better tell me what's got you so spooked."

Mahjtic just continued to look at Gus, the thought of chicken soup all but gone. It slowly turned its attention and head toward the now covered window.

"The Destroyer, hungry, bad, bad, ani . . . mal," Mahjtic said aloud. It still had its eyes locked on the window. Then it slowly said, *"Man is at . . . an end . . . Gussss."*

Gus paused while using the can opener on another can of soup, and he lowered his head and his shoulders slumped.

"I figured it was something like that."

The old man was shaking as he opened the can of soup and poured it into the pot, sloshing more on the stove than he got in the dented pan.

"When I was a middlin' boy, my ma told me there weren't nothin' in the dark to be afraid of." He stopped stirring and looked over at Matchstick, who had just turned away from the covered window. "Guess she was wrong, huh?"

NINETEEN

Collins, Everett, and the newly briefed Jason Ryan, now wearing his new blue Group jumpsuit, anxiously watched the activity in the Computer Center while they waited for the Europa XP-7 technician to join them. Director Compton saw them and yawned. He turned from watching a search grid and walked up the stairs to see them. They were all looking at the large screen on the far wall, which was a real-time display of southeastern New Mexico that the Group's satellite was beaming to them. The computers here were programmed to pick up every minute detail on the ground and search for any anomalies with the use of magnetometers, infrared photography, Doppler radar, and terrain-anomaly mapping. Collins nodded at the director when he joined them.

The pictures that were being sent to the center by the KH-11 were in small, red-lined, highlighted squares, so they could be broken down even further by technicians at their individual consoles, hoping to pick up the slightest trace of metal where it shouldn't be, or an anomaly in the surrounding terrain. As they watched, they saw a tiny car speed down a road outside of Roswell, as the computer digitally added a small blue compass showing the direction of the automobile.

Then the vehicle quickly disappeared as it didn't fit the programmed profile.

"I'm beginning to believe that damn thing didn't come down at all," Everett said. "They doubled the size of the search area to include most of western Texas now, and still nothing."

Jason Ryan watched the view change from the advanced KH-11 satellite. "From the view I had of the saucer it's my opinion"—he thought a moment, then corrected himself—"it's my guess, it wasn't going anywhere but down. It was damaged enough that it couldn't go back up, I'm sure of it."

Collins looked at the navy pilot. "The senator has a hunch that if it did, it would be here, and after what I heard, I tend to believe him. It's like whoever is piloting these things used a preset coordinate when traveling here that aligns their flight path to travel over lightly populated areas." He turned and watched the screen roll as the bird turned its cameras to infrared for night vision to gather objects in by their ambient light as it traveled farther east.

"I agree," Compton said.

"Just remember, it was too damaged, and after that second craft had shown up—"

"That's it!" Niles shouted. People at computer consoles frowned and looked up at the four men, annoyed at the noise. "Mr. Ryan, how far would you say the damaged saucer was knocked off course after the second one made its appearance?"

"I think I know where you're going with this, Doc, but it wasn't knocked off that far, if at all. Ryan here said so earlier," Everett said, looking at his boss.

Ryan shook his head. "He's right, Dr. Compton, in the distance that these satellites have covered, it should have been close to the search area. Believe me, I would like to find out what's going on. I lost a good kid in the backseat of my fighter and two pretty good guys in another, but you're grasping at straws." Ryan sighed and rubbed his eyes. Then he closed his eyes in thought. "Sir, I was dangling in a parachute at the time, remember? I just don't know what to tell you."

It dawned on Collins all at once.

"That's right; it won't be where it had been the first time in '47. In the past there was nothing but the second saucer that would have changed its course, unless you count the Cessna in '47, and that wouldn't have been enough of an impact to send a kite reeling. But this time there was actually one more event that occurred in its flight path that could have brought it down somewhere else," Compton said, still looking at the picture being broadcast by Boris and Natasha.

Jack remembered the Incident Report Ryan had filed about the attack. He quickly opened it and scanned the pages.

"Mr. Ryan, you said in your report you actually fired on the second, attacking craft, is that right?"

Ryan turned pale for a moment and turned away; he slapped his forehead with his palm. "My God, I fired a Phoenix at it. It was a snapshot and I know it hit, it must have. I had a solid tone and the Phoenix's warhead had locked hard on the target!"

"Damage to the attacker could have brought both ships down, not only the victim, but the aggressor also," Jack said aloud.

"Okay, I see your point; a missile strike would have brought it and maybe the other down sooner, but maybe even later. It's such a long shot I wouldn't put five bucks on it. But giving you the benefit of the doubt, where?"

"It's a matter of elimination that has nothing to do with the crash. West Texas is lightly populated; it may be there." Niles ran down to the large screen and slapped the monitor. "But if it was damaged, Texas may have been out of reach of it, even New Mexico." He walked down and plucked a digital plasma map from a desk and unrolled it. The map display automatically came to life, illuminating the sandwiched plastic pieces in a high-definition display. Niles, satisfied it was the right map, returned to the three men who were waiting. "There. We know if it came down anywhere in Southern California, there would have been witnesses. Hell, a crash there would have killed hundreds, or even thousands." He traced a line with his finger separating Southern California from the rest of the West. The spots where his finger ran changed color to an orange hue. "Even the Mojave Desert there to the east has a whole lot of people in it." Again he ran his finger in a circle around the desert area of California; again the digital picture changed the area to a soft orange hue. "But look here." He illuminated the eastern part of the Western states map to a pretty much blank area.

"Arizona?" Ryan asked.

"Why not?" Compton circled the map with his index finger, touching the plastic and changing the color of central Arizona to a bluish tint. "You get east of Phoenix and what do you have? Nothing but scrub and desert spotted with little one-stop café-and-gas-station towns all the way into New Mexico."

"I don't know, boss, that's awful thin," Everett said. But he still scanned the map just a little closer than he had been before.

"Thin? Yes, but impossible, no. This time there was something else that knocked it further to the west, Ryan's missile strike. In here would be the most likely spot. It's so thinly populated, the *Queen Mary* could fall out of the sky and not be seen."

"You've sold me on the possibility, Niles, but what you're proposing is a complete shift of search priorities. That could be disastrous if you're wrong," Jack said, looking closer at the director.

"Pete!" Niles shouted while holding Jack's eyes, then he turned and left and ran to the floor below. He found Pete Golding, his replacement long ago as department head of Computer Sciences. He had his feet propped up on his desk and was snoring. Niles hated to wake him because Pete had had even less sleep than himself. "Goddammit, Pete, wake up. I need you, man!"

Pete Golding felt his feet slapped off the desk and he came immediately awake. It felt as if he had been slapped off a cliff in his dreams.

"Damn, boss, what are you trying to do?" he asked, shading his eyes against the assault of the fluorescent lighting.

"Wake up; we have a search pattern we have to discuss."

"What in the hell are you talking about?" Pete Golding asked, putting his glasses on. Niles explained his reasons for the next three minutes, with Pete interrupting only once with a question. After Niles was done, he watched Golding and waited for his reaction.

Instead of arguing as Niles thought he might, he jumped to his feet, coughed once to clear his throat, and yelled to his tired computer department, "Alright, people, wake up! The director has a hunch we're going to bet the farm on." He turned to face Niles. "Remind me later we'll have to allocate about thirty million dollars in next year's budget for the shuttle to refuel these birds we're zigzagging all over the sky." Pete stretched, then grabbed his headset from his desk. "All right, boys and girls, let's get Pasadena on the horn and get ready to retask Boris and Natasha, now!"

Jack took a deep breath and watched as Pete was in his element; he was directing people left and right, arranging the right telelinks with Jet Propulsion Lab in Pasadena, California, to make sure they had the proper codes to push Boris and Natasha to a lower and more westerly elliptical orbit.

"I'm glad you think he's right, Major, because I think he's just screwed the pooch. He's way off," Everett said.

Jack didn't say anything. Everett and Ryan hadn't been privy to the story the senator had told, so they couldn't really understand the urgency. He couldn't tell them, but Niles understood completely; it was time to start taking chances, big chances. "Come on, let's find that damn computer tech and get to work. I feel fucking helpless." Jack turned and left for the mainframe center.

◆ ◆ ◆

en minutes later, during the retasking of Boris and
Natasha, the three military men were approached by a
man no more than five foot three inches in height as they
waited angrily outside the Europa clean room. He removed
his glasses and looked up at Collins as if sizing him up and,
by his expression, finding the major lacking in some way.
Then the lab-coated technician turned his attention to
Everett and Ryan and a look of utter disgust filled his features as the man exhaled loudly and rolled his eyes.

"Are you the Europa tech?" Jack asked impatiently.

"Your clothing just won't do. You're not going anywhere
near Europa wearing the clothing you now have on. If you
did, the Cray people would die of a stroke. Come with me,
you have to shave and disinfect." The tech started walking
away and the three men followed quickly.

Everett looked at Collins in horror as they caught up to
the speedy tech. "Listen, we've been cooling our heels here
at a juncture in this mission where action is dictated, and you
took your fucking time getting here."

The small man stopped and turned, his fists balling at his
sides. "Listen to me, you. I've been up forty-two hours with
my eyes glued to four fucking monitors searching for a
damn object that may or may not have gone down in an area
as large as Alaska, so don't you stand there and lecture me
on promptness. Now, shall we get to work?" he hissed dangerously, then entered the clean room.

"I'm glad he's working for us," Everett said as he quickly
followed the tech.

The hunt for Farbeaux and his employers was on.

New York, New York
July 8, 1920 Hours

endrix placed the phone down and activated the speaker
box, then opened the file containing the report he had
received from "Argonaut," the Secret Service asset they

had on the presidential protection team. The man would
have to be rewarded handsomely; he had come through with
a gem. With the file open he slid it over and retrieved another file and opened it. On the cover sheet he looked upon
the picture of Henri Farbeaux while the phone rang out
West.

"This is Legion," answered the irritated voice.

"Where is my Black Team?" Hendrix asked angrily.

"Reese told an interesting story that may or may not have
something to do with your mysterious Purple Sage file," Farbeaux baited his hook.

"You're playing games with us, Legion? You know how
dangerous that can be? Where is my team and why were you
in Las Vegas?"

"I'm afraid I am terminating my association with your
corporation."

"Listen to me, there won't be anywhere in the world
you'll be safe. We'll find you." Hendrix disconnected the
Frenchman, then punched in several numbers and waited.

"Johnson," the strong voice answered.

"This is Chairman Hendrix; our friend from Los Angeles
has learned more than he need know about Purple Sage, and
he may have eliminated the West Coast Black Team before
he fired on you and your men at the strip club. The bastard's
gone rogue on us. Right now, Compton and Lee may still believe he is working alone. Let's keep it that way. I suspect
he's still in Las Vegas."

"Yes, sir, we've been monitoring him since he escaped
the club."

"Good. Eliminate him at the earliest convenience, and
tell that arrogant French bastard I said *au revoir* just before
you put a bullet in his brain."

Las Vegas, Nevada
July 8, 1930 Hours

Henri Farbeaux left the restaurant and walked to his car
and saw it immediately. He was being watched from the
parking lot across the street. He didn't know of many
tourists, especially one with a black coat, who stood still in
the hot evening and stared at a drab-looking restaurant for
over an hour and a half. He held off smiling at the idiots as
he entered his car. He engaged the ignition without fear. He
knew Hendrix and his Men in Black liked to do things up
close and personal, to be sure there was no collateral damage and also to make sure the job was done.

It only took him thirty seconds to spot the tail. They were
in a white van that was parked across the street in a public lot
adjacent to Circus Circus. The idiots had forgotten to turn
their dome light off, and when the man who had been watching him entered the van, he had counted two in the front and,
coupled with the watcher, at least one in the back. Undoubtedly these were the same amateurs that had tried to ambush
him at the club, who'd missed him and only succeeded in
killing an old man. But knowing these killers and the way
they operated, he knew there had to be at least two more in
the vehicle. Farbeaux put the car in drive and left the restaurant parking lot, opening his cell phone as he did, pressing a
preselected number with his thumb, and waiting until his
call was answered.

"Now" was all he said.

The white van left the public lot and followed the Frenchman's Chevrolet out onto Las Vegas Boulevard and watched
as he sped up and darted quickly around the next corner.
They followed without fear of possible discovery because of
the amount of traffic on the streets this evening. There could
be no way that the Frenchman could have picked them out.
As they rounded the corner, they had to brake quickly as the
Chevrolet had pulled over and Farbeaux had exited the car
and was flagging them down.

"What the hell is this guy doing?" the driver asked as he

came to a stop. Too late, they realized they had driven right into a trap as another vehicle stopped immediately behind the van.

"What do we do?" the driver asked his boss.

"We do nothing. We're in the middle of Las Vegas with police all over the place. We've obviously been seen by him and that's all. No doubt he will puff his chest out and tell us to go away. I've heard plenty about this man, and I know the company overestimates his abilities. Besides, he's French."

The others chuckled.

Farbeaux walked up to the passenger window and waited until the man lowered it. The Frenchman saw that the men were dressed in black T-shirts and black Windbreakers. He smiled.

"You gentlemen really take this Black stuff seriously, don't you?"

"Now take it easy, we were told to make sure you come to no harm after your exploits this morning. All we want to know is where our other Black Team is."

The Frenchman looked at the man. The goatee must have been meant to scare those he was supposed to intimidate in his duties for Centaurus. The hireling never really looked at Farbeaux as he spoke. Henri smiled again and leaned forward, quickly examining the van's interior walls. They were standard. No reinforcement, and that was a major mistake.

"I guess Hendrix didn't inform you," he said.

"Inform us of what?" the man asked, finally looking at Farbeaux.

"That I am no longer in his employ," he said as he quickly raised his Glock nine millimeter and fired four quick rounds into the cab of the van, two each for the passenger and the driver, catching each twice in the side of the head. He then calmly took a step back. "That's for that old man this morning," he said quietly. Then he tossed the grenade he had been holding into the van, then quickly stepped forward of the front wheel well and ducked behind the thickness of the engine compartment as it went off with a crump, blowing out a bulge in the thin wall of the van and punching a hundred small holes as shrapnel blew outward.

Farbeaux quickly stood and made his way to the back of the van. The men who had driven up behind the vehicle sat and watched their boss at work. The Frenchman opened the back door without exposing himself to the open, smoky interior, and when no shots rang out, he deftly stepped up and started emptying his nine millimeter into the cargo compartment. The scene was one of shredded men who had not had the time to even start reaching for their weapons.

He calmly closed the door to the van and turned away. An old lady standing on the sidewalk with her dog about forty feet away was looking on incredulously. Henri replaced the Glock in his shoulder holster, then smiled as he raised his right hand to his mouth and placed his index finger to his lips.

"Shhhh."

The old woman turned her small dog with a hard yank and walked hurriedly in the opposite direction.

The mirth went out of his eyes as he waved his men in the sedan on.

He had just made a public statement against the secret Genesis Group and their Men in Black. Now Hendrix would realize that Farbeaux was someone who deserved respect.

He pulled up to the second car at the stop sign a mile away and didn't look over; they had their orders and no further discussion would be necessary. The men in the car and even more at another location had entered the country this morning through Québec and had flown to Las Vegas by charter jet. Now he had his own people on-site, men he had trained himself for black operations in the French army. The Event Group would have company when they went after that downed saucer and whatever riches it carried.

"Now, to find out where it is," he said as he whistled.

TWENTY

Dr. Gene Robbins was patiently waiting beside the clean-room doors for the three military men to adjust the uncomfortable antistatic and hermetically sealed suits. He explained as best he could about the experimental Cray system known as Europa.

"You see, gentlemen, the systems that came before the Europa XP-7 were good, fast, efficient, and reliable. The system that Director Compton and Senator Lee managed to procure has yet to be installed anywhere else in the world. Europa is made not only to compute its assigned tasks with lightning speed, but to compromise other systems. It's just simply amazing."

"In my experience a system, be it for military use or civilian use, is only as good as the people operating it," Jack said as he tied off his hood.

"That may be true for most, but not Europa, Major," Robbins said, shaking his head and gesturing for the others to step it up, seemingly hurt by the comment.

"Fine, Doctor," Jack said, patting the tech on the shoulder, "no offense, I'm sure Europa is everything you say it is. Now, can we cut the shit and get to it?"

Robbins looked hard at Jack, then turned and ran his key card through the door lock. The group of four had traveled down to level seventeen from the upper clean room in an air-tight, separate pneumatic elevator, to an area known as the Clean Level. The entire center had its computing main-frames located here along with biological testing labs. The level was always sixty-eight degrees and the humidity was also a constant. As the door hissed open, they were surprised by the simple room the Europa XP-7 was housed in. A twenty-foot acrylic desk lined one wall, with seven chairs with bendable microphones in front of them. A ten-foot-by-five-foot monitor was attached. A simple keyboard was in place on the desk. In front of this was a glass wall, which had what looked like a metal curtain hiding what was be-yond. Robbins gestured for the men to take seats at the seven chairs that were aligned in front of the clear desk.

"I expected something out of a science fiction movie," Ryan said.

Robbins looked at him and pushed his glasses back up onto his nose. He sniffed and took his place opposite the keyboard. He tapped a single key and the monitor above came to life. The view was of all four of them sitting and looking at themselves.

Suddenly the high-definition monitor separated the pic-ture of them and slid it to the right side. On the left, words started to appear in rapid succession. Under each picture was their name and date of recruitment and below that their department.

"It knows who I am, but I just came in today," Ryan said.

"Save it, we can wow ourselves another time. Doc, let's get on with it."

The doctor worked the keyboard and the metal wall started sliding into the sill; behind it was a triple pane of bul-letproof glass. And beyond that was Europa. The system was a marvel to behold. There was cylinder upon ten-foot cylin-der of programs that were stored. There were four sets of Honda Corporation robotic arms installed for placing and removing those programs.

"This is the automatic program loading system, or APLS. It will use the different programs for lightning-fast calculations and research." Robbins used the keyboard and ordered up a still picture the men had recovered that morning from the lounge. It was the man Gunny had identified as possibly being Farbeaux.

"Thank you for dumbing it down for our benefit, Doctor," Jack said, looking at the picture. "Let's save some time here and say Gunny was right, it's the Frenchman at the club. That means he and whomever he works for more than likely broke Reese and they know what we're after. That means we can expect a visit from either our French friend, or whomever he works for, or maybe the assholes that tried to kill him outside the club."

Jack watched as file after file, hacked system after hacked system, swam before his eyes. The three officers and Robbins had been into every hard drive and networking system they could think of trying to uncover anything that would lead them to Farbeaux's employers. It seemed that every computer manufacturer the world over was supplied with almost identical parts, and a few of those highly technical components had been hybrids substituted by the NSA and CIA. These reengineered microchips allowed a back door into every system using the components. That included almost every agency in every government and every system that was networked in every university in the world. Europa tapped into these deep-cover "spies" and activated them for piggybacking onto their host security programs and culled them for information, covering her tracks as she went. In other words, Europa would create a back door with the help of the magic chips, then cover that hole on her way out of the system, thus leaving no trace.

They had discovered that Farbeaux had started with the Antiquities Bureau after his discharge from the French army. That was obviously where he had acquired his taste for antiques and artifacts. Europa had discovered offshore accounts in the Caymans; the Swiss deposits they had uncovered were shallow to their prying eyes. It was Robbins who came up with an idea that none of them had caught.

"Maybe the guy isn't paid in money, maybe he's paid some other way," Robbins said as he looked at Jack and the others.

"You mean like artifacts and antiquities?" Everett asked.

"Why not? It's the hot investment of the last hundred years, safer than cash and easier to get rid of . . . or to hide," the doctor said. "Plus it would explain his high interest in our Group."

"Okay, where does that leave us?" Jack asked.

"Nowhere. We just may have figured out that however he's paid, we won't be able to trace it back to those people who are rewarding him with these items," Ryan answered.

Jack stood and stretched, then turned and walked to the glass wall and looked in at the now still robotic loading system that fed programs into Europa.

"Doc," Jack said while he was still looking at the interior of the clean room, "can you bring up his military record again and see if he had any service time at an embassy or consulate in the States?"

"Yes, I think we still have it out, let me see." Robbins typed in a command. "Yeah, the program's still up.

"Europa," Jack said.

Yes, Major Collins. The screen flashed the words in blue script.

"File, Farbeaux, Henri, Colonel. Question, any correlation between his duties in the French army and visits or duty in the United States?" Jack looked at the others, who were watching the screen.

The screen went blank.

"That would be too easy, Jack," Everett said.

"Maybe, but it's worth a try." Robbins looked at Everett. "I think the major may have asked something we just assumed would be covered up, but something like that could easily be overlooked."

The screen flashed back to life.

Five clandestine visits, 2002–2005. Discovered by FBI file examination of United States Customs videotape. One military assignment, February–December 1996, Europa typed out in blue letters.

"I'll be damned," Carl said as he leaned over the desk and wrote down the dates.

"Question. Duties involved with military assignment in 1996?" Jack asked before Robbins could.

Military Attaché, French Embassy, Washington, D.C., then assigned to French Consulate, New York, New York, September–November 1996.

"Question. Available diplomatic or public record photographs or reports filed by Colonel Farbeaux while conducting diplomatic business in Washington and New York?" Dr. Robbins asked.

Suddenly the robotic loading system sprang to life behind the glass, and the arms loaded at least eight new programs in a matter of a few seconds that would dig into every newspaper account, pilfered report, or tapped phone call the U.S. government had recorded on the Frenchman.

The screen went blank and then almost as fast came back on.

All NSA reports classified security sensitive and destroyed. All CIA reports classified security sensitive and destroyed.

"Now that's covering your tracks. Think he had friends somewhere?" Robbins asked, looking at the military men around him.

Jack looked at the screen but remained silent. The loading system placed one more program, then came to a stop.

Several pictures started to show up on the large screen. They looked as if they had mostly been gleaned from newspapers and looked to be coverage of the same event. They were pictures of Farbeaux, not dressed in a military uniform but in a tuxedo, but he was obviously not the subject of the photographer's lens. In almost every picture there was a dark-haired man, smiling almost arrogantly into the cameras lens; the Frenchman was always nearby.

Coverage is copyrighted material of the Washington Post.

"Question. Subject matter of the article?" Jack asked Europa.

Reception for the newly installed Centaurus Corporation CEO, in thanks for two-hundred-million-dollar endowment for the arts in Washington, D.C.

"Question. Name of Centaurus Corporation CEO, please?" Robbins jumped in.

Charles Phillip Hendrix II, Europa answered.

Jack was thinking back to the story the senator had told of the crash in 1947 in Roswell.

"Europa, any information on the Genesis Group, and what is the business of the Centaurus Corporation?" Jack asked.

Genesis Group, Strategic Military and Corporate Technologies Advisory Group to the United States Intelligence Community, United States Armed Forces. Centaurus Corporation, Advanced Electronics and Optics, Divisions in Aerospace, Communications, Genetics, and Optics. Current contractual obligations with NASA, Lockheed Martin, Boeing, Jet Propulsion Laboratory, Bell Laboratories—

"Europa, date of the founding of Centaurus Corporation?" Jack asked, interrupting the lengthy response of the computer.

Corporate papers filed in New York, New York, February 3, 1948.

"With contracts with companies like that, why haven't we ever heard about Centaurus? And I've never heard of a think tank called Genesis," Robbins said aloud.

"I don't know why—," Jack started to say.

"Europa, is there any listing for board of directors, Centaurus Corporation?" Everett asked.

The monitor cleared all the previous answers from the screen, and the system started reacting to the question, flashing newspaper filings and corporate reports.

No information filed publicly on sixteen-member board of directors, Centaurus Corporation.

"We need access to the Centaurus mainframe. Think you can do it, Doc?" Jack asked.

"I think she can, yes," Robbins answered.

"Hurry, Doc, things are moving too fast around us and we're running out of time, we need to catch up. I think the senator's right, I'm getting bad vibes about this encounter, and now we have these bastards to contend with."

"Europa, access Centaurus database," Robbins ordered.

Accessing, she said, then the screen went blank. *Unable to comply. Security system is unknown at this time, Centaurus mainframe inaccessible.*

"Incredible," Robbins said. "Europa, access Genesis Group, either mainframe or personal computer."

Accessing, Europa said, and then the screen suddenly came alive.

"Excellent, they have all that security for the corporate end, but they either didn't care or omitted the same standards for their think tank," Robbins said.

Ten personal hard drives found.

"Access Hendrix, Charles," Jack asked.

Hendrix, Charles. Program headings:

Defense at Sea.

Air Defense.

Subsurface—Offensive.

Viable Hybrid Aluminum.

Biowarfare—Altered Human Species.

Optical Warfare—Particle Simulations.

Wormhole—Opening the Gate—1947.

International Space Station Defense Platform.

Plastic Aluminum Composite Armor Pla—

"Stop!" Jack said, making the others jump. "Access Wormhole Program." He leaned over and watched the screen intently. "Synopsis of study?"

Evidence of wormhole travel, Southern Hemispheric Gate. Study indicates all UFO activity originates at 90 degrees south, 0.00 degrees east. Project Genesis confirms craft of same type as 1947 Incident. Photographic proof indicates use of wormhole corridor by enemy for planetary access, project code-named Crossroads. Air Defense Study, offensive operations by United States against attacking force.

"Good God, the bastards found out how they're getting here," Jack said. "They're actually formulating a plan for attacking them at this gate they've discovered."

"Just where in the hell are these coordinates?" Everett asked. "They sound familiar."

Robbins asked, "Europa, identify coordinates ninety degrees south, zero degrees east as noted in study file Crossroads."

Antarctica, polar south.

"The south pole," Ryan said.

"I guess that's why both incidents have them arriving from the south on the same track," Carl said, looking at Jack.

Collins patted the back of Dr. Robbins and nodded. "Make this program secure, Doc."

"Thank you, Europa, this search program is now coded level one security," Robbins said aloud, "director and his advisory staff Eyes Only. Personnel cleared for further research on"—Robbins looked up at Jack and he gestured at the three of them—"Genesis and Centaurus file are presently logged on to Europa, is this understood?"

File, new—coded level one, Eyes Only: Director Compton, Senior Adviser G. Lee, Special Assistant A. Hamilton; file research security clearance: Robbins, Everett, Ryan, and Collins.

"What do we do about this Centaurus Corporation?" Carl asked.

"I don't know yet, I've got to think. You guys get me some stills of that get-together in Washington and have them blown up and enhanced. I need clear shots of Hendrix," Jack said, then he used his key card to exit the clean room.

Ten Miles South of Chato's Crawl, Arizona
July 8, 2130 Hours

The Talkhan sat aboveground and seemed to study the desert surrounding its still form. There was no movement. The scurrying of the smaller animals had ceased and now they either sat still or had fled before the onslaught of slaughter. The beast was storing food, and her instincts dictated she needed even more. Every pore of its alien skin pulled in the aroma of protein near and far.

It moved its tail with a swish of air as it brought the stinger down with a thousand pounds of pressure to impact the cooling desert sand. It used the large stinger and flipped the now wet, cooling particles up and onto its distended belly, then repeated the motion, tossing venom-soaked dirt and sand into the still night air and allowing the cool soil to regulate its 180-degree skin and armor. The small movements inside her belly and increasing core temperature were indications that the nesting cycle would soon begin.

The offspring that were even now hatching inside her distended abdomen were developing quickly and were consuming the nutrients almost as fast as she could supply them. As studied by those of Matchstick's kind, its young, when born, would have abilities far beyond those of the mother.

The beast looked to the dark night sky. The bright, illuminated green eyes blinked as the moon was in its full bloom. The mandibles clicked together once, then the tail was brought up and the beast groomed the barbed tip. It licked some of the venom from its stinger, then used that substance to groom the thirty bubbled and spiky-haired parts of its long tail.

Then it suddenly stopped. The tail went into the air and it froze. Small openings in the creature's skin opened and closed. The feathered armor plates on its neck expanded out away from its body. It had caught a scent. The green eyes narrowed, and that brought the thick, hairlike brows to points resembling sharp horns. Three-quarters of the 22 million pores on its body needed for the intake of chemicals from the air closed down completely. It settled to no more than an intake of the oxygen environment every five minutes. Suddenly it sprang from its back and stood to its full height of over eighteen feet and then turned its monstrous head, first left, then right, sending its roosterlike neck armor swinging outward with the force of its action. The thickly

matted and coarse hair on its body stood up, sensing all that
was being transmitted on the night air. The billions of hollow
hairs twitched and moved, creating a rippling effect that
made its skin shimmer in the moonlight.

Suddenly the animal engaged its strong hind legs and ran
six feet across the desert hardpan, all the while emitting a
high-pitched buzzing from its palate. The unheard sound
softened the alien soil, making it lazily bubble, once again
changing the atomic structure of the earth. Then it sprang
into the air fifteen feet, closing its neck armor, making itself
streamlined, and hit the sand and small rocks claws first, burrowing into the ground as easily as a man diving into water.

In the distance, unknowing, the prey continued on their
way. The Destroyer was on the hunt and their fate was
sealed.

The machinations of most American police agencies were
slow at most times, but when it came to two of their own
officers who were missing, the wheels and pulleys
seemed to be a little better greased than usual. When Dills
and Milner hadn't shown up at shift's end, the machinery
started moving. All state and local agencies were notified,
and the hunt for the troopers had been on officially since
sundown.

The Arizona State police car was parked behind the Winnebago camper as the two troopers assisted the driver in
changing a tire. They were pulled onto the side of state
road 88. Ed Wasser held the flashlight while his partner,
Jerry Dills, Trooper Tom Dills's brother, waited impatiently
beside him.

Jerry didn't care for the fact that they were making this
courtesy stop in the first place when they should be out looking for his older brother. The tourist obviously had things
under control, Dills thought, except for his wife, who would
every once in a while lean over and say, "I told you so."

The trooper looked around and stomped his black boot on the macadam. It wasn't like Milner and his brother Tom to not check in upon shift's end and notify base if they were going to extend their patrol. That and the fact that they had tried for hours to raise them on the radio told him Tom and his partner were in trouble somewhere out in the desert. Tom had been on the state payroll three years longer than Jerry, but that didn't mean he had any more sense than Jerry did. At least Jerry knew George Milner to be a tough man in a pinch who would look out for Tom if it was at all humanly possible.

Jerry turned suddenly as the radio screeched and hissed their call sign. He quickly made his way from the camper and trotted to the cruiser. He was gone only a few minutes when he called, half in and half out of the car, "Hey, Ed, we have a call, code five down on Riley Road."

Wasser said something to the man changing the tire and turned away. He trotted back to the car and jumped in the driver's side. Jerry looked at his partner, just grateful to be moving again as every call could have Tom's life at stake. You just never knew out here. The desert was a killing place for even those who knew it well.

"Riley Road is right up here," Wasser said, taking the cruiser up to sixty, flipping on the overhead red-and-blues. "Hell, the only thing up there is Thomas Tahchako's ranch."

"That's what I figure too. There's the road right here." Jerry pointed to the right. "If I remember right, it's all the way down and just below the foothills."

"Right." Wasser swerved the patrol car onto the small sidetrack.

The washboard road played hell with the suspension on the state car. Jerry tightened his seat belt and hung on, using his right hand on the windowsill to brace himself as the bumping became worse. The high beams picked out several jackrabbits dashing not from but toward the car. Dills turned to look behind them in the road, wanting to say something about the bizarre scene, but staying quiet as his partner was concentrating on the rough road. The red taillights and dust made it impossible to see, but Dills thought he saw a few more jackrabbits running across the road after the cruiser had sped past. This time he had to say something. "Did you see that?" he asked, looking at his partner.

"What—oh, shit!" Wasser yelled, as he pulled the wheel to the right and narrowly avoided one of Tahchako's cows as it ran down the middle of the road.

"What in the hell is going on, a rabbit and cattle stampede?" he asked incredulously, straightening out the car and speeding up again.

Suddenly the headlights picked up the form of Thomas Tahchako standing on the side of the dirt road. He had an old Winchester .30-30 at his shoulder and was shooting into the darkness, the muzzle flare lighting up the scrub around him.

"What is he doing?" Jerry asked loudly, as the car skidded to a halt. They quickly opened their doors and ran to the side of the road, where the old Indian continued to fire his weapon.

"Thomas . . . Thomas!" Wasser screamed.

But the rancher kept ejecting spent shell casings and firing. Finally the state patrolman touched Tahchako on the shoulder and the man spun around. The trooper was quick to grab the barrel of the rifle and push it down until it was pointed at the ground.

"Oh, God, you scared the tiswin out of me!" the older man said, referring to the traditional alcoholic beverage favored by the Apache. The old straw cowboy hat was cocked at an angle on his head, his eyes still wild.

"What in the hell are you shooting at?" the state trooper asked, the gunshots still ringing in his ears.

"Goddammit, something's killing my cows!"

"Thomas, it's too dark to see out there! What in the hell is it you're shooting at?" Wasser asked, squinting into the darkness.

Jerry heard a cow lowing. Then the sound was cut off suddenly with a scream. He drew his nine millimeter out of its holster and flipped the safety off with his thumb. "Goddammit, cows aren't supposed to scream like that! What in the hell is out there with your cattle?"

"I don't know, but it's goddamned big!"

"Thomas, calm down and tell me what's going on here," Wasser said angrily.

"What is it, a mountain lion?" Dills asked, peering into the darkness nervously, pistol aiming first right, then left.

"We can't sit here and talk, man, my cattle are being killed," Thomas said as under control as he could manage, gritting his teeth.

That said, he turned and started walking slowly away from the road. He ejected a spent shell casing and raised the gun to waist level. The two state troopers followed. Wasser clicked the safety to the off position on his sidearm, and Jerry flipped on the large flashlight. He shone the beam in a wide arc as they proceeded away from the light cast by the cruiser's headlights. The red and blue flashers of the cruiser's overheads cast an eerie strobe effect onto the desert scrub. Wasser stumbled and almost fell when his foot came into contact with something big, and the sound it made told him it was wet. Dills heard the squishing sound and first put the powerful beam on Wasser, then on what he had tripped on.

"Good God almighty," Dills said with a sharp intake of air. His partner jumped back when he saw what he had stepped on in the dark. The cow's eyes were open and their whites were predominating in terror of what had killed it. The head looked as if it had been sliced cleanly through. The tongue had lolled out of the mouth and rested on the sand.

As Jerry Dills took this in, he felt the hair standing up on the back of his neck. There had to be more carnage waiting for the beam of his flashlight to illuminate. As he shone the light around, he heard the sharp intake of air by Thomas Tahchako. The bright light picked out the remains of the old Indian's herd. They were scattered here and there in different states of mutilation; for the most part, the bodies were gone.

"What in God's name could have done this?" Jerry asked, squeezing the handle of his nine millimeter tighter.

"Son of bitch, forty head of cattle, my whole western pasture," Thomas mumbled as his rifle slowly dropped from his

hands. "Goddamn cattle mutilations! The government's behind this!"

The two troopers watched as the man broke down and
started mumbling. Then they looked out into the desert and
wondered what was out there. Their eyes met for a moment,
sharing the same thought. They didn't believe for one
minute the government was out killing this Apache's cattle.
Whatever it was, they didn't think they wanted to meet up
with it in the dark.

Suddenly the ground erupted skyward and a wave of dirt,
sand, and uprooted brush screamed toward the three men.
The wave smashed into their feet and tossed the men easily
into the air. Tahchako, Wasser, and Dills came down hard
and immediately tried to gain their feet. All three were shaking badly as they scanned the darkness, but all that could be
seen was the wave dissipating in the distance as their invisible intruder crossed the dirt road and shook the lit cruiser violently before disappearing.

Around them, the desert grew still once again.

With the tire changed and the state troopers gone twenty
minutes now, Harold Tracy anxiously climbed the
steps into the huge Winnebago. He washed his hands
in the sink and dried them on a towel. He walked to the driver's compartment and climbed around the center console.
His wife was still reading the road map and shaking her
head.

"All set?" she asked without looking up.

Harold looked over at Grace and gave her the bird
quickly, while her face was still buried in the accursed map.

"That's not nice, Harold. That's why bad things happen
to you." Her face was still hidden in the map.

"That cop told me we have to go the other way on State
Eighty-eight to get even remotely close to the interstate." Digging it in the best he could. "You picked wrong again, Grace."

Finally she lowered the large map and carefully folded it.
The smile she wore didn't reach her eyes.

"Who was it that wanted to come on this desert outing in the first place, Harold, me? No, it wasn't, it was you, the great adventurer who scoffed so heartily at going to my sister's in Colorado. So if you insist on pointing fingers, point them at yourself."

"Believe me, if I could get this thing to fly, Grace, I would get you there right now and *drop you off!*" He yelled the last three words as he started the camper.

She was about to tear into him when they were both suddenly thrown from their seats and into the RV's roof. Grace hit so hard she dented the aluminum in the overhead. Then the camper came down, bounced once on its ten wheels, and tilted to the right and slowly rolled onto its side. For a moment, Harold thought they *were* flying to Denver. The crunching of glass and mirrors drowned out Grace's screams as the huge Winnebago settled on its right side. Then all was quiet. Harold had fallen onto his wife, who was trying to push him off.

"Get off me!" she yelled into his ear.

But Harold wasn't listening. He was looking out of the windshield with his mouth hanging open. Grace followed his gaze, and the scream caught in her throat as she came eye to eye with something she couldn't have dreamed in her wildest nightmare.

The beast blinked at the two people inside who were frozen in terror. The green and yellow eyes reflected their image back at them.

As Harold fought the urge to scream, the animal roared at the windshield, bringing up the armored plates around its neck. The window immediately fogged and then cracked into a million tiny wavy lines. But the image of the animal could, unfortunately, still be seen as clear as day. They were face-to-face with the largest set of incisors they had ever seen. The mouth was wide, and every time it opened its bonelike mandibles the rows upon rows of teeth shone clearly in its mouth. The beast roared again; the glass, unable to take any more acoustic hammering, fell from the frame. The man and woman screamed and screamed, until they noticed the sudden silence inside the camper. When they opened their eyes, the animal was gone.

Harold looked down at Grace. She was still staring out the window, and the shakes had taken over, making her entire body quake. The curlers she had placed in her hair earlier after they had stopped at that small bar and grill had for the most part fallen out. Some hung on for dear life, half on and half off.

"Harold," Grace said quietly, "I think I peed myself."

Harold thought it better not to comment for the moment and just sat there and thanked God they were still alive. And also that Grace hadn't again brought up that they should have gone to her sister's in Denver.

TWENTY-ONE

The Comp Center director, Pete Golding, and his tired team of techs hadn't found anything as of midnight and looked as if they were on a wild-goose chase in Arizona just as they had been in New Mexico. Boris and Natasha had burned most of its fuel and could not be retasked another time to a different orbit or track without running out. And that meant they would more than likely lose the bird because it was in such a low orbit now, it would soon come tumbling back into the atmosphere. Another move by the old and reliable satellite would be its last. It would take a shuttle launch to accomplish a refueling, and they all knew that couldn't be ordered like room service. Hours before, the president had been persuaded to give the NSA back its KH-11, Black Bird. The director of that agency was one of the few who knew about the Event Group and its front, the National Archives, and he was sympathetic and cooperative to a point, but with global terrorism still on the rise, their argument for having their bird back was valid and important to the nation.

Finally Compton had to sit at his desk and place his head down. The strain was finally catching up with him and he was on the brink of exhaustion.

Pete Golding, the head of the Comp Center and one of

Niles's closest friends, saw him and shook his head. He would let his boss get as much sleep as possible because he knew from watching him he was close to collapse.

On the many screens lining the curving wall and on the main viewing screen high above them, the expanse of desert kept rolling by as seen and sent along by Boris and Natasha, and still it showed nothing but vast emptiness.

N iles Compton was snoring lightly at his desk, his first sleep in forty-eight hours. His feet were propped up on the desk blotter, and this time the overworked director was making real progress with the much needed rest his body craved. The shifts had changed twice since they had re-tasked Boris and Natasha, and the results had been nothing but clear desert throughout most of Arizona. They were now taking wide-angle views of the small range of mountains everyone in the West had heard of, the Superstitions.

Pete Golding yawned and then pulled up a U.S. Geological Survey map of Arizona and used his mouse to place it in the right corner of the live feed from Boris and Natasha so he could study it and the terrain on the monitor.

"Damn closest town isn't a town at all. Chato's Crawl?" He shook his head. Chato had been a big man with the Apache a hundred odd years ago, a close friend of Geronimo's, if he remembered right, but what was this *Crawl* crap that tagged the name?

"Bingo!" a voice from the floor shouted out.

Golding looked first at the display and then quickly down at the row of operators who were gathering around one computer console. He hadn't noticed anything on the green-tinted, twenty-foot-wide screen at the front of the room that was showing the real-time feed from the KH-11.

"All right, Dave, what have you got?" he asked the operator.

The loud exclamation had startled Niles Compton from his slumber. He jerked awake with that odd feeling of falling one has when suddenly woken. He jumped to his feet and, wiping the sleep from his eyes, ran the three steps down to the main floor of the center.

"What have you got, Pete?" he asked, stretching his eyes wider as if this could make them less heavy. He slid his glasses on and looked.

"Nothing on the infrared, but look at the magnetometer from Boris, it's off the scale. Either we ran into an above-ground ore site or we have what we're looking for," Golding said as he stepped back so Niles could get a better look at the display.

The digital readout for indigenous metal was pegged out at over 442,000 parts per square mile. The metal detectors on board the KH-11 satellite were using a lot of power to focus on such a tight area of the earth, but the results, though now a little weak, were very positive. Compton looked at the big projection screen on the front wall. He could see the huge rocks and boulders this mountain range was made of. But the metal the detectors were picking up was nowhere to be seen, indicating it might be indigenous metal just below the surface.

"You know, Niles, I was just looking at the U.S. Survey map, and do you know where this signal is coming from?" Pete asked, but didn't wait for an answer as he had a horrible feeling that his boss was about to do something dumb. "That's the Superstition Mountain Range, you know, the historical myth of the Lost Dutchman Mine, it could just be either a gold or silver deposit we're picking up."

"Okay, I hate to order this, but let's take a chance and go to maximum magnification. Let's get us in close and maybe we can pick something up visually." Niles looked at the screen. "And I want it tight on that small valley right there, because Boris and Natasha is having a hard time seeing beyond the surrounding rock walls."

The other technicians looked at Golding, clearly expecting him to say something.

"Niles, a word please." Pete took him by the elbow and walked a few paces away.

Pete glared at the worried faces until they returned to their stations and the work they were doing. He removed his glasses and started to clean them with the white shirttail that had worked out of his black pants.

"Niles, we've used a lot of power on this. Boris and Natasha is damn near out of fuel and the batteries are down to darn near nothing. The solar cells can't keep up with the demands we're putting on them, and we have nothing going into the batteries." Golding looked at his boss and friend, then again at the main display as he put his glasses back on.

Compton removed his own glasses and used the earpiece to poke at his Comp Center director's chest. "Number one, Pete, we have to take this chance and use what's left in her batteries to bring the lenses to a nominal position. We need detail on that section. The metal could be in that valley or so small we can't see it. Number two, I don't give a flying fuck about the fuel state." He jabbed at Pete again, harder this time. "And number three, if you don't do as I say and we don't find that saucer"—he paused a moment to lower his voice—"we could be issuing a death sentence to everyone on this fucking planet. And four"—he gritted his teeth—"if we have to, we get into cars and planes and helicopters and go out there and find it ourselves if and when we lose REC-SAT." He put his glasses back on and stormed back onto the main floor.

"Lenses to full magnification on my mark," Golding loudly ordered, startling most of the technicians, who in turn started immediately complying. "Take communications to Boris and Natasha offline as soon as I give the word. I want a clear picture and I need that extra power when we reach maximum magnification." Out of the corner of his eye Golding saw his boss gently shake his head, whether feeling bad for his being a bully to his close friend or for sacrificing Boris and Natasha, he didn't know.

"Bringing maximum magnification onto site four two eight three nine, elevation four thousand three hundred feet," the man in control of optics announced. "Satellite altitude one two zero miles."

"Stand by to cut communications on my go. Remember, we'll have about three seconds of power from Boris to operate the lenses before he dies with the COM link. Another ten seconds of picture time from Natasha before everything goes, and with it, our picture, so be ready on infrared and magnetometers, and I want video and stills on this. Let's fucking be ready."

Niles knew how upset Pete Golding was. He had just given orders to basically kill Boris and Natasha, because without fuel and electrical power, the KH-11 satellite would be lost forever with a decaying orbit and no way to boost her back up without immediate refueling from the shuttle. But it couldn't be helped.

After the hastily relayed commands were sent through to Boris and Natasha, the picture cleared and they could now make out the small valley they had centered their maximum effort on. The infrared and ambient-light devices showed only rocks still heated from the day's dead sunlight. As they watched, the magnetometer shot off the scale once again, and Niles winced when he didn't see the wreckage he had hoped for.

"We lose power in five, four, three, two—"

But that was as far as Pete's countdown went. The picture turned to snow just two seconds off their projected time. The room grew silent as every man and woman knew they had just witnessed the death of the reliable old KH-11 satellite. Pete Golding slammed the clipboard he was holding to the floor, then kicked it in anger.

On the main screen and on several consoles in the computer center they saw the exact moment of death for Boris and Natasha. After the snow replaced the once clear picture of the earthbound valley, the test pattern for a lost signal came on the large screen as the communication link with the satellite was lost, possibly forever. Pete found a chair and sat down hard. Niles stood in a frozen stance and prayed he hadn't just lost their only hope. He swallowed and waited. The magnetometers had peaked out, but that could mean

anything from indigenous metal near the surface to a malfunction in an already overtaxed spy bird.

"Goddamn! Old Boris and Natasha may have kicked the
fucking bucket, but it sure as hell scored on its last play.
Look!" Dave Pope, technical specialist for optical enhance-
ment, yelled, and clapped. He quickly stood and jumped up
and down and started high-fiving his assistants.

Niles's heart raced as he focused on the still screen to the
right of the main viewing monitor as the operator calmed
down and punched a few command keys, then a crystal clear
image appeared. It was a still shot of the small valley, and inside it was the wreckage. It was scattered in a roughly two-
mile stretch. It was metal alright, twisted into all different
shapes. You could even see the point of impact and the crater
it had created and the earth that had been plowed up in its
slide before it fell to pieces. There were war whoops and
whistles, and every man and woman was on his or her feet.

Niles Compton closed his eyes and held them that way
for a moment, content to let the others applaud and yell. He
was still that way when he felt a hand on his shoulder. Niles
opened his eyes and looked up into the smiling face of Pete
Golding.

"You've got a pair of brass balls, Niles, my man," Pete
said, shaking his head. "But dammit, Mr. Director, it was a
good call."

Good old Boris and Natasha, Niles thought. He would
have it refueled and powered back up if it was the last thing
he did. He owed everything to the old KH-11.

Niles stood and took a deep breath, trying to compose
himself as best as he could. He removed his glasses and
rubbed his eyes.

"All right, Pete, put a call in to Alice so she can inform
Senator Lee." Niles paused as Pete started to lift the phone.
"Alert the complex and sound an Event signal and let's get
the discovery teams in the air. Let's do it by the book."

Niles watched his computer technicians work quickly for
a moment, never more proud of being a part of the Group.

He replaced his glasses and started for the door as first one, then another, and then all the technicians were up tapping on their small consoles in a semi-silent tribute to a man who had just risked everything on a calculated hunch. Niles didn't acknowledge them, he just opened the door and left.

As Pete made the call upstairs, he watched his exhausted boss leave and wondered if he would ever have had the courage to risk a $485 million satellite. Then he shook his head no, he could never have done it. But then again, maybe Niles knew something he wasn't telling him.

Pete looked at the crash site and wondered if there had been life on board. His eyes wandered over the hole at the center of the wreckage and wondered what that could be.

At the same time Niles Compton had ordered the retasking of Boris and Natasha, Jack had made his way to the cafeteria for some coffee. He wanted to think over the news of Centaurus before giving it to Lee and Compton. The ramifications of what had been discovered would shake the Group and other areas of the U.S. government to its foundations, if what Jack thought had happened had actually happened.

It was obvious that Hendrix junior was involved in running the Frenchman. They obviously dealt in high and cutting-edge technology. And the best part was, the company that friends of the elder Hendrix's had more than likely founded, so soon after the event in Roswell, was the direct result of the technology that had been examined and analyzed. Was the Centaurus Corporation responsible for the missing evidence from Roswell? Collins wasn't a big believer in coincidence. But the most disturbing factor was the possibility that a private company in this country was preparing for war without the backing or the knowledge of the government of the United States. He only hoped that Centaurus had done nothing since '47 to have provoked the second attack.

Jack was mulling these thoughts over as he entered the

cafeteria, poured himself a cup, and walked over to the closest table and sat down. He didn't see the figure as it approached his table until the shadow fell on him. Jack looked
up and saw it was Sarah McIntire.

"Hello, Major."

"Specialist," he said in short greeting.

"Well, I just wanted to say . . . well, sir, you have a
good—"

"What is your specialty again, Sarah?" he asked, then
brought the cup to his mouth and sipped the hot coffee.

"Mines and tunnels, soon to be an assistant director for
the Geology Department. I get my master's in three weeks
from the Colorado School of Mines."

"Think you'll stay in after you get your commission?"

"I believe so; I love the Group, but may be a tad intimi-
dated going back out into the real army as a second lieutenant."

McIntire smiled and looked into Jack's eyes and was
about to ask if he wanted to order something to eat, when the
speakers tucked away in the far corners of the cafeteria cut
her off.

"Will Discovery Team Odin report to the briefing room
please? Discovery Team Odin to briefing," the computerized
voice interrupted them.

Sarah lowered her eyes when the call came. Her team
name was Hokkaido. The name had never once been called
outside of drills since she'd begun at the Event Group.

Jack stood and pushed his chair back when he heard the
code name of the advance Discovery team.

"If you have need for a geologist or a tunnel team, think
of me and my geology team, will you? We're good, Major,
we'd be an asset," she said, saving Collins the embarrassment of asking her out.

Jack noticed the sad smile and said, "Will do," and winked.
"And, Sarah, if you weren't good, I doubt you'd be here."

Sarah watched him hurry through the double doors of the
cafeteria and suddenly realized what the call for the Discovery team meant.

"I'll be damned, they found the crash site," she mumbled to no one but herself. She glanced around the cafeteria at cooks hurriedly making up box lunches and throwing together coffee for the Discovery team to take into the field. How she wished she could be going out there with them.

TWENTY-TWO

Gus jumped when Mahjtic suddenly sprang from the bed and ran to the window opposite the door. The quick movement had to have caused great pain in the small being's body.

"What in the sam hell are you doin'?" Gus asked, getting to his feet.

Mahjtic had almost ripped the blind away and was gazing outside into the night through the dirty window. The bald head turned first to the left, then quickly to the right, and its eyes were wider than normal. It first growled low under its breath, then became quiet again as it searched the area around the small house.

Gus had given his visitor one of his old white shirts (white when Lyndon Johnson had been president anyway) after the small alien had finished eating. The shirt was overly large and was bunched around its small, slender feet, and Gus saw the movement of the cloth as the small alien trembled. Its long, strange fingers were gripping the sill tightly as it watched the darkness outside.

"What's eatin' you, son?"

Mahjtic continued to scan the dark night, head moving to a spot, looking intently for a moment, then moving on to another area in the darkness. Again it moved its head and looked toward the pen where Gus had kept Buck, and the chicken coop that sat beside it. Then it finally turned away and glanced back at Gus.

"Maybe you heard that damn mule coming back."

The large lids slid closed from the side of its head as it blinked again. That strange tilt of the head followed. *"Buck-kkk,"* it said in that cottony, buzz-sounding voice, trying to pronounce the word correctly.

"He's my mule," he finally said, then added quickly, "and my friend."

"He . . . is lost from . . . this . . . home?" Mahjtic asked, turning from the window.

Gus didn't know if not having the headaches and nose bleeds was worth the terrible noise of the alien's real voice. It was like scraping your fingernails across a chalkboard.

"Shit, Buck boy knows that damn desert better'n I do. Nah, he's not lost."

Mahjtic turned back to the four-paned window. It brought its hand to its bandaged head and touched it gingerly as its head turned left, then right, scanning the scrub and desert outside.

"The Destroyer is hunting."

The old man turned his eyes away from the window and looked at his strange guest, ignoring the pain its words caused. "You mean to say somethin's huntin' Buck?" Gus asked with raised eyebrows.

The small alien closed its eyes. The smooth nose twitched once, then it opened its eyes again and looked at the old man. *"Destroyer hunts,"* it said in its irritatingly gravelly voice, then pointed at Gus, and then its long finger turned and pointed at itself.

"And just what is this Destroyer?" the old man asked, walking slowly away from the window.

Mahjtic silently went back to the old bed and crawled up its height and sat down. Its small, three-toed feet dangled two and half feet off the floor as it looked from the old man to the window.

"*Aneemal,*" it said, mispronouncing the word. "*Destroyer is an aneemal.*"

Gus went to the table and sat in one of the two chairs. He put both elbows on his knees and looked at Mahjtic.

"Never heard of no Destroyer, Matchstick."

It looked at Gus and tilted its head. "*Maaaa-hJ-tiiic,*" it said, pronouncing its name phonetically and far more slowly.

The old man heard the correction and the indignant way it was said, but ignored it.

Mahjtic shook its head, then sat up and turned to the window above the bed and pushed the blind aside. "*Mine animal . . . my animal,*" it corrected. "*It is my animal captured for . . . work . . . other worlds, it is not from this . . . place?*" It thought a moment. "*It is not of Earth. . . . It . . . not meant for your—world.*"

"You mean you let an animal loose from your spaceship or somethin'?"

The small head shook back and forth quickly. "*Mahjtic not hurt life here. Destroyer escapes.*"

"You're sayin' this thing, this Destroyer, is dangerous?" Then Gus felt stupid for asking if something called the Destroyer was dangerous.

The head bobbed up and down, up and down, still looking away from Gus and staring into the darkness outside. "*It is danger, danger your world.*"

"That one animal brings all this danger? Then he better stay out of East Los Angeles," Gus said as a small joke.

Mahjtic looked away from the window and into Gus's eyes, confused. "*Forty and eight units, danger, forty-eight units of time from when . . .*" It was trying to think of the right word. "*I . . . I . . . boom ship . . . crash in ship, . . . forty-eight . . . hours?*"

"Why forty-eight hours?" he asked, not just a little nervously.

"*Babies come.*"

"I don't follow you."

Mahjtic squeezed its eyes closed in exasperation. "*Men*

come here, the mountain, tomorrow, maybe? Men help Mahjtic and Gus when sun comes again?"

"If you're askin' if the cops or army will be coming here, I don't know. In my experience the army sometimes can be a day late and a dollar short, and the cops will probably give you a ticket for crashin' your ship."

Mahjtic opened its eyes and looked at the old man long and hard. Then it slid from the bed and walked slowly toward Gus. It placed its small right hand on the table and looked at its host with its obsidian eyes. It tilted the large lightbulb-shaped head and concentrated, saying the words as clearly as its voice would allow it.

"The Destroyer has babies in ten more of your time hours. We need the many people of your species that will come to look for ship. When they find my ship, these mens will have to help find Destroyer soon, or too late, too many baby, overwhelm all life on this world. My Gray Masters live here then."

Gus blinked. The words had been pronounced slowly and clearly, even taking into account the bad quality of their vocalization.

"What makes you think the men will find your spaceship; maybe we should just walk into town and call for help."

"No, noooo, not in dark, never in dark. Never walk on ground in light-dark. Men will come to mountain, I feel it in here." The little green hand went to its head. *"Must tell mans about Destroyer, the Talkhan, or too late your world. Some of my Master kind, the Gray ones, want planet, Gussss."* It tilted its head and touched the old man's leg. *"Gus will help Mahjtic?"* it asked, eyes blinking.

Gus stood, the hand sliding away from his leg slowly. He felt Mahjtic's eyes on his back as he walked to the window once more and stared through the dirty panes.

"I s'pose I don't have much of a choice, do I?"

He turned from the window and looked at Mahjtic's downcast eyes and then shook his head.

"This is no way to impose on a new friend," he mumbled,

"by extinctioning him, whatever you just said. But again I ask, I s'pose I haven't a choice, have I?"

It looked up and the small mouth formed the wondering *O* shape again. *"Gus help?"*

"Yeah, Gus will help you, you little shit," he answered angrily, and pulled down the yellowing blinds to shut out the darkness.

"Gus help little shit," it repeated with awe. Then it thought a moment. The brow furrowed and the eyes narrowed. *"Not shit, Gus, Mahjtic name not shit. What is shit?"*

"Shit is what I have a sinking feeling I just stepped into, son."

TWENTY-THREE

Staff Sergeant Will Mendenhall placed the CLOSED sign in the window and turned the neon OPEN sign off, and for the first time in years the Gold City Pawnshop was closed for business. He glanced through the large plate-glass window as the buzz of the neon ceased, then he turned to the man standing beside him.

"Okay, that does it. This has to be something big for them to need all the security personnel," he said, looking at the lance corporal.

"What do you think it is?" the young marine asked.

"I don't know, but to close this gate down for the first time in twenty-some years is definitely out of the norm. The whole complex has gone on a war footing, or at least the highest alert level I've seen here since the attacks on the Trade Center and Pentagon."

Mendenhall had had little sleep that day and didn't feel like answering too many questions. The skeleton security staff they were leaving behind to guard the gate was on his mind more than whatever alert level they were currently on.

"That does it. We have to take one of the cars in through gate one to pick up some gear and then get to the briefing."

• • •

Henri Farbeaux watched the black man hold the door for the smaller one. He had come to full alert when the bright red OPEN sign had been turned off, leaving the area directly in front of the shop barren of light. After the information Reese had given him about the security gate that led to the Event complex and the security team there, he had been prepared to enter and do what he needed to do. But when the lights went out, he had to think on the fly. The pawnshop claimed to be open twenty-four hours a day, seven days a week, so Farbeaux instinctively knew this was the moment he had waited for. He would have either the complex location or the whereabouts of the crash site.

He placed two dental swatches into his mouth and firmly set them along his jawline, puffing his jowls out to the proper thickness, and then he smiled, not only happy with his disguise, but happy that the late Mr. Reese had been so forthcoming about this magical gate into the Event Group.

Farbeaux quickly opened the car door and crossed the street. As he moved, he took a tube out of his pocket and slid his thumb into position on the top of the small object and stepped to the sidewalk, narrowly avoiding a driver who swerved out of the way at the last moment. The Frenchman clicked the small button on top of the tube. He watched as the black man walked away from the door and toward a car parked in the front of the pawnshop. The other man went to the passenger side.

"Excuse me, gentlemen," Farbeaux called in his best down-home American accent. "This town's as confusin' as Houston in a snowstorm. Can you tell me where to find the Flamingo Hotel?"

Mendenhall looked closely at the stranger. The cowboy hat was cocked at a lazy angle on the man's head and his boots were the snakeskin sort he himself yearned to buy one day.

"Yeah, it's down three blocks. You come to an overhead walkway in front of Caesars Palace, make a right there, you run right into it," he answered.

Farbeaux was close enough, but to make sure, he stepped two feet closer to the big soldier.

"Three blocks you say?"

Mendenhall opened the car door. "That's right, can't miss it, buddy."

"Well, I'll be damned; I was right there and didn't ever see any walkway." The stranger turned to face Willie and held out his hand. "Thanks a bunch, partner, wife's gonna give me hell and rub it in eight ways to Sunday."

Mendenhall hesitated a moment, then took the man's hand and shook. "No problem, buddy."

The Frenchman coupled his other hand over the black man's, lightly pushing the button on the small tube. A fine mist of hydrochlorinolphysiline filmed the top of Mendenhall's hand. It was nontoxic and dried immediately with no odor or color. The man never knew he had been "tagged" by a substance that could be tracked by the molecule-sized plutonium abstract that had entered the pores of his skin. A Centaurus satellite would relay the information to a ground station, actually a small backpack-sized unit sitting in Farbeaux's car that Centaurus didn't know he had taken from company stores before he left L.A. The amount of chemical would only be enough to track, and the big black man would feel nothing other than the smallest of headaches. It would be four hours before the abstract wore off, and Farbeaux hoped this man didn't fully shower until he got to the Event complex or, better still, the crash site.

Farbeaux released the sergeant's hand and nodded once. "You gentlemen have a good night and thanks again."

The two men climbed into the car and never gave the well-dressed cowboy another thought.

He walked back and opened the car door and sat behind the wheel. He removed the mustache and dental wadding and tossed them and the cowboy hat into the backseat. As he did this, his secure phone started to ring, but Farbeaux ignored it. It was his secure line, so it had to be Hendrix wondering about his second team of missing men. Or maybe he had found them, Farbeaux thought. No matter, he was hot on the trail of the Event Group and the ultimate prize, a whole new technology to be sold off.

"Now, Senator Lee, make my year and tell me you have the saucer."

Jack, Niles, Lee, and Alice were in the Group's command room located just below the main conference room. Maps of southeast Arizona lay spread on the massive planning board. Alice was furiously scribbling notes and writing down directives delivered by Collins for his planning of the Discovery phase of the operation.

"Now, when do I let the rest of the Discovery team in on what we are really looking for?" Jack asked, looking from Niles to Lee.

"Hopefully never," Niles said.

"I'm not one who likes putting people's lives at stake by not giving them the full story. Their thoughts on-site could be very valuable," Jack said as he straightened up from the map table.

"What we suspect can never become general knowledge, even among our own people, Jack. The mere thought of some race of beings trying to wipe us out would run like a cancer through the Group. We have duties here that need to be done. If the animal is dead, I want all our people concentrating on their jobs, not what's coming next." Lee looked up from the maps.

Collins saw that the old man was speaking slowly, with a drooping mouth on his left side, as if part of the muscles in his mouth were failing. The white shirt was unbuttoned at the top and his silver hair was shooting off in different directions. Jack looked at Alice, who sat stock-still while taking the briefing notes. A few minutes before they'd started the breakdown and logistics needed for this mission, Jack had informed Niles, the senator, and Alice about the connection with Farbeaux, Centaurus, and Genesis. Lee had had his worst fears confirmed about another element operating inside this country. That they now knew it had to have been these people who had eliminated the Group's team back in '47 only underscored the fear that this company, Centaurus, was operating with impunity.

"If I have even an inkling of evidence that this animal has survived the crash, I will immediately inform not only the initial Discovery team, but anyone who comes on-site what we may be up against. There can be no negotiation on that fact," Jack said, looking from face to face. "I have never kept troops in the dark or lied to them about what they're up against. I hope I'm clear and you back me on that. I've had some experience with people above me not giving my men and myself a clear picture of what we were up against, and it always turns out bad."

"You have my word, Jack. If it's alive, you have permission to inform everyone."

They were interrupted by a knock on the door. Niles called out and Commander Everett entered and held out a file folder to Jack.

"The Discovery team is assembled and waiting with the exception of Mendenhall and Jackson, who will join us at the airfield."

"Thank you, Mr. Everett, we'll be right in." Jack took the file folder.

Everett left the command room and closed the door. Jack turned and faced the three expectant faces.

"I explained earlier about Centaurus and Genesis. Now I think you should know who is behind them. But I believe you already have guessed. We had this package made up for you and just received it back from photo recon." Jack handed Lee the red-bordered Eyes Only file. He dipped his head and left the command room to brief his team.

Lee turned the file over and peeled away a red piece of tape and reached in and took out first the hard copy of the report Jack had already covered with him. This he handed to Alice. Then he pulled the blowups and computer-enhanced prints from the file. He looked at the first photo of a dark-haired man taken at a banquet. The only indication he recognized the face in the foreground was the momentary widening of his good eye.

"Now that's a face I never thought to see again," Lee said as he handed the picture over for Alice to see. "It has to be his son."

After a moment, Lee removed the last picture from the file and looked at the smiling face of the Frenchman. "Well, Jack and the boys earned their money. With this photo we have visual proof of just who it was Farbeaux's been working for all these years," he said, shaking his head. Then he sat up and looked at the picture more closely. Standing behind Farbeaux and unaware of the camera, the same as the Frenchman, was a face that Lee knew. He lowered the picture and closed his eye.

"What's wrong?" Alice asked.

Lee opened his eye and looked at her and handed her the last picture.

"Farbeaux?" she asked.

"No, not him, the rather tall gentleman standing behind him."

"Oh, God, is that the president?"

Lee didn't say anything.

"You mean the president knows Hendrix?" Compton asked as he took the picture and looked at it.

Jack had confirmed what Lee had suspected for fifty years or more, that their enemy from the time of the Roswell Incident to the present wasn't a foreign agency, but the mythical Men in Black who had always been but a rumor. It was now highly likely that their foe was a privately held company that existed with the help of some of the federal agencies, at least initially in the company's earlier formation in the forties and fifties. The Centaurus Corporation, and the think tank Jack mentioned, the Genesis Group, also led by Hendrix, were the people who sat in judgment on how to exploit the finds and discoveries they had gleaned from the crash wreckage they had stolen almost sixty years ago.

"Let's keep this knowledge to ourselves for a bit, shall we? We don't know how deep the connection goes between

Centaurus and the president. After all, it was a Washington event and the president was a young senator then, no crime in his being there. I suspect that maybe it's only certain elements that are assisting this corporation and not the entire federal community. I couldn't believe that the president would be an accomplice in this. But still"—Lee smiled—"let's not take any chances."

Alice and Niles knew the look in Lee's eye. He was thinking about how to turn the situation in their favor.

"What do you think, Niles, did we find the saucer in time?" the old man asked tiredly, gladly changing the subject.

Niles stared at the far wall for a moment. Then he turned and removed his glasses and slid them into his pocket.

"I think I took too damn long to find it, Senator," he answered, walking toward the door.

Alice patted Garrison on the hand as they watched Niles leave the room to make his way to the briefing.

"Niles is too hard on himself," Alice said, "but Lord help us if he's right."

Lee used his cane to stand up; Alice quickly stood herself to help him into the briefing.

"I suspect we may need God's help, because for some reason I think it's going to happen this time around," he stated flatly. "Too damn many things happened differently, too many variables." He lightly took hold of Alice's arm. "And if the worst has indeed taken place, then God may be the only one who can stop it. Get the president and get Niles back in here. We'll find out real quick if the commander in chief is someone else's friend and not just ours, because we need to get Jack some help in securing that valley. Start working on a cover story for the army to move on. But make it one in which weapons, a lot of weapons, would be needed."

Nellis AFB, Nevada
July 9, 0200 Hours

A Discovery team as laid down by Department 5656 protocol is *an advanced team of required specialists and security personnel that will be present at the start of any field operation where security for the project and Group is of major concern. Deception to the general public is foremost to camouflage the nature of said Event.*

Jack's team had gathered in the main conference room in order for the senator to observe. Jack's first brief was to Denise Gilliam, a doctor of forensic science from the University of Maine at Orono.

"Dr. Gilliam, besides your forensic duties, you will also be our field doctor. We're cutting back on initial personnel."

"But I . . ."

Jack shot her a look.

"Alright, I can do that," she said.

"That's exactly why I put you on the Discovery team, one person—two jobs."

Jack looked next to Josh Crollmier, a former member of the National Transportation and Safety Board, who would be serving as the crash expert.

"Mr. Crollmier, initially you will concentrate on the possibility of survivors, and you'll be starting without your team or equipment." Jack looked to the next in line after Crollmier just nodded.

"Signalman Willing," he said, looking at Lisa. "You will handle ground communications and set up video links to Nellis and Washington with your four-man COMM team. You will be issued sidearms and will double as site security until I get more people in theater, are we clear?"

"Yes, sir, we'll have COMMO up in five minutes."

"Dr. Robert Randall, you will handle the zoology aspect of the team. I know you served your time with the Group, but our zoologist is off base. In short, Doctor, it doesn't pay to be at the wrong place at the wrong time. You should never have paid a visit to the Group. Welcome aboard."

"I was drafted," he said.

"We need evidence of any life-forms that may have arrived with the vehicle ASAP. And the rest of you, don't ask," Jack said, heading off any questions about why a doc from the San Diego Zoo was coming along.

Then Collins looked at the rest of the security element of Everett, Mendenhall, Ryan, and Corporal Jackson. Everyone with the exception of Ryan had assault experience and helio-cast jumps under their belt. Ryan would be backup cover along with the Blackhawk crew chiefs and gunners.

"Are two two-man teams on the ground enough?" Jason asked.

"Our initial Discovery team was kept to bare bones on my request due to continuing security concerns that have arisen in external matters outside the influence of the Group. But once we're in and secure, we'll get help on the ground. I have already initiated contact, with Dr. Compton's approval and through the office of the president, with certain elements of our armed forces, and they have been informed that they may be asked to take part in special desert operations. We can no longer wait until the last minute to have things to fall back on."

"Amen to that," Virginia Pollock said, wishing she were on the Discovery team.

"Besides the Event itself, there should be little collateral interference from the people who call the small valley home," the senator said from his seat on the couch. "There may be a few prospectors and maybe a camper or two about, but other than that, the desert should be void of onlookers."

"Okay, people, you know the plan. Site security will helio-cast in first, and then we'll clear a spot for the four Blackhawks with the remaining Discovery team and equipment to land up valley from the bulk of the debris pattern. Believe me, we would have liked to have entered from outside the valley, but the slope is too steep and we just don't have the time."

The senator watched all this with a sort of sadness. Besides the anger he felt at his failing body, he knew he was meant to be on this mission. He slowly raised his right arm and motioned for Collins.

"Yes, sir?" he asked, leaning over so the senator didn't have to rise.

"Jack, I wish you would change your mind about the med team," Lee said.

Collins thought about the absence of the Group's medical team. It would be hard on any of the wounded aliens if they were found alive, but it would be just more people to get in the way if the worst-case scenario happened. "Well, sir, the medical team will be with the fifth Blackhawk just two minutes out from the site, and Dr. Gilliam can triage until the med team arrives. We will hurry the initial recon as much as possible, and if we find any of the crew still breathing, we'll get them help quickly enough."

Collins straightened and held out his hand. The old man weakly took it into his own.

Then Niles Compton approached and lightly patted Jack on the back. "Wish I were going with you, Jack."

Collins looked at Lee a moment longer, then turned to face the tired eyes and worn body of Director Compton. "Niles, for as short a time as I've known you, you've done the most god-awful amount of work I've ever seen. You need to rest and let us handle some of the load now. The president placed several calls out to contacts of mine in the private sector; Aberdeen Proving Grounds is one of them. They're going to send out a few items they've been working on that may help us out here. Some cutting-edge technology couldn't hurt. Also the army is sending some state-of-the-art body armor our way that the CIA higher-ups have hijacked for us, and it should arrive in the morning. I hope we won't need it, but . . . anyway, that's what you can do now, Niles, make sure we get this stuff ASAP. Until then, rest."

Jack reached out and shook Compton's hand, then turned and ushered the rest of the Discovery team out through the door. The first response to an attack of extraterrestrial origin was now operational.

TWENTY-FOUR

The beast was once again aboveground. Its hunger was sated for the time being and it had even more nourishment stored deep in the earth at its nesting site. Now it was watching its new surroundings. The animal saw the lights in the distance and blinked as it licked the area between its claws. The millions of pores in its purple and black armored skin took in the scent of more prey. Its body was adapting faster each time it fed on the strange and rich proteins. It was becoming much stronger.

It would use its nest soon to drop its young. They would be born already acclimated to this world.

The beast suddenly looked across the desert at the distant lights. The enticing aroma of food was carried by the warm wind from the north.

The beast then leisurely moved its claws to the ground and gently leaned forward. The armored plates on its neck spread and its throat started producing the hum from the concave voice box, bounding it off the animal's palate. The sound, unheard by man or animal, rippled the sand and dirt, once again changing the atomic dynamic of the soil. Then the beast gently dove into the earth. The scent of prey had been much too strong for it to ignore.

Every few minutes the Destroyer would rise from the

ground as a dolphin would from the sea, bursting into the air fifteen and sometimes twenty feet in height to scan the area, then letting its massive weight send it back into the soil, and soon it was again parting the dirt in a massive wave as it drew nearer to its next food source, eventually going deep.

The small town in the distance was sleeping, oblivious to the threat and notoriety coming its way, as it would soon be on every news channel the world over as the beast had chosen the earth directly below the town as its nesting site.

The name of Chato's Crawl, Arizona, was about to become synonymous with the word *terror*.

The Superstition Mountains
Discovery Team Odin (Ground Assault)

The three Blackhawks were flying at terrain level. The collision-avoidance radars were on and running, freeing the pilot to stare in abject horror as the computers adjusted flight to avoid objects that loomed ahead through the windshield. Warrant Officer Jerry Brannon didn't care for the "hands-off" approach to piloting. He had been with the Event Group twelve years. Flying with your hands poised over the control collective of the huge helicopter was one thing he couldn't get used to doing. Technology, he reasoned with a pilot's mentality, sucked. He watched the collective, which was the control attached to his left that looked like an emergency brake. You twisted the throttle at the end and lifted if you wanted to go higher, or lowered it if you wanted to go down. Right now, looking at it operate itself was nerve-racking.

He glanced out the windshield at the passing terrain. The greenish image in the night-vision scope was eerily magical as it brought the desert to life around the streaking helicopter.

"Coming up on crash site in four minutes," he radioed back to his passengers.

The crew and security aspect of the Discovery team felt

the sudden shift in the Blackhawk's powerful twin turbines, and the steep climb it had to adjust to as the black-painted helicopter flew up the mountainside. The three other Blackhawks of the Discovery team peeled away and would hover at station just below the valley above. Collins felt the slight slowing of forward momentum, then Brannon flipped on the anticollision lights, which cast a red strobe-light effect against the coarse terrain of piled-up rocks that passed for mountains in this region of Arizona, the Superstitions.

Collins felt the old adrenaline rush of landing in an LZ again. The interior lights flashed once, then went to red to allow the advance team's eyes to adjust better to the darkness. Mendenhall, on Jack's orders, loaded and locked his M16. Mendenhall watched as all elements of his short-manned squad followed suit as they too inserted a twenty-round magazine and pulled back the charging slide on their automatic rifles. The indicators on the weapons remained on safe. Lisa had a nine-millimeter automatic pistol in a shoulder holster, as did Jason Ryan, who had been surprised to learn that Collins had included him on the Discovery team. After all, he was a pilot and knew nothing of ground assault or the tactics members of this team used. But Jack had explained he needed people who reacted quickly, and he knew naval fighter pilots were quick-thinking and weren't afraid of taking chances. He was quite comfortable with assigning Ryan duties on the initial team and later for duty in town. He knew Ryan would have the personality to handle civilians in the initial stages.

The Blackhawk had two sliding-bracket-mounted, five-barrel, mini-rotary cannons on each side, manned by two crewmen wearing night-vision eyewear. The hoppers to their left were full of the rounds that could tear into any target and shred it before it heard the noise of the electrically driven weapon.

The powerful UH-60 Blackhawk slowed, then came to a stop still a hundred feet off the debris field and automatically held position.

"Going to manual flight, people, you are a go for egress.

Good luck," Brannon called over the radio, then turned the red interior light off.

"Okay, watch your descent; don't land on anything if you can avoid it. We don't know what to expect down there," Collins shouted against the whine created by the twin turbines. "Are we ready?"

One by one his four-man security team gave the thumbs-up and answered into their built-in mikes, "Good to go!"

Collins slid the door back on its track, filling the compartment with a blast of cool desert air. He pulled his night-vision goggles down and adjusted the Kevlar helmet on his head. He also adjusted the harness holding extra magazines and water, then kicked out the first of four ropes, two on each side of the helicopter. They would make it a combat helio-cast into an unsecured area; it would be as fast as you could do it, in the safest amount of time.

"Okay, let's go."

He grabbed the rope on the steel extension arm that was four feet beyond the open door, then fed the rope into the metal ring just below where his belly button would be, then turned and faced the inside of the compartment to the opposite side of the Blackhawk. Mendenhall mirrored his leader's movements exactly. Then they both pushed off at the same time. Everett and Jackson followed a second later. Up front, Brannon prepared to bring the power down a touch to keep the Blackhawk level due to the loss of weight.

The four men slowed their descent on the thick rubber-encased-nylon ropes as they approached the debris field. They came to a stop fifteen feet from the ground and let their eyes roam the area where each would set down. The drop zone was strangely cast in the green glow one never really got used to when using the ambient-light devices the military had developed for night operations.

Collins released pressure on both hands and traveled the rest of the way to the ground, narrowly missing a four-foot piece of strangely shaped metal. He quickly released the rope and unsnapped himself from the ring, then tossed the rope to the side and brought the short-barreled M16 up from his belly pack. Jack clicked the indicator from safety to semiautomatic and watched as Mendenhall followed suit, placing his weapon from safety to full automatic, as the second part of one team.

Collins then felt the huge Blackhawk increase power and rise back into the sky. Brannon was good and quick. He had watched the helio-cast until its conclusion and hadn't waited for the all-clear before lifting the bird back up to a safe altitude so he could circle close enough to give the ground team cover fire if needed.

The major adjusted the small microphone to about an inch from his mouth. His voice would carry not only to his ground team and the helicopter, but also to the Group in Nevada. "All right, ladies, spread out and keep your eyes open."

Everett and Lance Corporal Jackson were teamed and walked side by side, weapons at eye level, sweeping the area before them. Carl couldn't believe the amount of wreckage before him. As he turned and scanned the area behind his team, he saw Collins turn over a big container, then move on. He thought nothing of it until he saw him repeat the same thing to another strangely shaped box. As he turned, wondering what Collins was up to, he didn't see the hole. The next thing Everett knew the ground gave way, and if it weren't for his quick reflexes, he would have fallen all the way. As it was, he was hanging on by his elbows. His M16 had come up and given him a good whack on the chin, putting a good two-inch gash just to the left along his jawline. He felt his feet swinging below him and knew immediately it was a deep crevasse he had almost stumbled into.

"Some help here," he called calmly into his voice-activated microphone.

Jackson quietly ran over and saw what was happening. He let his weapon fall by the strap to his belly pack and moved his hands to Everett's armpits and lifted. Once he was out of the hole, they both looked down into the black maw in amazement.

"Old mine shaft, you think?" Jackson asked.

"No," Everett answered, looking closer at the dirt and

sand with the night-vision scope. "Look at the dirt piled around the top, this was dug recently."

As they stared into the deep excavation, they saw it was smooth around the sides and went straight down. Everett broke a fluorescent nightstick and tossed it into the hole. Through the green-tinted limits of their vision the light told them it curved off somewhere around forty feet or so. They wondered why this hole was here right in the middle of the crash site. As they thought about the strangeness of it, both glanced around and brought their M16s up with renewed enthusiasm.

Gus's Cabin
0320 Hours

Gus was sound asleep. His snoring was loud and had kept Mahjtic on edge, and the pain wasn't helping it either. But far more than Gus's snoring or the pain in its ribs was the fact it knew the small house was being watched. Mahjtic's eyes were wide as it pulled the old blanket up to its small chin as it heard a shuffling noise outside.

"*Gussss,*" it whispered.

Mahjtic's call was answered by a much louder snore.

"*Gussss.*" A little louder.

A strange sound emanated from the front of the house. It sounded like small popping noises. Gus never stirred. Then a sound of the screen door hitting lightly as it was closed, as if something was testing it.

"*Gussss.*"

Mahjtic finally gathered up the reserve of courage to slowly slide up and off the bed, the pain in its ribs ignored as it leaned against the old clapboard wall and ventured a glance toward the front door and listened intently. There were scraping noises against the wooden door. The small alien's eyes went from the door to Gus, who was leaning back in the chair with his face toward the ceiling. Again it looked toward the flimsy door, and to Mahjtic's horror it heard the screen door spring being stretched open once again, and it saw the old glass doorknob slowly turn and then stop. It hadn't been turned far enough to open, but Mahjtic didn't care for the movement at all, and it had had enough.

"GUSSSSSS!" it screamed.

Gus was so shocked his legs pushed upward and sent him sprawling onto the floor. At that same moment a hatchet blade splintered the door and was quickly worked free. Mahjtic saw this, but Gus, who was trying to make sense of why he was on his back, didn't.

The small alien ran and jumped onto the bed and actually tried to climb the wall, only getting a few inches before sliding back to the old mattress. It was jabbering in terror as the hatchet again sank into the front door, and this time a loud hissing noise could be heard through the large crack in the wood.

"What in the—"

That was as far as Gus got as the center panel of the door gave way and a long, thin arm shot through. Small, clear claws were grasping at air, opening and closing. Gus's eyes widened as he saw that the arm was grayish and shot through with veins that revealed the dark blood that coursed underneath the sickly and wet-looking skin. As Gus started to gain some of his senses, he heard Matchstick scream again.

Whatever was at the door suddenly withdrew, and a moment later what remained of the center of the door came flying into the small house.

"Good God almighty," he said when the Gray stepped in through the doorway.

The creature stood outlined in the darkness outside. It was leaning to its left side and Gus saw the rusty roofing hatchet swaying in front of it. The Gray was almost as tall as Gus; its skin was dark and covered in small blackened and brownish flecks, like freckles, and they moved on the surface of its muscles. The head was large. The eyes were as small as a man's, but that was where the resemblance stopped. The pupils were yellow, ringed in black, and they were looking straight at Gus. It opened its mouth and hissed loudly, giving Gus cold chills as its clear teeth were exposed. It took a tentative step into the light of the kitchen. It was dragging its right leg, and Gus could now see the dark blood as it was spread across the linoleum by its high-heeled, double-jointed foot.

Matchstick ceased trying to dig its way through the wall and turned to face the Gray. Its small legs tried to steady themselves on the spongy mattress. Suddenly Matchstick let out a long stream of loud chattering in a language that was as far from English as Gus had ever heard.

Suddenly the Gray slammed the hatchet into the small wooden table. Gus quickly reached for the leg of the chair. The Gray quickly twisted the weapon free and advanced farther into the kitchen.

Gus slowly tried to sit up, trying in vain to untangle his boots from the legs of the chair.

"You were there in the mountains, weren't ya?" he said as if he were a bug to be stepped upon. "What do you want, you ugly bastard?"

The creature switched the hatchet to its left and suddenly lunged at Gus. He tried to grab at the small countertop but hit the hot plate with the pot of cold soup. The soup went flying across the kitchen, and Gus went back down and looked up to his left in time to see the sharp edge of the hatchet heading for his chest. The weapon buried itself in the wood only inches from Gus's upturned face. The Gray screamed in anger as Gus brought his fist up and connected solidly with the creature's jaw, hitting solid bone beneath the sickly skin, causing the alien's head to jerk back, but still it worked to free the hatchet. Gus heard the sound of cracking wood as it twisted the weapon back and forth.

Before either Gus or the Gray could react, there was a loud scream and then Matchstick had joined the fray. It had sprung from the bed to the table to the Gray's shoulders. It quickly started to attack the Gray's head and neck. The much larger alien momentarily forgot the hatchet and reached up and grabbed Matchstick and easily tossed it across the room, where it landed against the wall. The picture of the poker-playing dogs was dislodged from its nail and fell and hit the alien's large green head, and Matchstick momentarily saw stars. Then as it rubbed its bandaged head, the bow and arrow fell into its lap.

"You son of a bitch!" Gus yelled as he was punching and slapping at the Gray for all he was worth.

The alien used its free hand and slammed Gus's head into the floor, while its other hand started working at freeing the hatchet once again. Gus heard the sickening sound of the rusty tool being pulled from the wood and knew he was in dire straits.

"Gussssss!" Matchstick yelled.

The Gray stopped and looked up. The old man quickly grabbed for the right arm of the creature and tried to wrestle the weapon from it, but the creature's grip was iron. Gus saw Matchstick, but his view was upside down, but what he saw struck almost as much horror in him as the Gray with the hatchet. Matchstick had an arrow in its small hand, ready to throw it at the Gray.

Matchstick didn't hesitate. The maneuver was done to precision as its right hand let go and the arrow was loosed. It flew past the Gray's shoulder and embedded itself in the floor next to Gus's head.

The Gray actually grinned when the arrow missed, and it raised the hatchet to strike Gus. Then suddenly a strange look crossed the Gray's features, and the old man saw why: an arrow had pierced its back. Then Matchstick angrily crashed into the Gray and sent it flying off of Gus. As he quickly sat up to assist Matchstick, he saw the small alien atop the Gray, hitting it again and again with another arrow. The Gray was hissing and spitting angrily, but its actions were slow and growing slower. Gus quickly came to his knees and rushed over and grabbed the hatchet and went to assist Matchstick. He raised the hatchet high and brought it down with all his strength into the chest of the Gray. The large alien let out a scream of pure pain. Matchstick rolled off and scooted to the far wall of the house. Gus sat still for several moments.

"You okay, son?" Gus asked as he tried to gain his feet, but slipped in the blood on the floor.

Matchstick shook its large head. It brought its long fingers up and felt its head, then looked at the blood that stained its fingers.

"You started bleeding again, boy." Gus gained his feet and walked over to the small being. He gently reached down and picked it up and carried it back to the bed.

As Matchstick lay there, it rolled over as Gus went to get some water, stepping wide of the Gray as he did. When he returned, Matchstick was looking up at him.

"Thhh . . . thank . . . you."

"Yeah, well, it won't go botherin' us no more, not with you bein' as good as you are with that Indian arr'ah."

As Gus tried to wipe some blood away that had soaked through the bandage, Matchstick gently touched his hand and stopped him.

"Th . . . ank . . . you."

"A friend doesn't have to thank a friend for doin' what needs doin', son. 'Sides, I seem to recollect it was you who pulled my bacon out of the fire, so thank you," Gus said, smiling. "Now, what could be out there in the desert that's worse than this fella?"

Matchstick held Gus's eyes for a moment, then turned away and stared at the ceiling.

"Tell me now, boy, was that there fella one of your people, or that Destroyer thing?"

"It was . . . a Gray, Master of my kind."

"Well, I guess it found out we don't take kindly to Gray Masters' round here, huh?"

Matchstick closed its eyes. Gus thought it had gone to sleep when it slowly sat up and propped itself on one elbow.

"The Destroyer of Worlds, it is out there. We must find men, find good mens fast to help. Fast, Gus, very fast."

Las Vegas, Nevada
0430 Hours

Hendrix," a sleepy voice said on the other end of the phone.

"Johnson here."

"Yes," the voice said, annoyed.

"We have a problem."

"I'm listening."

"I have a verbal report from our Secret Service asset. The president has informed the Security Council that the saucer has been found. The Event Group has found the crash site of our visitors and is already on the ground. And it seems Director Compton is asking for military assets to help secure and control the area. I called our Black Team to make sure our former French friend was no longer in the equation, and there was no answer. They haven't been on the air all night, so I must assume they took his elimination lightly and paid for it. Therefore we must assume he is moving on the saucer."

There was silence on the other end of the phone for a moment and then a light chuckle. "What does that stupid bastard think he could do with whatever he comes across out there, sell it? Add it to his private collection? I'm afraid if what's out there is actually there, he won't want to take it home with him. If we can't get a team in there, I rather doubt he can."

"I hope you are not underestimating him, he's rather resourceful."

"No, my friend, let's just hope he has underestimated the corporation. In doing that he has underestimated America herself, and that has been the mistake of many an enemy." The line went dead.

The senator was at his desk. Compton, who was somewhat rested with a two-hour nap, sat with Dr. Pollock and Alice, who were behind him watching the hastily installed video feed from the crash site.

"The debris field is consistent with what the army ran into in '47, Dr. Compton," Collins said. His features were dirty in the yellow glow from floodlights. "So far we have no sign of any survivors." Jack turned and looked around him, then back at the stationary video camera. "We have two bodies, badly mangled. The third, if there was a third, is missing."

The senator looked at Alice and bit his lip in worry. Then he spoke into the small microphone that sat atop his desk. "Jack, have you found the enclosure?"

The major removed the Kevlar helmet, looked around him, then looked into the camera. "Yes, sir, it was badly damaged and empty, no biologic material at all, and we found the canisters damaged a few feet away," Jack answered quietly.

"Your first impressions, Major?" Niles asked.

Collins shook his head. "Niles, I need the damn sun to get up above these mountains and two hundred more men out here before I'll venture even a guess. Besides the hole Everett fell into, there's nothing but twisted metal," Collins answered, letting his frustration show.

That was the end of their quick and easy solution.

"Hole? What hole, Jack?" Virginia asked, leaning into the microphone.

"A damn strange one because it's not an old mine shaft of any kind, it's too perfect."

"And why do you think it's strange?" Lee asked.

"Because I normally don't get a sense of danger when I look into a hole, Senator, but when I look into this one, it seems like I'm looking into the mouth of hell, and I've learned to trust my gut when it comes to things like this."

"Thanks, Jack. If you think the area is secure enough, we'll get you some more people down there. I believe we must assume our worst-case scenario has occurred." Niles paused and looked at the others in the room, then said, "I hope we're not too late. Jack, you know how important finding the crewman is now?"

Collins just nodded into the camera.

"Good. As soon as some more security comes on the line there, your orders are to get forty winks. I need you fresh. Virginia will be there in an hour or two to take charge of field operations on the investigatory end, the cover story the CIA has worked out with the cooperation of the Centers for Disease Control is an outbreak of brucellosis, that's thanks to the cattle in the region. It's highly contagious and can spread to humans in the form of undulant fever, which means the army would have to destroy cattle by the hundreds if not thousands. That'll cover the weapons they're carrying. But for now, wait for Virginia, she'll get things going there," Niles finished.

"Glad to turn it over to her, sir. We'll see you soon," Collins said as the picture went to a blue field.

"God help us, it's out," Lee said.

"Now, we don't know that for sure, Garrison," Alice said.

Lee ignored her statement and turned to Compton. "You'll need some engineers out there and possibly a tunnel team. We may need to broaden the security aspects of this and bring in the element of airborne that the president offered to secure the town. Let the air force know we may need them." Lee thought a moment. "I'll ask the Chiefs in Washington for their advice and mollify them a little so maybe we can get the use of Rangers, and possibly some of those Delta boys we've been hearing so much about," he said, referring to the Special Operations men known as Delta Force, the unit that never officially existed, just like the Event Group.

"Yes, sir, we may just need to do that," Niles said.

A knock sounded at the door and Virginia answered it and took a note from one of the Group's communications people. She walked over to Niles and gave it to him. He read it quickly and lowered his head.

"What is it?" Lee asked.

"According to the Arizona State Police, they have a couple of missing troopers, and there was also a report of a mass killing of cattle not far from the crash sight."

"What's a mass?" Alice asked.

Virginia looked at Niles. He was now sitting with his head lowered and his eyes closed in thought. Then she looked at Alice and the senator and said, "Three hundred head were slaughtered from eight different ranches, all within the crash perimeter."

"Slaughtered?" Lee asked.

"Yes, slaughtered and eaten," Virginia said.

"My God, this must be more than one animal," Compton said.

Lee didn't answer as he moved to pick up the red phone he had left out on the desktop, fearing it would have to be used. He put the handset to his ear and waited a moment through the clicks and beeps. The voice on the other end was sleepy, but had a tone only a man who was used to these calls at any time in the morning.

"Sorry to disturb your morning, Mr. President," Lee said quietly into the phone.

Niles had informed the commander in chief earlier of finding the saucer. He didn't mention the president's possible relationship with the Centaurus Corporation, but he had alerted him to all the possibilities that could occur at the site, and the president was aware of what might happen, being fully briefed on the events of 1947. But the man held his breath while waiting for the statement he knew he would not want to hear.

"You don't sound happy, my old friend."

"Mr. President, we at Group believe we have been attacked. It's official, casualties have already been sustained on civilians of this country," Lee said somberly. "We are at war with sources unknown at this time."

The others in the room looked at him, and those looks were serious. No man had spoken any words like these since that day in September 2001, when madmen hit the World Trade

Center, and the only other time before that was in 1941 when Roosevelt had been informed of the attack on Pearl Harbor.

"Yes, the site is secure," Lee said in answer to the president's question. "No, sir, there's nothing to be done but wait and see what we can find. We will send people into the nearest towns and secure them as best we can without causing panic; we have a Case One scenario as a cover." He waited again for the president to respond. "No, sir, I believe we can consolidate and coordinate better at this time with just my people. But it may be prudent to have the elements of the 101st, the Third Rangers, and Delta if we can get them, standing by at"—he paused and looked at the map sprawled on his desk—"Chato's Crawl, Arizona. It's not that big and we believe if nothing's found, a cover story would be easier if we didn't have that many people to convince." Lee paused. "The base commander here at Nellis is cooperating nicely, thank you, sir. Yes, a special air force operations team will be on the ground to make sure the C-130s will have a clear landing zone.

"I believe also that Special Air Operations out of MacDill in Florida should be brought in. They are cleared for Event Operations." Lee paused. "Yes, sir, it very well may be that bad. And thank the Security Council for alerting the Eighty-second Airborne Division to be in the air in readiness for deployment to either Phoenix or El Paso, and for telling them it's only an alert exercise," he said, looking at the shocked faces around him. "Yes, sir, thank you, I do think it prudent as we aren't sure of this *thing's* capabilities." After hearing a few more words, Lee slowly hung up the red phone.

He took a deep breath and nodded at Niles.

Niles turned to Alice. "Notify the Group teams that are getting ready to leave what they face. Tell the major to let his team in on what we're up against. And then tell them that Operation Orion is officially your backup plan. Special Operations out of MacDill Air Force Base will be bringing in special packages for use if needed."

"Special packages?" Virginia asked.

"Tactical neutron weapons," Alice answered.

"It won't come to that because we will find that damn animal!" Lee said, grimacing and then tightly squeezing his eyes shut.

Niles, Alice, and Virginia reacted with dreamlike slowness when Garrison Lee leaned forward against the edge of the desk and then slowly fell to the floor clutching at his chest.

PART FIVE
EVENT FILE #457821:
EXTINCTION

War is all hell.
— GENERAL WILLIAM T. SHERMAN, U.S. ARMY

TWENTY-FIVE

In most cases the higher echelon of the U.S. government moves slowly, like a glacier that covers ground in increments of inches measured by years and multiplied by aeons. The country found out early on that knee-jerk reactions to situations brought innumerable consequences in losses of personnel and material. But when faced with a moment in time that had been anticipated for years and planned for by a man of former senator Garrison Lee's genius, he had no fewer than fourteen five-inch-thick files on different military responses to the Event in the desert. They covered everything from urban warfare with the animal to the scenario they now faced, but he had never planned anything for subterranean scenarios.

But now the senator was rumored to be dying. The story of his collapse had spread like wildfire throughout the Event facility and even as far as the National Security Council, giving ammunition to those who wanted the Event removed from the Group's hands.

Sarah McIntire stood in the Group's small chapel on that Sunday morning, watching as Father Carmichael went through the mechanics of his delivery. A standing-room-only crowd lined the areas along the walls. As Sarah listened, the sermon droned on. But her mind was somewhere other than the chapel that morning; she was wondering if the Discovery team in Arizona had yet been told of the senator's collapse. She hoped the news had been passed on to her roommate and other members of the advance team.

As the congregation was rising for a hymn specially selected for the senator, she was suddenly pulled away from the wall. She turned and saw a member of the geology team she had trained with for the past year, Steve Hanson.

"Come on," he said loudly just as her beeper went off.

Sarah closed the hymnal and handed the book over to a neighbor and followed the man out of the chapel. She raised the beeper and saw the word ALERT in small, neat letters across the top.

"What is it?" she asked, pulling her arm free of the excited man.

"Our team has been placed on full field alert status!" Hanson said excitedly as he hurried to the chapel doors.

Before they could open them, the sound of over a hundred other beepers started blaring around them, and others started to stand and leave.

The Event Group was going to war.

Superstition Mountains, Arizona
0740 Hours

The site on the rock-strewn mountainside was astounding. It had been transformed from a crash site into a small city of tents and trailers in less than two hours. All had been airlifted in by Pave Low helicopters, the largest that could be supplied by the Twenty-third Special Operations Group out of Nellis and the Seventeenth SOG out of March Air Force Base in California. The ground was littered with people as well as debris. A thousand little red and yellow flags had already been placed to mark pieces of wreckage from the vehicle.

A three-way COMM and video link was hooked up between Nellis, Washington, and the crash site, so Compton could see not only Collins, but also the president and his national security staff in Washington. Jack could also view them on two monitors that Lisa had installed moments before the link was brought online. Jack had already given a preliminary report to Niles moments before the others joined in.

"So what have you got so far, Major Collins?" Compton asked for the benefit of Washington.

"What we have here is a high-speed impact on solid terrain of a vehicle of *other* than Earth origin. The wreckage was spread out in a *V* pattern, indicating a high-velocity crash," Jack said as he looked into both monitors, which showed Niles at Group Center and the president in Washington. He knew the president had flown back to the White House in the middle of the night and was most likely in no mood for lengthy reports. He guessed right.

"Any survivors of the crash, Major?" the president asked pointedly.

"Our forensic team, led by the Group's Dr. Gilliam, have recovered two bodies of what she calls 'extraterrestrial beings,'" Jack answered, removing the Kevlar helmet and wiping his brow with a clean handkerchief.

"Okay, Major," General Wayne Crawford, Commandant of the Marine Corps said, the camera sliding over to his chair in the White House Situation Room far beneath the surface of 1600 Pennsylvania Avenue, "we received your request on Delta and Ranger reinforcement and have approved, they are in the air. Now, what of this animal, any remains found as of yet?"

Collins explained about their not finding any remains in any of the cages and the finding of the acid canisters.

"From this information from our ground team, coupled with the fact we now have two missing state troopers and a mass of cattle slaughtered, and with the holes we have discovered, we must conclude we have at least one burrowing-type aggressor species roaming the desert, sir."

"Damn," the president said. "Can you track this animal by using the tunnels it has dug?"

"Yes, sir, we are bringing tunnel and geology teams in and are going to reassess when they arrive. We are currently stripping all our department resources at the Group. Our security teams will be stretched the most, so the extra assault element of Rangers and Delta will be dispersed among them."

"The Joint Chiefs would like to send more, but they haven't any. They're recalling several strike units from Afghanistan."

Collins glanced over at his minimal security staff. Only fifty-two men sat at the tables inside the mess tent, not counting the twenty Event Group geologists and tunnel people getting ready to leave Nellis. He had dispatched Ryan and Mendenhall to the small town below to assist the air force in their drops.

"Thank the Chiefs for me, sir. We'll definitely need them as we don't exactly know what we'll run into down there, and I also suspect we'll find other points where the animal has entered and exited the earth, like out at"—he looked at his notes—"this Tahchako ranch that was hit last night and a few others that were also struck. We may have to break our geology and tunnel specialists into groups and divide a serious amount of security around them."

"What about secrecy matters at this point, Major?"

"Well, it shouldn't pose a problem due to the fact that they'll be led by actual military line officers from the Event Group. No need in telling them anything more about our little complex under Nellis. Also I have requested air cover for the valley until my teams can get into action, just in case the animal comes shallow before we're ready. Also, after they come in contact with the animal, Niles and the senator suggested not disclosing the animal's origin to the troops outside of the Group. We'll just say it is an engineered species."

The president turned and conferred with General Maxwell Hardesty, the chairman of the Joint Chiefs of Staff. "Can you take care of the air request, General?"

The air force general grimaced. "Yes, sir, air won't be a

problem. The town will be secured by a company from the 101st Airborne. They will also control access to the town; we are now in the process of shutting the door with the cover story. As the major stated, the 101st need not know about the nature of the agency leading them, and they have already signed secrecy and disclosure papers. Also I already have a fighter element in the air that will be on station over the valley momentarily."

"Very good, it's a start," said the president.

"What was the other item at the crash site, Major?" someone out of view of the camera's lens asked.

"Who is it I am addressing, sir?"

"This is Director Godlier of Central Intelligence."

"Well, Mr. Director, we have footprints. They were obviously made by a man likely arriving sometime after the crash as the prints are recent. We believe he may have possibly helped the surviving crewman, if there was one, escape the area."

The president looked around him, then at Collins two and a half thousand miles away. "Then we may have caught a break?"

"Yes, sir, this man may have been of some assistance to the survivor. We do suspect the crewman may have been injured because of the severity of the crash, but of course we would only be guessing at the extent of that injury or injuries."

"Very well, keep us informed." The president hesitated a moment. "Major, here is what we have done on our end. If our teams fail to contain the animal, I suspect we'll have a full-scale war on our hands that we can't keep from the American public. The Eighty-second Airborne is now on alert and already in transit for positioning in either Phoenix or El Paso in case the animal escapes containment. The Fourth Marine Expeditionary Force is on alert for possible action in Los Angeles and the bulk of Southern California. Fort Hood has been alerted and elements of armor CAV are being loaded onto trains as we speak to block any possible movement north into Colorado. That's it, Major, I'm afraid, as the general said, we are spread thin. So try and come up with a plan that will utilize those men we can get to that valley, and for God's sake, contain whatever this thing is." The view of the president and the Situation Room blacked out.

On the other side of the split screen, Niles looked grave.

"How is the senator?" Jack asked Niles as he tossed his Kevlar helmet to Everett, who had stepped out of the mess tent.

"Alice is with him at the center's clinic. He's due to be transferred upstairs to the Nellis base hospital in a while."

"Not good then?" Jack asked.

"No, I'm afraid not."

"Niles, we need to speed things up. Besides the special material I've requested from the private sector"—Jack looked at his notes again—"Dr. Gilliam here at the site has asked for a connection to be made to Helicos BioSciences in Cambridge. They have a high-speed DNA sequencer they've been working on that just may fit the bill here to get a firm grasp on this animal. She says our portable stuff is prehistoric when compared to what Helicos has in the works."

"I'll get on it right away."

Niles saw Josh Crollmier approach Jack from the side and tug on his sleeve, pulling him away from the camera. Compton looked at Alice in confusion as the voices off camera were muffled. But he was pretty sure it was Crollmier, speaking rather adamantly. He could also hear other members of the ground team shouting and carrying on. Suddenly an ashen-faced Collins stepped back into camera view. He ran a hand through his hair again and looked into the lens.

"What now, Jack?" Niles asked.

Jack once again focused on the camera. Others around the site stopped and watched him, eavesdropping for any information they could get. Collins reached out and snatched something from Crollmier and held it up. It was a piece of wreckage.

"The doc here says we have a problem. He says we don't

have the wreckage of one saucer here, we have two. Ryan's Phoenix missile must have caused the attacking craft catastrophic damage, enough to bring it down right next to the other ship."

Niles sat hard on the edge of the conference table.

TWENTY-SIX

Julie placed the plate of scrambled eggs in front of Billy as he pulled the napkin from the bar and placed it on his lap. He looked at the eggs and bacon without much enthusiasm as he yawned.

"Man, that sure smells good."

Billy turned and saw two men standing there. Juan and Carmella Lopez, his mother's cleaning people, were still in the midst of vacuuming and washing the last of Saturday night's dirty dishes. They went stock-still, looking at the two newcomers. One was a small, dark-haired man and the other a big black fellow who stood ramrod straight and smiling. They were dressed totally in black, weapons holstered across their chests and black helmets under their arms.

"Can I help you?" Julie asked suspiciously as she placed a knife and fork in front of her son.

"Well, ma'am, you can if you can serve us what that young gentleman is having," the smaller of the two said as he removed a pair of black gloves.

Julie gave the two men the once-over. They were dirty and, of all things, wore black nylon jumpsuits. Her eyes traveled to the black boots and bloused pants. As she watched, the small man unsnapped his body armor from his chest.

"This is Sunday, we're closed until noon, I'm sorry."

The small man looked around and saw the two cleaning people, then smiled and winked at them. "Yes, ma'am, that's exactly what the sign said in the window. But the sergeant and I would forever be in your debt if you could give us something that's not freeze-dried and full of sand."

"Marines?" she asked, noticing the word *freeze-dried* and the outfits.

"Not on your life, ma'am," the taller, black man said, not smiling a bit.

"Special Operations Group, Mrs. . . . ?" the smaller of the two started to ask.

She watched the two men for a moment, seeing the dirty faces around clean spots where goggles had previously been. She knew they had come in from the desert, because her son always had the same dirty face after riding around in the scrub.

"You don't look too special to me, and it's Ms."

The man stepped to the bar and looked at the boy, then down at his plate of food. "Hi, there, my name's Ryan," he said as he looked from the boy to his mother. "Well, my mama said I was special," he said in answer to her statement. "What's your name, little man?"

"B . . . B . . . Billy," he stuttered.

"This is my son, and I would appreciate you talking with me and not him," Julie said.

Ryan flinched. He was not used to having a woman come down on him that quickly, at least until they knew him a little better.

"Sorry, ma'am, didn't mean any harm." He brought his right hand up and lightly touched his chest. "I'm Lieutenant Jason Ryan, United States Navy." Then he stuck his hand out to the woman. "The prideful army-type fella behind me is Staff Sergeant Mendenhall."

Julie looked at the outstretched hand, then wiped her hands on the apron tied around her waist, then took the lieutenant's hand in her own and nodded over Ryan's shoulder at Mendenhall.

"Looks like no navy uniform I've ever seen, and I apologize, we're kind of on edge around here," she said, arching her left eyebrow.

Ryan looked down at his dusty black nylon jumpsuit, then the holstered nine-millimeter pistol. "Oh, this old thing." He looked up and met her green eyes. "Doing some fieldwork out there." He gestured out the window and into the desert beyond. "We're the good guys, really."

"What'll you have?" Julie asked in defeat.

"You mean you're open?"

"No, we're still closed, but I can make you something because the grill's still hot. Does your quiet friend want something?" she asked, going through the batwing doors that separated the kitchen from the bar.

"Yes, ma'am, eggs over easy and sausage would be fine, and some coffee if you have it," Mendenhall answered.

Ryan set his helmet on the long mahogany bar and pulled up a stool next to the boy. He heard and felt Mendenhall do the same to his left. Jason nodded at the boy. "Going to be some loud noises here in about ten minutes," Ryan said quietly, and winked.

Billy paused with a forkful of scrambled eggs halfway to his mouth and looked at the man in the funny suit. "Really?"

"Really. Going to be some very big planes setting down on Highway Eighty-eight right out there just about a half mile from town." Ryan looked at his filthy face in the mirror behind the bar.

As of one-half hour from now, the small town would be under quarantine. No one would be allowed in, and for the time being, no one would be going out until escorted out by armed security and placed in a safe hotel far, far away in Phoenix.

"All of this is for whatever's out there?" Billy asked, pointing toward the window with his now empty fork.

Ryan and Mendenhall exchanged looks, then Ryan smiled and looked down at the boy seated to his right.

"Out there?"

Billy took a drink of the milk his mother had given him. When he set the glass down, a nice white milk mustache covered the boy's upper lip.

"Yeah, whatever it is that's out *there*," he said, exasperated at the slow wit of the navy guy.

"You think something's out in the desert?" Jason asked.

Billy glanced at the batwing doors and heard his mother out in the kitchen making cooking noises. Then the boy just shrugged his shoulders and slid off the stool. "I have to go now," he said, grabbing an off-road helmet from the table behind him.

Ryan looked at the sergeant again, then back at the young boy. "Come on, you saw something out there?"

Billy placed the helmet on his head, squishing his ears against his head as he did so. "That's what I mean, mister, I haven't seen *anything*."

"What do you mean by that?" Mendenhall asked, leaning back on the barstool.

Billy stopped and turned. "Late yesterday I seen a whole bunch of rabbits and coyotes running away from the mountains, and since then I haven't seen anything, not even birds. It's like they were scared of something." The boy shrugged his shoulders, then walked out of the dining area.

"Hey, you stay close by because—"

But the boy wasn't listening. He was already through the door.

The two men were quiet as they watched the boy leave the bar and grill. Then they turned and Mendenhall shrugged.

Julie came through the door with two platters. She set them down in front of the two men and slapped napkins with silverware rolled up inside beside the two heaping plates. Then she wiped her hands and looked out of the large window in time to see Billy leave on his ATV.

"Damn, that looks good," Jason said.

"You didn't say how you wanted your eggs, so I just made them like I made the sergeant's," Julie said to Ryan, reaching for the coffeepot under the bar.

"Well, you guessed right," Jason replied, diving into his eggs and sausage.

As the two men ate their breakfast, Jason noticed a man

on the television set above the bar. He was holding a microphone to his silent lips, with a caption below it that read,
Capitol Building, Phoenix, Arizona.

"Ma'am, could you turn that up?" Ryan asked Julie.

Julie reached up and turned up the volume on the television set.

". . . said the disappearance of the two state troopers has
law enforcement agencies statewide on the alert. Now *Eyewitness News* has learned of a possible military deployment
to the mountains just northeast of the small town of Chato's
Crawl. What this means is anyone's guess, but there is a rumor starting from the halls of the capitol stating there may
be some sort of outbreak among cattle in the nearby area.
This is Ken Kashihara, Channel Seven, *Eyewitness News*, at
the capitol building in Phoenix. Back to the newsroom."

"Well, that's got to please everyone from the president on
down," Mendenhall said.

"Just what are you guys doing out there? You helping
look for those bikers and state troopers?" Julie asked, hands
on her hips.

Before Ryan or Mendenhall could think of what answer
to give her, a thunderous roar filled the interior of the bar.
Mirrors shook and glasses clinked and chimed as Juan and
Carmella, who had been dusting around the green-felt-
covered pool tables, turned and grabbed for Julie's antique
storm lamps. Then the two cleaning people crossed themselves and cowered in the far corner by the dance floor.

Ryan swallowed the last drop of coffee in his cup and
threw two twenty-dollar bills on the counter, then stood.

"Thank you, ma'am, it was delicious. Have to go to work
now," he shouted over the noise. "I'll stop back by if that's
alright with you, I like the way you cook." Ryan turned and
followed the sergeant out the front door.

Julie ran to the window and watched the two men climb
into a Humvee. The vehicle tore out of the parking area and
headed out of town. She shook her head in amazement at the
forwardness of Ryan, but pleased for some reason, she had
to smile as the noise that surrounded the small town contin-

ued to grow louder. Then she looked to the right and left and saw both patrons and owners alike empty out into the street eager to find out what was shaking their quiet world on this Sunday morning.

The ten U.S. Air Force personnel Ryan had left on the highway one mile out of town had been busy. They had placed blue and white strobe lights every ten feet on both sides of the highway, and they were now flashing brightly. They were similar to the ones seen at any airport. This part of the highway had been picked for its flatness as there were no large dips, and it looked as if it would bear up under the excessive weight that was to be placed upon it. As Ryan and Mendenhall pulled up, an army specialist from the Event Group staff ran forward and saluted. Ryan returned the salute as he scanned the sky overhead. The security man was wearing a regular army BDU so he would blend in and wouldn't be asked any questions about his real outfit.

"All ready?" Ryan asked.

"Yes, sir, so far no one has entered the landing zone. But we do have a report from a Kiowa scout ship of a state police car heading this way from a dirt road about three miles to the east," the specialist said. "And three news helicopters out of Phoenix coming in from the west. The Apaches won't be here to intercept, sir. They just left Fort Carson and Fort Hood two hours ago."

Suddenly the first giant C-130 Hercules filled the sky, rising over a small hill two hundred yards in front of them. The huge C-130 banked sharply, its left wing seemingly only feet from the top of the rise, and at that moment it suddenly straightened and brought its nose down. Jason had never witnessed an air force combat landing before. The plane was down to a hundred feet before the nose came up. The landing gear exploded downward out of its belly as the wings of the giant plane caught the air. It flared, bringing the nose up suddenly, and the wheels chirped loudly as the "Herky" bird came into contact with the hot macadam of the roadway. The noise increased as the pitch on the sixteen propeller blades was reversed and the flaps popped high on the wing, further braking the great aircraft and slowing it even more. The rear ramp was coming down just as the plane hit the ground, and the brakes screamed as it came to a stop.

Immediately troops of the 101st Airborne Division ran deliberately down the ramp carrying equipment and weapons. Ryan was approached by a man wearing a tan desert BDU. His helmet was the same Kevlar German-type Ryan himself had been wearing the night before.

"You Lieutenant Ryan?" the man yelled over the noise of the aircraft.

"Yes, sir." Ryan saluted.

"Lieutenant Colonel Sam Fielding, 101st Airborne advance recon unit," the man said, returning the salute. "I'll tell you right now, mister, I was only authorized ten percent of my manpower for this, and they claim security reasons. Now I expect someone to explain."

They both turned as the thirty-five men of the first unit moved away from the Hercules, followed by a Humvee that shot down the ramp, its fifty-caliber machine gun and TOW missile launcher strapped down for safety while in transport. The plane suddenly revved its four engines to a high-pitched whistling whine while the pilot applied the brakes. Then when the engines were at full power, he released the brakes and the Hercules started its turnout roll. It quickly came up to speed with an assist from eight rockets and was in the air in less than 150 feet, climbing steeply into the sky.

"Colonel Fielding, you can get your men settled just over there, sir. We don't know the full story yet, but my on-site commander is Major Collins, U.S. Army," Ryan said, holding his black helmet against the thrust of the departing Hercules.

"Jack? They have Jack Collins in on this?" the colonel asked.

"Yes, sir."

The man looked around and spit onto the roadway. "Take me to him, young lieutenant," Fielding said. "If Collins is here, then the *real shit's* here."

◆ ◆ ◆

The two state troopers were spent after their long night out at the Tahchako ranch counting slaughtered cattle and trying to find out what had killed them.

"Say, what's this?" Dills asked.

Two men appeared in the middle of the road, rifles slung on their shoulders. They wore black and had the same color baseball caps on their heads.

"I don't know, but I smell military," Wasser said from the driver's seat.

The two troopers reached down and unsnapped the straps holding their automatics in their holsters. They stopped a few feet in front of the two waving men.

Wasser opened the door and stepped from the car.

"What's this?" he asked loudly to the first soldier.

"Sir, we have an airplane about to utilize this roadway."

"The hell you say!" Wasser replied, not too gently. His sense of humor had left with the thousandth mangled cow part he had viewed the night before.

"Sir?" the soldier asked.

"We can't be havin' planes coming down on state highways, boy," Dills chimed in, puffing his chest out.

The two soldiers looked at each other, then hurriedly moved to the side of the road and knelt down holding their hats.

"Ain't you hearing me, boy? We're not allowing any planes to come down on this or any other highway in this state," Dills said, sunglasses reflecting the morning sun.

"Yes, sir, we heard," the first soldier said.

The two state troopers were suddenly knocked off-balance, and they grabbed the open doors of their cruiser to keep from being thrown face-first into the roadway. Their hats flew from their heads and they dove to the hot asphalt when the noise hit them full force. A windstorm blew sand and scrub brush against their bodies and rocked their cruiser as the giant C-130 touched down two hundred feet in front of them.

After the strangest night shift of his life, Trooper Dills had reached a point where any more input would just swirl around in his mind and not take hold anywhere.

"Jesus Christ, how can I put all this in a report?" Wasser yelled.

But Dills was already up and climbing into the police cruiser, mentally clocking out for the day.

The *News 7* chopper was speeding to the scene at Chato's Crawl. The word was out that the army, in conjunction with the State of Arizona, was quarantining the town and closing the airspace within a hundred miles. The race was on to get there before they could enforce it.

As reporter Ken Kashihara watched from the backseat of the newsroom's Kiowa helicopter, he saw below them the blue-and-white Channel 4 bird slightly ahead of them.

"Goddammit, Sydney, I thought you said we were the only ones up in the air. Look at that asshole," Kashihara said, pointing down. "That's that Janice Mitchell bitch from *News 4*. If I lose an exclusive to her one more time, it's your ass!"

As the pilot started to tell Kashihara to go screw himself, the helicopter was buffeted so hard he thought he'd lost the entire tail boom. He fought to maintain control of the Kiowa as a giant C-130's tail section screamed over them, and then they saw the Hercules turn for the roadway outside Chato's Crawl.

"Goddammit, you see that, you almost got us killed. And for what? Because you got an inferiority complex about that chick from Channel Four!" the pilot said loudly into his mike.

Kashihara was bone-white after the near collision with the Hercules. He looked at the pilot shakily. "Just get me to that town, *and watch the fucking road!*"

The cavern was from an ancient underground river that had dried up a thousand years before the creature's arrival. It was spacious, and here the beast had chosen to nest. Meat was stored all around the huge cavern, and the smell of blood was heavy as the beast made its way to the birthing chamber where she had collected water. Her distended belly was ripe with the offspring that were only moments away from taking in the food she had waiting for them. They would be born starving.

The beast roared as the first dilation of her exoskeleton began. The thick armor plate protecting the animal's reproductive organs split with a loud crack and widened with a sickening ripping noise reminiscent of tearing paper. The creature slammed its claws into the side of the rock-lined chamber and roared again. Her legs buckled at the knees and she squatted, bringing the dripping birthing orifice close to the water that lay beneath. Slime dripped from the opening, creating a natural lubricant for the young as they fought their way out. The beast screamed and slammed her massive claws again into the rock as the first of the new generation slowly slid out. The purple mass fell free of the mother and into the water below. The hardened eggshell of the baby sizzled as it began to expand. This egg was already cracked open and had the remains of one of the small animals sticking out of it, being eaten by the occupant of the egg. Another fell; again its shell hissed and cracked. The first baby, free of its shell, was already attacking the second egg as the mother reached down and slapped it away. It flew completely clear of the water and next to the gathered food. She would have to repeat this a hundred times in the next hour as she pushed the newborns toward the stored food.

The last of the offspring was the most difficult because of how large it was. By instinct the mother understood that if the creature wasn't expelled quickly, it would eat its way free, thus killing her. The single male left inside was the largest of the offspring and the last to be born. It would be killed by the mother to keep it from mating with other females in the hatching cycle because she carried enough eggs for millions upon millions of generations, and the male she had originally mated with had been enough to fertilize her eggs—she'd synthesized more sperm after her initial mating, copying the cells that were needed to reproduce. But if this male lived, it would kill everything in its path to protect this cycle of females until they too gave birth, to its offspring. It would kill her because she carried and copied another's sperm.

Even the small beings of which Gus's new friend was a part didn't understand the true nature of the horror that they had brought. The beast crushed her clawed hand into her abdomen and tried desperately to expel the male. The small creature was clawing and ripping at her insides until she finally reached into herself and grabbed it. She brought the struggling male up to view. Its shell had already been shed and it had started to form what would become its armor. Its neck armor was already intact and merely held to its neck by a mucous membrane that would soon dissolve. It snapped and hissed at the mother as she roared and tossed the creature hard into the wall of the cave, but failed to kill it.

The two-foot-long male struck the rough wall and immediately gained its feet. It snatched at a female and took it into its claws. It started devouring it even as the mother slapped at it, knocking it farther away into the darkness. Then she started screaming and throwing mutilated cattle toward it.

The male saw its parent in the darkness as it started in on the bloody meat. The yellow and greenish tinted eyes never left its current threat, the mother.

For the next few hours, as the animals grew and learned their abilities, the real Destroyer ate and grew faster, and it continued to stare with hatred at its parent, only shifting its gaze to the others if they came too near it. And coming near it was the last thing its siblings ever did. Soon they would gather around him and him alone, forsaking the parent that had brought them into this world. Then the work of devouring all life on this world would commence.

PART SIX
THE VALLEY OF THE SHADOW OF DEATH

Riders on the storm, into this house we're born, into this
world we're thrown . . .

—THE DOORS

TWENTY-SEVEN

After shaking hands and quickly catching up, Jack explained Fielding's mission. He took it well that he was here in an unofficial capacity of "advisement" only, and that he would have to take orders from a major. He didn't bat an eye as Jack led him to a table to sign an extensive secrecy and nondisclosure form.

Fielding looked at Jack and rubbed a hand over his bald head. "Just who in the hell are you working for, Jack?"

Collins held the colonel's gaze a moment; an unvoiced answer seemed to flow between the two officers.

"Why, the same man you work for," he finally said.

"Got it, don't ask."

Jack nodded.

Collins entered the tent with Colonel Sam Fielding close behind. The colonel had taken the rest of Jack's briefing without batting an eye, only commenting, "Should have fucking known the government was covering up at Roswell."

Sam's element of 101st would be split to secure the town for the quarantine cover story and Site One security. That would free up the Event Group personnel and the Delta/Ranger contingent for tunnel teams. Jack had all of the incoming troops sign secrecy and nondisclosure orders, basically assuring the government they would have to keep their mouths shut forever.

The two men put on surgical masks as they stepped through the makeshift autopsy area. They were met by a staff doctor and shown the way into the examination area of the spacious army tent. There were several of the strange metallic boxes found at the crash site. Teams were using small tools, brushes, and cotton swabs as they gathered minute samples from the containers. To the left was a paneled-off area with a large see-through window that showed teams inside working with other high-tech gear, but most were bent over microscopes.

"Hello, Jack," Denise Gilliam said as she walked up and removed her surgical gloves.

"Denise, this is Colonel Sam Fielding. He and I served together in the Gulf a million years ago. Colonel, Dr. Denise Gilliam, our chief forensics pathologist."

The colonel and the doctor shook hands.

"What have you got so far, Doc?" Collins asked.

Gilliam turned and took in the scene around them. "Well, we have collected the DNA samples of over three hundred different species of alien life in these twenty-seven containers," she said, then saw the look of confusion on their faces. "We believe the containers are like cargo bins, they get used over and over. We also know they were empty on this particular trip, as none of them have any recent bodily material inside of them. We have sent off slides and specimens by fighter jet to Helicos BioSciences in Cambridge. But as I was saying, the cages were empty."

"All of them?" the colonel asked.

She looked at Jack, who nodded his head for her to continue. "No, sir, we have one here that was occupied upon impact." She gestured to a large crate that was mangled and torn apart. "We were successful in collecting DNA of a species of creature that is not found on this planet." She placed a hand on the ripped-open section of the metal container. "We've found hair, or what we would consider hair. Actually it's more like a porcupine quill. We believe it's part of this particular animal's sensory input mechanics as the follicles on the ends have bits of nerve ending on them. Now we're running the samples again to be positive of the results, but what it looks like is that whatever was shipped in this container is anatomically different from any life-form we know of."

"How do you mean?" Jack asked.

Denise turned and walked over to the window and looked in on the other pathologists, who were busily working alongside the paleontologists. "Its atomic structure is out of whack," she said, looking away into the area her team was working. "It shouldn't be able to exist," she said with awe in her drifting voice.

"I don't follow," Fielding said.

"It means its body should sink right to the core of this planet, Colonel. Its structure is so dense it shouldn't be able to live on this world, or any others that our space probes have reached thus far."

"Can you expand on that?" Collins said.

"I'll try, gentlemen. Have you ever tossed a rock into a lake and watched it fall once in the water?"

They both gave a quick nod.

"Well, that's what this creature would be able to do here on this world. The ground would be like water is to you or me. It would literally be capable of swimming through our soil."

"You mean it can tunnel or dig?" asked the colonel.

Gilliam looked at him for a moment in thought. "The atomic structure of this animal is not like ours and everything around us. You see, every atom that makes us or even the ground we stand on, or the furniture you sit on, is always in motion to some degree. One atom spins around another, that spins around yet another, never connecting but giving the illusion of being a solid to the naked eye. This animal is made up of atoms that are attached to each other in groupings of eight and ten, no single atoms like us, thus its structure is far more solid than our own. So, no, not tunnel or dig, Colonel. It would be able to run or whatever it does in the ground a lot faster than we can walk or run in our own atmosphere. I just used water as an example for lack of a better example. In our air or aboveground if you will, it would be eight or maybe even as much as ten times faster than we are. Just conjecture at this point because it being here and living is still, at least according to our science and universe, an impossibility."

"That means it could be a threat to my men if it finds us first," Fielding said. Like any good commander he feared for the well-being of his men above all else.

"Okay, what about these others?" Jack asked hurriedly.

"Well, they're not too dissimilar from us. They definitely died due to impact trauma. Wounds on one were severe enough that he must have died instantly. The other looked almost as if it were asleep. There was old scarring on both of the subjects, as if they had led a harsh existence. Some here think they are fighting scars, as many of them look like they were made by claws, or nails if you will, while others were clearly teeth marks. These beings may be from a harsh or combative society, or they may be a subservient species of something else."

"Doc, right now let's make the priority this creature that treats alien steel like it was tissue paper," Jack said, touching the ripped-open areas of the cage. "I think we have to—"

Jack was interrupted by shouts and warnings outside.

The three people turned and listened as yelling filled the camp and crash area. They started for the tent flap but were met by Mendenhall, just returned from town with Colonel Fielding.

"Major, we have a visitor out here, and he asked to see the man in charge of the flying saucer crash; his words, sir."

"So much for securing the area before the cover story hit the news," Collins said.

They walked outside, removing their surgical masks. The sun was blazing and made their eyes water. They stood and watched as an old man was escorted by two armed security men to where they were standing. The man wore an old brown fedora and newer-looking jeans, battered brown cowboy boots, and looked as if he had just shaved. He had at least three pieces of toilet paper stuck to his cheeks and chin, stanching the flow of blood from the nicks that were obviously inflicted by a hurried job with a dull razor.

"This man just walked up the mountain, sir. Right to where we were hiding and said he wanted to speak with the man in charge," one of the men said. "We would have just sent him on his way, but he said he wanted to talk to the fella that was in charge of the saucer crash. It's like he knew we were there, sir."

Collins stepped up to the taller, much older man. He looked him over, then held out his hand. "I'm Major Jack Collins, U.S. Army, and you are . . . ?"

The man looked from Collins to the crash area around them and then at the huge tents that had been erected overnight.

"Gus Tilly. I prospect this part of the mountain." He didn't take the major's hand right away, instead eyeing the strange black Nomex uniform a moment. "Don't look like what I wore in Korea."

"U.S. Army, sir, that's what and who we are," Collins said, gesturing to the men and women around him. He was still holding his hand out, but with his other he reached over and pulled down a Velcro patch on his right shoulder and revealed a small American flag underneath.

The old man looked relieved, then took Jack's hand and shook quickly.

"Now, why do you think this is a flying saucer? We can't tell what it is."

The man turned and shaded his eyes against the sun. Then the old gray eyes fixed on Jack. "You're not gonna tell me it's a plane crash or some horseshit like that, because I'll call you a liar, sir."

"Whoa, take it easy there, Mr. Tilly. All we're saying is we're not sure what it is. Now, why do *you* think it's a flying saucer?" Jack asked.

"Because, youngster, I have the guy . . . er, uh, pilot or whatever it is that flew the goddamn spaceship thing here,"

Gus said, looking from Collins to Colonel Fielding. "And I'll add one more thing, fellas. You better listen to what he has to say, because we have a whole lot of trouble on our hands."

The rocky valley had turned into an armed camp above and a civilian holding pen on the highways below. News crews from as far away as Los Angeles had picked up the rumors of the mutilated cattle and the two missing state policemen, and now even a story that maybe a rogue motorcycle gang had been responsible.

The element of the 101st herded them together one news crew at a time as they came into the small town of Chato's Crawl, ignoring the shouts and curses that they had rights. As soon as the army had shown up and corralled his news crew, Ken Kashihara knew this wasn't about a rogue biker gang. He was worried because three full busloads of reporters and conspiracy nuts had already been moved out of town. He didn't believe for a second the cattle-disease story; his gut was telling him something else was going on and it was big.

Ken grabbed his cameraman and walked to the rear of the roped-off area. He at least wanted to be one of the last reporters removed from the area.

Event Group Complex
1015 Hours

Sarah went through the logistics line collecting her field gear. She had collected a set of ambient-light (night-vision) goggles, web belt, and canteen, a portable VDF, which she had trained on extensively for use in locating underground rivers, and a black set of Nomex BDUs. Then she was surprised by receiving a weapon that she had only fired once in her time here; it was still experimental, she thought. The Event Group quartermaster handed her an XM8, the newest assault rifle developed for the U.S. Army. It came with an SMG/PDW package. That meant it was configured with butt plate slid in and had a short barrel, excellent for Sarah's line of work, in tunnels or other tight spaces. The quartermaster issued her three hundred rounds of 5.56 mm armor-piercing ammunition in thirty-round magazines.

"Jesus, where in the hell are we going to deserve these kind of weapons?" asked Steve Hanson.

"The weapons are courtesy of Major Collins. I don't know how he did it, but he pulled some strings and we got a hundred of these just an hour ago."

Sarah accepted her weapon and signed for it. She couldn't help but wonder where they were going and just what in the hell was out there that they needed these.

"Sarge—"

"Before you ask, you'll be briefed on-site, young lady. Now get to the transport level," the gruff quartermaster ordered.

"Well, you wanted your field mission, Sarah, I hope you're happy," Steve said as they gathered their gear.

"Yeah, and now I'm a little worried," she said as she raced him down to the cargo elevators to be one of the first on the helicopter.

Military Airlift Command, Flight 241 Bravo, over Taos, New Mexico
July 9, 1025 Hours

The four jet engines of the giant C-5A Galaxy whined a sleep-inducing lullaby for the one hundred soldiers in her cavernous belly. They sat in canvas seating strapped along the side and center of the aircraft, instead of the more comfortable airline seats on regular military charters.

Thirty of the U.S. Army's elite and highly secret Delta unit, sometimes known as Blue-light, watched the more boisterous elements of the seventy-man team derived from both Companies B and C of the Third U.S. Ranger Battalion (Enforced) as they talked about home and girls. The Delta

teams checked their weapons and conversed in soft whispers. They removed their black helmets and readjusted their
chin straps before placing them back on their heads. Before
leaving Fort Bragg, where they had been training for the last
few months with these very Rangers for a mission in Africa,
a mission that had suddenly been scrubbed, they had been
issued small oxygen cylinders and new night-vision goggles.
They also received the new multi-use vibration-direction
finders, or VDFs, the kind geologists used to detect minute
tremors and anomalies and the direction they came from.

"What the hell is up with these things?" a young Ranger
PFC asked.

"Who the hell knows? Maybe they're lowering us into
volcanoes now," his sergeant whispered, as he checked the
loads in a magazine of 5.56-millimeter rounds.

"Did you hear the latest?" the PFC shouted over the engine whine, succeeding in getting the attention of the rest of
the Deltas and Rangers. "I heard that we're going after
something in a desert somewhere."

"What? Here in the States?"

"That's what I heard, probably some more training for
Libya or something."

"Well," the sergeant said, patting the stock of the special-
order Barrett fifty-caliber rifle, "whatever it is, I hope it
doesn't like breathing."

Chato's Crawl, Arizona
1120 Hours

Farbeaux watched his men and was pleased with the way
they were preparing. All former French Army commandos, they had experience ranging from assaults in Africa
to clandestine actions in South America.

They were arranged around the hydraulic lift in Phil's
Texaco. The station was closed, and Phil, Farbeaux guessed,
was out with the rest of the town's people, wondering what
was happening. Farbeaux had indeed lucked out when the

tracer he had placed on Mendenhall's hand had led him straight here. He and his men had dodged a search team twice as they searched the town for stragglers that they could hustle off to that bar and grill and detain. He and his men had come inside one of the now quarantined helicopters shortly after the arrival of the first American C-130 this morning.

Farbeaux was dressed casually and was waiting for his phone to ring, which he knew it would, and this time he decided he would answer. He only had to wait another minute. He looked down at the incoming number, then placed the cell phone in the portable scrambler.

"Legion" was all he said.

"May I be so bold as to ask what it is you are doing?"

This was the man the Frenchman was hoping for, Hendrix himself.

"You fool, if you go in without Centaurus expertise to back you up, you and whatever idiots you have following you will be chewed to pieces. You have eliminated two of my teams, that I can forgive, but if you fail to satisfy me in this matter, there won't a safe place where I can't get to you. Now fulfill your contract to Centaurus!"

"I wouldn't have lived long enough to say thank you for the bullet you placed in my brain. I will collect what I can of the technology and—"

"You dumb son of a bitch, is it technology you think we are after? We have all that we need." Hendrix laughed. "The thing that may be out there is far more than even you have bargained for. Even if you live through this without getting mauled, I will burn everything in your private collection right in front of you, and then I will personally put that bullet in your brain, do you unders—"

Farbeaux pushed the button on the scrambler and ended the call.

No, my friend, you won't be doing that. And please, "mauled"? Besides, I have learned enough about you and your little basement secrets that it should make interesting reading to a certain senator, he thought to himself as he picked up a handheld electronic computer and started writing his "get-out-of-jail-free card."

Eight Miles South of Chato's Crawl, Arizona
July 9, 1300 Hours

Billy turned the ATV off and coasted the final ten feet. The four-wheeler had enough forward momentum to roll through the scruffy yard to barely bump the rotting slats of the wooden front porch before coming to a full stop. The boy removed his helmet and looked around. The chicken coop was full of chickens, but unlike on Billy's previous visits they were all huddled together in one corner of the pen with a large Rhode Island Red rooster walking guard in front of them. He then looked at Buck's stall and noticed the mule was gone, and that meant Gus was still up in the mountains.

He was just about to put his helmet back on when he saw out of the corner of his eye a flash of movement at the kitchen window. He swallowed and wondered who, or *what*, was watching him. The boy knew without a doubt eyes were on him because the hairs on the back of his neck were standing on end. Gus once told him that usually meant danger to a man attuned to the desert. Billy tried to slide the helmet on, but it seemed his arms wouldn't work anymore. He turned slowly and looked at the window. It was empty.

He shook his head, still trying to build up the bravery he needed to get out of there. It was for reasons like this his mom never let him watch those old horror movies she sat up late watching on television. She told him kids of today didn't have the patience to be frightened as she had been when she was young. Billy had thought that was just about the dumbest statement he had ever heard. He shook his head, unable to believe he was actually as afraid as he was, so he guessed he had learned patience.

Instead of placing the helmet on his head, he took a deep breath and forced himself to calm down. He wouldn't let the fear of something that wasn't there scare him. What would Gus think? He sure wouldn't think Billy was ready to accompany him to the mountains to prospect, that was for sure.

Billy placed the helmet on his handlebars and looked at the house. It looked normal.

"Hey!" he shouted bravely at the house.

His eyes roamed over the front windows quickly, looking for any signs of movement. He took another breath. He didn't see motion but he felt he was still being watched. Then a horrible thought struck him: What if Gus was hurt? Maybe Buck was still in the desert, but Gus had come back and had a stroke or something?

That helped him find his bravado. He jumped from the ATV and ran to the porch, and that was when he saw through the old screen door that the front door had recently been repaired. Nails were crudely pointing this way and that, and a few were even bent over. Billy stopped and examined the situation again.

"Hey, I know you're in there!"

Still nothing. He took one step and then another. He placed one foot on the first step and then evened it out with the other foot. He swallowed and watched the door, and then he suddenly looked to the window that sat above Gus's old cot in the corner. Did that window shade move? He started to back away, then thought about Gus again. He took the next step, and then he was at the front door. He placed his hand on the screen door and easily pulled it open, flinching every time the spring made that popping noise. Then he placed his shaking hand on the glass doorknob and closed his eyes. He turned the doorknob, but stopped and thought, what kind of an idiot was he? He had put one over on his mom on occasion and seen too many movies where a door had been the only thing separating a stupid kid from the horrors of a slasher that waited just the other side of that door. Then he looked down and saw that the wooden door's center panel hadn't been nailed down all the way and one corner was sticking out.

Billy swallowed and backed away a step and examined

the repair job. Yeah, it was Gus's work alright. Bob Vila he wasn't. With one hand holding the screen door open he leaned over and peered through the crack. All he saw was darkness. He knew then that he was being silly, but still wasn't in a hurry to throw open the door. He looked behind him to make sure nothing was sneaking up there, then went to one knee and looked again. This time the space seemed even darker. So Billy leaned closer—and saw the huge black eye blink. Billy stood straight up and the screen door slammed him in the ass, knocking him against the door. He stood motionless as he heard something move on the other side of the door.

Suddenly the windows started shaking and the door was rattling in its frame. The screen was flapping like a bird's wing, and that made him move, almost tearing the screen door off its old hinges when it slammed back on him. He stumbled and fell backward, rolling down the steps of the porch, and then a hurricane of wind and dirt and dead grass started pummeling him. The noise came from the back of Gus's house, hesitated there, then started forward, seemingly coming from over the roof. Billy screamed, but no sound came out of his mouth as the world became a swirling storm of desert sand and wind. Finally one of Gus's front widows shattered and glass flew everywhere. Then a shadow fell over the porch and front yard as the horrible noise and vibration not only continued but increased twentyfold. Suddenly he felt the evil was out here and not in the house, so he quickly gained his feet, but it was like one of his horrible dreams where you try to run but your shoes are sticking in syrup or something equally thick and sticky. He finally pulled the screen door open, and it flew back with a crash as it hit the house and the spring snapped. Then to his horror the screen door went flying away off the porch.

"Oh God, oh God, oh God," he cried as he turned the doorknob and opened the front door and ran in.

He was halfway through the kitchen when he saw Gus's

back door crash in and a large, dark forbidding shape crouch and then stand motionless. His mouth widened to scream, but again nothing came out. And then to top off his day, he saw something rise up off the floor and go screaming away from the menacing dark figure. It was small and wearing a white shirt that caught the wind from the open front door and flew back like a cape.

Billy finally managed a loud and convincing scream as a small green creature ran right for him with the taller black thing in the shadows starting forward into the house. Billy immediately turned with both pursuers screaming after him. The smaller of the two hit his back and they both crashed onto the porch and right into the arms of another figure that towered over him. Billy screamed and then Matchstick screamed as they both fell onto the porch after bouncing off the thing standing before them.

"Hey, hey, easy," the tall figure said as it removed its black face and head.

"Ahhhh!" Billy screamed again.

"Ahhhhhh!" Matchstick screamed behind him.

Billy turned back toward the scream and his eyes widened when he saw what was there. Matchstick's eyes went from Billy to the taller figure and then back to Billy, and they both cried out simultaneously.

"Hey," a voice called among the wind and debris. "Billy, Matchstick?"

Billy stopped screaming and looked up and finally saw the first sane thing he had seen since arriving. Gus was running from a settling black helicopter, then Billy looked up and saw a dark-haired man looking down and holding a helmet, tossing a black nylon mask into it. He smiled and pulled the boy up. Then he hesitantly reached for the thing behind him, but decided to hold off.

Sergeant Mendenhall called from the interior of the house, "All clear!"

"Clear here!" Jack called out, still staring at Billy and the small alien, then quickly stepping aside for Gus.

The old man reached Billy and picked him up off the porch, then Gus reached for Matchstick, who looked to be in shock and was shaking as heavily as Billy.

"I see you two have met," he said as he turned and winked at Collins.

The alien was nervously looking around and sitting upright on the bed. The visitors crowded into the small one-room house. Matchstick eyed each man in turn and listened as they talked, every once in a while tilting its head and then with shaking hands taking a sip of water from the glass Gus had given it.

"You feel better, Matchstick?" Gus asked.

Jack turned and looked at the old man. He met his eyes and gave him a small smile. "Matchstick, that's its name?"

"As close as I can get anyway. He can talk like us," Gus said, "but he's just being stubborn right now. But sometimes he does his talkin' through me; brain chatter's what I call it."

Jack walked over and joined Mendenhall, who had slid the dirty sheet away from the body of the Gray, which was still lying on the floor.

"One ugly son of a bitch, Major," Mendenhall volunteered.

Jack took in the malevolent features of the Gray compared to the soft features of the smaller Green. Like Gus, he didn't think he had an imagination capable of thinking this thing up. He thought the two races were as dissimilar in looks as they were in temperament.

"Not exactly something you would take home to meet Mom, is it, Sergeant?" Jack turned toward Gus. "Did this being have the same telepathic ability as your friend, Mr. Tilly?"

"I didn't exactly invite it in for drinks and mild conversation, so I couldn't tell you."

Collins turned and looked at the alien sitting with its back to the wall on the old bed. Its eyes narrowed and the small mouth set itself in a straight line. Then it finally looked at Gus, its features softening, then turned back to Collins.

"Destroyer, feeding?" came the buzz-filled voice. It was like hearing someone through a wet pillow using a voice synthesizer.

"Yes, it's feeding," Collins answered after a moment's hesitation caused by the strangeness of the visitor's voice.

Babies, babies, babies, babies. This time it closed its eyes and only spoke with Gus through its telepathy.

"Matchstick says it's laid little monsters, babies, it says," Gus interpreted for them, wincing at the pain. "He gives me headaches when he talks like that, nosebleeds too. Matchstick, talk like regular—" He caught himself. "Just use your voice."

"So it's definite, it has the ability to project thought," Jack said.

"You could say that," Gus answered.

"Matchstick, this is Colonel Sam Fielding of the United States Army," Collins said softly to the small being while raising his left eyebrow toward Gus, who in turn looked down, knowing he had been a little rough on the major.

The colonel stepped forward and gave the alien an awkward smile and almost saluted, having actually brought his hand halfway up, then, embarrassed, looked at the others in the room and lowered his right hand to his side.

Collins smiled. "I'm Major Jack Collins. Do you know your race has been here before?" Collins bent down and looked the alien over.

Mahjtic looked from one man to another, each human in turn, still confused. Then it looked at Gus and then to the boy, not saying anything.

"Over fifty years ago," Collins continued. "I believe you are going to tell us about a faction of your race, who look to take this planet from us?"

The alien suddenly looked just at the major.

"This part of your society has acted upon itself to end life on this planet with the thing you call the Destroyer, am I right so far?" Collins asked.

"Those that would make us crash . . . your world with

Destroyer, attack us." It closed its eyes in thought. "*Damage on . . . to our craft.*"

Collins nodded. "A being like you told a man a similar story a long time ago." Jack sat on the foot of the bed. "The being like you told him it might happen again. Why did they wait?"

They watched as the alien's eyes widened. It brought its large head down, then up. It understood now.

"*Talkhan, the Destroyer, hibernates. Have you animals here . . . sleep for long time frames?*" it asked, looking from face to face. Collins noticed it was shaking, perhaps afraid they would blame it for the danger they were in.

"Yes, we have animals that hibernate," Jack answered.

"*The Destroyer kind wake fifty year on its world. . . . We take Destroyer for use by Masters on other world, easy way to—*"

The men looked at the small being, waiting for it to finish, but it was looking at Billy.

"Matchstick, don't stop now, you go on and tell 'em," Gus said.

It swallowed and then looked away from Billy and out the kitchen window.

"*Is . . . is easy way . . . clean your world. Gray's use . . . animal to clean undeveloped planets of life for harvesting of . . . resources and . . . settlement. The Destroyer exterminate man and . . . all life on this . . . world,*" it said sadly, looking into the water glass. "*We take animal to other world, not this one. Gray attack us and bring here.*"

"Your kind is against this action?" Fielding asked.

Matchstick looked up with his large eyes and blinked. "*We teach and work machines . . . We are . . . worker? Is this your . . . word?*

"*My kind, we . . . we are afraid and . . . can do . . . not much,*" it said sadly, shaking its head. "*I want help . . .*" It pointed and then spread its fingers out at everyone in the small kitchen. It slowly rose from the bed and stood on unsteady feet and walked to the window. "*Too late, babies come. Not stop now, but baby have baby in twelve . . .*" It placed a finger to its mouth and thought. *"Baby have baby in twelve . . . hours. Then more baby."* It kept shaking its head. *"And more baby, more smarter baby, smarter baby more."* It looked to the floor, not able to look at the men.

"How many babies right now, Matchstick?" Jack asked.

"Numbers one hundred, little more, maybe one hundred twenty, depend food source? Yes, how plentiful food animal to feed on."

"How much food is there from three hundred head of cattle and some bikers?" Fielding asked out loud. "Pretty good welcome-to-earth banquet, I would say."

Jack walked to the window and placed a hand on the being's shoulder. "We need your help."

Matchstick looked up and held Jack's eyes.

"If Destroyer and baby killed, the Gray will not stop. This planet is theirs. We cannot help your kind much. We are teachers . . . doctors . . . servants. Soon the Gray will tire of easy fight and come here. That you will never stop."

"First we have to stop this animal. Can you come with us?" Jack asked.

Matchstick walked away and stood next to Billy, staring at him, blinking its eyes, then smiled at the boy and touched him on the shoulder. Then it looked at the black Kevlar helmet Mendenhall had placed on the kitchen table.

"Mahjtic and Billy, we will help you."

"Good, we'll leave right—"

"Want soldier helmet," it said, looking from Jack to the helmet on the table and then at Billy.

"Yeah, a helmet," Billy said, looking defiant.

"Tough negotiator," Fielding said.

"That's a high price, but, okay, you have a deal," Jack said in all the seriousness he could muster.

Mahjtic walked over to Gus and took his hand, then pointed at the picture on the small table by the bed of the young Gus in uniform.

"Gus, fight with Mahjtic, make young again," it said, still pointing at the old black-and-white picture.

"Looks like you've been drafted, Mr. Tilly," Jack said.

Gus Tilly looked at the picture and then at the others around the room. "S'pose it wouldn't do any good to call my congressman right about now, would it?"

All three soldiers shook their heads no.

TWENTY-EIGHT

Julie Dawes had been forced to enlist the aid of Tony, who was sober this afternoon because he had misplaced his truck again the night before and hadn't been able to get to the bar. Now he was up for waiting tables to deal with the army-induced rush of business. Juan and Carmella were in the back helping with the dishes. Julie also asked Hal Whikam, her weekend bartender and full-time bouncer, to run the kitchen while she took food orders.

Big Hal had a huge red beard and was wearing one of his many slogan-riddled T-shirts. His current shirt read KIRK OVER PICARD AND JANEWAY UNDER ME! It wasn't as funny as the one that had said IT'S GOD'S JOB TO FORGIVE OSAMA BIN LADEN, BUT IT'S A MARINE'S JOB TO MAKE THE INTRODUCTIONS. Hal barely fit his bulk into the shirt, he was so large. Not fat large, but hulk large. Julie counted on little trouble from the people who plied their trade at the Broken Cactus because the ex-marine kept anything from getting out of hand, and if it was going to get out of hand, today would be the day.

The army had started collecting all the field reporters, cameramen, and tourists, and thank God, most had already been bused out of town, but because the Broken Cactus had food and water, it naturally became *the* place in town for those remaining to be removed from the quarantine zone, waiting on the next round of transport.

Most of the remaining townspeople were sitting off in the twenty-two corner tables and booths in the café section, watching events unfold around them. They were amazed at the way all the field reporters were shouting into cell phones explaining to their producers the predicament they found themselves in. All the while cameramen were getting all the background footage they could, which of course entailed bright lights aimed in other reporters' faces. Then at exactly 1:45 in the afternoon, all cell phone service in the valley was interrupted. Jason Ryan, USN, had just finished placing the last inhibitor around the town that blocked any signal from leaving. So now all that was heard were the thirty or so reporters and crew simultaneously cursing their cell service for their loss of signal.

Ryan had come in twice since this morning and announced that they were under quarantine because of a serious outbreak of brucellosis in the valley. When pressed for answers, Ryan had coolly explained that Thomas Tahchako had lost most of his cattle already, and the disease could easily spread out of the valley and even into humans. Julie had watched through the hail of protests and questions as he calmly gave out copies of a prepared press release. Julie had also noticed him look her way and smile on his way back out. That smile had caused her to get the "schoolgirl" goose bumps that had lain dormant in her all these years. It had been a while since anyone had given her that kind of feeling.

Julie was harried, though grateful for the extra business, but it didn't belie that something was seriously wrong out in the desert. She couldn't wait for the final word for her to close down and head for the buses that were due to arrive anytime. She kept looking for Billy through the crush of strangers since it had been several hours since he had left the café. She only hoped he was somewhere in town.

"Hello," a man said loudly while half leaning over the bar with his feet on the barstool.

Julie looked his way and noticed the stranger smiling at

her. He was good-looking, probably in his late thirties or early forties. His hair was blond and combed straight back. The small, circular lenses of his glasses gave him that bookish look that was the fad these days. He wore simple Levi's and a blue denim work shirt.

"Hello," she answered back loudly, walking up and flipping open her order pad.

"Is it always this crazy around here?" he asked, smiling and gesturing to all the reporters.

Julie looked from him to a cameraman who was holding a Minicam just a foot from her face, the light atop it blinding her. The reporter she recognized as that irritating Kashihara guy from Phoenix. He was doing some background and was speaking into a microphone to kill time until they were let go, which Julie heard wasn't going to happen this side of Phoenix. Squinting her eyes from the glare, Julie deftly tossed one of the soaking bar rags over the lens of the Minicam.

"Hey, what gives?" the camera jock yelped.

"Lady, you just ruined a pretty good voice-over," Kashihara said loudly.

The stranger at the bar stepped in front of the newsman and said, "I guess it means the lady doesn't like being window dressing, and my boss wouldn't like seeing me in your shot either, I'm supposed to be working. Now go and play somewhere else." He gently turned the reporter around and gave him a gentle shove.

"Who the hell are you, her father?" Kashihara asked, but still moved along as he spoke with his trailing cameraman about going to the Ice Cream Parlor, where it was calmer.

"Thanks," Julie said, raising her voice a little to be heard over the noise of the crowded bar. She smiled at the newcomer. "Can I get you something?"

The man looked around the crowded room and then leaned closer, placing both hands on the bar, and said, "Water and a ham-and-cheese sandwich would be great."

"It'll have to be on white, out of wheat and rye."

"White is fine."

"One ham and cheese on white, Hal," she yelled as she pulled a glass from below the counter and poured her only sane customer that day some ice water. She set the glass in front of him and looked him in the eyes. "In answer to your question, no, never this crazy. Are you one of them?" she asked, nodding toward the reporters.

He held out his hand. "Henry Tomlinson, Department of the Interior."

Julie took the offered hand and shook. "Julie Dawes, owner of this madhouse. I take it you're a part of that quarantine thing the army claims is going on?"

The man lowered his glass after taking a long swallow of the cool water. His eyes focused on the body of the woman behind the counter, appraising her a moment as he deftly displayed nothing. "Let's just say I'm here to evaluate the situation. If you don't mind me asking, why say the army 'claims'?"

Julie wiped her hands on the dish towel and looked the man in the eyes. "I wasn't born yesterday. All those guys walking around in CDC coveralls, they're armed. Strange way of fighting a bug, isn't it?"

"I wouldn't know about that, only what my boss in Washington tells me. But I do know one thing for sure: someone could open up a used-helicopter dealership out there."

Julie smiled at his reference to all the news choppers sitting just inside town. Most of them had been forced to land by the lethal-looking army helicopters, which had *very nicely* told them to set down, *or else*.

The man watched as Julie made her way down the bar removing dishes and replenishing water glasses. Somewhere in the back, the jukebox started up, and an old Creedence Clearwater Revival song, "Hey Tonight," began to play, and it bounced its way through the crowd with some cheers and some boos.

He sat and took it all in as Julie returned and placed his ham and cheese in front of him and started writing his ticket.

"One ham and cheese on white, anything else?"

"No, this is it. Can you tell me where the army has set up?" he asked, then took a bite of his sandwich.

The question made Julie hesitate a moment as she wondered why this man didn't know where the army had their camp since he was from the government. But she decided it was probably innocent. "All I know is they're everywhere. But you may want to look for a Lieutenant Ryan. He seems to be in charge in town." Julie looked up into the man's eyes. "Do me a favor. If you see a little boy hanging out with him on a four-wheeler, tell him his mother needs him back home, would ya?" she asked, batting her lovely eyes.

"My pleasure, ma'am, and the name of the guy is Ryan, gotcha. By the way, how will I recognize the boy?"

"Easy, he's the only child in this madhouse."

The Talkhan watched as her young started their separate journeys to the surface. They had eagerly devoured all the nourishment she had stored for them, and still their added abilities demanded more for their burning metabolisms. They were again starving.

The activity felt and sensed from above was enough to set them on their instinctual path to the outside world.

The only offspring to lag behind the others was the male. It sat far away from the females and watched. The mother had approached it earlier in an attempt to wrest one of the smaller females from its clawed grasp, but it would have none of it. Already as large as her, it puffed out his purple neck armor and backed away a few steps, its horrible eyes never leaving her. The mother, sensing danger, moved off to tend to the females. The brooding male dove into the earth, its instincts taking over and driving it away from the others for survival. The females, their food exhausted, went separate ways, diving into the soil in all directions.

The mother watched as they went, then she too dove upward from the birthplace and into the soil. She would hunt separately.

The extinction of mankind was now beginning in earnest, and a new king was about to sit alone at the top of the food chain.

Ryan was trying to hold his rising temper in check with the state trooper as best he could. He felt for the man, but missing brother or not, he couldn't let him go back out into the desert. The other twenty state troopers that were also surrounding him all shouted their curses at the same time.

The forty members of the 101st Airborne who had been assigned to Ryan were spread throughout the town, but some were starting to make their way to the assembled crowd of policemen, as their shouts of protest were becoming a little more threatening.

"Look, we have men out there right now. We didn't try and hand you a bullshit cover story like the rest, and you saw yourself what this animal is capable of from the cattle you found. Do you want to run up against that with just a sidearm and riot guns?"

"We can take care of ourselves and don't need the fucking army to hold our hands, goddamm it!" Dills shouted back, and the other officers nodded in agreement and shouted epithets like *Damned straight*. "We're willing to go along with your bullshit cover-up about a disease, but you have to give us a break. Let us go back out there and do our jobs. We have missing men and my brother is one of them!" Dills shouted.

At that moment, Ryan felt someone tugging at his sleeve. He ignored the shouted curses of the state troopers and turned. At his side were a man and a woman. They were disheveled to say the least, as the older woman's hair was loose and going in every direction of the compass and still had a few curlers hanging on for dear life. The older man was pale and had small cuts on his face and neck and was sunburned.

"Yes?" Ryan said, looking at the two people as if they had fallen from the sky.

The state troopers settled for a moment and they too looked at the couple, who seemed to have just stepped off the elevator from hell.

The man cleared his throat and looked from Ryan to the staring state troopers. Dills and his partner had a vague memory of helping these people change a tire last night.

"I would like to report an . . . an . . . an accident," the man said haltingly.

The woman rolled her eyes. "Accident my ass, Harold," Grace Tracy declared a little too calmly. She looked from her husband to Ryan, staring at him, and without blinking said, "Our camper was hit by a monster in the desert and tipped over, and I want to know what you are going to do about it, young man?" Her eyes were wide, moving from Ryan to the state troopers.

Ryan and most of the troopers blinked under the woman's maniacal glare.

"Well, are you going to do something about it, huh . . . huh?"

Ryan was just going to ask her to give a report to one of the state cops when he heard yelling and screaming coming from the center of town. As he watched, people broke out running from the Broken Cactus in a steady stream. Someone even threw a chair out the big plate-glass window in the front, followed quickly by people jumping through the empty frame, some knocking others down in their frenzy to get out of the Broken Cactus. Ryan stared for just a moment at the strange spectacle before him. Then he shook himself and started running toward the center of town, quickly followed by his men, and then, drawing sidearms and yanking shotguns from their patrol cars, the state troopers came.

Harold and Grace Tracy decided they had dropped back into Chato's Crawl at a bad time. Only one thing ran through Harold's mind as they turned away from the horrible scene once again unfolding around them in the very place they had had lunch the previous day. He really regretted not having gone to Colorado to visit his sister-in-law.

• • •

Julie didn't realize the attacks had started until the floor exploded under her. The music had been playing loudly, but not loud enough to cover the ear-shattering crack of the flooring as it exploded upward into the milling crowd of reporters. Screams sent chills down Julie's spine as the crowd parted and she saw people being pulled down into the now missing floor of the diner.

Tomlinson reached over the bar and shoved Julie to the left as the part of planking she was standing on cracked and splintered. She screamed and moved quickly around the bar.

Suddenly, a dark, nightmarish form jumped from the hole behind the bar and roared, sending the featherlike armor plates lining its neck and head outward from its body. The crowd around the bar stared in shock and added their screams to that of the creature. The beast was about eight feet in height with shimmering thick, black hair that caught the light streaming in through the window. The claws were huge, and they came down and sank into the mahogany bar and snapped the three-inch-thick hardened wood as if it were made of balsa. The green eyes fixed on them, its mouth opened, and claw-tipped mandibles parted to show three rows of sharklike teeth. The ears were sharply pointed over a snout that was huge and curved off into the jawline with bunched muscles. The thick brow was covered in sharp points of protruding plate that highlighted its terrible eyes. The tail, its barbed stinger dripping venom, shot forward and missed Tomlinson by an inch as he fell back into Julie and they both tumbled to the floor.

"Run!" he shouted at Julie, who was busy pushing herself out from under his weight and scooting backward on her ass. She didn't need to be told by any stranger to get the hell out of there.

With lightning speed he pulled a hidden pistol from somewhere on his body and started firing at the beast, which had deftly jumped to the bar and was ready to spring. The huge head swayed left and right, surveying the area for threats; the armor plates around the neck were now relaxed and swayed with the movement like a large headdress. Out of ten bullets fired, one missed and five hit the thickest chest armor of the animal and ricocheted off. But then the next four of the Frenchman's shots found a weak spot in both its eyes. The nightmare roared again and swiped at its assailant, missing him by mere inches. Its momentum carried it over and off the bar and crashing to the floor. As it hit, two huge claws of another yet unseen animal burst through the wood and tile and grasped the dying beast and pulled it under with a sickening crunch.

Tomlinson quickly turned over and gained his feet, picking Julie up on the way out of the slaughterhouse.

"What in the hell was it?" Julie screamed.

He turned and pulled Julie close and yelled, "Just get the hell out of here. I have to find my men."

As he was shouting at the woman, the crowd started pouring out of the Broken Cactus, pushing the two apart and carrying Julie away outside.

In the kitchen another of the creatures burst through the flooring and black and white tile went flying. When he realized what was going on, Hal quickly grabbed the first weapon he could, a large, lethal cleaver, and he immediately went on the attack. As he moved forward, Tony stepped in his way with an armful of hamburger patties just retrieved from the freezer. Hal pushed a wide-eyed Tony into the large walk-in refrigerator and quickly swung it closed, saving Tony and making more room to fight.

The beast circled the big ex-marine. Saliva dripped from its mandibles as it clicked its huge claws together. The green eyes looked into those of the man who had the nerve to confront it and glared in all hunger. The tail was constantly swinging in quick arcs behind it, and once every few seconds its stinger would stab into the stainless steel countertop, sounding like a gunshot and leaving a clean hole dripping with a bluish green liquid. The feet were large and they too scratched the black-and-white-checkered floor with curving claws. The weight of the beast must have been tremendous, Hal saw, because every step it took cracked and separated the tile and broke wooden beams beneath its feet.

"Come on, fuckhead, you want some of this, come and get it! Come on, Charlie, get some."

The beast bent at the waist, roared, and charged the cook, head down.

"Oops, fucked up!" Hal screamed as he quickly side-stepped to the right, allowing the animal to barely graze him on its way past. He quickly brought the cleaver up and brought it down again with all the strength he could muster. The blade sank deeply into the shoulder of the refugee from a B movie.

The animal roared and turned, its momentum slinging the cleaver from its back. It sprang quickly onto Hal. The man punched with his fist as the animal sank its teeth into his shoulder. Hal screamed and started to gouge at the animal's right eye. The beast roared and jumped high into the air while still holding the big man and dove into the hole it had entered from. Hal was quick enough to grab a large, sword-like butcher knife from the counter as he fell into oblivion.

Kashihara couldn't believe what he was seeing from the Ice Cream Parlor. He had just arrived and was shooting a spot he might or might not use when he got back to Phoenix. The old woman, Gail Ketchum, was good color, slamming the army for driving off her business. That was when he heard the screaming coming from the place they had just left. *What kind of luck is this?* he thought as he and his cameraman ran to the front window.

"You getting this?" he asked.

"You bet."

Ken turned when he heard a noise behind him.

"Thanks, ma'am, we'll get back to you in a—"

That was as far as his words got. As he turned, there was the old woman, mouthing words that could never be voiced because she was being held in one clawed hand of something Kashihara knew had nothing to do with any brucellosis outbreak. The beast squeezed the old woman and stared right into Ken's eyes. He was watching the animal and at the same time reaching and slapping for his cameraman to turn around. As he did, the camera almost slipped from his hands, and he stared in terror at what was happening behind him.

The animal roared and raised the old woman higher, then wrapped her into its other claw, as if protecting its catch from the two terrified men.

Kashihara was holding on to his cameraman for all he was worth when out of the corner of his eye he saw men and women breaking for the helicopters outside.

"I think we have enough to go on!" he shouted as he broke for the front door, quickly followed by the cameraman, who was now dragging the Minicam by its strap.

"It better be enough because I quit!"

Ryan and the twenty troopers around him watched as soldiers and civilians alike were pulled into the ground, and their jaws went slack when the first animal made its appearance.

The beast turned as it sprang from the hole and landed ten feet in front of the shocked men. The tail was swinging as rapidly as a rattlesnake as the animal blinked in the bright sunlight. It then bent at the waist and jumped into the air. The gathered men watched in horror as it traveled at least 130 feet into the blue sky, coming down right in the middle of the troopers.

Screams filled the air as the beast started swiping at the men. Entrails spilled out of open wounds as the sharp claws grazed midsections. Pistol shots started almost as quickly, and as soon as the attack had started, it seemed to end as the animal dove back into the earth screaming and taking one of the state troopers with it.

"That's what got my brother!" Dills screamed.

Their attention was diverted as a helicopter with a big

blue 4 painted on its side started to lift off from a clearing just out of town. Two men and at least one woman were hanging on to the skids of the Bell Ranger.

The helicopter slowly rose and started a slow turn to the northwest, toward Phoenix. The Bell Ranger was two hundred feet up and it looked as if they would make it when suddenly the ground erupted in front of Ryan and the troopers. Three of the strange animals roared as they cleared the soil. It was as if they had been shot from cannon.

Ryan and the others almost lost their balance from the impact the animals had on the roadway. They watched in astonishment as the three creatures, dirt and sand trailing them like rocket exhaust, shot upward. One slammed the helicopter low and grabbed the right skid, pulling a well-dressed woman free and dropping her screaming toward the earth, while another crashed into the side window, punching through to the interior. The last of the three slammed into the whirling rotors. The impact shattered them like glass, sending pieces flying out over the town. The helicopter started to autorotate with the stubs of its rotors, but instead of its automatically circling and spinning as its designers intended, because it no longer had the full length of its rotors, it came down like a rock. It hit the center of Main Street and burst into flames with a loud whump. The state troopers and soldiers watched in horror as the animal that had crashed into the interior burst from the flaming helicopter in flames, a man screaming and also on fire held in its clutches. The beast roared in pain and shock, its strange armor smoldering as it ran for a hole and jumped into it, taking the screaming man with it.

Soldiers of the 101st Airborne were firing automatic weapons in isolated pockets all over the small town. Amid the shooting were the louder screams of the people as they tried to get away from the attack.

"Come on," Ryan yelled to the troopers. "We have to try and get these people away from here and set up some kind of defense."

"How in the fuck are we going to fight these things?" Dills screamed back.

Ryan looked around, then had a thought, a quick moment of clarity. "The roofs!" he screamed. "Get these people to the roofs of these buildings . . . now!"

The Blackhawk was in the air just two minutes after Ryan had made the frantic radio call. Other Blackhawks were coming in from the crash site bringing more troops onto the scene.

"What did the lieutenant say, Major?" asked Mendenhall, screaming over the roar of the helicopter.

"All hell's broken loose, they've sustained a lot of casualties, both civilian and military." Collins looked from the sergeant to Sam Fielding. "He said they've been overrun."

Mahjtic and Gus exchanged glances. The small alien sat next to Billy, who was looking out the side window.

"Your mama will be alright," Gus said, watching the boy.

Billy turned and looked at the old man, then at the Matchstick man. His eyes were all that were needed to express his feelings about what could be happening to his mother. The small alien closed its eyes, the vibes making clearly evident where responsibility lay for the nightmare around them.

As the helicopter approached town, it was joined by six more of the Blackhawks that had been sent from the 103rd Special Aviation Battalion out of Fort Hood, Texas. It made them feel a little easier knowing they were packed with airborne troops from the crash site, leaving the crash site with a skeleton security force, which Collins didn't like.

"Look at that!" Fielding said, pointing out the window.

Below was a sight that amazed them all. Ryan had managed to gather the remaining survivors and get them safely to the rooftops of the town's buildings. The townspeople, three or four surviving reporters, state troopers, and only a few soldiers were high on the large steel awning of the Texaco station, the remains of the hardware store, which sat at a crazy angle after most of it had collapsed into the ground, and even on the flat and false-fronted roof of the Broken

Cactus. More soldiers were on the flat roofs of the Ice Cream Parlor and Snake Farm. These were also firing into the trenches that surrounded all of the buildings.

"Jesus Christ, it looks like Custer's last stand!" Fielding yelled.

The firing had ceased, and the town lay quiet. The troops were now deployed around the buildings, but the activity of the animals had ceased. There had been no attacks for the last ten minutes. Still Collins had M60 machine guns placed on each of the buildings in case the animals returned.

"Report, Mr. Ryan," Collins said as he gained the roof of the Broken Cactus.

Ryan, looking dirty and bloody, stepped forward, holstering his nine millimeter as he did. He looked a lot older than he had this morning.

"We lost at least ten state troopers." He cleared his throat and looked around and lowered his voice. "Twenty-five or thirty of the airborne troops, we haven't had a chance to count yet, but I think I've only counted ten or so left." He looked at Fielding, who just clenched his teeth. "They fought like hell, Colonel, trying to get these people to safety. The state men also, they didn't die for nothing. God, Jack, maybe twenty or twenty-five civilians were taken in the first assault, mostly the remaining reporters, and . . . it's just a god-awful mess."

Fielding removed his sunglasses and harshly rubbed his eyes. He turned from the devastation of the town and slapped Ryan on the shoulder. "Isn't much like the navy, is it, son?"

Ryan lowered his eyes and shook his head.

Billy was standing behind Collins and shifted positions looking at the faces of the survivors, and that was when he saw his mother. She was treating one of the soldiers leaning against the building's waist-high false front.

"Mom!" he screamed, and ran into her arms.

Julie reacted immediately to her son's voice and gently laid the soldier's head against the wall and ran to her son.

"Oh, God, I was so worried about you, baby, are you alright?" she asked, crushing him into her chest.

Gus, who was carrying Mahjtic under a sheet he had removed from his cot, smiled. The small being mentally felt the relief flood through the old man.

"What about these animals?" Collins asked, unzipping the vest armor from his chest, letting in some needed air.

Ryan looked from his boss to Sam Fielding, then reached over and patted Billy on his head. He looked into Julie's eyes a moment, seeing the relief she was expressing because she had been near a panic during the operation to get everyone up top. Then he looked back at Collins.

"They're straight out of a fucking nightmare, Major. Fast, strong, and you're damn lucky the freakish bastards stopped their attack and went away, because these sons of bitches can jump. They took down one of the news choppers from almost two hundred feet." Ryan stepped closer and whispered to Collins and Fielding so Billy couldn't hear. "They're definitely eating the ones they take, Major, we all saw it."

The White House, Washington, D.C.
July 9, 1500 Hours

The hookup between Washington, Event Group Center, and Chato's Crawl had been hot for the last ten minutes. Niles was holding his own against the top military leaders of the country in defending the actions of the 101st and his ground teams.

"As I stated, Mr. President, there was nothing that could have been done to change the outcome of this first engagement. The animals hit us while the ground teams were still in the process of evaluating the situation." Niles paused for a moment. "The tunnel assault elements are being organized now."

The president turned to face the director of the CIA and air force general Max Hardesty, chairman of the Joint Chiefs.

"Okay, I'm sticking with Compton and his team as to rec-ommendations on how to fight these things. Now, and most importantly, Operation Orion will only be ordered as a last resort. Understand, gentlemen, no nukes unless you have my specific authorization."

All the directors of the national security staff nodded their compliance.

"Now, what does Major Collins need to"—the president held a finger up—"one, rescue all the civilians in that town?" He held up another finger. "Two, what equipment can we rush in there to help fight these damn things?" Then he held up a third finger. "And number three, what course, other than nuclear weapons, can we use to contain these things if they escape the valley?"

General Hardesty stood and went to a large back-projected map of the western United States.

"Mr. President, we have brought in elements of the Sev-enth Aviation Battalion from Fort Carson, Colorado. They just arrived on-site." Hardesty drew a line down from Col-orado to Arizona. The plasma in the screen reacted to his fin-ger, and a red line traveled the length of the map from Colorado to the Superstitions. "We will have ten Apache gunships on station in a little over an hour. They will provide cover for the four MH-53J Pave Low IIIs that have just ar-rived from MacDill in Florida. They will be used to airlift the civilians from the town. Collins and Sam have come up with a plan to lift them directly from the building rooftops. The Pave Low is basically a huge flying gun platform with large enough cargo facilities. We believe four will be enough to evacuate all collateral personnel out of the town."

"What about containment?" the president inquired.

"There we are committing a number of F-15 Strike Ea-gles and F-16 Fighting Falcons for use in ground assault. They will be loaded with type-N Bunker Busters and stan-dard cluster munitions that should give the burrowing bas-tards something to write home about. If we have to, we can ring the entire valley with bombs. We are scraping anything we can package, Mr. President, and will have more as soon as we can get them online. We are also airlifting a squadron of Paladin tanks for cover if and when the tunnel teams go in."

"What about the special troops Mr. Compton has asked for?"

"They just landed outside of the town and are being airlifted to the site by Blackhawk. The best we have, sir. Major Collins will have a strong element of Delta and Third Rangers to add to the Group's tunnel and mine teams."

The president turned and looked into the camera. "Mr. Compton, I know this is a lot to throw at you, but what have we learned from the crewman of that saucer?"

Niles pushed his glasses back up on his nose and looked into the camera.

"With maybe only two or three of the offspring killed or wounded, that leaves approximately ninety-plus healthy ones, not counting the adult, which hadn't been present at the attack that we know of. The surviving crewman assures us if we can kill all the young and then get to the mother in another"—he looked at the clock on the wall—"nine hours, we can avoid having to deal with another, even larger hatching cycle, as each surviving animal will give birth to another hundred young."

"And if even one of the offspring survives?" the director, CIA, asked.

"It starts all over again," Niles said.

The president looked from each of his highest advisers, then back into the camera. "Mr. Compton, you are to take complete control of the visitor, and Major Collins and your Group are still in charge of everything underneath the soil of that valley. Tell Major Collins to kill the bastards, Niles."

Chato's Crawl, Arizona
July 9, 1410 Hours

Julie watched as the giant MH-53J Pave Low IIIs of the Third Special Operations Squadron circled the town. She felt somewhat safer after she noticed the large ro-

tary cannons sweeping the desert below from the side doors
and rear ramps. Also crisscrossing the town were ten AH-
64D Apache Longbow attack helicopters with their lethal
load of sixteen Hellfire missiles, and seeing the chin-
mounted M230 thirty-millimeter chain guns moving and
covering the area around the buildings at least gave the survivors the illusion of safety. Above even them were hordes
of streaking fighter aircraft. Upon their arrival, the few surviving townspeople and news crews gave a loud cheer.

But Julie's mind was somewhere else. She looked at the
injured soldiers and civilians spread out over the rooftop of
her once quiet and out-of-the-way bar and grill, their awful
wounds being tended to by army medics, and bit her lower
lip as she made a fateful decision.

"Mom, what are you doing?" Billy asked, trying to
catch up with her retreating form. "Lieutenant Ryan said to
stay put."

She quickly walked to the small trapdoor that some of the
fleeing patrons had used to access the roof. She looked around
to see if anyone was watching, but they were still staring skyward as the giant twin-turbocharged helicopters started making their run for the rooftops.

"You stay here, I've got to find out if Hal and Tony are alright," she yelled over the rotor noise. "I just can't leave
without knowing."

"Mom, that's nuts. Ryan said he would be right back, and
that major guy will be seriously pissed," Billy pleaded, tugging at her shirt. "Let them check, Mom, they won't leave
anyone."

"They're our family, Billy. We have to be sure. I'm only
going in for a minute." Then she opened the trapdoor and
disappeared down the darkened staircase.

Billy looked around nervously and wished Gus were
here, but he and Matchstick had been lifted off with Ryan,
the colonel, and the major twenty minutes before. He was
guessing they were at the crash site. He bit his lip as he too
made a decision, then followed his mother.

TWENTY-NINE

Superstition Mountains, Arizona
July 9, 1440 Hours

You're going to what?" Lisa asked a little too loudly.

Sarah checked her pack one more time, then she looked around at the preparing Delta and Ranger teams as they checked their equipment. Only a few of them looked their way when Lisa raised her voice. Sarah looked at her friend and nodded toward the commandos sitting around them at tables. Then she withdrew the nine-millimeter automatic from the shoulder holster and chambered a round, checked the safety, then replaced it. She checked for the fifth time the small oxygen tank that was lying on the cot and saw the needle well into the green. Then she turned and faced her friend.

"I'm leading the main excursion into the first excavation made by the parent, right here at the crash site," she finally answered as nonchalantly as she could.

"That's nuts, sister of mine. Did you hear what those things are capable of? Did you see the wounds on some of those airborne guys?" Lisa looked around her and stepped closer to Sarah. "Does Major Terrific know about this?"

A few more of the Delta and one or two of the Rangers looked up at the two women, who stood toward the front of the huge tent. Lisa eyed them until they looked away.

Sarah held the night-vision goggles to her eyes and adjusted the width of the eyepieces. "Lisa, it's my job, and, yes, it's the major's plan. He chose me. The geology teams are split up among the other tunnel teams." She lowered the ambient-light device and looked at her taller friend. "Look, we have to find these things in less than nine hours, and if the air force is cut loose on them, we won't be able to piece together enough bodies to tell how many we bagged. It's not like I won't have company. Other members of the mine and geology teams, plus the zoology members, are leading groups into over fifty holes. Besides, since those Delta guys and Rangers arrived, our odds of surviving have gone up substantially."

Lisa walked over and closed the tent flap, cutting off some of the sunlight and noise from the helicopters coming and going.

"That's those *things'* turf down there, and now you're volunteering to go into those holes? Has the major lost his fucking mind?"

Sarah turned and looked at her roommate while inserting a thirty-round magazine into her XM8 light assault rifle. "Why aren't you that concerned about Carl or the commandos going down there? Why me?" she asked, looking her friend directly in her eyes.

Lisa didn't back down. "Because, goddamn you, they're macho schmucks with not one fucking ounce of brains, which I used to believe you had, but I guess not."

"It's my *fucking* job, Lisa," Sarah said in a harsh whisper. "What do I say on my first mission, 'Oh, can't do it . . . a little *too* dangerous'?"

Lisa lowered her head and bit her lip, cutting off more of her argument because she knew her friend was right.

"I'll be okay. If I have to, I'll toss a few of those Delta Force guys in front of me and run like hell, alright?" Sarah looked over and smiled at the few of the elite troops who were still watching them. They nodded.

Lisa smiled for the first time since her friend's arrival. "Just watch out for Carl, he thinks he's the hero type."

"I would, but he's not on my team. But he's with Jack,

that spunky little navy guy, and Will Mendenhall, so he'll come back, I promise," Sarah said, taking her friend's hand into her own. "I've got to go, Lisa. We have a briefing in five. Those things don't know it yet, but it's our turn to start hunting *them.*"

Chato's Crawl, Arizona
July 9, 1420 Hours

J ulie slowly stepped off the bottom rung of the ladder, afraid the noise of her tennis shoe coming into contact with the broken floor would be enough to bring one of those things up through the broken tile and grab her away. But all was quiet in the kitchen. She saw a hole that had been made during the attack and stared into the dark and forbidding pit and shivered. Blood lined the mouth of the hole, and she silently prayed it hadn't been Hal or Tony who had been pulled down to their death. As she moved forward, she heard the hiss and pop of the jukebox as the needle was stuck and kept hitting the stop and sliding back.

Overhead she heard the powerful turbines whining from the large helicopters settling just above the rooftops. Things in the kitchen began to rattle loudly as the down blast from the powerful five-bladed rotors hit the Broken Cactus. She jumped when one of the hanging frying pans fell from its hook over the stove and clanged to the floor. Then her heart fell to the floor as she was touched on the shoulder from behind. She gave out a yelp and quickly covered her mouth. Billy placed his small hand over his mother's and held up a finger to his lips.

"Shhh," he hissed. "Come on, Mom, what're you doing?" he whispered, removing his hand.

"Goddammit, Billy, get your ass back up those stairs, now," she half whispered, thanking God for the loudness of the turbine-driven engines of the Pave Lows.

"No way, not without you," Billy said, looking around for any sign of the animals that had so ravaged everyone in the town. He had yet to see one of them and didn't ever want to. He was putting up the best look of bravery and defiance he could muster; he just didn't feel either of those at the moment.

Julie pursed her lips, trying hard to hold her temper. Then she consciously counted out loud to ten, angrily forcing out each number as she did. She calmed a little and opened her eyes.

"Alright, it doesn't look like anyone's here anyway, so let's get back upstairs and the hell out of here."

They were just starting to turn when, over the rumbling sound of the settling Pave Lows, they heard the sound of voices. They weren't traveling down the stairwell from the rooftop, but were coming from the dining area just around the corner out of their vision. Julie raised an eyebrow.

"There must still be people in here," she whispered a tad nervously, as she knew that everyone was supposed to be on the roof.

She took Billy's right hand in her own and gently pulled him out of the kitchen and around the bar. They crept as quietly as they could, stepping lightly over fallen barstools and broken tables, and as they moved, the voices grew louder.

"Whoever they are, they don't speak English. It sounds like French, I think," Julie said in a whisper.

They finally reached the corner of the bar and looked around it. Julie quickly counted sixteen men. They all wore black suits like Ryan and the others who had come into the bar earlier, not the brown desert fatigues of the other soldiers of the 101st. These soldiers were different somehow from the black-clad men of Lieutenant Ryan's outfit. Their uniforms were a different make, and some of these men had beards. They looked, in Julie's unprofessional opinion, lethal.

As Julie started to pull Billy back, a hand fell on her shoulder. She couldn't help it; she hated being this scared and tried not to, but she screamed anyway.

"Hey, can I pay you later for this?" Tony's slurred voice asked loudly.

The men that had been sitting around loading weapons

suddenly stood, and the ones who had already been standing brought their weapons up and ran to a better angle inside the dining area and aimed at the intruders. A dozen pinpoints of laser-red light hit the intruders' chests and didn't waver an inch. All Julie could do was raise her hands to show she wasn't armed.

"I'm glad you're okay, Tony, but you couldn't have picked a worse time to wake up," Julie whispered out of the corner of her mouth, taking a deep breath.

"Miss Dawes, what a surprise. I was sure you had vacated the premises with the others," the blond-haired man from the Interior Department said, as he stepped away from his companions.

Gone were his casual clothes, and in their place was this military, black jumpsuit. He had a large pistol strapped to his side and the most lethal-looking knife Julie had ever seen on the black belt across his chest.

"Mr. . . . uh . . . ?" Julie stuttered.

The man just smiled and stepped up to the three intruders. He placed his hand on Billy's head and rubbed his hair. The smile, all three noticed, didn't touch his now cold eyes.

"We'll leave my name out of it for now, Miss Dawes. And this must be the man of the house. I'm glad you located him. Today isn't one to be roaming around outside."

"My son, Billy," Julie said, looking worried.

"As I said, Miss Dawes, you really should have left on the evacuation helicopters with the others. But as it stands, I'm afraid you'll be accompanying us. I am sorry."

"Okay, okay, what'd I miss?" Tony said, taking the cap off the bottle of Jack Daniel's.

The four F-15 Strike Eagles out of Nellis streaked through the blue sky at twelve hundred feet off the desert floor. Lieutenant Colonel Frank Jessup led the flight of air force jets, who were on temporary duty from Japan, here to take part in Red Flag, a rigorous course to train pilots to fight foreign aircraft and their tactics. And now they had been summoned on the most unusual CAP mission he had ever been in command of. He scanned the ground, watching for any kind of activity out of the norm. He was trying to figure out just what the norm should be when his wingman, Major Terry Miller, called over the radio:

"Drover lead, this is Drover Two, they said unusual activity, correct?"

Jessup thumbed the transmit button on his joystick. "That's what they said. What have you got, Drover Two?"

"Look to your nine o'clock and tell me what you see."

Colonel Jessup looked to his left and down, but his weapons officer in the backseat saw it first.

"What in the hell is that, Colonel?" he asked.

Jessup stared in wonder as the ground below rippled as if a small speedboat were traveling across the sand. Just behind the advancing wave, the ground was caving in as if whatever was causing the wake was traveling close to the surface, weakening the tunnel it was making and causing the ground to fall in just as it passed.

"All right, Drover flight, we have a target of opportunity as per orders. Our ROE are still the same." Jessup didn't have to remind his flight that the rules of engagement were simple: sight the enemy and attack. "Drover Three and Four, sight on target and attack" was Jessup's brief command. "Drover lead will ride high cover."

"Drover Three and Four, sighted and locked."

In all three locations, ears listened anxiously to the radio conversation between the air force pilots as they rolled in and dived on what must be the leading element of the animals as they were exploring the valley. The president's attention went from the live feed in the desert valley to the monitor hooked into the Event Center for a reaction from Niles Compton. But Niles was busy listening to the radio transmission and watching the live feed himself. Then the president looked at the Joint Chiefs in the room, then to another monitor showing the crash site, where the largest audience by far, made up of Event Group technicians, were gathering to hear the exchange between the attacking fighter bombers.

T he F-15E Strike Eagle is an amazing aircraft, capable of dogfighting with the best fighters in world, belying that it also has a bomb load capacity almost equal to that of the venerable old B-17 bomber from World War II. The bombs on this flight had been researched and specially chosen. If the animals were traveling close to the surface, the pilots were to use the general-munitions cluster bombs. They didn't have the shaped charge or the weight of the Bunker Busters that the F-16 Fighting Falcons were carrying above the larger fighters at ten thousand feet, but they were accurate, and they exploded with a large bang and killed well for their size. Before the human element went below to fight the creatures, the air force had been given the green light. Now they would see what air power could do to help right the situation in the valley.

The two fighter-bombers streaked in low, maintaining their height at three hundred feet, a dangerous altitude for the large fighter, even in the relatively flat terrain of the desert. Then, at three miles out, the fighter-bombers nosed up and climbed, water vapor pouring off their wingtips as the Eagles fought for altitude. At a thousand feet they leveled off, and Colonel Jessup watched as both Drover Three and Four dropped their munitions wing abreast. This tactic would expand the area of impact and make their killing zone wider, rather than longer, for the best chance of taking out the lead elements of the animals. The colonel watched as four small wing-brakes popped out from the back of the eight six-foot-long bombs, retarding their speed and rate of drop to give the fighters time to get out of Dodge before they impacted. At 175 feet of altitude, a pressure-sensing device activated and blew the outer casing off the eight bombs, loosing two hundred softball-sized bomblets. They struck the ground just two feet in front of the wave of dirt and sand that was caused by at least two of the moving animals, causing what looked like a fireworks display gone awry and exploding on the ground. To the men and women at the crash site it was if someone had set off two hundred grenades at once.

"Direct hit," Jessup said in a businesslike manner into his oxygen mask.

As Drover Three and Four banked hard to come around for an assessment pass, they didn't see another two waves approaching the first set until they were almost on top of the strike zone. Jessup saw the twin waves breaking fast from above his pilots, who were too busy to notice the approach. In horror, he watched an animal they thought had been stopped in the cluster munitions strike rise from the dirt and sand and shake itself.

"Drover Three and Four, pull up, abort pass! Bandits are approaching the strike area, and the active target is now aboveground!"

The call came three seconds too late. As the colonel watched in horror, two of the animals approaching the first exploded out of the sand and dirt of the desert. Bunching up their muscled legs and using their powerful tails as a natural catapult, they sprang into the air at incredible speed. The first one caught Drover Three in the left air intake, smashing into the fuselage and being sucked in, exploding through the Pratt & Whitney engine, causing a catastrophic failure and explosions that ripped through the cockpit and fuselage of the heavy fighter, tearing it apart. The second animal ricocheted harmlessly off the remains of the disintegrating jet, falling onto the desert floor, along with the mile-long stretch of settling wreckage of Drover Three. To the amazement of all watching, the animal rose and stumbled, fell to the ground, then rose again. This time it shook its massive bulk, jumped into the air, and dove into the desert soil. Drover Four banked hard and climbed, pushing the big fighter to afterburner in its attempted escape, taxing the huge jet's airframe as it did so. The first beast was on the surface of the desert floor below and was watching the F-15 Eagle trying to make her escape. The beast timed its jump perfectly and leaped just as Drover Four went to afterburner and started climbing. But before the full effect of the powerful twin engines could provide enough thrust to propel the heavy fighter forward and up, the animal struck hard. It hit the Strike Eagle's left wing and punctured straight through it, tearing out control surfaces and bending and weakening the struts until the wing creased and folded inward toward the cockpit with a pop that sounded as if a bomb had exploded. The wing then slammed hard into the glass-enclosed canopy, crushing the life from the two men inside instantaneously, seconds before the aircraft slammed into the desert floor and disappeared in an expanding fireball. The Talkhan that had embedded itself in the fighter's wing rolled free of the wreckage. It was burning as it gained its feet, stumbled three steps, then collapsed dead to the sand.

"Jesus Christ!" Jessup yelled into his mask. "Drover Three and Four are down. Repeat, Drover Three and Four are down, no chutes. Drover lead is on the attack."

Jessup banked hard to the left, bringing the fighter to a nose-down attitude. His wingman mimicked the move as he followed. The colonel brought his cannon to bear on the still form of the animal that had downed Drover Four. The cannon embedded in the left side of the aircraft just aft of the radar dome in the nose erupted with all six barrels with a short *bruuuuuup*. Rounds from the powerful minigun struck the remains of the invader, tossing pieces in all directions and further disintegrating the wreckage of the downed Drover Four, pushing the carcass hard across the desert floor.

Jessup applied power and pulled back on his stick, bringing his fighter back up to a safer level, then he called, "Drover flight, climb to five thousand feet and hold for targets."

Lieutenant Colonel Jessup removed his oxygen mask as he made the fast climb to altitude and rubbed a gloved hand across his sweating mouth. In all the missions he had flown in deserts just like the one below him, in all the time he had spent in, over, and around the battlefields of Iraq and Afghanistan, he had never lost anyone, not even an aircraft, with all his aircrews coming home safely. Now four men lay crumpled and dead in their aircraft on American soil. Dead because someone on the ground had underestimated the ability of the enemy they were facing. Jessup had become like most commanders in the opening phases of war. He took it for granted that he had superior firepower and numbers, the same mistakes that had been made by men of his nation since the times of Washington, Lincoln, Custer, and Westmoreland.

Once he made it to a safe altitude, he thumbed his transmit switch and raised his mask to his face. "Drover base, Drover base, this is Drover lead. Inform National Command Authority, the enemy is a viable air threat."

Superstition Mountains, Arizona
July 9, 1425 Hours

Billowing clouds of black smoke that marked the remains of the two downed air force fighters and crews could still be seen from their high vantage point above the mountain valley. They had all listened and watched in horror as the aircraft and four brave men were lost, and that made for the grim determination they felt as they gathered in the large command tent.

Collins watched Specialist Sarah McIntire as she spoke with a member of Delta, obviously a part of her tunnel team. He waited until she looked up and made eye contact with him. He had been tempted to place her on his team, which had been assigned one of the town holes, but they needed one of the tunnel experts to go in after the mother, and Sarah was it. Since she was the most experienced in tunnels, she would be making a few points about the geology of the valley during the briefing.

"Alright people, let's settle in and get started, we're damn near out of time," Colonel Fielding said, standing at the head of the one hundred men and women of the tunnel assault teams.

Behind Fielding was a three-dimensional computer blowup

of the surrounding mountain and desert floor. Marks in a dozen places indicated the routes the squad-sized tunnel teams would take. Larger dots indicated a parental hole and the smaller ones the offspring.

"Before we start out, we wanted you to hear what we're up against here. It's nothing you have trained for, but your units have been chosen for your ability to adapt to a fluid situation. And make no mistake, people, your enemy is ruthless and cunning, as we just witnessed in the valley."

The absolute quiet of the gathered soldiers told the colonel they understood.

"Very well." He turned and looked at Collins. "Major Collins, if you would, please."

Collins stood and stepped forward. "Here's what we know. They are diggers, as you've heard. Our soil is absolutely nothing to them because their body is so much denser than our own. They can be killed, even though they're heavily armored. Hit it where it is weakest, where the armor plates meet, but even then it will take a pounding before it dies. As search teams, your job is simply to search and destroy and count. I can't stress this point enough, count.

"I'm sure some of you are wondering why we just don't bomb the valley from the air. We need to keep them confined. If just one escapes, the cycle will start over and we can't control it. Airpower is never a certain thing, especially after the events of this afternoon; the creatures actually sacrificed themselves for the well-being of the group, so the air campaign is not the answer. I believe along with the docs here that all the animals would have to do is go deep. Dirt and sand is the best bullet and bomb stopper there ever was.

"When you leave the briefing, we have a gift that has been supplied by the army and a very special engineer from the University of California at San Diego. We're pulling in a lot of favors here today." Jack turned away and retrieved something from behind him. When he held it up, it looked as if it were another piece of body armor that covered the chest and back and zipped up like all others. "This is a new piece of armor developed by Kenneth Vecchio, a mechanical and aerospace engineer. He has developed new armor made from, of all things, abalone shell. The shell has undergone what they call 'depth of penetration' testing and can resist a steel rod traveling at two thousand miles per hour. In our language, people, it is what is called a bullet stopper. And that means this animal may have a hard time biting or clawing through it. As you can see"—he laid the vest down and brought up leggings, which resembled shin guards like those a catcher would wear, and thick arm bands—"these are made of the same material. Each of you will be issued a set after you leave this tent." When Jack saw the doubt on their faces, he said, "Welcome to the world of biometrics, people. We are imitating other life-forms from our own world to survive." He paused for a second. "In this case an abalone." That elicited tension-breaking chuckles from these hardened soldiers. "Now, a quick brief by our geology element, Specialist McIntire." He indicated Sarah, in the front row.

McIntire walked to the front with a rolled-up virtual map. She unrolled it and placed it on the easel Colonel Fielding had placed there.

"As you can see, our operational area is ringed with granite mountains. This will be the outermost area of the assault. The tunnels lead off in all directions as if the animals are seeking the quickest and easiest way to get out once the food supply is gone." She turned away from the map and picked up a softball-sized instrument and held it up. "This is a remote-sensing device that will be air-dropped onto the valley below. It will sense the vibrations underground just like the VDF remote devices each of the teams has been issued. These aboveground units will send a signal to an orbiting global-positioning satellite and an AWACS that will relay the coordinates to our teams to allow you some warning. Of course they have never been used in this manner but—"

"Thank you, Specialist," Collins said, purposely cutting her off. The men didn't need to know the what-ifs if all this technical stuff failed.

McIntire looked at the major, then caught the innuendo about morale and turned and sat, leaving the virtual map out and displayed. The mountains were by far the predominate feature as they circled the valley like wagons in defense against Indian attack, only the Indians were in the circle with them for this fight.

"Okay, assemble to your assigned assault teams and good hunting," Colonel Fielding said.

The men and women of the tunnel assault teams moved out of the tent with not much said. Jack watched them leave with doubt flitting at the edges of his thoughts. They needed more time to plan this assault. He could be leading them into a massacre by not knowing the animal's full potential.

The tent was near empty as Commander Everett and Lisa Willing stepped inside.

"Jack, you wanted to see Signalman Willing?"

"Yes, I did," Jack said.

Lisa swallowed. She didn't know what was to come; Carl had said he didn't know.

Sarah was rolling up her virtual map and gathering her equipment, just getting ready to join her tunnel team.

"Specialist, if you would join us here, please," Collins asked her.

Sarah looked from the major to Lisa and received the slightest downturn of her lips to show she had no idea what was happening. Sarah laid her gear down and joined the small group at the front of the large tent.

Collins nodded in the direction of Colonel Fielding, who quickly pushed the entrance flap aside to allow a tall, lanky man inside. He was carrying something in his arms that was covered with a white sheet. He walked quickly to the briefing table and set his small burden down, but still held on with his old and scarred hands. He lifted one of his hands and quickly removed his fedora and nodded in deference to the ladies in the tent. Then he looked at Major Collins.

Jack half smiled and looked at Sarah and Lisa. "McIntire, Willing, we have something to show you. Colonel Fielding brought it to my attention that in case something happened to those who are privy to what you are about to learn, we had no one else in the field that could possibly protect the most vital asset we have in the coming fight. Therefore you were chosen by me in case something happens to those who are in the know. You are to make sure that this item gets back to the complex unharmed. Your lives are expendable in that pursuit. If none of us return from the assault in the tunnels, Willing, you are to immediately leave Site One with this package and return to Nevada and personally turn it over to the director. If you make it out of the tunnels, McIntire, you're part of the chain. Others have the same orders; you're just the end of the domino line. Am I understood?"

They both nodded.

"Good. This is Mr. Gus Tilly, the man responsible for us even having a fighting chance is this mess. Gus, this is Lisa Willing, U.S. Navy, and Sarah McIntire, U.S. Army."

Gus smiled and again dipped his head in acknowledgment. "The military's changed a mite since I was in, progress ain't all bad, I guess."

"Gus, will you make the introductions?"

Gus took a deep breath and removed the bedsheet from his friend. Lisa and Sarah both stared wide-eyed at the small being that stood on the table, its large eyes blinking in the bright light. Matchstick looked around nervously until it saw the friendly faces of Gus, Jack, and the colonel.

"Ladies, this is Matchstick. He's what you might call one of them little green men."

Lisa allowed her mouth to do what it wanted. It fell open. Sarah actually laughed and clapped her hands just once. Her smile was from ear to ear as she stepped up to the small alien. She looked at Jack, who in turn mouthed the words *Go ahead*. She slowly brought her hand up and held it in front of Matchstick.

"Well, don't leave the lady hangin', son, shake her hand," Gus said.

Mahjtic looked from Gus to the woman in front of him. Then it slowly brought its small hand up. The long fingers gently touched and slowly wrapped around her smaller ones.

Sarah turned to Lisa and took her hand. "Kind of justifies what we do here, doesn't it?"

Lisa just kept her eyes on Matchstick as she slowly closed her mouth and smiled.

Jack pulled Sarah away from the small group and walked her outside.

"Listen, I have been thinking of something. Do you have your virtual map of the geologic formations of the mountains surrounding us?"

"Yeah, I have it right here," she said.

"Can I see it? I have an idea."

Julie, Billy, and Tony were now being led into the very hole Julie had stared into when she'd entered the kitchen. She had pleaded with the blond-haired Frenchman to let her son and Tony stay behind. But he'd insisted, although politely, too politely Julie thought, and they went along.

Three members of the Frenchman's commando team were the first to rappel into the hole. It wasn't but thirteen feet deep below the surface of the kitchen when it trailed sharply off to the south and down. The tunnel was about six and half feet in diameter and smooth around the circumference. The smell was that of a slaughterhouse, with that coppery odor. Julie noticed as she inched her way down the rope that blood was smeared and splattered on the tunnel's smooth and shiny surface. She silently prayed it wasn't Hal's.

She waited for Farbeaux to land on the tunnel floor, then she approached him, shrugging off the hands of one of his men.

"What is it you expect us to do?" she asked.

"Do? Why, nothing. You may buy my men and me some valuable time, if and when we run into our guests down here." Farbeaux smiled and not too gently moved past her and deeper into the black void beyond. He knew a small sample of this animal's DNA would be highly valuable on the open market, and he might need the lives of the three Americans to deal his way out of town.

Niles was on the video link with Virginia Pollock discussing the autopsies of the animals they had recovered. Alice listened in.

"Basically, we're in deep if that third generation is born. There'll be just too many of them to contain. And you saw the confrontation with those air force fighters. They had adapted well to the lightness of this atmosphere, although we are not sure the parent doesn't have that same ability because we haven't seen her yet. In any case, they were trying to seek the limits of the valley and were possibly sending scouts out before heading for greener pastures when they were attacked by the air force."

Niles rubbed his weary eyes and looked at Alice, then back to the camera.

"What makes you think they haven't already escaped? They could be well on their way to Phoenix, or Albuquerque."

"The autopsy of the mangled animal we pulled from one of the holes that were bombed indicated they were void of digested food. That's why they broke from the main pack, to scout the surrounding area because they're hungry. We've removed their food source by evacuating the civilians, so we believe the rest will seek nourishment anywhere they can before setting out," Virginia answered.

Niles gave her a worried look. "The only food in the area is the teams on the ground."

"Yes, that's the obvious conclusion."

Suddenly Jack appeared on the screen with Sarah by his side.

"Niles, I've come up with something here. It might be the backup plan we need." Jack nodded toward Sarah, who removed her helmet.

"Mr. Compton, do you have virtual reality map 00787 there with you?" she asked.

Niles reacted quickly and punched in the command on his desk keyboard. As they watched, a tight, multicolored view of the valley popped up on the screen. Niles quickly looked it over and made sure the map numbers matched.

"Got it," he said as Alice joined him in front of the large screen.

"Do you see the eastern end of the valley?" Sarah asked.

"Yes," Niles said.

"Now, the major caught this little item and I missed it. See the rock stratum goes down into the ground at some points more than two thousand feet, but at the eastern end it tapers out to almost nothing, and there is an actual gap in the ring of mountains at the easternmost end. The rock stratum is virtually nonexistent."

"I don't get it, what are you saying?" Niles said.

"Niles, the animals will try to exit the valley through the point of least resistance. They may just choose the eastern range, because of the shallowness of the mountain stratum in that area. It's a funnel, Niles, a funnel!" Collins said.

Compton finally got it. "A trap of some kind?"

"Right, we need an engineer company at the point where the mountains dip down to nothing, where there is no rock deep enough. We need them there with one of the packages from MacDill, placed about a thousand feet down ought to do," Collins said.

"I get you, Jack, but what in the hell is going to keep them from heading to the shallow point before we're ready?" Niles asked.

Alice understood and grabbed his arm. "The tunnel teams have to keep them busy for a while, Niles, that's all."

The director stood and looked at Jack and Sarah. "The only way you can do that is to make yourself targets, Jack. You're there to try and flush them out, and that's their god-damn territory down there!"

"Niles, can you get the engineers there ASAP?" Jack asked.

"They'll be there, Major," said a voice from the doorway that caught them off guard.

Both Alice and Niles turned to see Senator Lee standing in the doorway leaning on his cane. He was wearing a red

robe and slippers and was staring at both of them. Alice and
Niles both stood in shock at seeing him there.

"Thought you could get rid of me that easy?" he said as
he glared at Alice. "You have to do more than hide my pants,
woman, you . . . you usurper."

Alice finally gained back some of her senses and threw
her pad on the desk. Niles didn't know what to do, so he did
what came naturally lately, he plopped back down into his
chair, shaking his head.

"You need to be back at the clinic!" Alice said, going to
Lee's side and helping him to the couch.

"Now, can someone fill me in on how this war is going?
Or do I have to wait for the damn movie?"

Niles explained Jack's plan to the senator, who sat and
listened with his eye closed.

"Jack, I know exactly what you need, and maybe I can get
you some bait out there to ensure the animals' participation
in their destruction. You two go on with your mission and
we'll take care of everything from here."

"Yes, sir, nice to see you decided to go to work today,"
Jack said, and smiled into the camera, placing his hand on
Sarah's shoulder and walking away from the camera.

"Okay, smart guy, what do we do to take advantage of
knowing where they will run if they get by the tunnel teams?"

"Well," Niles said while eyeing Lee, "as Jack said, we order some engineers into that gap in the mountains and drill a
hole as deep as we can and then booby-trap it. One neutron
bomb should do, no radiation. That may just finish them and
break their backs, unless they just go deep under any rocks
in the immediate stratum and go under the mountains at
some point."

"We may be giving these animals too much credit," Lee
said. "I mean, are they sentient or just wild beasts? We don't
know, and our only choice is to treat them as animals. So
maybe they will take the path of least resistance just like the
major said and go where they don't have to dig deeper. We
must hope they are driven by their metabolism, not their
brains. So, where we stand is, we need their path to be fail-

safe and very, very tempting. Get every head of cattle left in that valley and get them to that gap."

Niles didn't comment but just nodded and marked the break in the mountains with his finger, drawing a line that bled into the map as his finger passed.

"So there it is, the line has been drawn, huh, Niles? Now get on the horn and tell the president Jack's fallback plan," Lee said. "If the tunnel teams fail, Major Collins may have to do the unthinkable."

Niles looked at Lee and shook his head, hoping it wouldn't come to that.

"After you get done there, Niles, we have to sit down and discuss a little e-mail I just received from a traitor in the midst of *our enemies*. It seems after this is all over, we have an old friend we have to go meet in New York."

Alice and the senator sat on the couch exchanging gentle words. It seemed whatever e-mail Lee had just received was like a tonic that gave him a breath of new life and a new mission.

Niles connected with the president. "Sir, Major Collins has come up with a rather ballsy backup plan. Are you ready for this?"

Collins followed Sarah, catching her just as she was walking up to Everett and Lisa. "You watch yourself, don't pull any hero crap out there." He stopped and looked her in the eyes and then at Lisa. "Because in my experience, a hero is a sandwich." Then he gave her a soft smile and turned away and left.

Sarah smiled sadly at Lisa and Everett, then joined the line to get her body armor, leaving Lisa and Everett alone.

"I've decided something," Lisa said as she watched her friend leave.

"And that is?" Everett asked, not caring who saw them talking with each other. At this point, Congress could climb into one of those cursed holes and go straight to hell.

"I'm resigning from the navy."

"No, now that Jack is on board, the Group's security is in the best hands possible. It's me who's resigning."

Lisa couldn't speak.

"That means as soon as this thing's over, we're going to your folks in Houston and we're getting married. That's an order."

She smiled and hit him in the shoulder. "Ow" was all the big SEAL said.

PART SEVEN
I SHALL FEAR NO EVIL

Man has always been wary of the darkness and thus has followed the path laid bright by the moon; therefore I shall steal the moon glow and blacken the night . . . and show him just why he is afraid of the dark.

—ANCIENT HEBREW TEXT

THIRTY

Sarah turned and watched the Blackhawk carrying Jack and his tunnel team to Chato's Crawl. She thought he was looking down at her and she gave a halfhearted wave as the big helicopter lifted skyward. She turned and counted the heads that made up her team, then looked toward the command tent. Lisa was there with her arms crossed over her chest. She waved and Sarah just smiled as she threw her nylon rope down the dark hole. Thirteen more ropes followed, and two by two her team rappelled into the darkness.

The heat and humidity hit her immediately as her light searched for the area where the hole became a tunnel. She came to a stop with her partner on the opposite side and scanned the area with her helmet light. Then she snapped it off and lowered her night-vision goggles and the world became a greenish hue. She nodded and they continued the final few feet to the floor, landing softly and pulling the ropes from their rappelling rings. They both lowered to an assault crouch as they scanned the emptiness of the tunnel ahead of them. Sarah raised her goggles and turned her helmet light on and off twice, signaling it was safe for the next two to finish the drop and enter the hole. Sarah moved to the mouth of the tunnel as the rest of the team came down in twos. Sarah raised her XM8 and stepped into the blackness.

She moved twenty feet into the darkness before holding her hand up in a stop gesture. She removed her glove as the team assembled behind her and felt the wall. It was sticky, not to the point it made her fingers stick together, but it felt moist and tacky. The tunnel had a musky odor, like a lot of caves that host large bat populations, and some ammonia smell, but the humidity was the worst aspect thus far. Sarah replaced her glove and started forward.

Her team had only gone two hundred yards into the increasingly deepening tunnel when a Ranger, a young sergeant, started talking loudly and shaking his head. He slid down one of the shining walls, losing his weapon and placing his hands over his face, knocking his night-vision goggles from it.

Sarah turned and made her way back. The man was now screaming.

"What in the hell is going on?" she asked as she knelt before the young soldier.

"I gottta get outta here, the walls are closing in on me, I can't stand it!" he screamed.

Sarah reached out and grabbed his right arm and shook it. "Calm down, calm down," she said as she reached out and took his oxygen tank and unclipped the plastic mask and quickly placed it over his mouth. "Breathe, troop, breathe, easy, easy."

The sergeant started taking deep breaths, his eyes closing as he finally started calming.

"Anyone else?" she said loudly. "Come on, you're no good to us if you're going to freak out, so is anyone else claustrophobic?" she said, looking around.

The sergeant removed the oxygen mask and looked at Sarah with pleading eyes. "Sorry, sorry, I need someone to take me back," he said as he slammed the mask back over his mouth.

"I'm the one who's sorry, Sergeant, but I'm not going to

spare a man walking you out of here. You get back the best way you can. The rest of you, let's go."

With that, the sergeant's eyes widened as Sarah abruptly turned and went back to the head of her team. The other Rangers and two Delta men didn't look back, but joined their team leader. The young sergeant scrambled to his feet and started back to the tunnel opening.

Sarah shook her head as she once again started forward into the dark and humidity of the tunnel. If the truth be known, she wanted nothing more than to follow the kid out of there.

As Collins hit the bottom of the hole, he was hit immediately by the heat. Everett landed easily on the opposite side. This tunnel was far smaller than the one Sarah was currently struggling in. It must be one of the offspring holes. They had to bend slightly to keep from scraping their heads on the rounded ceiling. Jack turned his night vision on and saw the small, sparkling elements of sand and dirt that made up the compressed walls. They were smooth and warm to the touch. Everett looked his way and shook his head.

"Goddamn, Jack, but it's blacker than a well digger's ass down there," he said as he brought his XM8 up, thinking it was too light to do any good, armor-piercing rounds or not.

Collins watched as the tunnel sloped down into nothingness. He looked at the ground and saw large marks gouged into the earth. He reached down and saw they were scrapes made by the passing of the animal. He was looking at what were claw marks. He shook his head and moved forward so Mendenhall, Ryan, and the rest of his team could crowd in. Then Everett stepped aside and allowed a master sergeant from Delta to take the lead. The Delta sergeant went forward, held his hand up, then slowly lowered it, indicating that they should follow.

Before long the team halted and Jack was asked to come forward. As he did, he nodded for Everett to follow. The

Delta point man was kneeling and examining something on the floor of the tunnel. Jack looked down and immediately knew he was looking at an arm. It was severed at midforearm and had a watch that was still ticking off the seconds. As he looked up the tunnel, he could see a darker hue from his glasses as they were now able to follow the blood trail left by the animal and whatever victim the arm belonged to.

Jack nodded for the team to move on. The coppery odor of blood was becoming more apparent the deeper into the tunnel they progressed, but in their minds it had become even stronger with the finding of the arm. Jack stayed behind with Mendenhall for a moment and indicated he should go ahead and take a reading on his VDF. The sergeant shouldered his weapon, raised his goggles, and removed the steel probe from its clip on the box and slowly pushed the spearlike instrument into the compacted earth. He removed his hand and looked at the lit gauge. One of the needles pointed west, toward the center of town, while the other needle picked up minute vibrations coming from underground, which they could only assume were the animals as they dug.

"Looks like we're headed in the right direction, Major," Mendenhall said.

"Keep that thing on and check it every sixty feet or so, it'll make me feel better," Jack said as he patted Mendenhall on the shoulder.

Mendenhall quickly pulled the probe from the wall and decided to just let it dangle by its cord for quicker reach. Then he turned and hurried after the major, deciding the one with the VDF box should be in the middle of the team.

Group geologist Steve Hanson, Sarah's friend, led his team of fifteen soldiers through one of the small holes. They had found nothing significant since coming into this underground hell. He had called a stop at a junction where their smaller tunnel joined one that was far larger. Unlike any of the intersecting tunnels before, Steve investigated and found that the musky odor they had noticed in all the other small excavations had changed significantly. This stench was far sharper and made him wince. He placed his mask over his mouth and took three deep breaths and headed back to his men. Jackie Sanchez, an Event Group army sergeant, raised her night-vision goggles and asked if he was alright.

"Something's different here, you getting that smell?"

"Just what I'm getting off of you, that's bad," she said.

"That tunnel is far different than what we've seen. Any luck with the radio?"

"Nothing but intermittent chatter. Other teams, I think, trying to get Site One."

"Doc, I'm picking up something here," a Ranger spec five said. He had his VDF probe stuck in the wall to his left. "Not strong, but it's steady, seems close, but can't say for sure."

The rest of Hanson's team started looking around. There were three holes besides the large one that Hanson had just investigated, plus the one they occupied, and one more that seemed too small for one of the animals. The Ranger removed the probe and stepped to the smaller hole that was right in the middle of the team. He placed it into the loose earth that had been pushed out into the larger tunnel. The gauge moved minutely and held steady. The red indicator light came on for the first time and stayed on.

"We definitely have something," he said, replacing the probe.

"Go to the end of the line and make sure we don't have something coming in behind us," Hanson said, as he brought his XM8 around and kept it pointed at the larger hole ahead.

The Ranger squeezed his way past the other Rangers until he came to the end of the team. A lone Delta commando covered their rear.

"Excuse me, Sarge," he said as he placed the probe into the wall. As he started to take his reading, he noticed the red light on his VDF had become brighter. He lightly hit the box and was starting to question the sensitivity of the machine when he felt movement to his left. He looked back along the length of tunnel; there was nothing but blackness in the area they had already covered. He turned and looked at the Delta sergeant, who was taking a drink from his canteen. He could have been picking up his movement. He lowered his ambient-light goggles and turned back to his rear. He didn't catch it at first because it was so close it was unrecognizable. The creature was there, staring right at him. The eyes were actually glowing bright yellowish green as it tilted its large head and studied him for a moment. He quickly brought up his weapon and pulled the trigger; nothing happened. He had forgotten to remove the safety he had put on as he maneuvered around the team.

Suddenly he was blinded as the Delta sergeant opened fire. The armor-piercing rounds flew by his head and struck the animal dead center in its broad chest. Then three more Rangers added their fire to that of the Delta soldier. Rounds were ricocheting off the creature as it roared. The Ranger was still blinded as he was grabbed by the lethal claws of the enraged animal. He felt the air being crushed from his lungs, and though he wasn't aware of it, three armor-piercing rounds went through his own armor where it met his hips, and then through his body, and struck the animal. He saw one round hit an area uncovered by the beast's exoskeleton, the pain causing it to squeeze him even harder. But still the animal had shown no ill effect from the bullet penetrating its body.

The Delta sergeant lowered his weapon and was joined by two other Rangers as they tried in vain to pull the first man free of the clawed monstrosity before them. Hanson was there, adding his firepower to those trying to find a weak spot on the creature. Suddenly the wall exploded outward onto Hanson and the would-be rescuers. The creature that struck them in force was larger than the tunnel and brought down the rounded ceiling on them as they turned in terror. Hanson felt a powerful arm as it raked by his face and grabbed someone to his right. All he could hear was a scream of pain as the man was pulled over him through the loose collapse of dirt. He couldn't breathe as the sticky dirt fell into his mouth. He tried to pull back on someone he had grabbed on to when the roof fell in, but as he pulled, he realized it was someone's weapon and not an actual person. Then he was suddenly free of the cave-in as he was turned upside down. He spit out dirt as he felt blood rush to his head. He heard firing in all directions and just knew he was going to catch a wild round in the back. The screams were now reaching his ears as he finally focused his night vision on what had him. The beast roared and quickly bashed him against one of the hardened walls. His senses flew out of his body and he became mercifully numb as he heard his back and legs snap into several pieces. The beast screamed again, then threw him to the ground where he lay in a slumped position against the wall. Still alive, he saw around him at least five of the smaller animals as they attacked what remained of his team.

The last thing Hanson saw was the larger of the animals as it lowered its large head toward him and the eyes blinked, as if it was smelling him, studying something it hadn't seen before. He didn't feel the roughness of the black tongue as it slowly curled free of the mandibles and delicately licked his face. The odor was the same as what he had smelled in the tunnel. Hanson's senses were gone forever as the beast started feeding.

The first tunnel team to meet the enemy had been wiped out within two minutes of first contact.

Ryan pushed the earpiece as deep into his ear as he possibly could and still the static was too much. He removed his Kevlar helmet and shone his light at Collins's chest, making sure not to hit his goggled eyes. He wiped sweat from his brow and shook his head.

"Still can't make it out, Major. It may be Site One, or one of the other tunnel teams, I just can't be sure." He reached for his oxygen to get a breath of clean air.

They had been deep underground for almost an hour and forty minutes and hadn't made contact with as much as a ground squirrel. Collins shone his light ahead of the others in his team and noticed a branch in the tunnel up ahead. The men were squatting and taking some of their own oxygen. The humidity was off the scale and the heat was close to unbearable. They would have given anything to leave the O_2 masks on because of the stench clinging to the tunnel walls, but they knew they might have at least a few more hours of this, so they conserved as much as they could.

"Being underground is hell on the COMM links. Where do you estimate we are, Sergeant?"

"I believe the center of town is just that way," Mendenhall answered, pointing to the right. "Maybe a thousand yards or so. The depth of this tunnel is making the GPS signal we're receiving from base sporadic at best and nonexistent most of the time, but my last fix was pretty dead-on, so I'd say not far ahead."

Collins had chosen this particular hole because it seemed to be the freshest and hottest of the many trails. It seemed to have been created by two animals traveling side by side because it was wide enough for the men to get around without too much difficulty. He looked at the other members of his team. They were hot in the new abalone-shell armor and were using too much of their water.

He placed his hand on the wall and felt the eerie smoothness through his glove. It was almost crystalline in feel and shimmer. He glanced again at the other fifteen members of his tunnel team. The Delta men were in the lead, then him, Ryan, Mendenhall, and Everett, and the last five were Rangers bringing up the rear.

"Well, if the town is that way, I'm thinking the branch to the left, away from the town. Thoughts?" Collins asked them all, not just the officers.

They all concurred with silent nods.

Suddenly, the VDF Mendenhall held started blinking. Something was moving toward them and it was coming fast. The lights started blinking on and off at a faster rate, and the needle on the motion sensor went into the yellow. Mendenhall raised the small stainless-steel probe that was attached to the side of the handheld VDF device and shoved it into the wall of the tunnel. The lights became brighter and started blinking even faster. The gauges were starting to really move into the higher ranges, indicating extreme movement. He then removed the probe and jammed it into the wall to his right; the blinking lights slowed and dimmed at the same time. He returned the probe to the other wall but farther to the left, then he pulled it free and placed it in the wall farther to the right. The lights again sped up their blinking and glowed bright red. The directional indicator showed the vibration coming straight at them, and the motion sensor was now pegged in the red.

"Uh, we have company headed this way, Major."

"Which direction?" Collins asked, bringing his XM8 rifle up into firing position.

"Shit, sir, now in every direction." Mendenhall took his eyes off the VDF and raised his own weapon. He glanced down at the signal once he was prepared to defend himself. "Shit, the needle first points to the south, then jumps to the east, then west." Mendenhall kept his eyes on the device. "The only place they're not coming is from behind us."

"You men, bunch up, four-man teams. I want weapons coverage in all directions. Keep fire discipline, you are now weapons-free."

He watched as the team broke up into the four-man groups they had rehearsed before coming down. It was a tactic Jack and Sarah had devised to protect against sudden attacks.

The machine was no longer emitting a chirp or a beep, but a solid buzz. The blinking lights were now a steady red glow, casting those around it in an eerie shade.

"Shut that off, everyone use your regular lighting, no ambient devices, they'll blind you if there's shooting."

Suddenly the wall exploded right behind Mendenhall. The shattered wall threw him to the ground. Lights immediately illuminated the animal as it shook itself free of the clinging dirt and sand, slinging outward its armor neck plates. The plates dug into both walls of the tunnel creating deep gouges in the rock and dirt. The beast roared, then leapt for the fallen Mendenhall, who screamed and rolled just as the creature swiped with its claws. Collins and Everett opened fire at the same time the group to Mendenhall's rear did. Over one hundred armor-piercing rounds hit the animal simultaneously. All but a few glanced off its purplish armor and embedded in the walls. As the tracer rounds struck, it stumbled forward and leapt onto the sergeant. At that moment, another animal burrowed into the tunnel somewhere in front of Collins. He heard the loud pops of automatic fire as well as screams of terror and pain. Jack saw the bright flashes as the Delta and Ranger teams opened up.

Everett used the muzzle of his short-barreled XM8 and lifted one of the plates of armor just below the Talkhan's skull and fired a twenty-round burst of 5.56 mm rounds into the back of the animal's head. It roared and shook its massive head, then collapsed heavily onto the sergeant and firmly pinned him to the tunnel floor. They could barely hear Mendenhall screaming below the heavy carcass of the dead creature over the screams and bursts of gunfire in the enclosed tunnel. Collins and Everett both reached down and quickly pulled him out from under the animal.

"Goddammit, sirs," the sergeant said loudly and breathlessly, "just a little fucking faster next time." Mendenhall started checking himself, making sure he was all right. The new armored vest had paid major dividends for the sergeant because when he turned, the officers saw three large gashes almost through the back of the abalone-shell protection. One of the animal's teeth was still lodged in the collar of the new armor vest.

They didn't have time to answer Mendenhall or comment on the armor as more shots rang out down the entire length of the tunnel, each weapon sparking a myriad of bright colors on the crystalline walls. Screams and yells could be heard, along with cries of horror and injury. Suddenly, the firing stopped. Then started again as another animal broke through the wall. They heard Ryan's shouts as he directed fire down the tunnel. Collins reached for a flare, popped it, and threw it into the darkness. It settled and revealed a nightmarish scene as the Delta front guard was battling for their lives against three of the animals. One of the lead animals struck out with its tail and caught a Delta sergeant in the throat, impaling him and yanking him away from the others and into the midst of the flailing claws of the attackers.

Suddenly a clawed hand burst through the wall and creased the air in front of one of the men just before the entire bulk of the animal crashed into the tunnel. The claws had slashed a specialist from Delta almost in two, catching him between the neck and shoulder. The beast had blindly ripped down, severing flesh, bone, and cartilage as easy as a knife slices through paper. A corporal was too close to use his XM8, so he pulled his combat knife from its scabbard and leaped onto the creature's back when it became fully exposed. He thrust the knife between and under its flapping neck armor and into its neck three times in rapid succession before the beast reached behind and grabbed the soldier with its long claws. The stinger swiped and nicked the corporal, but the claws were already doing the necessary damage. The sharpened points pierced the soldier and he screamed in agony as the beast brought the struggling Ranger toward its face and roared in anger and pain.

"Yeah," the soldier screamed back into the gaping, teeth-filled maw, "fuck you!" He then quickly plunged the knife into the animal's left eye. The Talkhan screamed in pain, slamming the soldier again and again into the hardened wall of the tunnel. It pummeled the lifeless body until the corporal simply came apart.

"Move!" Collins's shout filled the tunnel as others rushed up from behind the wounded and enraged beast. Collins, Everett, and Ryan opened fire at the same moment, taking the animal first to its knees and then to its side. The rounds followed it down and kept striking it as it lay prone on the blood-slick floor, the tail and stinger still twitching. Then abruptly, the animal at their feet roared and staggered to its feet. It swung outward with its claws, seeking out anything it could kill. Collins quickly removed a grenade and pulled the pin. He waited until the beast had swung and

missed, then while it roared, Jack quickly jammed the
grenade into its large mouth, scraping his arm and hand on
its teeth as he did so. He threw himself at the creature's feet
as the grenade went off with a muffled explosion, and Jack
saw the head come apart, spraying him, Everett, and
Mendenhall with gore.

An eerie silence then filled the smoke-shrouded tunnel as
the flare sputtered and died, leaving them in total darkness.
Seven men were left standing. Two were only slightly
wounded with gashes and cuts from the sharpened claws.
Seven men had been lost during the brief two-minute encounter with the four Talkhan.

"Okay, let's get ourselves together and start moving. I
don't like just standing here like ducks on a pond. You have
anything on the VDF, Sergeant?" Collins asked while reaching for his oxygen.

Mendenhall was shaking badly. He wiped some of the animals' blood from the OD-green face of the small device and
examined the gauge. "No . . . uh, no, sir, needles are flat and
steady."

Collins lit another flare and examined what was left of his
team. The mangled bodies of the dead littered the floor.

"Pull these men back against the wall. If we can, we
come back and retrieve them." Jack focused on one of the
Rangers who couldn't be more than nineteen.

As they started forward, the first Delta man to the branch
in the tunnel called back behind him using his radio, "Major,
you better have a look at this."

Collins squeezed past the others and knelt beside the
highly trained commando from Fort Bragg.

"What have you got?" Collins asked.

"It looks like we're not the only ones to come this way."
With his flashlight the Delta man pointed at the footprints
clearly evident in the soft floor of the tunnel.

"This looks like it may be one of our teams, number's
about right. Maybe fourteen to eighteen men, give or take a
couple," Jack said.

"Normally I would say you're right, sir, but look at this."

The flashlight fell on a set of prints that were too small to be that of a soldier. And they were obviously made by tennis shoes. "And this set here, they're not military boots, they're probably cowboy boots." Then the beam swung forward about a foot and illuminated another set. "These are small and are like nurse's shoes, maybe a waitress; my wife wears something like these."

Collins straightened and cast his light down the tunnel. The beam seemed to trail off to nothing as it tried to push its way through the blackness and smoke ahead.

"Whatever unit is down here, they've taken along at least three civilians. A man, a boy, and possibly a woman, Major."

At the same time Collins had started worrying about possible civilians in the tunnels, Carl Hastings, one of the Event Group's most experienced tunnel engineers from the Colorado School of Mines, was in a frightened, head-long flight from the hole his team had entered. The Delta teams led the way as the Rangers brought up the rear as they carried what wounded they were able to snatch away from the attacking animals. Their team was down to only seven men, not counting the four wounded. Bobby Jenks, a friend of Sarah's, had been pulled screaming into a hole that had suddenly appeared out of nowhere, crashing into him and knocking him off-balance just long enough for the beast to grab him.

The sheer numbers of the attackers had caught them off guard. They thought that maybe they had killed at least one of the animals, but could honestly account for no more. The Delta teams in the front took the brunt of the attack while those in the rear tried to help, but it had been hopeless from the beginning, and by the time the attacks were on in force, the Delta teams were using their nine-millimeter handguns at close range. Some even had to use knives in the closed spaces. The animals had knocked several of the soldiers down easily by collapsing walls of dirt and sand upon them, then struck at them while they were in the worst possible position to fight. Now they only prayed to make it to the surface and not die in this underground hell, but to do it fighting in the light of day.

Hastings pressed his earpiece into his ear. "We have a break in the tunnel up here, there's sunlight. Let's move and get the wounded up front and out."

"Oh, thank you, God, thank you," Hastings said aloud.

As they moved into the sun that was cast down into the tunnel from a hole, they saw the shadows and heard the distinctive thumping of rotors. The breach in the ground was being circled by at least three AH-64D Apache Longbow gunships. The dispirited group of soldiers and Event members could never have imagined a more welcome sound.

Two Delta men used one of the XM8 weapons as a step as they thrust first the wounded and then the rest through the opening. Once up and out, they helped pull their comrades to safety. As the final Delta sergeant cleared the hole, they collapsed down on the hardpan as the Apaches continued to circle.

The pilot of the lead Apache, a veteran of the Event Group for eight years with his team, Chief Warrant Officer Brett Jacobson, watched as the tunnel unit emerged from the hole. He quickly counted the men on the ground and shook his head, knowing the number they had started with.

"Those guys were mauled," he said into his mike.

"Yeah, and it may not be over. Look, Chief," his weapons man in the front nose of the Apache calmly called.

As the pilot turned, he saw with horror the speeding animals as they parted the sands in their rush toward the grounded troops, two from the north, a third from the east. He estimated a closing speed of close to sixty miles an hour as one of the creatures breached the surface as a dolphin would, most likely to spy its quarry, only to disappear again into the soil as quickly as it had breached a moment before.

"Jesus! Predator flight, we have men on the deck and three, I repeat, *three* targets closing on their position. Let's move!" he called to his attacking wolf pack. *"Break, break, break!"*

The other two Apaches broke formation and started their run for the fast-attacking animals. They aligned themselves and targeted two Hellfire missiles each; in moments the laser-guided weapons were streaking toward their intended targets. But they would never make it as two of the animals came to the surface and sprang into the blue sky. The relatively slow-moving Apaches were easy targets as they slammed into the first gunship, jolting the big chopper and breaking the Hellfire's laser hold on the target. The second of the two beasts hit the Apache's tail boom and rebounded to the ground, stunned for a moment before it shook itself, then dove once again into the sand. The Hellfires remembered the last position the laser designator targeted before it was knocked offline, but the speeding creatures were by the point of the missiles' initial impact by twenty yards, as they missed the animals totally. The warheads struck the hardpan, sending surface sand one hundred feet into the air. The pilot regained enough control to bank hard and bring the Apache under control. But he didn't know the first animal was still attached to the Apache's undercarriage until the beast brought its claws up in a swinging arc and punctured the armored belly of the attack bird.

The lead pilot saw what was happening and he brought his stick forward. His Apache shot toward the dangling animal. His gunner aligned his eyepiece and targeted the clinging beast on his wingman's underside, and the thirty-millimeter chain gun erupted. The slow-operating weapon sent large tank-killing rounds forth in a perfectly straight line, catching the animal in the large bulk of its torso, severing it from the remaining parts of its body. What was left fell three hundred feet to the floor of the desert. Only four or five errant rounds hit the Apache.

"Now that was never put in the book by the manufacturer," the weapons officer shouted in triumph.

Jacobson then turned his Apache and the chain gun fired at the distinctive lines of thrown-up soil made by the attacking Talkhan. Another animal had joined the other two on their ground attack. The explosive rounds found the first animal as it breached the surface. The thirty-millimeter shells tore through its armor, stopping it dead in its tracks. Then a Hellfire caught the second, exploding a foot in front of the parting wave of dirt, sending chunks of purple and black skyward.

The pilot pulled back on his stick, but as he did, the third animal suddenly surfaced and shot like a homed-in missile toward the hovering Apache. The pilot watched in horror as everything seemed to slow to a crawl. The animal was traveling so fast that the Apache's computer took it for an incoming missile and started to automatically pop off chaff and flares. The animal hit the cockpit with so much force, the front half of the attack helicopter separated from the back, sending the chain gun, weapons officer, and most of the fire-control system tumbling three hundred feet to the ground. The army warrant officer was inundated with flying glass as he fought for control as the huge machine started a plunge for the desert below. As the men on the ground watched in utter horror, the Apache hit hard, tearing away the wheels and weapons pod on the right side of the gunship. The rotors dug into the ground and sheared off as they struck. Jacobson was pelted with dirt and pieces of flying metal as he fought to hold on. The Apache skid along the sand and dirt, tearing access panels and the left-side weapons pod away as it hit a small rise in the earth and bounced into the air, then it flipped over once and came down on its side, sliding to a stop in two pieces.

Two Delta sergeants broke for the fallen bird to try to free anyone alive. As they approached, they saw Jacobson fighting his harness trying to get out as aviation fuel was pouring all over the two engines. The first Delta man started cutting away the damaged harness with his knife, and the other started pulling and tugging at Jacobson, who was screaming for them to hurry as he spied one of the dirt waves approaching at breakneck speed. As they finally released him and pulled the pilot from the broken Apache, the animal surfaced and jumped, missing the three men by a foot. It struck what was left of the cockpit and became entangled in wiring and broken glass. One of the Delta sergeants stopped and took out his nine millimeter and emptied his clip into the engine compartment of the Longbow. Suddenly all three were knocked flat by the explosion as one of the bullets made the spark the soldier was hoping for. The aviation fuel went up with a loud *thrump* and the animal was caught inside. It fought free of the remains of the chopper and started toward the prone men. Then fifty rounds tore into it and dropped the flaming beast mere feet from the three men. The remaining tunnel team was there and was now helping the men up. Then they retreated from the remains of the animal and the crash site in case any of the other creatures had the same idea.

The other wounded Apache was coming down also. The remaining arm and claw of the destroyed animal had kept working, its nerve endings continuing to fire. It tore the fuel lines and severed the tail-rotor wiring harness, stopping the thrust the bird needed to counter the main-rotor torque, thus sending the chopper into a spinning hell ride. The whine of the two turbines wound down quickly as it slammed into the ground. The Apache bounced once, breaking off all three landing gear assemblies. Then it rolled, tilting over onto its side until the rotor blades struck the rocks around it, disintegrating, sending composite metal shards in every direction.

The third Apache was a smoking ruin in the distance.

The remaining troops on the ground had watched the incredible air battle around them as at least twenty of the animals made a run for them. They stared in stunned silence, the wounded pilot, Jacobson, among them, as the creatures swam toward them in a huge dust cloud. Jacobson slowly stood on a broken leg and drew his .45 automatic from his shoulder holster. The others picked up their weapons and waited.

· · ·

From the monitor in the White House, the president and the National Security Council members watched as the animals rose in the last fifty feet, then dust obscured the remaining men of one of the tunnel teams and the pilot who had at first rescued them, and then they him. A moment later when the dust cloud cleared, the men were gone and the only thing that remained was the large hole where they had been making their last stand.

The president lowered his head, and the other members just closed their eyes against the scene.

Sam Fielding adjusted his binoculars and scanned the area below them for any sign of life from the brave stand the tunnel team had made on the open plain of the valley. Then he tensed as he saw another of the teams exiting the earth about a half a mile from the massacred first team. Then he shifted position and saw they had already been spotted by the animals. At least three of them were now streaking toward the second tunnel team from two miles out.

"Sir," Lisa said at his side. "I have Colonel Jessup on the radio asking permission to cover that team."

"Tell them permission denied. I have a small surprise for those motherfuckers. Tell them to hold position for two minutes. I'm going to buy them some time," Fielding said as he lowered his field glasses. He looked at Lisa. "Go, go."

Lisa turned and sprinted into the tent, knowing the pilots on the radios were going to scream bloody murder because they were now ordered to watch the men on the ground get chewed to pieces.

But Sam Fielding knew they would never have time for the fighters to cover them, nor the helicopters to land and get all of the survivors on board before the animals struck. So he would buy them the time they needed with something he had had the foresight to airlift in.

He heard the sound of the engines and looked up. The

AWACS was there, and he knew the big 707 had painted the desert terrain and was sending out a position on the attacking creatures. He smiled and turned for the command tent.

Lisa was trying to pacify the angry Jessup and the Blackhawk pilots when Fielding ordered her to contact his field artillery, code-named Gunslinger.

The commander of the three M109A6 Paladin self-propelled howitzers received the radio call from Command Site One.

"This is Gunslinger. Affirmative, we are tracking on GPS relay from the air force. Standing by for fire mission, over," said the captain in the lead Paladin.

"Fire at will, Captain," came the call from Fielding.

"Lock and load Excalibur!" the captain called from his command seat.

The loader opened the automatic ammo-storage door and pulled a brand-new piece of untested ordnance straight from the Aberdeen proving grounds. The Excalibur round weighed forty pounds and had compressed, funny-looking fins on the back end that told any expert in the world this couldn't be an artillery round.

The round was loaded into the M284 cannon and it immediately started communicating with the Paladin's computer-fire system. The round was fed constant updates as to its target, and the fins, which were still compressed against the sleek shell, would automatically be set accordingly after it left the tube. The information was relayed by military satellite to the orbiting AWACS and then to the small dish antenna atop the strange-looking tank.

"Fire!"

The three Paladins simultaneously spat fire and smoke as they hurled three GEO positioning smart rounds from their 155 mm cannons at the three moving targets. The Paladins were fed constant information from the AWACS overhead, and their own Global Positioning Systems cross-referenced with the big plane, which received signals made by the animals' vibration caught on the portable VDF bomblets dropped on the valley floor earlier, and now the targets were painted, as the tank commander had told Fielding earlier, three ways from Sunday.

After leaving the muzzle of the cannon, the fins popped free of the outer warhead and started to make their minute adjustments of trim and angle, sending the rounds right or left depending on the changing aspects of their individual targets. This is what basically amounted to an enemy's worst nightmare, a smart bullet.

The heavily damaged team that had just exited the ground watched as one of the animals split off and the other two stayed together in tight formation as they sped toward them. The soldiers as one all stood and started aiming their weapons at the large plumes of dirt and sand as the wakes grew closer to them, a mere two hundred yards away.

Suddenly a thunderbolt wrenched the sky overhead as the first Excalibur found its mark, exploding exactly on top of the creature on the left, sending pieces of it flying skyward. The second animal veered away from the explosion and altered its angle of attack, but it only made it another thirty feet before the second Excalibur round also changed its aspect to target via a minute adjustment at the last minute by its small tail fins, changing the flow of air over the surface planes of the fins and sending the warhead to the right, with the Global Positioning System calling the shot. That round exploded three feet in front of the beast, tearing it apart and flooding the surface with its flesh and blood and immediately collapsing the tunnel it was in back sixty yards.

As the soldiers and Event Group members stood stunned, the third Excalibur caught the other animal as it came from a roundabout direction from the first two. They were silent at first, then they collapsed to the ground in exhaustion. They had been saved, at least for the moment, by something none of them ever knew existed, a lightweight, forty-pound artillery shell with a brain the size of Einstein. It was a new sword for the working soldier called Excalibur. But they also couldn't know there were only three hundred rounds in the entire American arsenal. And that the three Paladins had only fifty on hand.

Fielding was pleased as he watched the attack and knew the pilots in the Blackhawks were satisfied as they swept down to evacuate the team on the ground.

"My God, that was impressive," Virginia Pollock said at his side.

"Yeah, it's too bad we only have forty-seven more rounds, and those will be used to save the lives of any more survivors down there." He looked at Virginia. "We're going to need a lot more than a few experimental artillery shells to survive this day."

"Well, the engineers that my boss requested are here, and so is the president's special gift. They're drilling as we speak.

Fielding removed his helmet and rubbed his forehead. "God, I hope those murdering bastards cooperate and head to the exit door."

Sarah watched as two Delta Force men stabbed the darkness ahead with their powerful lights. The tunnel was wide, almost like that of a large concrete storm drain. Sarah chipped away part of the wall and looked it over in the light.

"This has been compacted, that's why there's no excess dirt from the tunneling, only at the surface. It's literally compressing the soil as it drives through the ground," she said, looking from the sample to the man next to her.

The hole was hot and humid and smelled badly of rotting meat and sweat. They had been traveling downward for the past hour and forty-five minutes and had to stop and breathe the clean air supplied by their oxygen tanks. Now two point men waved them forward, and once again they started moving.

Suddenly one of the men held up a hand and made a fist, then opened it and gestured for them to lie low. He then waved for Sarah to come forward.

"What is it?" she asked in a low tone.

"Listen, sounds like a freight train," the Delta sergeant said.

Sarah placed a gloved hand to the smooth wall, then she removed her helmet with her other hand and listened.

"Whatever it is, it's coming this way," the commando said in a whisper.

"And coming fast," added Sarah as she stepped back from the wall and removed the safety on the XM8, making the deadly automatic ready to fire.

The remaining thirteen members of her team did the same. They took up various positions for defense, using the four-man pack defense they had discussed. The one thing they did that was exactly the same was to point their weapons at the far wall as the vibration grew louder in the tunnel. Dirt and sand started to slowly come off the roof of the unnatural cave in soft splatters, then in whole chunks.

"It has to be the mother," Sarah said softly, almost speaking to herself. "It's too damn big to be the smaller ones. Look at the VDF, it's off the scale."

As quickly as the vibration started, it stopped. Whatever was on the other side of the tunnel wall was only feet from where they were standing. Sarah and the others could feel it, it was a palpable thing. Most of the soldiers brought their automatic weapons up to eye level, focusing on the spot. As they did, the vibration and noise of the displacement of soil began again, coming closer. It seemed to have turned their way and was coming on in small advances. They felt it in their feet first, then the vibration caused by the movement traveled up their calves to the thighs. Then it stopped. As they watched the wall, small pieces began to fall. They were still and quiet.

"Hear it?" Sarah whispered. "It's right there," pointing the muzzle of her weapon to her right. "It's definitely the mother."

Suddenly a roar shook the air and brought an avalanche of dirt and rock down upon them. Then the noise started growing fainter. It was moving away, back up the mountain.

"What the hell?" the Delta sergeant asked. "Why didn't she attack?"

"I don't know. This thing has to have senses that should have felt our heartbeats through the soil. It should have attacked."

Suddenly a horrible thought crossed Sarah's mind as she was shaking dirt off herself and she froze. They had been briefed on the animal and how it would adapt to whatever it was up against. Now that, coupled with the fact it was heading away from the desert floor and traveling up the mountain, seared the answer to the sergeant's question in her mind. Not only was it going after a bigger target, it was going after *the* target that was controlling the fight against it and its offspring: the crash site and all the support personnel gathered there. The thought of Lisa, Virginia, and the unsuspecting Event teams working at the site raced through her mind. She quickly hit the transmit switch on her radio, hooked to her web gear at her side.

"Site One, come in. Site One, come in!" she said loudly into the mike just inches from her mouth.

The other members of her tunnel team quickly realized what she was thinking. The sergeant grabbed Sarah by the arm and turned her roughly as they started running back the way they had come. They knew down to a man they had been outmaneuvered.

THIRTY-ONE

Lisa sat in the communications tent with Virginia. They had heard little in the last few minutes, and from what they had monitored, a massive slaughter was obviously taking place beneath the surface of the earth. Lisa had tried for forty minutes to recall all the tunnel teams after the initial attack just outside one of the town holes. But thus far, she hadn't been able to raise a single team. Being deep underground was taxing the systems they currently had. As usual, the army had delayed sending the more reliable M-2786 radios out from Fort Carson, radios that were in use in caves and tunnels in Afghanistan. Lisa wished now they had at least had time to run antenna relays throughout the tunnels; they could have been placed as the troops went deeper, like bread crumbs. Now the softball-sized ground-penetrating radar units were not furnishing anything on the animals' movements as they had obviously caught on to the attacks and moved deeper under the ground, thus defeating the weak signals of the small units.

"S . . . t . . . ne, Si . . . One, come . . . !"

The static was cutting off whoever was calling. Lisa took a chance.

"This is Site One. Repeat, this is Site One, over."

"Get the hell ... o ... of there, the mother ... heading ... way."

"That sounded like Sarah," Virginia said.

Lisa didn't wait as she clearly understood the broken message. She threw off the headset and ran for the front of the tent. She hit a large red button on the way out that had been mounted to the main support pole, and a Klaxon started sounding throughout the crash site.

Colonel Sam Fielding was standing on a rock with field glasses pointing toward the valley floor when the alarm started. He immediately jumped from his perch and ran to organize the Event staff and remaining Rangers and Airborne personnel.

The state troopers or what remained of them drew their nine millimeters again and started scanning the area.

Gus grabbed Mahjtic and heard him say one word in a frightened voice with its eyes larger than normal: *"Destroyer!"*

Lisa grabbed an M16 from the arms locker and started back for the COMM tent. On the way she yelled at the remaining state troopers, "Get your asses over here and get something with a little more kick to it than those potato guns!"

They all immediately ran for the arms locker where Lisa had been a moment before. Trooper Dills arrived first and grabbed for an M79 grenade launcher. He smiled as he hefted a bandolier of grenades over his shoulder, saying, "Payback is a motherfucker!"

Fielding slammed into the COMM tent and yelled, "Get the goddamn Apaches up here, *now!*"

Lisa immediately put the M16 down beside the radio gear and started calling for reinforcements. Everyone from the White House situation room, Nellis, and the Event Center, to a few of the newly surfaced and severely damaged tunnel teams, heard Lisa's call for assistance.

The remaining Event staff were starting to run from the saucer's crash area to the tent site. Before most of them made it clear of the debris field, the ground rumbled beneath their feet and a high-pitched whine came to their ears. Suddenly, the ground exploded in the middle of the site, and the large, thick-haired form of the mother burst from the hole, sending pieces of the broken saucer flying in all directions, with some of the debris striking a few of the technicians, knocking them from their feet. The large beast roared, flaring her neck armor, and immediately went on the attack.

Virginia ran out of the tent in time to see Dr. Thorsen from the anthropology department picked up and torn in two by the massive animal. He was ripped like a rag doll and tossed aside. But still she couldn't bring herself to look away. The brutal life-form was horrible, but still a mesmerizing sight to the scientist in her.

The mother quickly grabbed two of the staff as they tried to dodge the towering beast. The mouth opened and the mandibles worked at an incredible speed, almost undetectable. The tail swiped at another doctor as she ran the opposite way, sinking the stinger deep into her back. As the barbed tip pulled free, it took with it most of her coverall and about eight inches of flesh. She collapsed and her skin instantaneously shriveled and collapsed in on the bone, as her insides, including the hard muscles, were reduced to jelly by the alien's venom.

The team member it held in its right claw was dispatched quickly with a bite to the top of his head as it casually tossed the man aside. It threw the other scientist against an outcropping of rock, smashing most of the bones in his body.

After the initial shock of seeing the parent and its size for the first time, the few Rangers, Airborne, and Arizona State troopers opened fire on the animal. It easily dodged most of the flying bullets, and most of the projectiles that hit ricocheted harmlessly away after striking the hardened chest plates of the beast. The Talkhan sidestepped Dills's grenades as it leapt into the air and sank into the soil. It surfaced again in the center of the gathered policemen to quickly seize three troopers, one in its maw, the other two in its huge claws as they cried out in sudden pain, then disappeared with the beast below the surface. The others watched; a few, out of frustration, fired into the sand and rock in which men and animal had vanished.

Fielding grabbed a few of the remaining 101st personnel and set up a perimeter around the command tents. It seemed as if an hour had passed, when it had actually been only a moment since the attack had begun. Finally they heard the sound of rotors as the Apaches fought for altitude and climbed the mountain.

The ground once again exploded as the beast breached the surface twenty feet in front of the command tents. Fielding saw it first and fired a burst into the animal. The bullets bounced harmlessly off the armored chest and side as the Talkhan swiped at him. Dills quickly saw an opening and, without aiming, fired a grenade from the M79. The round exploded at the animal's feet, and it quickly turned and jumped through the air, landing in front of the state trooper, swiping at his chest and driving him to the ground, snapping ribs and breaking one arm. Fielding saw the animal's amazing leap and ran forward, still firing the M16. It swiped at Dills's prone form, claws barely scraping through his shirt as it missed. Then Virginia screamed as Fielding fired more rounds into the creature's back. It forgot about Dills as two of the bullets found the mark between the two plates that protected the animal's shoulder blades. It roared in pain and confusion as it turned from Dills and swiped at Fielding's still form. The huge claws easily separated the muscle, sinew, and vertebrae of the colonel's neck, sending his head flying thirty yards to strike the side of the forensics tent. The Talkhan immediately dove into the earth, again creating a soil eruption that covered most of Dills's agonized body. Then they all saw the wave as it sped for the COMM tent. As they watched, the battle started up again in the huge command enclosure, with Lisa facing the Destroyer of Worlds, alone.

• • •

Gus grabbed Matchstick into his arms and ran for their tent opening. The sight that met his eyes stopped him in his tracks. Bodies were lying everywhere, mutilated and smashed, crumpled and discarded as easily as one would toss away dirty clothes. As he was looking at the scene of slaughter, the whine and zing of bullets sounded in his ears, bringing back memories of his taking fire in Korea. And then he remembered what he'd wanted to do back then and couldn't. But now he could, he thought. The bullets barely missed him as they thumped into the tent flap. He ducked and ran in the direction of the crash site. Mahjtic, sensing the thoughts of the old man, said, *"Bug out, bug out, beat feet!"*

The animal came straight up through the ground and into the tent's plywood flooring. Lisa was lifted up into the air as the wood cracked and separated. As she hit the ground hard, landing on her back, knocking the wind from her lungs, she came face-to-face with the mother as it roared, shaking its head and sending its mane flaring and slicing through the sides of the tent. She roared again, sending spittle mixed with the blood of Lisa's comrades to soak Lisa's fatigues and face. The animal cocked its massive head and looked with hate-filled eyes at the weak creature staring up at her arrogantly.

Lisa stood stock-still, looking directly at the animal as it stood before her. Drool slowly fell from its open mouth as it leaned forward toward the diminutive human. Lisa swallowed as the creature seemed to be looking her over, possibly smelling her. Her right hand slowly started reaching for the M16 that was caught between an upturned desk and a support pole.

It suddenly and deftly reached down and plucked Lisa up in both of its massive hands, its claws digging deep into her sides and back, and Lisa screamed in pain and anger. The mother Talkhan roared again as it looked at the woman in her clutches. Lisa yelled right back, partly in terror, but mostly because she knew her death was imminent and she was angry. With great effort against the pain, she worked her right arm free and grabbed for the nine millimeter in her shoulder holster. Seeing this, the Talkhan squeezed, sending two of the sharpened claws deeper and puncturing one of Lisa's lungs, as it brought her toward its gaping, mandible-snapping, tooth-filled mouth.

As blood flowed freely from Lisa's lips, she weakly brought the pistol up and fired three times in quick succession into the beast's face. She was so weak by now the recoil after each round almost made her lose her grip on the pistol. One of the nine-millimeter rounds caught the raging animal in the right eye, knocking its head back and making it reach for its wounded face. The claws of the right hand severed a main artery in Lisa's stomach as they tore through her body and the screaming mother dropped her to the floor. It covered the wounded eye and roared, shaking the ground and rippling the tent as if an internal wind had erupted. The Destroyer then shook its head and brought the powerful tail up, and instead of stinging Lisa, it smashed the tail into her skull with bone-breaking accuracy. It repeatedly slammed the tail down, trying to obliterate the small creature that had caused it so much pain and anguish. It finished by repeatedly stabbing the now mangled body with its stinger, sinking the barbed tip deeply into the naval signalman's remains.

As the Talkhan stood glaring one-eyed at Lisa's body, the tent suddenly erupted as hundreds of thirty-millimeter rounds exploded into the interior. A number of the armor-piercing shells found their mark, neatly punching holes into the mother. It roared in pain and stumbled forward toward the opening. Then another two rounds exploded into its shoulder and upper chest. It screamed in outrage again as it leaped and dove into the earth just outside the tent, taking most of the canvas front panel of the communications and command enclosure into the hole with it.

The three Apaches circled the camp and saw nothing but

broken and lifeless bodies. Their thirty-millimeter chain guns turned and scanned the area of the crash site. Here and there men and women slowly stood and shook themselves off. Most were half-deaf from the loud explosions brought to bear by the attack helicopters.

Sarah had a horrible feeling. They had been unable to raise the crash site for the last half an hour, as they sprinted through the tunnel and up the mountain. Suddenly the radio crackled in her earpiece as they came shallow.

"I repeat, tunnel missions canceled, over."

Sarah bit her lower lip as she realized it hadn't been Lisa on the radio. But she couldn't wonder about her friend's fate just now.

"We have movement!" shouted one of the point men with the VDF device.

They stopped and the entire team brought their weapons up, and the laser sights pierced the darkness and ran off into the blackness settling on nothing. They waited. Finally, they saw movement, and then the old man suddenly appeared moving fast down the tunnel. He didn't notice at first he was being targeted as several laser sights settled on Mahjtic's wide eyes.

"*Sonsbeeeech, Guss, sonssssabeeeeches, don't shoooooooot. Gus and Maaahjtic!*" the small being cried, covering its head and burying its face into Gus's chest.

Gus threw his one free arm into the air, turning to the side to protect Matchstick the best he could. "Whoa there, get them laser beams off us!" Gus called out breathlessly.

"Mr. Tilly, what in the hell are you doing down here?" Sarah asked as she lowered the submachine gun.

"Escaping little missy." He placed his other arm around Mahjtic once again and hefted him higher onto his chest. "I guess no one told you. We just got our asses kicked up there," Gus said, nodding upward.

◆ ◆ ◆

Farbeaux had felt them coming long before they made an appearance. Despite that, the animals struck so fast that five of his men had been taken in the first few seconds of battle. They looked like the same monstrosities he had come across in the Broken Cactus, only now they had grown considerably. But as the smoke from the automatic weapons cleared after the beasts' lightning-quick assault, he quickly counted. He could account for only two of the creatures' bodies. Not a good kill ratio at all. The animals were clearly hard to kill, and he suspected they would be much harder later in their lives. Now he was getting an inkling of the reason his former employer Centaurus was interested in such an animal. The rewards in bioengineering alone could be a bottomless pit of money. And Hendrix would be just the man to head a project that would bring a creature as destructive as this onto some future battlefield. Even Farbeaux understood the ramifications of this animal. Left alone, mankind would never stand a chance against these creatures' abilities en masse.

They had been traveling slowly through the tunnel, stopping every few minutes for a VDF check and some oxygen. They hadn't even noticed that the creatures had been right there among them. Some were half-buried in the walls of the tubelike excavation and others half-burrowed into the floor. One had even struck from above. It was a trap that foreshadowed the grisly loss of a third of his men.

"It seems we are up against a species that is calculating enough to lay ambushes," Farbeaux said, looking at the faces of his remaining men. He glanced over at Julie, Billy, and Tony. "You there, hand me that bottle," he ordered, holding out his hand to Tony.

Tony looked from the bottle of Jack Daniel's to the Frenchman. He held it out and watched in horror as the bottle was passed back and forth between the Frenchman's mercenaries using the whiskey as disinfectant. Watching this made Tony madder than being kidnapped.

"Why don't you guys do what comes natural to French soldiers?" Tony said.

Farbeaux looked at the man a moment, then asked, "And what would that be, my drunken friend?"

"Give up and let Americans get a handle on this."

Billy couldn't help it, he laughed, lowering his head as his mother tried to stifle him by quickly placing a hand over his mouth and pressing hard.

"Still trying to save the entire world, huh? Well, it looks like you may have an enemy you can't bully, it looks—"

"I hate to interrupt, Colonel, but we may want to leave this place. I heard on the radio the Americans are pulling out of the tunnels in anticipation of another strategy," the bearded radioman said.

Farbeaux held his gaze on the three Americans a moment longer. "I believe we can learn no more from this excursion," he said, lowering his eyes. "Either way, Hendrix would have killed me." He looked at his men. "Come, I see no profit in dying here. We shall choose our own time and place, and we'll make it for money, not this dark death."

Julie was having difficulty taking a deep breath in the enclosed and claustrophobic tunnel. She wished they would just let them go.

Farbeaux was just starting to move away when he saw one of the dead animals. He held his light on what looked to be small, round grapes. The light caught a shadow inside that suddenly jittered. His eyes widened in amazement as he realized what he was looking at. Eggs! They were purplish in color and half the size of a wine grape. He looked around quickly, then removed his combat knife. He quickly emptied his canteen and stuck the knife into the membrane that held the hundreds of eggs. He gathered twenty or so on the edge of his knife and scraped them off into his plastic canteen. With his gloved hand he scooped up a few ounces of the clear viscous membrane and also deposited that in the canteen. He replaced it on his belt.

They were just getting ready to start out when the animals attacked again. Farbeaux was just missed as the first animal grabbed one of his men and pulled him into the earth. The colonel yelled and dropped his knife, then quickly fired at the retreating animal. He turned and started pushing his way to the front. Suddenly the whole side of the wall caved in as four of the beasts struck. It was all close-in fighting after that.

Julie pushed Billy and Tony ahead. "Run!" she shouted as she felt more than saw one of the animals turn and start coming their way, screeching and shaking its ugly head.

The screams coming from behind them in the tunnel intensified as they fled as fast as the darkness would allow. Suddenly Julie felt searing pain slice across her back as one of the animals leaped. Her blouse was torn in two down the middle of her back as she yelled for the others to run. She stopped and turned, facing the nightmare in front of her. The animal rose to its full height and roared, but no sooner had the sound emerged from its mouth than it staggered under an onslaught of bullets. Pieces flew from its body as the tracer rounds struck nonarmored areas of its torso. A few of the bullets whizzed by her head, missing her by mere inches. She then noticed a dozen thin red beams of light dotted all over the animal's chest and torso. Amazingly, they were coming from the direction the three had been heading. Everywhere a beam of red light hit, a bullet soon followed, either bouncing away harmlessly or digging into the purplish flesh. She slammed herself into the dirt and covered her head. Then suddenly the animal dove into the wall, cascading dirt and sand over her.

At the same time, the screams and gunfire in the section of tunnel they had just fled subsided to nothing.

Julie was shaking uncontrollably as she felt movement around her but was afraid to look up.

"Miss Dawes, you alright?" a familiar voice called out, barely audible to her through the dirt.

"Mom, hey, Mom, it's the major and Lieutenant Ryan," Billy shouted.

Julie slowly turned over, rocks and dirt sliding away as she winced in pain. She brought up a hand to shield her eyes from the harsh glare of the flashlights.

"That was pretty close," Ryan said, bending over and helping her to her feet.

With a trembling voice she hissed, "A little too close."

Collins stepped forward along with Mendenhall and Everett. Their weapons were still smoking and held at the ready.

"Who else is back there, ma'am?" Collins asked.

"Probably no one now," she answered, hugging Billy and Tony. Ryan pulled the two pieces of her blouse together from behind. "But there *were* soldiers or mercenaries, French-speaking." She gingerly turned and faced them. "The leader was a man that passed himself off as an Interior Department person in the Broken Cactus. A *colonel,* I think he had been called by one of his men."

"Farbeaux, Mom, his name was Farbeaux."

"Son of a bitch!" Everett exclaimed as he pushed by the others and made his way farther down the tunnel, squatting and holding his weapon high.

As Collins turned and followed, shining his powerful light after Everett's retreating form, he saw the carnage of what remained of the group of kidnappers. Most of them were, he assumed, missing. He looked down and saw a set of tracks leading the other way, away from where they stood and heading back into the tunnel.

Everett returned with a foul look on his face and looked the major in the eye. "It looks like one or two got away. And you can bet your ass on which one was among the two. Permission to give chase to that bastard," Everett asked.

Collins looked around, then at his watch. "Negative, let's get the hell out of here."

They both looked down the tunnel, knowing that the Frenchman was in there somewhere and there was nothing to do but hope he met a fate he deserved.

Thomas Tahchako was helping to unload what remained of his herd. The government boys had offered a good price for the lives of his now depleted number of cows, but he was secretly willing to sacrifice them all if he could just be a part of killing the horrible creature out there. He watched as the other ranchers in the valley unloaded their herds from trucks of every size.

As he turned his attention from the gathering cattle herd, he looked to the bright sky and prayed that this beast could be lured to this spot. He lowered his gaze toward the strange-looking drilling device and the heavy equipment that was busy smoothing the ground. He didn't really care to know what they were drilling for.

The army engineers that had been brought in from Fort Carson, using heavy drilling equipment they had confiscated from several construction companies in Flagstaff, had completed drilling the quarter-mile-deep pilot hole, between the two eastern edges of the Superstitions that slacked away to mere foothills and then nothing, as the mountain edges created a natural doorway out of the valley, or as Jack had earlier thought of it, a funnel.

With the hole drilled and all the sensors in place, the Special Ordnance Division of the U.S. Army out of Fort Carson, Colorado, started lowering the one device nothing could escape from, a fifteen-megaton tactical neutron warhead.

Operation Orion was about to be put into play with Jack's added plan of the funnel, if the animals could be lured to the open back door of the valley.

Collins was called forward by the Delta sergeant who had point. Jack left Ryan with the rescued civilians and patted Carl on the shoulder as he went by him.

"Everyone take some water and air," Jack ordered as he gave his canteen to Everett to pass back to Julie and the others.

The point man was kneeling and had his night-vision goggles raised as he peered into the shaft. He kept his eyes forward as he was joined by the major.

"What've you got, Sergeant?" Collins asked.

"We have another tunnel merging with this one. Looks

like one of the town's buildings from above has fallen in, must have been a lot of animal activity. See how the two converging tunnels have been widened, like they were foraging for food or something?"

Collins saw that the two tunnels made up a good-sized cavern. He thought he saw trash cans, bright and shiny new, racks of hand tools, and other racked and shelved items.

"Looks like the hardware store fell in here," Jack said as he waved forward two of the Rangers. "You take some water too, sergeant, we'll check it out," he said as he lowered his ambient-light goggles and started forward.

The hollowed-out space was riddled with items of every description. He easily stepped around a rack of lawn rakes and hoes. He held his hand up and pointed to the right for the two Rangers behind him to take that area. He continued forward as easily as he could. The expanded tunnel had a heavier than normal musky smell. As he looked up, he could see into the darkened recesses of the first floor of the hardware store. This must have been its basement as he saw large blocks of concrete that had once made up its foundation. From underneath one of the large blocks he saw an arm protruding. As he leaned over and felt for a pulse, he heard the shouts of the two Rangers as the far wall exploded in toward them. As Jack straightened, he felt the first shower of dirt as the roof of the tunnel fell in on him. He heard the screams and shouts as those men still in the tunnel rushed forward, but as quickly as it had started it was cut off like a radio being shut down. The tunnel behind had caved in, effectively sealing him and the two Rangers from the others.

The roar of an animal made Jack freeze as he tried to free himself from the fallen roof. He heard one of the men open fire and then the other started screaming. Collins moved from side to side, trying to push away the accumulated wall that encased him on all sides. Finally he felt his right arm free up, and he pulled himself up and out, spitting dirt and sand as he did.

Silence greeted his return to the air. He silently rolled down the hill that had been his own cage a moment before and found himself lying against plastic bags of fertilizer. Jack raised his goggles and reached into his vest and pulled out a flare and struck it. He tossed it over a jumble of wheelbarrows and immediately saw one of the creatures strike out at the light with its tail. Jack rose and fired a ten-round burst at the beast, which roared and turned on him. Collins fell backward over the fertilizer and landed with a thump into sacks of something whitish gray that plumed into the air around him. He fought to quickly right himself and came to his knees. Still off-balance, he saw the animal charge in the glowing red light of the flare. As he fired, the first three rounds hit the fifty-pound sacks of the whitish material in front of him, sending a cloud up as his other rounds passed through. He heard a roar and then the scrambling noises of the animal as it suddenly changed direction. He then heard the screams of the beast as it momentarily went crazy, slamming into the fallen racks and fixtures of the sunken hardware store.

Collins heard shouts coming from behind him as the rest of the tunnel team on the other side of the cave-in fought and dug to get to him. He saw the animal as it swiped at the white dust that clung to its sickening armor. Jack quickly fired ten rounds at the beast, and to his surprise he saw no ricochets as the armor-piercing ammo found weak spots all over. They seemed to stitch right up the animal's side armor as it screamed and fell forward, unmoving. Jack couldn't believe the easiness of this creature's death as compared to the others they had met up with. As he limped forward, he saw that the fifty-pound bags were full of potash. He figured some of the bitter-tasting stuff that he thought was used in planting may have blinded the creature, making it an easy target. He came forward and looked the animal over in the flare's light and could see where the armor had cracked as the bullets pierced it. Parts of its exoskeleton were lying beside it like fallen eggshell, and its blood was soaking into the ground.

Everett finally pushed the last of the dirt aside, and he and two others slid into the remains of the hardware store.

"Jack!" he called. "Where are the other two?"

Collins lowered his weapon and just nodded toward the far side of the tunnel. He reached out and rubbed a finger across the creature's armor, and his glove picked up a heavy coating of potash. He rubbed it together with his fingers and some soaked into his gloves; he felt a tingling but nothing any more significant than that.

"They're dead, Jack," Everett said as he returned.

Collins looked up from his fingers and into Everett's face. "We're all going to be if we don't get out of here," he said as he studied the unsteady and crumbling foundation of the hardware store, then finally turned and went back to the main tunnel.

It took thirty minutes for Collins's team to retrace their tracks through the tunnel to a large branch that he hoped led to another opening in the surface. The VDF machine had picked up nothing on their return but a far-off target that seemed too large to be one of the animals. Besides, the ghost target appeared to be at the far end of the valley where there had been no animal activity. The absence of any closer targets meant the offspring were heading out of the valley or were congregating somewhere else and keeping still, waiting around the next turn of the tunnel in ambush.

They moved closer to where they thought the town lay. Suddenly the small column stopped and Jack leaned against the wall and waited for Everett to report. It didn't take long.

"Major, you better come up here and look at this."

Jack took a deep breath and made his way past the others, winking at the small boy as he did. He found Everett looking to the right. Jack's eyes widened as he took in the massive tunnel. It had been excavated close to one of the offspring's burrowing and had partially caved it in, the one Collins and his team were currently inside. The large tunnel was three times the diameter of the tunnels they had been traveling through, and its odor was different from the stink they still couldn't get used to. But far more worrisome was the twenty-five-foot width of the hole.

"The mother?" Everett asked, shining his flashlight around the circumference of the shaft.

"Has to be, we haven't seen anything this size out of her offspring. But if it is, she's grown since she dug the tunnel at Site One."

"Can't tell which direction it's heading off in."

Jack lightly slapped Carl on the back. "Come on, we don't need to run into her right now, we're beat and low on ammo."

Carl turned away and started forward again.

Jack took one more look at the size of the tunnel and shook his head. The mother would have to be close to twenty-five feet tall to have made this. He turned his back on it and found the others.

Twenty minutes later Everett again held a hand into the air. They stopped and waited.

"We have a light up ahead, Major," Everett said into his microphone.

Collins eased his way past the others until he reached the front. Then he clicked his light off and waited for Everett, who turned and looked at Jack. Their faces told a story of hardship and terror he never wanted to see again. He had been through some bad situations before, but none that were this oppressive to the mind. He had started to think of the creatures as being much more than mere animals. They had to be sentient beings, with the intelligence to know when their lives were threatened. As he looked at his small group, he knew there could be no other conclusion.

"It looks like it leads up into some kind of bar or café or something, Major. No sign of the animals."

Ryan, who had left Julie, Billy, and Tony only after promising he would be right back, joined them. He had taken his nine millimeter and chambered a round, removed the safety, and started to hand it to Tony, then caught a whiff of whiskey from the man and handed it to Julie. "It's ready to fire, so be careful," he had told her.

"Hey, guys, what's up?" Ryan whispered when he found Jack and Carl.

"We have an entrance hole up ahead," Everett said.

"I smell cheeseburgers," Ryan said, sniffing. "Must be the Broken Cactus, Julie's place."

"As good a place as any to get the hell out of here." Collins adjusted his mike to his mouth and spoke softly to his remaining nine men. "Alright, listen up, we found a way out. Let's move quickly and try and make as little noise as possible."

Ryan returned to Julie and the others and let them know they were home.

"After you, swab," Collins said, smiling at Everett.

"Yeah, SEAL would probably taste better to it than some old leathery army type."

Everett slowly approached the hole and noticed ropes hanging down. This must have been some other team's point of entry, but he couldn't remember ever seeing it on the chart. Then he thought about Miss Dawes and her kid; this must have been the point where they had been taken into the tunnel. Everett tugged on the first rope and was satisfied it was secured well at the top, then he tested the second. Slowly Carl pulled himself up. When he was a foot from the top, he freed his automatic from its holster and peered over the top. He was looking into a kitchen. There were stainless steel counters, pots, pans, and dishes lying smashed and bent everywhere. He listened for any sign of movement, then sniffed. The odors of old grease and coffee assailed his nostrils. Then suddenly he heard it, a soft crunching sound he couldn't place. As his eyes roamed over the remains of the kitchen, he froze. One of the animals was hunched in a corner near the stove, and it had a man and was slowly eating him. Everett let his eyes adjust for a moment, then made out a Channel 7 Minicam lying next to the former owner. Carl grimaced and carefully eased his nine millimeter back into his shoulder holster and removed a grenade from his web belt. He placed pressure on his boots and held himself in place as he quietly pulled the pin. He quickly rolled the round grenade over the broken floor, where it bounced twice and landed at the creature's feet. As it tilted its head in curiosity, the grenade exploded. Everett had ducked down into the hole and was holding on tightly when the flash and loud boom shook dirt down on him and the others waiting in the tunnel.

He didn't bother to explain to the major and the rest of the team as he scrambled up the rope again and peered over the flooring and into the smoke-filled kitchen. He looked through the swirling, acrid smoke caused by the grenade and at first only saw the damage it had caused to Miss Dawes's kitchen. Then he saw movement. The creature was down but still alive. Shrapnel had found a weak spot somewhere on its armored body, but Carl didn't know how seriously it was wounded. He reholstered his weapon to free his hands again and climbed the rest of the way up and gained the kitchen floor. He rolled as quietly as he could and pulled his automatic again. But just before he could fire, an angry scream filled the kitchen as a man with a giant butcher's knife fell from the rafters onto the wounded animal. The beast roared and tried to stand, but its assailant plunged the knife again and again under its neck armor until the Talkhan finally collapsed from the shrapnel wounds and the plunging knife.

Everett was shocked when he saw the filthy and blood-covered man as he moaned loudly and then rolled off and lay spread-eagled on the damaged floor. Carl holstered his nine millimeter and knelt down beside the man and looked at him curiously. The T-shirt of the large, bearded man read KIRK OVER PICARD AND JANEWAY UNDER ME!

"Like your shirt," Everett said, quickly checking the man's wounds.

The animal grunted and lay still in the far corner, and Everett stood and walked over to it and, to be sure it was finally dead, kicked it. Then he looked at the remains of the Channel 7 cameraman and grimaced. He then moved his weapon from side to side, sweeping the area for anything that so much as moved. Satisfied, he whispered into his mike the all clear while assisting Hal Whikam to his feet.

"What happened up there?" Collins asked from below.

"Don't let Ms. Dawes and the boy hesitate in the kitchen on their way through. It's not pretty, looks like the Channel Seven camera jock wasn't as fast as his reporter friend."

One by one Everett helped the others into the kitchen of the Broken Cactus. Julie was the first up and saw the man lying against the stove breathing hard. He was bloody and cut in so many places she couldn't believe it.

"Hal!" she screamed and ran to him. "Billy, Hal's alive!" she called back over her shoulder. "Hal, oh, Hal . . . God, what happened to you?"

Hal opened his eyes and focused on Julie. He smiled at her and then Billy as he joined her.

"That was one tough motherfucker, Jules, I'll tell you that," Hal said weakly. "We fought back and forth down in those tunnels for what had to be the longest four hours of my freakin' life. Then I made it back up here and the bastard had me cornered. Luckily for me, that reporter guy, you know, the one from Phoenix, Kashihara?" Hal grimaced in pain as he tried to raise his head. "He came in the diner screaming about being left behind." Hal focused on Julie again after drifting for a moment. "Well, I guess you could say he saved my life. That monster thing went for him and the chickenshit bastard actually pushed his cameraman in front of him and ran. But he got his when he turned and another one of those ugly bastards got him and took him under. That gave me time to scramble up in the rafters, then Captain Marvel there chucks in a grenade and almost made mincemeat outa me."

Julie hugged Hal and with Billy's help assisted him to his feet, and they slowly made their way out of the kitchen.

"But I finally got that fucker," Hal said with his arms around Julie and Billy. Hal gave one final look at the beast and shook his head admiringly. "What a tough SOB," he mumbled.

Collins immediately ushered everyone into the dining room and then called the base camp, looking around as the others found places to sit and rest. He watched Julie as she went behind the bar and filled glasses full of ice and water and passed them around. As Jack listened to the report from the base camp, he was glad his remaining men had removed their earpieces and let them dangle as they removed gloves, helmets, and the new body armor that had saved most of their lives. Collins turned away while listening to the voice on the other end explaining the details of the loss of life belowground and at the base camp. Collins shook his head as he listened to the numbers. When he was done, he turned and slowly walked up to Everett, who was just staring out the window. The major took a deep breath when he saw that the big SEAL still had his radio on and his earpiece in. In exasperation Jack removed his helmet and took his gloves off and threw them inside.

"We don't know for sure if she was one of the casualties, Carl," he said softly. At first it didn't look as if Everett was going to respond. Carl, for his part, was surprised that Collins had seen through his ruse with Lisa so quickly. But what did it matter?

"You didn't get a chance to know her, Jack. Most people just looking at her would've thought she was just another dumb blond or some stupid crap like that. But she was smart." Carl spit some dirt from his mouth. His voice lowered as he again looked out the window. "And brave? I've never known a braver woman. If the parent hit the base camp, she would have done her duty," he said as he turned and faced Jack.

Collins patted him on the back and turned to the others. "They're sending a Pave Low to pick us up. Is the way to the roof through there, Ms. Dawes? I came up the outside stairs earlier and I don't fancy going out there and doing it again."

"Yes, back through the kitchen," Julie's tired voice answered, and then she winced as Ryan applied ointment to the nasty cut running the entire length of her back.

"Don't bother to hand out menus," Everett said from the window, "Major, we're about to have company."

Collins ran to where Everett was looking out the window. Jack made no reaction for Julie's and Billy's sakes as he watched four or five waves of parting concrete and street asphalt head right for the Broken Cactus. Two zigzagged and crossed the road, sending up huge chunks of roadway as they crossed Main Street, then suddenly they swerved back toward them.

"Site One, Site One, we have company. We're headed for the roof, repeat, we are headed for the roof," Collins said as calmly as he could into the mike, then put his gloves back on. "Okay, kids, let's head up. Ryan, you first, take the civilians. . . . Where is the other one?"

Everyone looked around, but Tony had disappeared.

"Don't have time for this, let's just hope he knows what he's doing," Collins said, as he placed his last magazine into his XM8.

The navy pilot led the protesting Julie, Billy, and the wounded Hal to the stairs as they yelled about not leaving Tony. They were quickly followed by the remaining five Delta and Rangers. Collins called for Everett, who was still looking out the large dining-room window. Carl silently watched the advancing animals while shoving a new magazine into his own assault rifle, then he suddenly turned and dove as the floor exploded in the exact place he had been standing. He rolled and came up firing into the animal as it cleared the wall and floor. The rounds struck but only a few caused any noticeable damage.

The beast struck out and its claws sent Jack's XM8 crashing against the wall. Then it quickly turned on Everett and swiped, catching him on the new vest. The nylon covering material separated easily, but then the steel-like claws struck the packed-abalone-shell case and ricocheted off. Still, Carl was thrown across the room, the rounds from his weapon stitching a pattern in the wooden ceiling and sending 5.56-mm rounds slamming into the headboard of Billy's bed upstairs.

Now the Talkhan turned its full attention on Jack. He quickly pulled his personal combat knife from its scabbard and faced the inhuman form before him. The beast roared, shaking the remaining dishes and pans in the kitchen. Jack quickly glanced in the direction of Everett, who was just starting to regain his senses after striking the far wall.

The beast watched Jack, its brows arched to show the full glory of its yellow eyes, then it charged, head up and claws extended. Jack didn't move at first. To a layman it would have seemed Collins was frozen in fear, but Jack had a mind that always planned three moves ahead. As the beast charged and swiped at Jack, he ducked, barely escaping being raked by the death-dealing talons. As he did so, he quickly brought his black-painted, stainless-steel-edged knife up and slashed at the creature's leg tendons that were exposed when its leg muscles flexed. The Talkhan screamed in pain as the knife severed the tendon in its right knee joint. Before the beast could turn on Collins, he had come up behind it and instantly found a vulnerable spot in its massive shoulder armor. He quickly sank the blade in and out three times in succession, wounding the animal to the point it was delirious in pain and outraged at the assault.

Everett shook himself and looked about for his assault rifle. He found it three feet away.

Jack was surprised how quickly the animal recovered and regained its momentum. Instead of turning around to face its enemy, the beast quickly brought its tail up and slapped at Jack. The stinger caught in the front of his vest and pulled him down to the floor, slamming him into the bloodstained linoleum.

"Stay down, Jack!" Everett cried.

Collins quickly covered his head as the XM8 opened up.

Taking advantage of the animal's distraction as Everett slammed rounds into it, Jack rolled free, dodging two quick stabs of the creature's stinger, and recovered his own weapon. He opened up, adding his firepower to Everett's. Somewhere in the firestorm of tracers and smoke, the animal dove back through the hole it had entered by. Jack stopped firing, then watched the SEAL as his weapon finally ran out of ammunition.

"What do you say we get some sun?" Jack asked, eyeing Everett closely.

"Let's go," he said, turning and quickly running for the kitchen and the safety of the roof.

As they broke free of the stairway and into the bright sunshine of the late afternoon, they saw the other members of the team firing their weapons over the false front of the building. Julie was holding Billy in her arms and had an arm around Hal as they huddled at the feet of Ryan as the flier fired one shot at a time from his nine-millimeter handgun.

Collins and Everett ran to the front where Ryan was standing and looked out over the small town. The creatures were everywhere, diving back into the ground, then surfacing a moment later.

The soldiers watched incredulously as round after round bounced from them and into the dirt or into a wall after slamming into the creatures' armor.

"Shit," Collins said under his breath.

Two loud explosions rocked the building as the Rangers tossed grenades over the side. A Delta sharpshooter brought one of the animals down with a perfect shot into one of its eyes. It stumbled and skidded into the side of the building. A Ranger popped up and threw another grenade down right next to the fallen beast and it went off, jolting the creature away from the wall. Other animals fell upon the still-smoldering carcass, tearing huge chunks of flesh from it, devouring their sibling.

Then, as suddenly as the attack began, it ended. The animals had stopped dead in their tracks. The only movement was a gentle swaying as though they were listening to music only they could hear.

The strange thing was the soldiers *were* hearing music, as the sound of the jukebox was coming from the barroom below. The animal's landing against the building must have jarred it and shorted something out, and Collins shook his head as he watched the strange behavior of the beasts and listened to Guns N' Roses singing "Knockin' on Heaven's Door."

"Things have taken a turn for the fucking surreal," Jack said under his breath.

The others heard the music and watched the creatures as they swayed back and forth. The remaining troops looked

from the Talkhans to each other. They were totally surrounded by the mass of animals, and everyone knew it was
just a matter of time before they started to attack again.

The gathered survivors on the buildings' roof may have
thought the creatures were swaying to the soft rhythm of the
song. But what had caught their attention were the minute vibrations coming from the desert valley. They were also picking up signs on the wind that humans couldn't smell. It was
the distinct odor of food, a lot of it. Also, an invisible wave
was striking the animals that called them away. The male
was aboveground and signaling in the center of the valley.

As those on the roof watched, all the animals save for one
dove into the earth and started heading away from the town,
at least ninety of the animals, Collins quickly counted. The
one remaining had stopped swaying and was looking
straight up at them. As they watched, a blackened tongue
shot out of its mouth and it lowered itself closer to the
ground.

"Son of a bitch is going to spring!" Collins shouted, taking aim with his weapon.

The animal crouched, gathering and bunching its muscles
for the short leap to the rooftop. The huge tail coiled behind
it for use in tandem with its legs to shoot itself toward its
next feeding.

The men gathered quickly, raising their rifles, and a few
pulled the pins on grenades.

"Get ready to repel boarders," Ryan said, quoting the famous naval order, only half-jokingly.

The animal launched itself.

Things of a terrifying nature sometimes seem to happen
as mere snapshots of the event, creating a slide show for the
observers. None of the gathered soldiers would ever remember how the pickup truck had gotten so close without any of
them seeing it or hearing it. And with that surreal slowness
to it, they watched as the animal just cleared the ground and
the front bumper struck it. The truck sent the beast in a head-
long tumble ending in a crunching impact on the street, with
the pickup careening into the Ice Cream Parlor. The creature

hit in the middle of Main Street and skidded. It was hurt, but had not been killed. It slowly gained its feet and looked at its attacker and roared, then started forward, slowly making its way to its assailant. But it never made it. None of the people on the rooftop of the Broken Cactus saw or even heard the scream and thump of the hovering air force Pave Low III as the twenty-millimeter cannon at its rear ramp opened fire, sending two thousand rounds hurtling at the creature. The weapon was fed ammunition by a giant hopper attached next to it and wasn't going to run out soon. The large bullets struck the animal, sending it forward until it slammed into the protruding back end of the truck. Stuck there, it was slowly pounded to nothing by the Pave Low and her Gatling gun.

Five minutes later several happy men pulled the drunken Tony from the front seat of his battered pickup. He'd received a rather large cut to his forehead after smashing into the beast, but smiled as Julie handed him a fresh bottle she'd grabbed on her way back down from the roof. She hugged him and admonished the older man for disappearing on them and for doing something as stupid as saving them, but Ryan pulled her away as everyone to a man wanted to pat him on the back.

Only after they had been loaded up on the huge Pave Low did Tony venture any comment.

"I guess I don't have a truck anymore, Miss Dawes, so I can drink all I want," he said, looking at the smiling Delta and Ranger troops.

Farbeaux waited for the big helicopter to leave the roof of the café and then made his way out of the Texaco station where he had holed up while the town was under attack. He was the only one of his team to make it out of the tunnel and he felt lucky at best. He had a canteen full of the eggs of the creature, but he wouldn't even be able to sell that if he couldn't leave the town.

He took the last swallows from a bottle of warm Coke, then slowly made his way toward one of the six remaining helicopters lining the road across town.

The Frenchman's liftoff was noticed by the orbiting AWACS, but it was paid no mind as it was thought to be an army Kiowa helping to evacuate the remaining ground teams.

Colonel Henri Farbeaux had managed to survive the impossible once again, only now he was on his own and dangerous as he was in a flight for his life.

J ack, Everett, Ryan, Mendenhall, and the remaining tunnel team were on a Pave Low III that had diverted to Chato's Crawl on its way to refuel. As medics started treating the wounded and Ryan helped Julie, Billy, and Tony, who in turn assisted Hal into a corner out of the way, Jack was surprised to see Virginia Pollock standing before him with a grave look on her face.

"We heard about the base camp," Jack said, tiredly looking from Virginia to Carl.

"That's not it," she said, leaning down so he could hear over the turbines. "We finished the analysis on the creature's exoskeleton, Jack. Your plan won't work. No matter what weapon you use, it won't penetrate their armor. Unless they are right on top or just below an underground detonation, the heat and X-rays won't kill them."

Collins, his face filthy and body hurting, closed his eyes. "There was no luck on the analysis of the chemical in the cage tanks that reduced the creature in '47?"

"No, it's not even an acid that we can tell. We did identify a minuscule amount of an agent that is found here on earth in the largest of the three tanks. Alkali, it was alkali-based, but that's a base, Jack, not an acid," Virginia said as she patted his leg. "I wish I had better news." She straightened and looked from Jack to Everett and placed her hand on Carl's shoulder. "Lisa . . . ," Virginia started to say, then stopped, putting a finger to her trembling lips. "She . . . saved my life, Carl," she finally said, then turned away.

Everett looked at Jack and nodded, as he finally heard it officially.

"Wait a minute," Jack said as he struggled to his feet. "Virginia, what in the hell is potash anyway? Is it used for planting or something?"

Virginia swallowed and stared at Collins with a questioning look.

"It is, well, lime, potash, they're both used as soil enrichment, they're both alkali . . ."

"Did you test alkali against the exoskeleton?" Jack asked.

"No, we only found trace amounts in the one canister . . ."

"In the tunnels, I was about to die at the hands of one of those beasts when it stopped suddenly. I couldn't figure why it didn't attack me through the remains of the hardware store that had fallen through to the tunnel. I looked around me and I must have been in the garden section of the store, fertilizer, plant food . . . and potash."

Virginia didn't respond at first.

"It was an entire pallet of potash, Virginia. The fifty-pound bags were all busted open and the stuff was everywhere. That's why the beast didn't come after me, and when it got some of the stuff on it, it flew into a rage, rolling in the dirt and slamming into walls, and then I dropped it with a few rounds. They penetrated its weakened armor because it was dusted with the stuff. Dammit, Virginia . . . the potash!"

"Alkali," she said to herself. "Alkali was the catalyst that allowed the acid to work in the cages!"

THIRTY-TWO

A t the confluence of the small range where the edges of the mountains joined together and formed the small valley that Chato's Crawl sat in, the combat engineer company from Fort Carson was beginning their evacuation as the special ordnance section wired the remote firing trigger and placed the portable antenna that would send a signal to the fifteen-megaton neutron warhead buried a quarter mile beneath the target area. The remote sending unit, sitting in the back of the engineer's Humvee, would now be placed under the orders of Jack Collins, who was in total control since the death of Colonel Sam Fielding.

"That does it, Captain," the communications technician said to Captain Reggie Davis. "The antenna is hot. Now all you have to do is enter your code to arm the device."

Davis had done this over a hundred times in simulation and knew the procedure by heart. But as he lifted the transmitter that would send the signal down the shaft and arm the weapon, he knew this was the first actual nuclear device he had ever activated.

Davis punched into the transmitter, which was no larger than a handheld calculator, *1178711 code 1T2 actual,* and pushed ENTER. As he watched, the small window at the top went blank, then showed in red letters, *Code accepted. Field device 45145 activated.* Davis swallowed and held his breath, then pushed ENTER again.

Armed.

"Let's get the hell out of here and inform base camp they have a live nuke on their hands."

As they were the last two in the target area, they were alone as they climbed into the Humvee. Davis climbed into the right-side seat and let the COMM tech take the wheel. He reached into the back and brought out a black case, making sure to keep his hands away from the telescopic antenna attached to the side. He clicked open the box and made sure the remote detonating device was working. In the window at the center of the box was the word *Activated.* The keyboard below was live, and all the triggerman had to do was enter *1T3* and raise the clear plastic cover, then push the red flashing button. Then all hell would break loose underneath the sands of the valley. Captain Davis closed the case, checked the antenna once again, and carefully replaced it in the backseat.

"Okay, let's go, and hope they don't have to use this godforsaken thing."

The technician gunned the engine and started speeding across the valley toward the base camp.

Site One, Base Camp

The Pave Low III settled onto a high ridge. It would have to stay put and be refueled when the other helicopters returned because she was now nearly empty. Jack ran to where they had placed some backup command radios and started asking everyone from Washington to Nellis about the location of large amounts of alkali.

"Niles, I'm not even sure, but it may just weaken the animals' armor enough for the X-rays and gamma rays that the neutron bomb releases to penetrate and kill them. As it is right now, the bomb won't get them all. I need that stuff before they make a run for freedom."

No one knew what to do about getting the quantity they needed to them in time. Jack slammed the microphone down onto the table and bashed it a few times in frustration. He ran a hand through his filthy hair and looked up in anger.

"Let's get a team together and go gather what we can from the remains of the hardware store," he said to Everett.

Billy, who was sitting in the shade with his mother and Tony after seeing Hal into the first aid tent, overheard what was being said at the communications table. He stood and shrugged his mother's restraining hand off and approached Jack.

"M. . . . M . . . Major?" he said, tugging at Collins's armor.

"What is it, Billy?" Ryan said, trying to get in between the boy and Jack.

"Alkali—will that hurt those things?"

Jack turned and looked down at the boy, then quickly lifted him to the table. "That's exactly what we need. Do you know where we can get some?"

Billy looked from Jack to Ryan. "Only a whole big lake of it. But Gus told me never to go there. He said I could get really hurt by it."

Jack couldn't talk; he didn't know how to pursue his questioning.

"A lake?" Ryan asked.

"He means a dry lake bed, it's called Soda Flats," Julie said as she stepped up to the table and took Billy's hand. "And he was supposed to stay away from there; the damn place is clearly marked as a danger."

Everett took the map from Virginia as she ran up to the group after overhearing Billy. He quickly spread it out on the table. "Where, son, where is the lake?"

Billy half closed his eyes as he found Chato's Crawl, then ran his finger east. "Here, right here," he said as he jabbed his finger onto the map.

"God, it was right in front of us the whole time, Soda Flats, looks like about three miles in diameter," Jack said. He

quickly ran his own finger from the dry lake bed south. He
jabbed hard at the confluence of low hills that marked the
funnel end of the valley and where the engineers were placing the bomb. "Goddammit!"

"We can't catch a fuckin' break!" Everett said loudly as
he turned. "If the animals are afraid of this stuff, Jack,
they'll head straight for the back door and won't go anywhere near the damn alkali."

"The cattle, the cattle have to be moved!" Jack said as he
reached for the radio.

Valley Forge, Valley Forge, do you have indication of
movement on GPS ground sensors? Over," Ryan called
from the open rear hatch of the Pave Low III. At first
Ryan got only dead air, then the AWACS finally reported:
"Negative ground contact at this time. Valley Forge will advise, over."

As Collins and the remaining members of the tunnel assault teams watched from a ledge just sixty feet from the
recently destroyed Site One base camp, Everett held up
a map and explained where Soda Flats was. They didn't notice the beast watching them from its high vantage point in
the rocks. It was badly wounded. Blood coursed down into
its thick hair, matting it together as it dried in the sun. The
mother leaped from the rocks toward the unsuspecting group
of soldiers.

Sarah and her team had just crawled from the large hole
and into the battlefield of the crash site. She removed the
night-vision goggles and tossed them aside, breathing in
the fresh air.

Sarah saw the creature just as it jumped. She brought her
weapon up and fired, knowing as she did she was too late.

The large animal struck Collins with its shoulder, sending him over the ledge from which they had been scanning Soda Flats. It then landed and swiped at Mendenhall, catching him in the chest and flinging him into Everett. They both crashed to the ground as if they were made of nothing more than paper, leaving a fine mist of red that swirled in the air as the animal moved again. The Talkhan raised her head and roared, catching the pilot and copilot of the Pave Low that had ferried Collins and his team from the town with one blow of its massive claws, decapitating both. She then turned to leap at two Blackhawk pilots who fired point-blank into its exposed back. The beast turned with lightning speed and grabbed one of them by the head, squeezing until the pilot's skull exploded under the pressure, the body falling onto his bleeding copilot.

The creature turned to the spot where Collins had gone off the small ledge and had landed on another outcropping of rock instead of falling a hundred feet to his death. The Talkhan easily hopped down, fully intending to finish what it had started. Standing over the major's still form, it brought its right set of claws up to swing downward, and its tail, with venom dripping from its stinger, rose into the air, then suddenly something small and almost insignificant jumped onto its back. It hesitated for a split second, then easily reached back and pulled the screaming Matchstick off and angrily tossed it over the cliff. But the small alien's attack hadn't been in vain. It gave Everett and the remaining soldiers enough time to get over their shock and start firing at the beast.

Bullets ripped into the mother from all directions. Some bounced off and one even grazed Collins on the forehead, but others found damaged places in the already battered armor of the mother Talkhan. It staggered backward and lost its footing, trying in vain to straighten as more rounds tore into its armored skin and found soft spots. The tail swung in a slow arc, trying to strike something, anything. Finally it made a last lunge toward Sarah and its antagonists as it stumbled one last time and fell to the ground, unmoving.

A moment earlier Gus had been unable to control Mahjtic. As soon as they saw what was going to happen to Major Collins, the alien, without a moment's hesitation, jumped from the old man's arms and leaped onto the Destroyer's back in a show of pure hatred. Gus had seen it all as if he had been watching outside of his own body. He remembered his own screams as the mother had grabbed the little being and thrown it off the cliff. Now he just went to his knees and placed his hands over his eyes.

M ajor, Valley Forge is broadcasting; they say they have something moving on the valley floor."

Collins turned to look at his second-in-command, wincing as he did from at least two cracked or broken ribs.

Collins looked at Sarah. "You stay until Gus is out of here; nobody gets near Matchstick unless it's someone from the Group, clear?"

"Yes, sir, nobody will touch them."

Collins and Ryan turned away, and with Everett helping them they climbed back into the base camp. Jack went to the Pave Low ramp and took the headphones from the 101st sergeant who was already holding them out.

"This is Site One Actual, what have you got exactly?" he asked, wincing at the pain in his ribs.

"Site One, we have an intermittent contact bearing on heading 445, moving east at a high rate of speed. Contact is larger than previous targets, repeat, larger than previous targets. It comes shallow then goes deep; we lose it at that point until it comes shallow again. GPS confirms from remote sensors. Contact is definite and now is being joined by at least ninety smaller targets. Over."

"Roger, Valley Forge, Site One will advise," Collins said as he quickly tossed the headset to Ryan and turned, and, in pain, ran for the cliff overlooking the valley. Ryan looked at Everett and followed.

Sarah left Gus and Matchstick and climbed the cliff face and joined them at the edge, wondering what they were looking at.

So far they hadn't seen any indication of movement from the sand and scrub below. When Jack locked his eyes on the prone body of the mother, he saw a few underdeveloped eggs that had burst from her abdomen wounds, and that started him thinking.

"How big around was that hole we came across near the diner?" he asked, still looking at the dead form of the parent Talkhan.

"Twenty-three, twenty-five feet in diameter," Everett answered, following Jack's eyes to the mother.

"Too big," Jack mumbled.

"What do you mean 'too big'?" Sarah asked.

"Look, this has to be the mother. It's larger than the ones in the tunnels, the tail and stinger are more developed than the smaller ones, and if I'm not mistaken, those are eggs. That hole we saw down there was too damn big for this animal. Whatever made that hole is huge, much larger than this creature."

"God, I didn't see it," Everett said.

"What in the hell do we have out there now?" Jack said.

As they watched, they saw the sands below the mountain about two miles distant shimmer and start jumping and vibrating, creating an eerie blurred effect.

"What the fuck?" Ryan asked no one. "Look!" He pointed to the right. "Who in the hell is that?"

Collins looked but didn't see it at first. Then he hobbled over to one of the tables and started slashing reports and other equipment from it until he found what he was looking for. He grabbed the binoculars and turned and focused on the thing that was kicking up dust to the west of where the AWACS said the target was.

"Damn, is that the engineers? They were the only unit east of us, correct?"

"They reported in about ten minutes ago. They confirmed Orion was active," Ryan said.

"Shit, get on the radio, Ryan, and warn them off, they're heading right for whatever that is down there!"

THIRTY-THREE

The White House Situation Room

The president was standing and drinking a glass of water when General Hardesty leaned over and saw the remaining command element at Site One as they were gesturing wildly at something below in the valley. Then his attention was diverted by the frantic call from Ryan in Arizona.

"Mr. President, something seems to be happening," he said.

As the president turned toward the large monitor, the general turned up the volume on the radio frequency.

"It's huge, Site One, and it's breaching now!" they heard the call from the AWACS.

"For God's sake, what now?" the president asked the room, but they all were busy standing and pointing at the remote camera relay from the valley.

The sight was one that all who witnessed it would never forget and would in the years to come haunt their nightmares. The undiscovered male breached the surface of the valley floor and shot into the air fifty feet, trailing dirt and sand in its wake. The multicolored armor plates of its neck were caught in the rays of the sun and sparkled, sending reflections of deep bloodred against the purple of its body armor. Then suddenly at least eighty or ninety of the smaller offspring shot up and out of the desert floor, mimicking the male. They formed their arches on both sides of the larger Talkhan. The animal was huge. Collins estimated from head to foot it was at least thirty feet fully erect. The male Talkhan hit the top of its arc and gracefully curled and rolled and entered the desert hardpan on its back and disappeared beneath the splash of sand and rock, quickly followed by the others.

"God, they're headed right for the Humvee," Jack said. "Ryan?" he called.

"Can't raise 'em!" Ryan called while still holding the headphones to his head.

As everyone from the valley, the White House, and the Event Center watched, the male surfaced again exactly in the path where the Humvee was speeding back to Site One. It sent the vehicle into the air 150 feet, paying it no more attention than it would a small bush. The beast roared as it started its fall back into the soil. The Humvee crashed hard back to earth; the entire armored vehicle was now upside down and crumpled.

"Site One, this is Valley Forge. Target has changed aspect and is moving toward sector 327. Repeat, target is now moving toward sector 327," the AWACS reported.

"Roger, sector 327," Ryan said. Jack was already heading to the Pave Low where Ryan had a map laid out on the ramp. Ryan quickly circled the area in red marker. "Goddammit, Major, the bastards are making a run out of the valley."

"Right for the funnel, into the last line of defense," Jack said as Everett joined them. "Contact Niles and relay to the ranchers to get the cattle moving."

"Then let's get ready and blow the crap out of it," Everett said.

Jack thought as he looked below at the line of collapsing tunnel as the beast ran for the eastern gate of the valley, quickly followed by its siblings. His eyes went to Sarah and the others.

"Gentlemen, the remote trigger for the weapon is in the Humvee," Jack said simply.

"Then we better go get it," Ryan said.

It was Everett who knew what Jack already did. Carl turned and watched as the surviving tunnel teams and Event personnel were covering the remains of the three pilots killed in the mother's final attack and helping the fourth, who was lying on the ground bleeding to death.

"Jesus Christ! Can we get a break here?" Carl said for the second time that day, then looked to the sky in frustration.

"Is someone going to let me in on what's going on?" Ryan asked.

"By the time we get to the Humvee, the animals will be out of the valley and gone," Everett said with his eyes closed in frustration. "The Blackhawks and other Pave Lows are all refueling."

Then Ryan caught on. He threw the headphones onto the back ramp of the huge Pave Low in frustration.

"You're a pilot, aren't you?" Jack said to Ryan, looking at the grounded Pave Low.

Ryan was confused. He looked around and then caught on to what Jack was asking.

"Major, I've never flown one of those in my life. I don't even like riding in the fucking things."

"What about the smaller one?" Collins asked, heading for the lone Blackhawk.

"Are you nuts?" Ryan asked as he chased Collins.

"Where is the crew chief for this aircraft?" Everett called out.

"Right here, sir," a young spec 5 called out.

"Can you fly?" Everett asked quickly as he started gathering weapons.

"No, sir, I'm just a crew chief."

Jack slapped the young man on the back and shoved him toward Ryan. "Well, you've now been promoted to warrant officer, and you will assist your new pilot in the copilot's station. Move."

"Major—"

Everett and the injured Collins just turned and glared.

Ryan grimaced and ran for the imposing Blackhawk.

One minute later Ryan was sitting in the left seat of the Blackhawk staring at the flight panel of the huge helicopter.

The crew chief leaned over and studied the buttons and switches angrily. He pointed quickly. "This one, this one, and this one," the boy said as he pushed two buttons and threw a switch.

"Power coming up!" Ryan called out more for himself than the others.

The four blades of the composite rotors started turning and coming up to speed. Ryan studied the controls. He knew the collective throttled both of the powerful engines when twisted and raised the helicopter when pulled up, and he knew the pedals operated the tail rotor to compensate for the torque of the main engines, but he didn't know how they actually worked. This was no Tomcat and he was totally uncomfortable without any wings.

"Come on, Ryan, get us in the air!" Collins yelled. He was listening on the headphones as the AWACS was calling out the position of the animal. It was only five miles away from the mouth of the funnel and closing on it fast.

Ryan closed his eyes and twisted the throttle on the collective with his left hand. That brought a burst of power to the main rotors and the tail boom. He opened his eyes as the rotors started really spinning and thumping. Then Ryan gently pulled up on the collective, which manipulated the rotors that supplied the Blackhawk with lift, but the helicopter didn't lift. He twisted the throttle to its stops.

"Oh, shit, we're going to die!" Ryan said aloud.

The young, just promoted spec 5 just stared wide-eyed out of the windshield as the large helicopter just sat there. Ryan gulped and again pulled up on the collective and immediately felt his stomach lurch as the heavy bird lifted suddenly with a jolt. It slowly started to spin to the right and Ryan applied foot pressure to the left pedal. It was harder to push than the foot pedals in his Tomcat, but it was pressed hard enough to slow the rate of the Blackhawk's spin. They had made two complete circles before Ryan finally stopped the spin. He shook his head in the affirmative though no one had asked him anything.

Out of the open side door Jack saw Sarah wave with a sad look as the helicopter started to lift into the air. Then she seemed to come to a decision and looked angry. She dropped her hand and sprinted for the Blackhawk. Jack started shouting for her to get out of the way and screaming also for Ryan to hold it. But it was too late; Sarah placed her right foot on the left wheel of the helicopter and used it as leverage to launch herself up and into the cabin. She flopped on the deck and winced as she looked up into the angry face of Collins.

"Look, I'm the only one that isn't injured, you need me!"

"When this is over, we're going to talk, McIntire," Jack said as he reached down and pulled Sarah to her feet.

Ryan slowly pushed the control stick forward and the Blackhawk lurched and lost altitude. He quickly twisted the throttle and its descent was halted, but not before the left wheel assembly hit a large rock outcropping, tearing the wheel away. Everett and Collins were thrown forward in the back compartment and looked out the door and watched the wheel and gear fall and strike the ground below, bouncing and just missing several men and women on the ground.

"Goddammit, Lieutenant!" Everett shouted.

"Sorry, sorry," Ryan said. Cursing under his breath, he spared a glance over to the specialist who was holding on for dear life. "Relax, trooper, I got it now!" Ryan shouted as the Blackhawk shot out over the cliff and started its jerking run for the crashed Humvee.

Event Complex, Nellis AFB, Nevada

I didn't know Ryan could fly helicopters," Niles said as they watched the video feed.

Alice was staring at the monitor. "According to his file, he can't," she said as she patted the nervous Lee on the leg again.

Three minutes later Ryan was hovering three hundred feet above the crashed Humvee after passing it twice while trying to figure out the best way to set the helicopter down. Then he swallowed and twisted the collective power down and slowly brought the control stick back toward his chest. He breathed easier when the Blackhawk started to settle easily.

"To the right, to the right!" Everett called out. As Ryan couldn't see right below them, he didn't notice he was coming down right on top of the mangled wreckage.

"Jesus!" he said as he pushed on the right pedal and swung the stick to the right. Then he felt the left wheel touch down with a groaning bang.

"Hurry, I can't hold it here forever," Ryan said into the back, then looked over at his young copilot. "Are you going to do anything this whole trip?"

The specialist chanced a look at Ryan and shook his head. "No, sir, I am not."

Everett, Sarah, and Jack jumped from the Blackhawk and ran for the crashed Humvee. They scrambled inside. They first checked the driver and then the captain sitting beside him. They were both dead.

"It's a black box the size of a laptop," Collins called out over the noise of the helicopter.

"Got it!" Everett called.

Jack looked up and saw Carl was holding up the black box. Then all three ran back to the Blackhawk and jumped aboard, making Ryan lose control for a moment because of the sudden weight change. Then he lifted too quickly into the air, slamming both Everett and Collins to the floor. Sarah quickly followed, landing on top of Jack.

"Head back to Site One," Everett ordered Ryan.

• • •

All was quiet on the valley floor where the gathered cattle from the surrounding ranches grazed, only a half mile from the exit to the valley, the place where Jack Collins had first guessed the Talkhan would turn to run. The state police and the FBI had combined all the assets the surrounding ranches could provide. Every truck, trailer, and even the expensive air force Pave Lows had been used to get the makeshift herd together. The six hundred head of cattle were lowing, unaware of the role they were about to play in the drama getting ready to unfold, or the part they would play in the fate of mankind. But they would be there for only another minute as the horsemen surrounding them started to get themselves ready for the run of their lives.

Two miles from the cattle, the ground began to shake and part violently in ninety-plus different waves. The creatures appeared and disappeared as they went high, looking for danger, then sank again, going even deeper. They were traveling as fast as they could to the tantalizing vibrations and smells produced by the confiscated cattle.

Look at them go!" the president said in awe at the speed of the animals.

Senator Lee sat forward on the couch and leaned his chin on his cane as Alice lightly squeezed his thigh. Niles walked over to the screen in the Event conference room and watched as the beasts seemingly took the bait.

Niles picked up the phone and called the base camp. "Virginia, radio the ranchers to get the cattle moving, now!"

• • •

On the valley floor, Thomas Tahchako and his eight ranch hands had volunteered to get the cattle to the middle of Soda Flats. They knew the risks, but they also knew the cattle could not be moved by truck or helicopter fast enough. He watched as the first of the animals breached the surface. His eyes widened when he saw the size of the first one. Thomas immediately spurred his horse forward and at the same time drew his old-fashioned six-shooter from his holster and fired three times in the air, startling the cattle into movement. The other ranch hands yelped and whooped as they started the organized stampede toward the dry lake bed. As Tahchako turned, he saw the first of the animals turn toward the feel and sound of the thundering cattle as they ran in the direction of Soda Flats.

The Apache spurred his large horse ahead of the stampeding cattle and was only a thousand yards from entering Soda Flats when the first of the cattle started being pulled under. He looked back and saw one of his ranch hands disappear into the ground as he and his mount were suddenly gone. He kept whipping his horse until he was far out ahead of the herd, his hat flying free and his long braids whipping in the wind as he and the cattle ran headlong onto the alkali flats, sending up large plumes of bitter-tasting silt.

Thomas fired his three remaining rounds from his six-shooter and the cattle started spreading out. The animals were attacking the herd in force now; he counted at least eight animals as they breached into the alkali. They were in such a killing frenzy they couldn't feel the alkali as they became coated with the stinging particles.

Tahchako turned his horse and was quickly followed by his remaining hands as they sped south, away from the flats. He once again spared a look to see the animals jumping and then diving back into the dry lake bed, each time taking a terrified cow beneath with them. He turned away from the grisly scene and prayed that this would lead to the beasts' end.

* * *

It took the animals a considerable time to realize they were in danger. As they started to feel the alkali eating at their armor, they became frenzied in pain and haste to get free of the burning substance.

Jack quickly put on headphones and listened to the position report on the creatures. They had fallen for the alkali trap and were now back on course for their escape. He was happy to hear that at least thirty of the smaller creatures actually perished at Soda Flats, having been overcome by the powerful corrosive. But the survivors were less than one mile from the target area. Jack nodded and threw his headphones down and quickly opened the remote transmitter. He brought up the code relayed by Compton from memory. With Everett sweating beside him, Jack entered 1T3, then lifted the plastic cover and quickly pushed the red button, not wanting to even think about what he was doing.

"Shouldn't there have been a big boom about now?" Sarah asked.

Jack pushed the button again. The light went out, then it came back on.

"That's not good," Carl said.

"There's a thirty-second delay in the warhead."

They both counted down . . . and nothing.

"Fuck!" Jack said as he pushed the button again, then again. In frustration he remembered the antenna and turned the black box on its side. His heart skipped a beat when he saw the leads but no antenna. In the crash of the Humvee it must have been torn away. He hit the diagnostic switch on the side and the screen started flashing *Malfunction,* over and over, casting a red strobe across Jack's face.

Everett saw what Jack was looking at and just sat hard into his seat. Then he placed the headphones over his ears and started telling everyone connected to the radio link the bad news.

◆ ◆ ◆

After hearing Everett's report, the senator stood and paced, using his cane as a support. Compton and Alice watched as the weakened Lee swayed.

"What are you tossing around in that mind of yours?" Alice asked.

"The unthinkable, and if I've read between the lines in the major's file correctly, he should be thinking the same horrible thought right now."

Jack set the black box down and placed his head back against the headrest. Then he closed his eyes thinking about what had to be done. It only took him a moment to realize the answer, and then he quickly sat up straight and placed a headset on. "Mr. Ryan, head those fucking animals off and get ahead of them," Jack said as he looked at Carl, who raised his brows. "Head for the Orion site."

"You got it." Ryan knew when not to ask questions.

What in the hell is he doing?" the president asked. General Hardesty stood and walked to the wall map in silence. Even the director of the CIA understood and lowered his eyes.

The president turned to the camera. "Director Compton, what is Collins attempting to do?"

Niles looked into the camera, then removed his glasses and placed them on the conference table. "He's going to do his job, Mr. President, that's all Jack Collins knows how to do."

"Don't want to hear any more, swabby, I outrank you and that's that." Jack turned and looked out the door at the passing desert below. Sarah sat staring at Jack, not believing what was happening.

"We can find some other way, you can't do this!" Sarah shouted over the turbine roar.

"Goddammit, Jack, it's time I did the duty, you're all busted up. Stand down, for Christ's sake."

"Sorry, mister."

"Look!" Ryan shouted as he fought the pedals and control stick.

When they looked out the door again, they saw the giant wake as the animal rose to the surface and breached, making Ryan swerve at the last moment, and the Blackhawk leaned on its side just in time as the beast reached its altitude. They couldn't believe the size. The animal's eyes were different from those of the other creatures. This beast had what looked like blue pupils, and it clearly had a larger head. The thick, hollow strands of hair were finer as they shimmered in the sun. Jack and the Talkhan's eyes seemed to lock as the creature again turned on its back and dove for the ground. They watched until it splashed into the soil heading for the funnel.

"That was different," Jack yelled.

"Did you get the distinct feeling it knew exactly what it was doing?" Sarah asked.

"I'm only interested in what was covering its armor," Jack said.

"What?" Sarah asked.

"Alkali."

The Blackhawk sped ahead and Ryan saw the cleared area where the engineers had placed the device.

"Coming up on-site, thirty seconds till touchdown," Ryan yelled. "I hope," he finished under his breath.

Jack held out his hand while holding his broken ribs with the other.

"Dammit, Major, this isn't right," Everett said.

"What in this fucking world *is,* Commander?" Jack answered as his right hand didn't waver.

Everett frowned but took Jack's hand. Then Collins turned and looked at Sarah. She looked hard at him. "You piss me off, Jack. There's plenty of bravery to go around out here, why does it always have to be you?" she shouted.

"Watched too many John Wayne movies, I guess," he said, holding her eyes with his own.

Sarah leaned over and hit Jack's mouth so hard with her own he thought she bloodied his lips. The kiss lasted only a second, but Collins drank it in as if it were a lifesaving swallow of water.

Jack pushed away and smiled one last time as the Blackhawk hit the ground with its left wheel. He winked at Sarah and started for the door with the trigger.

"I have to at least touch these leads to the antenna; you have about thirty seconds before this end of the valley changes forever. Now get the hell out of here!" Jack jumped from the Blackhawk and ran out into the heart of ground zero.

Sarah closed her eyes and fought back her anger at Jack. She opened them to see Collins limping toward the tower that marked Operation Orion.

Everett felt Ryan lifting off, bouncing twice as he did so. Then Carl leaned into the cockpit and started to say something, but Ryan cut him off.

"Go back and get ready, Commander. Did you think for one fucking minute I would leave him out there?" Then Ryan smiled and looked at the specialist in the right seat. "Ready to be a hero?"

"No, sir!" the young man answered.

Jack saw as soon as he opened the remote case that he wasn't going to have the time to set off the device. The dirt waves were a thousand yards from the dust cloud that was Soda Flats. They were breaching and then diving back into the earth, and they would eventually rise within a hundred yards of the very spot where he was. He frantically started to pull on the broken electrical leads on the case anyway.

The captain in the lead Paladin snapped up when his GPS came to life with target-tracking information. The orders had gone out to give the ground team added time by covering them with their remaining rounds. The numbers were streaming in from the circling AWACS above them. He quickly got on his radio and started shouting orders to his tank platoon as the Excalibur rounds were loaded into M284 cannon.

"Excalibur up!" the loader shouted.

Over the radio they heard a voice call out, "Fire until all rounds are expended."

"Gunslinger, fire, fire, fire at will!" the captain shouted into the radio.

The platoon of M109A6 Paladins opened fire, and the Excalibur rounds flew up and out toward their preprogrammed targets. As the gunners reloaded, another GPS signal imprinted on the rounds, initiating contact with the circling AWACS overhead. It was feeding constant target-aspect changes to each individual round as it flew from its tube. The small directional fins popped free and guided the smart rounds to their targets.

Jack heard a tearing overhead as if the sky were ripping apart. The vibration of the approaching animals was actually making the ground around him shimmer and jump. The first rounds exploded on top of the lead offspring running ahead of the male, a mere 250 yards from Orion. These animals vaporized in a flash as the second volley fell on even more of the shallow-traveling creatures. Jack threw himself to the ground as the next three Excalibur rounds tracked the largest target. The male, sensing danger, dove deep as the rounds dug into the dirt and sand, exploding harmlessly thirty feet above it.

A number of the other creatures were faring far worse as they were left behind by their larger and much swifter brother. They became easy targets as their wakes were clearly marked by the cameras of the AWACS, and it computed in a millisecond targets where the Talkhans would be, not where they currently were. The movable fins guided the rounds perfectly, outsmarting the offspring at every turn.

The Paladins fired what ordnance they had. By the AWACS count they had taken out at least twenty-five of the smaller animals, with the largest Talkhan and possibly twenty to thirty of the smaller females still missing.

J ack saw his reprieve and started working as fast as he could. Then he saw the wave approaching at breakneck speed. It was as if the animals knew what was planned and were trying to speed by before detonation.

Collins looked around at the emptiness of the desert and knew in fifteen seconds it wouldn't look the same, having turned into a giant hole in the ground. He bent down and opened the case and tugged hard on the broken antenna leads, taking away the built-in stress relief all manufacturers place in wiring. He looked up just as the giant animal breached the surface of the desert, followed into the air by the surviving thirty females. Jack didn't know how, but he knew the beast had seen him in the expanse of machine-cleared dirt and sand. The Talkhan roared and dove for the ground, sending up a wave of atomically altered soil that rushed toward ground zero. But Jack smiled as he saw the trailing grayish alkali dust cloud follow the animal down.

"Well, Niles, Senator Lee, it's been fun." Jack placed the box close to the small antenna and wrapped the wire leads around the steel, then pushed the button.

This time the screen flashed red with the words *Detonation 30 seconds*. Jack relaxed and sat down and placed the case beside him. He knew the fuse had been lit and there was nothing to stop it now.

The wave diminished as the beasts approached and started making their run for deep soil. Jack smiled, knowing no matter how deep they went, they would never escape the inferno of gamma rays coming their way.

• • •

Senator Lee lowered his head. Niles Compton placed his head in his hands and waited. Alice was angry as she quickly swiped a tear from her eye, then glared at the senator for having known exactly what Jack was going to do.

As they all waited, they heard shouting over the COMM link. It was the White House.

"What in the hell are those maniacs doing?" They could tell it was the president yelling.

As Niles looked up, he was amazed to see the Blackhawk slowly zigzagging and bounding its way back to ground zero at a horribly slow rate of speed.

"Ryan, you crazy bastard!" Niles screamed, jumping from his chair and clapping once, knowing there wasn't a chance in hell the slow-moving, terribly piloted Blackhawk would make it, but cheering the fools on nonetheless because he knew a neutron bomb didn't have the same explosive effects as a nuclear weapon. It would be less violent and they would be shielded somewhat if they could get at least two hundred yards from ground zero.

Jack stood suddenly when he heard the thud of rotors and saw the helicopter approaching. "Good God," he said as he saw the Blackhawk slewing first left, then right, all the while losing altitude too fast. There was only fifteen seconds left to detonation. The vibration of the approaching Talkhans indicated they were close to dead center of ground zero. "I'm going to hang you three," Jack said as he saw Everett hanging out of the door and bracing himself on the remaining wheel and Sarah behind him, grasping his waist.

The beast was past dead center as the Blackhawk swooped in dramatic fashion toward the desert floor. Jack saw a worried look on Everett's face as he reached for all he was worth. Collins jumped, sending a jolt of searing pain through his chest from his broken ribs. Everett caught him, but Ryan was having trouble stopping the Blackhawk as Jack's feet dragged along the topsoil for twenty feet. Then Ryan applied everything he had on the collective, twisting the throttle and adding all the power he had, and the helicopter shot straight up. He had just pushed the control stick forward and the nose had just dipped, gaining speed as they shot away from ground zero, trying desperately to escape the conventional explosive of the weapon, when suddenly the world changed below them.

The desert floor first lifted, sucking the air away from the Blackhawk, making Ryan lose control, then the ground fell back. The eruption was white-hot and only the falling soil saved them from being fried to death by the expanding X-rays. The very edge of the Superstition Mountains vanished as they fell into the giant hole created by the device after it evaporated a half-mile section of desert. The creatures had been only a hundred feet from the neutron weapon when the electrical charge detonated the conventional explosive, sending a compressing impact into the uranium core. The animals had vaporized as the power of the sun struck them and gamma radiation coursed through their armorless bodies.

Ryan had totally lost control of the helicopter. Jack was still dangling precariously above the giant crater in the desert, only holding on because of the sheer strength of Everett and the willpower of Sarah, who was holding the weight of both men. The Blackhawk threatened to force Collins off by centrifugal force as it spun out of control over a hole that now resembled a giant meteor strike.

Ryan was also being forced away from the pedals due to the force of the rotation. The specialist, who saw what was happening, and against the forces being applied, fought his foot to the left pedal and jammed it down, helping Ryan slow the spin. The control panel started flashing several warnings. The engine-fire light went on and Ryan was at a loss as to what to do.

"Sit it down, sit it down, you crazy bastard!" the specialist screamed out.

"You waited long enough to say something besides 'Yes, sir'!" Ryan screamed back. "And now you're giving orders!"

In the back, Everett and Sarah had finally managed to drag Jack up and over the wheel, and then he jumped into the back compartment of the helicopter and collapsed on the deck. As Everett was pulled sharply backward by Sarah, and they both tumbled into the cabin on top of Jack. They all watched breathlessly out the door at the slowly spinning world outside. Jack saw the giant depression in the ground stretching at least half a mile in a circular pattern and knew the beasts couldn't have lived through that. He nodded, satisfied, and collapsed, not caring that the added weight of Sarah and Everett were crushing him.

"In case you didn't know it, Mr. Everett, that arm of yours is broken," Jack said as he saw the twisted limb resting beside his own face.

Collins was breathing hard and grabbing his left side. He rolled over as the Blackhawk finally straightened out and they were descending at a normal rate despite the alarms sounding from up front and Ryan yelling about what a great flier he was.

"Just wait until you see the shit details I'm going to give you three when we get back," Collins said as he reached out and squeezed Sarah's hand.

"We were only passengers, Jack," Everett replied. "I was trying to jump out of this thing when I hooked you. That fucking Ryan can't fly worth a damn."

THIRTY-FOUR

Gus was still sitting on the hard rock beside the still form of his friend; he hadn't allowed anyone to help him or remove Matchstick's body. Julie was standing and holding Billy as he cried. Ryan was there with one arm on Julie and the other arm supporting the still-shaken Collins. Sarah was on his other side, staring at the fallen alien.

Collins watched the old man holding the small being's hand. Mahjtic was still lying facedown in the rocky soil where he had landed after his forty-foot plunge from the cliff behind them forty-five minutes before; he hadn't fallen all the way thanks to another of the many rock ledges that lined the mountainside.

"He was as brave as any soldier I've ever served with, Gus," Jack said, looking down. "He saved my life."

Gus just nodded his head and continued holding the small hand.

"Sonsabeeeeech."

Gus heard it and slowly looked up at the others. Jack was looking astounded, and Sarah had her mouth frozen momentarily open and Ryan mumbled, "Holy shit."

"Matchstick?" Gus said as he squeezed the small hand.

"Gussss, I hurting badly," said the cottony voice.

Jack looked around quickly; besides themselves, there were Billy and Julie, but they hadn't heard yet.

"Gus, listen to me," Jack said in a deadly serious voice.

The old man was smiling with tears in his eyes when he looked up; then he saw the serious look on the major's face and the smile faltered.

"They'll come for him, Gus. They'll want Matchstick, dead or alive." Jack winced as he stepped closer, dragging Sarah and Ryan with him. "He's *dead,* do you understand? He didn't make it and the body cannot be recovered," Jack said, holding the old man's eyes. "Damn it, Gus, do you understand me?"

Gus swallowed and nodded his head, looking around.

"Only my people can know about Matchstick being alive. We'll debrief him and help you keep Matchstick hidden, but, Gus, right now you have to get up and get the hell out of here or people will come for him and there'll be nothing we can do to stop them. He was a part of an attack on this country, they'll want to know what he knows. I think our people can get that information without keeping him locked away. I want you and Julie and Billy to get him the hell out of here."

Gus nodded and mouthed the word *Thanks.*

"Ooooh, Gusssss hurt Mahjtic's hand."

"Oh." Gus eased up on squeezing the small hand. Then he looked at Jack again and lost the words he wanted to say in the emotion of the moment.

"Go now!" Jack hissed.

An hour later at the crash site, Jack and Sarah were watching the bodies of all the Event staff and soldiers being removed with reverent slowness when Carl walked up to them.

"How are you doing, Mr. Everett?" Collins asked.

Everett lowered his head and adjusted the sling on his broken arm, then he looked up into the eyes of the major and at Sarah, who couldn't stand the haunted look in his eyes, so she looked away and once again fought her tears.

"Look, we can stand here and cry about Lisa until the sun comes up, but I really don't think she would like that too much," Everett said. Instead he pulled out a note one of the security men had just given him. "We don't have a lot of time, Jack. I just heard that the president is going to officially turn the remains of Matchstick over to the CIA. Compton and Lee, well, they're throwing a fit about it, but it looks like they're going to get outmuscled."

"The hell you say," Collins said, standing a little straighter, gasping a little in pain, but angry enough to shrug Ryan's arm away.

Everett smiled slightly, all he could muster after officially finding out about Lisa. "The senator said you would know how to handle it."

Eaten?" the field officer from CIA asked, hands on hips. Collins watched the agent. Sweat was freely rolling down the man's face as he stared incredulously at the major and Ryan. Collins took a step forward menacingly.

"That's right. Tell your director he has the sincere apology of the ground commander, but as I said, the extraterrestrial was eaten by the mother creature."

The man removed his sunglasses and looked the two men over in the fading sunlight of a day most here would never forget. "Where's the old man . . . this Gus Tilly?"

"Went home," Collins answered, taking another step toward the CIA messenger boy with the sweat stains covering most of his white shirt.

The field officer took a step back and looked the haggard soldier in the eyes, then as quickly looked away. "Then may we speak to him there? You know, to debrief?"

"No, no debrief. The president of the United States said, I quote, 'Anything Mr. Tilly wants, he can have,' end quote. Mr. Tilly wants to be left alone." Jack came within an inch of the other man's nose. "And he will be left alone. He's under the protection of our department, and if there is any debriefing to be done, we'll do it."

The intelligence man stepped back and stumbled on a rock, caught himself, then straightened. He looked around at the remaining 31 soldiers, Event staff, and state troopers of the 152 who had fought the battle under- and aboveground. They were all watching him. Some were badly wounded, lying on stretchers, and the doctors treating them were also watching. Others were standing dirty-faced and injured to one degree or another. The surviving state troopers didn't know anything about Matchstick but were downright angry about everything else and looking to kick the hell out of him or anyone giving the soldiers a hard time. Though the different groups were all in disarray, the one thing they were all doing was staring at *him,* he noticed. To the men who'd survived, all involved in the battle were now a part of themselves, comrades, many fallen, few alive, and all deserving of each other's protection.

The man placed his sunglasses back on and turned to face Collins. He nodded his head, then turned and left. He would let the director of the CIA fight his own battle later. Right now, the agent thought, discretion was the better part of valor.

Everett watched, blank-eyed, as they loaded the body bag containing Lisa's battered remains onto a stretcher and took her to a waiting Blackhawk. He blinked and tossed the XM8 down upon the littered ground of the crash site.

Sarah and Collins watched from a short distance away as Everett's proud form followed the stretcher.

Sarah quickly swiped a tear away and looked at the major. "You think it's over?"

"That can only be answered with time, I guess. God only knows what would have happened if that damn saucer had been forced down in some other part of the world where the response wouldn't have been as quick." Jack looked down at her with a sad smile. "I guess we'll all be looking for the monster in the closet or under the bed for quite a while."

A red-eyed Virginia Pollock interrupted them. "Jack, have you seen Mr. Tilly? The director would like you to bring him back with us, we have some information Niles wants to give him."

Collins shook his head sadly. "He went down the mountain with Ryan, Miss Dawes, and her boy. I'm afraid Mr. Tilly wants nothing more to do with us, at least for a while."

Virginia's eyebrows rose. "But, Jack, he . . ." She stopped and just lowered her head.

"How's Sergeant Mendenhall?" Sarah asked, trying to break the tension.

Collins looked from Virginia back at Sarah. "He'll make it. The docs say he has four broken ribs to my two and a pretty good gash to his head. He's still able to say we officers were too slow in our reactions." Collins smiled. "Personally, I think he's still trying to get out of OCS, which I've decided to send him to."

Virginia stepped up closer to Collins and Sarah. "Jack, I do want to see Mr. Tilly at least one more time before we head back." She paused and held her hand into the lighting that had been turned on at the site. "I was checking the mother animal and . . . well, look at this."

She held her hand out to the major, and on it was a substance that glimmered in the light. Jack and Sarah stared in amazement as the large particles of gold filtered through Virginia's fingers.

The last tunnel the Destroyer had dug had cut right through the no-longer-mythical Lost Dutchman Mine.

Event Complex, Nellis Air Force Base, Nevada
July 14

The president of the United States had flown out for the memorial service for the Event personnel that had been lost. He meandered through the milling crowd, shaking hands and giving his thanks for the job that had been done. All told, they had lost 32 Event staff on the Site One team and another 41 of the geology and security staff in the tunnels, and all this didn't account for the 99 other soldiers, airmen, and state troopers involved in this catastrophic encounter with life from outside this world.

Earlier the president had met with Lee and Niles, and they had explained in detail the items Europa had uncovered about the Centaurus Corporation, the Genesis Group, and the Hendrix family. The president had made certain calls and the teams in New York and Virginia were awaiting the personnel additions for the final chapter in the Roswell Incident, which had covered the past sixty years. The president had a copy of the e-mail that had been sent to Senator Lee from the Group's number one enemy.

My Dear Senator Lee & Esteemed Company—

We have been at odds for several years now and I fear all good things must come to an end. I must intrude upon your organization this one last time to assist me in breaking an obligation to a man and organization that may hold some interest for you. In a cavernous basement on Seventh Avenue in New York, a basement that has only one entrance, I believe you may find the very items you have most desired since a stormy night lo these many years ago in New Mexico.

For cooperation in allowing me egress from your wonderful country, I am forwarding two gifts of goodwill. First, for Senator Lee, if you examine the relics from the past, you may find one that interests you the most in the previously mentioned building in New York. Second is the gift of knowledge I myself have only learned of recently. I must insist you understand that this information has left a terrible taste in my mouth, as it reeks of amateurism. At a spot not three hundred paces northwest of the exact impact center on a ranch once worked by Mr. Mac Brazel, you will find buried the sad finale of the Roswell Incident and Operation Purple Sage.

I must admit I am tempted to offer these gifts for free,

but alas, I do need to leave, and you have the power to allow that to happen.

Until we meet again, you have my fondest thanks.

Regards,
Colonel Henri Farbeaux

THIRTY-FIVE

Charles Phillip Hendrix II was in the middle of a presentation to several high-profile investors from Germany and Taiwan in the boardroom of the Centaurus Corporation. Arrayed around the room were models of the various weapons systems the company had contracts in either building or providing vital systems for. The younger Hendrix had brushed the whole Farbeaux incident under the table until the Frenchman could be caught by the corporation's security teams. Then that bastard would learn what it was to betray him, for in his opinion, if you betrayed Centaurus, you betrayed America herself.

"Gentlemen, if you will look at the growth factor for our peripheral military contracts, you will see that Centaurus has the outlook to achieve—"

At that moment the double doors of the boardroom opened and his assistant backed through them and then turned apologetically toward him. She was followed into the massive boardroom by at least ten men in navy blue Windbreakers, and as they spread out into the plush conference room, Hendrix saw FBI was printed on the backs of all of them in bold yellow letters.

"I'm sorry, Mr. Hendrix, they say they have a warrant . . ."

"Charles Phillip Hendrix the Second, I am Special Agent

in Charge Robert Martinez. You are under arrest for the crimes of conspiracy to commit murder, industrial espionage, and treason against the people of the United States of America." The agent took Hendrix by the arm and gently made him place his hands on the polished table.

The prospective investors slowly stood and moved away from the table and tucked themselves into a far corner, distancing themselves as far as they could.

"You have the right to remain silent . . ."

Hendrix wasn't hearing his Miranda rights being read to him, he was looking at the man standing in the doorway, wondering why a naval officer was here.

Lieutenant Commander Carl Everett watched with his saucer cap tucked under his broken arm as Hendrix was placed under arrest. He removed a cell phone from the sling his arm was in and punched in a pre-programmed number and waited.

"Everett," he said when the phone on the other end was answered, then he held the phone out to Hendrix.

"Yes!" he growled into the phone.

"Hendrix, do you recognize my voice?"

"Yes, Mr. President," he answered as his shoulders hunched and his voice emptied of hope.

"I take it you have been placed into custody?"

"For the time being. I'll plead my case in court direct to the American people," Hendrix answered with as much cockiness as he could.

"I think we're going to leave the courts out of this one. You are hereby divested of all businesses in the United States, and your personal and company assets are frozen. You are now an unpaid consultant to the federal government on the knowledge your company has discovered about extraterrestrial technology and their intentions toward us in the future. You will offer this information in exchange for your life. If at any time you renege on this arrangement, you will be arraigned in a court of law and found guilty of treason at a time of war. Be fruitful and very forthcoming with your information, Mr. Hendrix, your worthless life depends upon it."

Everett saw Hendrix close his eyes, signaling the end of the conversation, and then Carl removed the phone and gestured to a woman who was waiting just outside the doors.

"This is Mrs. Celia Brown; she will be the caretaker for Centaurus for the foreseeable future, at least until the IRS and the General Accounting Office can auction its divisions off."

Celia Brown of the Event Group walked in and past Hendrix. She held her hand out to the two investors who were sitting dumbfounded on a couch in the corner of the office.

Everett leaned toward Hendrix and whispered, "Compliments of the Event Group."

Hendrix didn't respond, he just allowed the FBI to drag him away and into his future as a guest of the country he loved, giving up everything he had ever worked for.

The Oval Office, White House

The president hung up the phone with Everett, then stood and stretched. He yawned and sat back down in the large overstuffed chair and finally looked at his three directors of the FBI, CIA, and the National Security Agency. He then looked to the far end of the Oval Office and nodded to the two Secret Service agents who stood on either side of another man.

The president ignored the three and turned his attention to the phone and punched the intercom. "Marjorie, you can connect the call now."

"Collins."

"Major, we're done here, and New York corporate is in the bag. Tell Senator Lee to have fun," the president said.

"Yes, sir."

"Oh, and, Jack, I want you to know I couldn't have been more wrong about trying to hide you away like I did. That was some damn good soldiering in the desert; I want you to know that you can have any combat command you so choose."

There was silence for a moment, and then Collins said, "I

have a command already, Mr. President, I think I'll stay in the desert air for a while."

"Then, good luck, Jack, you take care of Director Compton for me." The president silently laid the phone into its cradle, then he looked up at the man standing handcuffed between two Secret Service agents.

"Now, what to do with you, Agent Davis," he said as he closed his eyes in thought.

The Sage Building, Midtown Manhattan

Collins looked at the senator, who was quietly sitting in the foyer of the Sage Building, as Jack closed the cell phone after speaking with the president. The receptionist was sitting in a chair behind his ornate desk in a shiny new pair of handcuffs not saying a word as two agents from the FBI's New York office flanked him on either side. The senator tapped his cane, and Jack stood and assisted Lee to his feet. Alice had wanted to be here but Garrison wouldn't allow it.

Collins winced from his healing ribs as he helped the older man to his feet. Everyone had tried to convince him not to go, but he had to be with Lee when he did this.

"Before we go down there, Jack, I want to say thank you for staying with the Group. We need you here. Niles will need the strength of a strong arm as the Group starts recruiting replacements for all the people we lost," the senator said sadly.

"Niles is going to be just fine, it's an honor to stay and help him."

Lee nodded his head. "Let's go down and meet an old friend, shall we?"

On the ride down on the ornate and secure elevator, Jack looked at the senator and knew that time had finally caught up with the old man and he was showing his age.

The cane wasn't much of a support anymore, and his hair had thinned since the Event in the desert had started. It seemed Lee had come full circle from Roswell to Chato's Crawl and the time had come to pay the bill. Jack looked away toward the five FBI agents who were accompanying them to the sublevels of the Sage Building, which had been a gift of another scoundrel who would be Jack's headache in the future: Colonel Henri Farbeaux.

The basement was where they were to meet the founder of the Genesis Group and Centaurus. The double doors slid open and the agents were the first out with their handguns drawn but placed at their sides. They had been the souls of propriety as they had taken all the security people into custody an hour before. Most of the detained men were former soldiers of the U.S. armed forces and were quite surprised at being pushed around by federal agents. *They must have been used to doing all the pushing,* Jack thought, then wondered if he had just witnessed some of the infamous Men in Black. If they had been, they didn't look all that formidable when faced with men who could shove back.

Jack helped the senator out of the elevator, and they turned to see a well-lit riser with two large glass enclosures. In the left enclosure there were three aluminum cases, tilted up at an angle, and they could see these contained the original bodies from the Roswell crash site, as they were illuminated with spotlights hidden in the ceiling above. Lee shook his head and then looked at the reconstructed saucer in the giant glass-walled viewing room on the right. Then he let his eye settle on a lone figure sitting in a large wheelchair facing the viewing area. Collins helped the senator down the small incline and past rows upon rows of theater seating. They approached the man cautiously as the FBI agents had their weapons drawn and half aimed at the figure sitting in the chair. Collins helped Lee into another, smaller chair to the right of the solitary man, and then Lee waited, placing the cane between his knees and leaning on it.

"You were alive all this time," Lee said aloud.

The old man in the large high-backed wheelchair didn't turn at the sound of the voice. He continued to stare at the saucer behind the glass.

"My son tells me that you had another encounter. This is true?" Charles Hendrix the elder asked.

Garrison looked at the haggard form of Hendrix; he seemed to be aging right before his eyes. The man who had been helped by Curtis LeMay and Allen Dulles to disappear in a false death these many years.

"Yes, another came down," Lee answered as he turned away and looked at the saucer encased in glass.

"The animal and crew?"

"All dead," Lee answered.

Hendrix sat motionless for a moment. "You know, I've had years to think on this. The Grays will soon tire of doing things the easy way, and sooner or later, for better or for worse, they will come themselves," Hendrix said as he finally looked his old antagonist in the eye.

"That's what we at the Group conclude," Lee said. Then he looked away, then slowly back. "Hendrix, I believe your Mr. Farbeaux has given the location of my men from 1947."

Hendrix smiled and chuckled and then pointed to his right temple. "They're right here, Lee, they never left. They've been with me and have never left. So why don't you just leave them there? Remember what I told you a long time ago, *controlled violence*. You never had the guts to carry inside of you the responsibility that had to be taken upon oneself to truly secure this country. I did, and I have the ghosts in here to prove it." Hendrix tapped his head hard with his right finger. "Right in here, Lee," he said louder, then grimaced for a moment as he was momentarily frozen with pain.

"All my staff, the civilians and the young soldiers and airmen that were lost, and you may have been able to help them with the knowledge your company has learned over the years from Roswell. Why didn't you help?" Lee asked.

Hendrix looked at the senator again and once more grimaced in pain. "In many ways Centaurus helped those boys,

helped with some of the equipment they used to fight the animals with. The same equipment that will be used time and
time again to defend this country." He grabbed lightly at his
chest, wrinkling the large coat he wore. "You are still a Boy
Scout war hero, Lee," Hendrix said too low for anyone but
Garrison to hear.

The old man reached for the inside of his coat and shakily brought out his nitroglycerin pills and fought with the tin
lid of the ornate pill carrier. Then he fumbled it and the
small pills fell to the floor, a few landing in Lee's lap. Hendrix looked at Lee with sad eyes and the senator returned the
stare. Then Lee brushed off the fallen pills and stood, waving Jack away as this time he did it without the use of his
cane. Then he bent down as Hendrix's eyes started to flutter
as he went into the opening throes of a heart attack.

"*Controlled violence?* I guess I finally understand what
you were getting at after all," Lee said. "It seems I just now
realized *I am* capable of it."

He gestured for the FBI agents to assist Hendrix, but
knew the old man had only moments more to live.

"Let's go home, Jack."

Near Roswell, New Mexico
July 22

On a desolate piece of land once worked by a rancher
named Mac Brazel, Senator Garrison Lee felt he had
come home. He stood leaning on Collins and had an
arm around Alice Hamilton, who raised her sunglasses and
wiped a tear from her eye. As Lee watched, Niles Compton
was leading the actions of the forensics team, who were removing the first casualties of the invasion from another
world.

"I hoped not to get too emotional over this," Lee said as a
light, cooling breeze sprang up.

"Old man, it's all over now. You owe those men your
emotions, they deserve anything we can give them, the least

of which is the memory we have of their friendship," Alice said as she used her handkerchief.

"You did the right thing, exchanging *this* for letting Farbeaux out of the country," Jack said.

Senator Garrison Lee lowered his head, and finally a tear was shed as he watched Niles and his team bring the last body out of the ground where they had been buried and hidden close to sixty years before. Dr. Kenneth Early's body was the last to be identified and the last of the skeletal remains to see the bright sunlight. Lee watched and stood straighter as his old friend was quickly covered by an American flag that caught the light breeze and rose slightly, then settled over the last member of the Event Group to finally be thanked for his duty to the country.

EPILOGUE

Two days later, after the quiet arrests and the return of their long-lost heroes, a loud cheer erupted in the Computer Center of the Event Group complex. The large back-projected viewing screen came alive for the first time in days.

The space shuttle *Atlantis* had successfully refueled the KH-11 satellite 41672, otherwise known as Boris and Natasha, from their own fuel stores, saving the flamboyant KH-11 from a fiery death. The shuttle crew had also had her solar batteries replaced and a new charger put in. When the old girl was turned back on, the picture was still locked on that small Arizona valley, cleared of all debris of the crashed saucers. As the applause died down, a tune could be heard coming from the speakers set behind the main viewing screen, courtesy of the shuttle *Atlantis*. Frank Sinatra was singing "Fly Me to the Moon."

As Collins, Niles, Alice, and the senator watched, the picture became clearer as it zoomed in on the valley floor. They were amazed at the clarity as Boris and Natasha centered her picture exactly where it had been prior to the satellite's supposed demise.

"We have something," one of the computer techs called out.

As they watched, the valley and its occupants came into the camera's view. "Go to maximum magnification on my count," Niles called out. "Three, two, one, now, max-mag on-site."

They all smiled as the images became crystal clear. Jason Ryan, on a thirty-day leave from the Event Group, held hands with Julie Dawes, and she in turn was pointing a finger at Billy, partially hidden under a large beach umbrella, who looked to be teasing them. Then Gus stepped into the picture, pointing at a large hole in the ground and gesturing wildly around the rocks. He was holding something out to the others, and you could tell he was smiling and happy as he danced an old-time jig. Then he clapped his hands together and the gold dust shimmered in the sunlight and fell to the ground as the old prospector kept dancing.

Another beach umbrella was next to the one Billy was under. This was brightly colored in a pattern resembling a galaxy of stars, and a large pair of cowboy boots were sticking out from under it, both gifts of the Event Group. As the wearer of the overlarge boots leaned forward and caught some of the gold particles before they hit the ground, the assembled Event staff saw it. The hand that was reaching out was green and protruded from a long-sleeved white shirt that was obviously overlarge. Then the small figure moved from beneath the beach umbrella and the arms reached around the old man's legs and hugged him. The full view of the body was hidden beneath a giant white cowboy hat, but they could tell it had cutoff Levi's shorts on.

They couldn't help it, they all laughed as Mahjtic stumbled in the oversize cowboy boots he was wearing and caught himself on Gus's trousers. Then for no apparent reason and to the complete surprise of all the people at the Event Complex, Matchstick looked skyward.

"I suggest you leave them be for a while before fully debriefing Mahjtic and questioning him about the Grays and when he expects them to come visiting again. I suspect Hendrix was right, next time they will come themselves, and my guess is we'll be fending off a full invasion," Lee said.

The others looked at Lee and said nothing. They all knew the Grays wouldn't stop at sending an animal; they would eventually take care of Earth the hard way.

"So, we're sure at this point the Gray that Gus and Matchstick killed was the lone survivor of its vehicle?" Jack asked.

"As a matter of fact, while you were recuperating, the army found the remains of the second and third crewmen of the hostile ship. They had ejected over the desert in the moments leading to the crash. I'm afraid they ran into the animal life indigenous to this planet and found them much smaller than the Talkhan, but just as unforgiving," Niles said.

Virginia Pollock entered the Computer Center and nodded at her colleagues. She carried a file and handed it to Niles.

"The autopsy report?" he asked.

"Yes."

"This time we hung on to the bodies long enough to finally complete our files from Roswell. The other intelligence services threw a fit, but the president stalled until we got our answers. He said the government owed Dr. Early and his team at least that much," Niles said sadly.

Garrison Lee lowered his head as he spared a thought for his long-lost men.

"Anyway, if we knew at the beginning what we were up against, a lot of boys would be alive right now," Niles said. "Virginia . . ." He gestured that she should explain.

"First, the results of the animal, or Talkhan, won't be available for many years. I suspect our friend Matchstick, who knows the animal better than anyone, will be able to shed some light on its planet of origin and biological makeup. Second, the three Grays that were recovered: the two in the desert, what was left of them anyway, and the being that was dispatched by Mr. Tilly." Virginia looked from one person to the other. "They were dying. It will take years to figure out the toxicology, but it looks as if they were a victim of their environment. Their world must be in the final stages of a massive breakdown of their ozone layer. Not only that, their bodies were so full of toxins from their natural environment that we can only conclude that, besides the two different forms of skin cancer they displayed, and also the cancerous nature of their reproductive systems, they have mere generations left to them."

"So, that means they will not delay in moving on Earth."

"We notified the president. This time I think we'll let someone else do the fighting. We lost a lot of good friends this time around.

"There is one more thing," Virginia said.

Niles was puzzled. "Yes?"

"You're not going to like it, I know I didn't," she said, looking at her feet. "We did the blood workup on Matchstick." She frowned and couldn't look anyone in the eyes. "He has the start of the same symptoms, but I think we can help him. You see, Matchstick is very young in his years, he'll fight this off, but the rest of his race, if they stay in their current environmental conditions, they'll die."

Silence greeted her comment. Jack looked away and over to the monitor where there was a still shot of Matchstick smiling up at Boris and Natasha.

"You mean to tell me that the Green species were willing to die out instead of taking the easy way out and siding with the Grays?" Jack asked while still looking up at the screen.

"Hard thing to try and live up to, isn't it?" Lee asked no one in particular.

"At least Gus and Matchstick won't want for anything," Alice said, finally forcing a smile.

"Yes, Gus and his friends are about to become very well-off," Lee said, smiling. "Imagine, the Lost Dutchman Mine, we should have known it was real. There's a lesson to be learned there." He shook his finger. "No matter how ridiculous the myth, they always have a basis in fact, always. It seems we forgot that for a while. This was a nice way to be reminded," Lee said, looking back at the screen as he took Alice by the hand.

"Yes, they are going to be very well-off," Niles said absently.

"Just like you kids will be well-off without the likes of me bitching all day. Niles, call me from time to time just to say hi to an old man, and let me know how that new head of security is doing tracking down our Colonel Farbeaux now that his immunity is at an end," Lee said, looking at Jack and winking his one good eye. "And by the way, Alice is taking the rest of the month off."

Without a word, Senator Garrison Lee left the Event Center for the last time, placing his arm around Alice. She smiled like a coquette, looking back at the others as she placed her arm around Lee's waist.

Collins and Niles returned her happy smile as they watched the couple leave.

The major was off the next day. He, Virginia Pollock, and Everett were flying to MIT and from there to New York University for interviews for replacement personnel for those lost. From there Jack would meet up with a field team and fly to the University of Washington to investigate a diary from a man who had supposedly escaped from Custer's regiment at the Little Big Horn.

On his way out of the Computer Center, Jack ran into Specialist Fifth Class Sarah McIntire, soon to be promoted to second lieutenant. As he stood and looked at her, they both heard through the closing Computer Center door, "Alright, boys and girls, let's retask Boris and Natasha and see if we can get some film on this lost Inca city! And someone get Sir Basil on the phone at the Royal Geographic Society in London and tell him we'll return the remains of King Arthur, in exchange for a year's worth of study on that Roman execution order for Jesus of Nazareth." Niles was now in his element and happy.

On the screen, with Frank Sinatra still crooning away, the picture of the four people and one alien dimmed, then was gone.

"Well, Specialist," Jack said, "I can't officially ask you to dinner until you're an officer, but would you like to bump into each other at Gino's Spaghetti House later tonight?"

Sarah looked at the major's blue eyes and then looked around her to make sure no one was near.

"I think I would like that . . ." She hesitated, then lowered her voice. "Jack."

As she turned and walked away, Collins smiled and watched her a moment, then looked around him at the clean, plastic-lined walls outside the Computer Center and knew he was now at home at the Event Group.

Read on for an excerpt from the next novel by

DAVID LYNN GOLEMON

LEGEND

COMING SOON IN HARDCOVER FROM ST. MARTIN'S PRESS

"A quest for the riches of the earth brought them to the waters of legend and the greed of man came and destroyed the way of innocence, and the ancient one rose from the depths to consume them."

— FATHER ESCOBAR CORINTH
CATHOLIC PRIEST TO THE
FRANCISCO PIZARRO EXPEDITIONS

Amazonian river basin,
Summer, 1534 A.D., 56 days out of Peru

The survivors of his once proud and now cursed expedition were holed up in a large green basin that was fed water by the large and very deep tributary of the Amazon, at least ten leagues from the site of last night's massacre. The large lagoon, which for all practical description was much more like a small lake, lay before them. They had waded along the shore of the tributary, following the treacherous rapids to gain entrance into this hidden Eden that had trees so tall they stretched away and over the dark waters.

It was something Captain Padilla had never thought to see in his lifetime. Beautiful as it was, it was not the kind of place one would choose to conduct a massacre of the small people if they chose to attack them here. It truly was a place God had sculpted when last upon this earth. Tree branches hung out over the water and soft grasses grew all the way to the slow-flowing lagoon. The walls of what had to be an ancient and extinct volcano rose on three sides, actually leaning out over the lagoon, creating three natural shelves.

Flowers of every variety bloomed and nourished honeybees that gently moved from species to species, never noticing or caring about the sudden invasion by the Spaniards. The strange flowers that grew with only small dapples of sunlight were large and the most fragrant Padilla had ever smelled.

The ancient volcanic bowl was not only fed by the Amazon tributary but also by a mammoth waterfall that fell from high above on the far end of the large lagoon. But that was not the outstanding feature of the small valley. There, flanking either side of the tumbling waters of the falls, were pillars. They were at least a hundred and twenty feet high and carved from the surrounding rock, and they supported an arch that vanished into the white waterfall of the river above. Vines coursed through the cracked and weather-worn pillars and in several places had separated the stone completely, making them look as if they would fall at any moment.

Now here he stood, trying to decide if he should make their last stand or continue the insanity of running deeper into the green hell beyond the lagoon. The men knew there might be something here because of those giant pillars, but they had lost all interest in riches and just wanted familiar sights, even Pizarro was preferable to this madness.

Maybe the villagers would take the decision out of his hands and just leave them be, allowing them to go back and skirt the village to the north or south on their trek back into Peru. He would then personally report to the fool Pizarro that the expedition had been for naught, there was nothing but death waiting for any man in the distant valleys of the Amazon.

While he wrote his thoughts down in his personal diary, the map he had made of their travels fell from the back pages where he had placed it. As he bent over to retrieve it, he hesitated momentarily as he was suddenly tempted to leave it to rot on the ground. Then he considered his men and picked it up and placed it back into his journal.

His thoughts of leaving the map so no one could follow were broken by the harsh laughing of the very man who had caused so much horror in the last twelve hours. Such laughter after the spilling of so much blood seemed wrong. The captain looked over at his men. Joaquin Suarez was kneeling by the water with his hair freshly wet after washing the blood from himself and his armor. The soldiers around him looked on and shook their heads, all knowing this man was a danger to them all with his recklessness.

Padilla reached down and retrieved his helmet and that was when he caught a glimpse of a strange visitor to their makeshift rest area. The huge eyes were there for the briefest of moments before whatever it was scurried off through the thick foliage, using it as cover as it slid silently into the waters of the lagoon. Captain Padilla looked around to see if his men had seen the strange little creature, but they were busy washing and lying on the thickly carpeted grass; some of the more experienced soldiers were even knelt in prayer. He once again peered into the thick undergrowth for some sign that the little creature had been there at all, but there was not a trace. He quickly came to the conclusion that it had been nothing but a trick of his overtaxed mind and the darkened jungle floor. Suddenly there was a rustling of bushes behind him and his hand went to his sword.

"My Captain." Ivan Rodrigo Torres, his friend and second-in-command, stepped from the dense growth of the forest. "The Indians have disappeared." He removed his helmet and his long black hair fell free as sweat poured from his face and beard. "One minute we were watching them from a clearing about half a league from here and the next minute they fell back into the jungle and were gone. Our trail into this valley was so obvious they must know where we are." He took a breath and looked around him as he loosened his armor. "I expect them to double back this way, so I placed the men in an excellent position for ambush, but thus far they haven't come."

Padilla patted his old friend on the shoulder. "That is just as well, I can't do this any longer." He lowered his hand and looked around at the darkened area under the thick canopy of trees. "I just feel like resting here for a month before returning and reporting this horrible thing we have done." He pulled the front collar of his armor away from his soaked tunic. "Maybe I'll swim out to the only spot here that has sunlight hitting it and remain there until the Lord pulls me under." He looked at the magnificent waterfall and then back toward the center of the large lagoon and the bright dapples of sunlight that lit the blue waters and made them sparkle.

"I, like most of the men, feel like cutting Suarez's throat for bringing this evil to our doorstep," Torrez said angrily.

"I can't think on that now, my old friend, I am weary to my very bones. Besides, in the end, it is I who will be judged for this debacle, not Suarez."

"Surely Commander Pizarro will not blame you for the actions of this maniac?"

"Pizarro is not an ordinary man and he has little or no patience for incompetence. I can assure you I will be judged harshly for losing his nephew and a chance at finding the *Sincaro* gold source." He looked at Torrez and smiled. "For my failure the *Sincaro* will be extinct or enslaved by this time next year," he sighed. "I had the arrogance to believe I could do this another way, I am but a fool."

Loud laughter once again sprang up from the beach area. As both officers turned and walked toward their men, another round of loud and raucous howling came from the lagoon. Upon entering the small clearing, they saw Suarez holding something in the air as the other soldiers hooted loudly, several even patting each other on their backs. As they looked closer at the strange object the soldier was tossing into the air, they saw it resembled a small monkey. Then Padilla realized it was the same creature he had spied looking at him from the bush only moments before. The captain could clearly see the small animal and its remarkable resemblance to their chattering companions that lived in the trees. In his diary Padilla had listed many different varieties of monkey and other strange animal life, but this was unlike anything he had ever witnessed before in his many travels. On this expedition he had become quite knowledgeable on the far-ranging species that inhabited this new continent; thus the animal that Suarez held in his hands so casually was something he knew to be very special.

"Captain, we have a captive, this little clown tried to steal my satchel with the last of our bread," Rondo Cordoba, the quartermaster, said while gesturing toward the small creature Suarez was toying with.

Padilla and Torrez joined the men, and both were amazed to see the small creature up close. It was a monkey, or what a monkey would look like without so much as a hair on its body. The facial features were close to that of a man, except for the lips. They framed many sharp teeth and were thick, with the upper lip much larger than the bottom and the ears were but small holes in the sides of its head. The tail was slick as a taskmaster's whip, and it swung back and forth quickly as, Padilla surmised, it was agitated at being thrown into the air by Suarez. He saw small protrusions of skin, like a spiny sail, as it flared outward down its back every time it was tossed upwards.

"Stop tormenting that creature, you ignorant fool!" Torrez commanded loudly.

Suarez stopped, looked angrily for a moment at his captain and then at Torrez, and without removing his eyes from the two men, arrogantly tossed the small animal in the air again. He caught it and then concentrated his look on the captain in a silent challenge. Padilla drew his sword and pointed it at the larger man's throat, pressing the blade enough so that blood was soon collecting on the steel blade. His eyes were locked on Suarez and a ghost of a smile touched his lips. He would enjoy sliding his sharp blade into the throat of the very reason for their current predicament, no matter if they needed all the men they could get at that moment.

"As you can see, you fatherless child, our captain is of ill humor today," Torrez said smiling, as he watched his captain and a seemingly unshaken Suarez.

Suarez only ignored the sword and the neck wound and was still holding the animal tightly. He quickly changed his grip, now holding the choking animal by its throat. Its tail was now jittering in small movements that were more of a spasm.

Padilla pressed the blade further into the man's throat, and the arrogance that had been there a moment ago was quickly replaced by a worried frown. Suarez just then noticed there was no laughter from the men around him. He saw there were only looks of anticipation at his seemingly imminent death.

All this time the animal's eyes never left Padilla. It was as if the small creature knew it was the subject of the standoff and was awaiting the captain's next move. Suarez slowly lowered the creature to the white ·sand that made up the small beach, and the monkey-like animal scurried not towards the jungle or the water, but behind the captain. The beast jumped up and down and spat at Suarez and jabbered as if cursing the large soldier. As Suarez straightened, Padilla pushed the gleaming sword forward, bringing a more satisfying flow of blood to the blade, where it rolled slowly down the shiny surface and dripped onto the few feet of pure white sand.

"We may need this fool, Captain," Ivan Torrez said loudly so all could hear. "We may still have him up on charges upon our return, but we need his strength to fight, or to flee from this place, and God willing, he may even redeem himself at some point in this nightmare." He placed his hand on the captain's arm, but gave Suarez a withering look.

Padilla, without dropping his gaze, slowly lowered the sword and just as slowly wiped the blood from its tip onto the red sleeve of the big man, then he slowly slid the weapon back into the ornate scabbard at his side.

The small creature was still holding onto the captain's leg and hissing at Suarez as if cursing its antagonist. Padilla reached down and, using both hands, gently picked the animal up and looked it over. It was breathing through its small nostrils and open mouth, but it also had what looked like the gills of a fish right where the small neck joined the head, three rows of soft skin arranged along its jawline, flaring and then closing, as they too sought life-sustaining air. There were fin-like features along its forearms and a small spiny dorsal fin, again like a fish, on its back traveling the length of the animal's spine. It had sharp clear claws arranged on its fingers, and the toes were like equipped. The tail wasn't as smooth as he had first thought. It had small fish-type scales all the way to its tip where it suddenly flared and tapered to a paddle-like feature resembling a shark's tailfin, and as Padilla watched, it swished through the air in what seemed a contented arc. The beast was as foul-smelling as a fish that had washed up on the shore.

"This is the most amazing animal I have ever seen in all of our travels," Padilla said softly, as the large black eyes of the creature blinked, not with eyelids like his own, but a set of clear membranes.

"I think it looks like my mother-in-law," Torrez shouted to the staring company as he slapped the captain on the back in an attempt to lighten the darkened mood.

The men laughed, even Padilla smiled as he chanced a wary eye toward Suarez.

"Captain, look!" one of the men shouted.

Padilla lowered the small creature and looked to where his men were pointing toward the calm waters of the lagoon, as another of the small animals stood holding a struggling fish in both its clawed hands. The first animal scurried up to the newcomer, waddling bowlegged on its paddle-like feet, and started jabbering loudly. The animal looked on and then tossed the fish underarm toward the group of Spaniards. It landed on the sand and flopped around, then lay still, the small claw marks evident on the smooth skin of the large catfish.

As they watched in amazement, another and then another of the animals exited the water, stepping up tentatively and tossing more flopping fish onto the small shoreline as the soldiers looked at each other and nervously laughed.

"Maybe it's an offering?" Rondo ventured to no one in particular.

"Gather the fish, men, we will not waste this gift brought by our new friends," Padilla ordered. "Collect them all so we can also feed the men who are guarding the perimeter."

As the men moved forward to collect the offered bounty, they failed to notice as large bubbles appeared in the middle of the lagoon and slowly circled under the sunlight, then vanished after a moment. Nor did they hear the sudden silence that filled the trees around them as the birds grew momentarily still in their high nests and roosts, but they did see the small creatures look at one another as they jabbered back and forth and then slowly headed back toward the water. The first one, the one Padilla had saved from the murderous Suarez, was looking back at the newcomers to its beautiful world. To the men who were watching the strange exodus, it looked as if the animal were saddened at leaving.

Padilla looked away from the lagoon and was amazed at the horde of fish as he counted over ten species of varying types. But just one caught his eye, and he bent over to examine it. He called Torrez over to see this wonder. The fish had huge scales and very strange fins on its lower belly toward the thick and powerful-looking tail. These most unusual fins looked as if they had small feet-like appendages on the very tips. The mouth was huge and filled with lethal-looking teeth, the jaw jutted far forward, unlike any fish he had ever seen, almost like a barracuda's, only far more pronounced. As the two officers examined the strange fish, its eye seemed to roll and look at them, and as it did, the mouth snapped open and closed. They quickly straightened up and looked at the men who were starting to build fires for cooking and to guard against the coming night. Padilla once again bent down toward the large fish. He was looking at something on its blackened scales; he reached down and lightly rubbed the strange, coarse scales. The fish moved momentarily and then lay still. Padilla held his fingers close to his face and rubbed them together; small gold flakes gently fell to the tips of his worn boots.

P adilla lay under one of the many ancient and beautiful trees that permeated the area with their massive roots projecting from the earth like a giant's arms ripping through the fabric of a blouse. He had his booted feet close to their small fire, drying the thick leather as best he could. His diary was in his hands, and he had just finished recording the observations of this eventful day. His last entry written before he closed the small book declared that the battle with the *Sincaro* was due to his own negligence.

He had considered not recording evidence of gold found lodged in the scales of the fish. But he had never omitted anything from his observations and would not start now. Pizarro would be startled to read about a source of gold so abundant that it was actually brought to the surface on the backs of fish. The captain shook his head at the thought as he placed the diary back into his tunic.

Torrez lay beside Padilla, playing with one of the strange monkey-like animals that had appeared after the sun had set behind the dense jungle. The other men played with the numerous animals that came and went with their strange jabbering and constant curiosity of the many fires the men had built up. They were a nuisance as they emptied rucksacks and even a few of their precious black-powder bags, actually spilling the contents dangerously close to the fires. Padilla had eight of the men out on watch making sure the *Sincaro* didn't make a return visit.

"What do you make of them, my Captain?" Torrez asked, holding a small piece of bacon out for the visitor who sat on his chest, its tail swinging back and forth like a happy puppy. Its little claws finally stabbed the small piece of meat and popped it into its mouth, smiling and jabbering softly at the man, the mouth working frantically along with the small gills.

"I think they are an offshoot or very close relative of the monkey, just one that happens to live in the water, surely not a design that God had intended." Then the captain laughed. "But who knows the mind of God, but God himself?" Padilla watched Torrez and the animal a moment. "What is truly amazing is the fact that you can see their small gills working, moving like those of a fish, but then you notice that the rise and fall of its breathing is light, almost as if it is taking air through both systems. It must be so for them to live out of the water for such long periods of time."

"We need such devices, my captain, for breathing on board those stinking vessels of ours."

"Yes, if our friend Rondo over there gets a bellyful of beans and pork fat, the whole ship is in danger of choking to death or exploding like a musket," Padilla joked.

The two men were silent a moment as they listened to the comforting sound of the men as they spoke and talked of things other than death and this accursed mission. Then Padilla placed his diary in his belt pouch and looked over at his friend.

"When we entered the water in the outer valley, the stone monoliths, what did you think of them?"

"I was hoping that subject would not have arisen after the sun went down, if at all," Torrez said as he gently laid the small animal on the ground and watched a moment as it scurried away. "As for what I thought at the time? They scared me." He looked over at Padilla and could make out the captain's eyes on him. "You know me, I fear no man, or for that matter, nothing I have come across before. But those carvings gave me chills as I looked upon them, even as I ridiculed our men for the same reason."

"The Watchers of this valley, gods of the lagoon, that's what I called them in my diary. They were very old carvings, I suspect even older than some of the Inca dwellings we found in Peru."

"The age isn't what concerned me, my Captain, it was the forms themselves. I would hate to run into one of those while bathing, I'll tell you."

Padilla laughed loudly and was about to comment when a shrill piercing scream ripped through the night around them. The small creatures screeched and jabbered at the noise and shot off for the water, making little splashes as they dove for the safety of the lagoon. Padilla and Torrez were up in a second, Ivan with his sword drawn.

"What is it?" Padilla called to his men as they entered the circle of light cast by the fire. The men were angry, yelling as they pointed forward toward the small shoreline.

One man stood at the head of the others and was holding the limp and obviously lifeless body of one of the little creatures. He had the small animal clutched by its broken neck, and it dangled, almost formless in the firelight.

"You bloody bastard!" one of his men yelled. "Why did you have to do that?"

The man who was standing and facing everyone was none other than Suarez. The huge man stood his ground and stared back at the men, almost daring them to make a move toward him. He had no armor and his scarlet shirt glimmered as if with blood in the firelight.

"What is happening here?" Padilla asked, knowing all too well the answer to his question.

One of the soldiers stepped forward, a boy of only twenty, pointing to where the big man stood.

"That bastard did that for no other reason than the want of killing."

"He bit me and I will kill anything I wish, man or animal," Suarez said, still looking at the group rather than at his captain, shaking the lifeless body of the harmless creature.

"The man is mad, Captain, we must put him down as we would a dog with the foaming sickness," Torrez hissed, stepping closer to Suarez and forgetting his earlier words of restraint. His sword was pointing straight at the big man's chest.

"He bit you by accident, you're the one who pulled the

bread away and allowed his teeth to strike you instead of the bread," another man said as the others shouted agreement.

"Suarez, you have caused enough trouble, and it ends here, now, tonight," Padilla stated flatly and without emotion. He reached over and made his lieutenant lower his sword. "This will be my responsibility; you will stand down, my friend."

"You must not go into armed combat, my Captain, we cannot risk you. I will do it."

Suarez tossed the dead creature onto the sand, backed up three paces to the water's edge, and slowly drew his sword.

"I will make quick work of the man who comes for me," he said, slicing the sword through the air.

The rest of the men placed hands on swords or pistols, demonstrating their willingness to dispatch this man. They would make sure he brought them no more ill will.

"Stand down, all you men," Padilla said as he advanced, drawing his own thin blade, not removing his eyes from Suarez. "This is your captain's duty."

Suddenly small explosions of water erupted from the lagoon as dozens of the small creatures burst through to the surface, some clearing the water by two and three feet. They hurriedly swam to the far side of the lagoon, and before the men knew what they were looking at, the fast and agile animals were all scrambling up trees and large bushes on the opposite shore. They jabbered back at the water they had just exited and then grew suddenly quiet. That was when the men noticed that the animal sounds in the deep night had ceased, as if the entire jungle had grown mute as the two Spaniards faced each other.

Suarez had backed further into the water waiting for the advance of Padilla. But he had turned at the sound of the small creatures and their noisy flight from the water.

"Rondo, take five men and follow the shoreline and see what you can see. Something has frightened them," Torrez ordered.

Rondo pointed out five men, and they broke free from the group and started to walk slowly down the slim shoreline, buckling their armor and drawing their swords as they did. Rondo cocked his two pistols and then placed himself at the head of the small band of Spaniards. They walked cautiously, and then they disappeared around some bushes at the turn in the lagoon.

Padilla was as calm as the night around them as he advanced on the larger Suarez. He slowly brought his sword up toward the other man's barrel chest. Suarez smiled and moved deeper into the water and swung his own sword in a slow deliberate arc, parting it with a swish. Then as he saw the anger etching the face of Padilla, he backed deeper into the dark water.

The remaining men in camp froze when they heard the large man shout in terror as he was grabbed from beneath the water, his legs jerked out from under him so hard that one moment he was screaming and the next he had vanished. The big man surfaced briefly, splashing and in shock with the whites of his eyes showing brightly, and then he was quickly pulled into the lagoon before he could utter a second cry of pain or terror at what was happening. Suarez quickly disappeared below the roiling surface with nothing but bubbles and two quick slashes of his shining sword to mark his trail to death's door.

"What in the name of God was that?" Torrez yelled as he ran to the water's edge.

Men pointed, and then they all saw the bubbles and a sharp "V"-shaped wake surface as something was traveling fast toward the far side of the lagoon, toward the spot that Torrez had sent Rondo and the five others. They soon heard splashing and screams of terror splitting the quiet night, and two loud reports as Rondo fired his pistols. Then amongst the screams of men and the dying echo of the gunshots, they all heard a sound they would take with them to their graves. The roar was like a deep echo of an enraged demon from their nightmares. The horrid sound reverberated and sent chills down their spines.

The screams of his men ended as suddenly as they had begun, and in an instant the night became still once again.

Torrez was suddenly at the stunned Padilla's side, pressing his armor into his hands. The captain sheathed his sword and slipped the heavy iron onto his back and chest. Then they watched the spot where the men had disappeared just moments before. Suddenly a dark figure of a man emerged through the bushes and stumbled forward, obviously wounded. Two soldiers ran to the man and brought him into the bright circle cast by the firelight. There were deep gouges in the man's face and arms as if he had been mauled by a tiger. The punctures in his armor were deep and ragged. The soldier's left eye was missing and he cried out, claiming for all to hear that the Devil had risen from the water.

Padilla ran over, knelt next to his soldier, and grimaced as the young man's wounds were some of the worst he had ever seen. The rest of the men turned to the lagoon and watched. The jungle had grown quiet around them as the captain heard the man cough out the same words as before, only the ending was different. *The Devil has risen from the water and he has come for his offering.* Then the man's eyes were void of life as his pain ended and darkness covered him.

Padilla didn't hesitate in ordering his men to form up. The sentries had entered the campsite with swords drawn and flintlocks aimed. They had lost seven men in as many minutes to something in the lagoon that he cared never to see or even hear again. He would leave this place, retreat, and never venture into the jungle again. They would return to Pizarro and tell him they were cowards and that he could punish them however he deemed fit, but he could never send them here again and that was good enough.

"We march west tonight, and we stop only when we are under the light of the Lord's sun once again."

The Devil can have his home, Padilla thought, and he prayed that no man would ever find this place again, for men were not meant to be here. He would give the map he had made of the valley to Father Corinth and warn him that this was truly the playground of demons.

With the night sentries on the point, Padilla ordered his soldiers forward. But just as they nervously took their first step, the night exploded around them. The animal came at them, not from the water, but from the bush. It seemed to have followed the tracks of the soldier who had escaped it. The darkness around the screaming men was rent with the powerful and enraged cry of the beast as it attacked. Padilla felt the warmth of something striking his face, and then the coppery taste of blood filled his mouth.

"Captain, into the water while there is time. Fall back, men, into the water and swim for it!" Torrez screamed as he pushed the shocked Padilla into the cool lagoon. "We can gain the trail on the other side."

Padilla was still trying to peer into the blackness as he was pulled away by Torrez. That was when the beast stepped closer to one of the open firepits and swiped its strangely formed hand at one of his men. The soldier was silent as the claws raked down his face and tore through his chest armor. As the Spaniards watched in horror, the animal was struck from behind with a sword, and then a shot rang out from a pistol. The beast did not slow down, even though Padilla saw the ball strike the animal in the upper chest, slinging scales and red meat into the air. The beast screamed a cry of outrage and quickly reached out and grabbed the hand that wielded the sword and easily lofted the man over its head. Then it threw the body against one of the large trees as if he weighed no more than a piece of firewood.

Another Spaniard made a break for the trail they had used to enter the valley, and that was when Padilla saw the real speed of the creature. It easily headed off the soldier and attacked from the front, throwing its massive weight against the man and driving him to the ground.

"Look at the size of this devil," Padilla mumbled while Torrez pushed his captain into deeper water. "It is a man!"

Padilla snapped out of his shock as the cool water closed over his head. He reached for the buckled straps that held his armor in place and quickly shrugged out of it. The heavy armor was sent to the bottom as Padilla pushed his way to the surface. As his head broke free of the surface, he saw Torrez ahead of him swimming for all he was worth for the far side of the lagoon. He started after his lieutenant while the screaming of his remaining men continued on shore.

Padilla was starting to lose the strength in his arms after ten minutes of swimming blindly across the lagoon. His ears were filled with his own struggles and the roar of water ahead of him emanating from the waterfall. His arms were flailing and his knee-high boots had filled with water, and he was finding it very difficult to maintain the momentum needed to keep his head above water. He was starting to swallow more and more of the strangely cool and sweet water. He felt himself go under and was aware of water flowing down his throat. He thought he heard shouts as he began to give up his struggle and let the cool water embrace him.

It was comforting because now he wouldn't have to face any of his men who had survived and he could accompany those who hadn't on their final journey toward forgiveness for what they had wrought on the innocent *Sincaro*. Captain Padilla even managed a smile as his lungs took in his last breath of, not air, but water. Suddenly he felt hands grabbing at him from above. Even his beard was pulled on as he was lifted up out of the water. His eyes rolled as he tried to catch one single blessed breath but found his lungs were full.

"Captain, Captain," Torrez shouted.

Padilla felt himself rolled over and his back struck as if it were an anvil. He felt his spine pop as he was pushed on heavily by Torrez trying desperately to expel the water from his lungs.

"Breathe, my Captain, don't you leave me here in this black place!"

Padilla felt the warm water vomit from his stomach and lungs, and the pain hit him in earnest when he tried to replace the water with precious air. He felt his body spasm as his lungs slowly brought in the needed oxygen. A loud moan escaped his shivering lips, and he slowly brought in another breath.

Padilla rolled over and tried to sit up but failed miserably. Other hands quickly grabbed for him, and he was lifted to his feet. He looked over and saw that the two soldiers were

Juan Navarro, a cook's assistant, and Javier Ramón, a black-smith. The captain saw they were only feet from the water-fall. He looked up and saw where the water cascaded from somewhere high above. He coughed, trying to clear his throat of the remaining water in his throat. He saw Torrez standing at the small shore, staring out across the lagoon.

"The screaming of our men has stopped," he said without turning as Padilla approached and watched the distant, dwin-dling fires of their destroyed camp across the lagoon.

After a moment, Torrez took Padilla by his shoulders and turned him away from the distant scene of destruction. As they walked toward the wall of rock that ascended straight up from the lagoon and bordered the waterfall, Torrez knew they were being watched.

"Look," he softly spoke, not wanting to attract the atten-tion of the other men.

Padilla looked up at the spot Torrez had indicated. An-other of the statues carved into the wall looked down upon them. It resembled the same beast that had just attacked them, and the same as the two images that guarded the tribu-tary. It had been hidden from their vantage point across the lagoon. This one was larger and it stood alone. How had they missed seeing it during the daylight hours? Padilla didn't know.

They both turned as they heard a loud splash in the water. The noise had come from their destroyed campsite. Both men watched and saw the ripples and large wake that was streaking toward their side of the lagoon.

"Captain, Lieutenant, there is a cave rising above the wa-terline under the falls," Navarro said as he approached. "You won't believe it, there are stairs."

Torrez turned and looked at the sheer cliff in front of them which held only the carved figure of the animal that was now their God of judgment. Then he looked down the shoreline at the distant jungle. Surely, whatever this creature was that was coming after them would surface long before they could reach the trees. He frantically looked around, and then pushed Navarro forward.

"Take us to this cave, soldier," he shouted as he started pulling Padilla after him.

The three men joined Ramón the blacksmith, who was waving for them to hurry. He had caught sight of the underwater demon as it sped to this side of the lagoon. As they came upon the waterfall, the roar drowned out all talk. Torrez looked up and then down at the point where the water struck the lagoon. Then he saw it. It was just a darker outline against the cliff face, but it was there. The cave rose about ten feet above the water and then disappeared into the depths. He saw no other choice. He dove headfirst into the water, the others, including Padilla, followed. They had to dive deep to avoid the crushing water of the falls, the vortex of which pushed them even further into the depths as they fought to swim into the dark and forbidding cave. As they disappeared, the creature changed its underwater course and swam toward the white water of the falls.

Two months later, a lone survivor was saved from the river. At first the Spaniards who discovered him thought him to be an Indian, but soon realized the man had been part of Captain Padilla's expedition. The men had struggled to carry the survivor back into Peru but knew they would never make it. Word was sent to Father Corinth and the survivor, knowing this, had miraculously clung to life. The man was dying from exposure and a strange sickness the men in camp didn't recognize but could only guess at. His only possession was a book the men had mistakenly taken for a Bible that the survivor held tightly to his injured chest. Every time they tried to relieve him of the book, the man would rise like a tiger to protect it. They even tried to pry his fingers from it when he had passed out, but that had proven just as futile.

When Father Corinth arrived at the small outpost with a rank of Pizarro's personal guard, the man was waiting for him, only he waited on his deathbed. For hours the lone survivor of the expedition spoke softly with Corinth. The priest had listened, never interrupting the soldier while he examined his wounds and nursed him through the strange sickness. As he spoke, gasping in inner pain and getting weaker for each word he managed to hiss out through clenched teeth, he reached into his tunic and withdrew two small objects. One was a large golden nugget. The other was a strange green mineral, a strange chalk-like substance imbedded in stone. It was strangely warm to the touch. The soldier pulled Corinth close to him, close enough that the priest could feel his high temperature rising from his face. A dire warning was told, barely audible and with fetid breath. Corinth removed his large cross from around his neck and removed the bottom portion. The inside of the cross was hollow and he easily slid the small mineral samples into it. The cross was made of a soft metal covered with gold, not only for beauty but to give the cheap metal more strength. It was of a sort the church frowned upon as being arrogant, but it had been a ceremonial gift from his dead mother given to him on the day he took his vows. It was very beautifully engraved and far too large, and she had spent every ounce of her meager savings to present him with it. He put the end back on the cross and placed it around his neck.

It was long after sunup when Father Corinth finally emerged from the small hut, and he carried the book with him.

"How is he, Father?" one of the soldiers asked. "Is there any news of our friends? Is Captain Padilla still alive?"

"The soldier is dead. His name was Ivan Torrez."

"Lieutenant Torrez? We know this man, he looked nothing like him," another soldier said as many of the escort gathered to hear the Father.

"The plague will change a man's features so you would not even recognize your own brother."

The men stepped away in fear. That one word was enough to weaken their knees and make the brave conquerors cringe.

Father Corinth brought the book to his chest and started to turn from the gathered soldiers.

"What of the expedition, Father, did he give a location of their whereabouts?"

He stopped and turned. "Captain Padilla and his men will

stay where they are. Get your men ready to break camp, and bury Lieutenant Torrez deep. Honor him, he was a brave man," Corinth said as he bowed his head and crossed himself. The Padilla diary, which contained the unholy route the doomed expedition had charted, was clutched tightly to his chest.

He slowly moved away from the stunned men. The Father knew he would have to either destroy the diary and the map that would again take the greed of man to follow Padilla's directions, or bury them so deep no one could ever find them. The diary was the only proof of what wonders the captain had found under the falls of that lost lagoon, but because of men like Francisco Pizarro, the contents could never see the light of day. For only death could come to those that ventured into that dark lagoon and he would take it upon himself to make sure the pope sided with his decision.

A few months before the death of Francisco Pizarro, the general ordered one last expedition sent out to try and trace the route of Captain Padilla's ill-fated journey. The Spaniards found only helmets, rusted armor, rotted clothing, and broken swords on a path that stretched for thirty miles along the Amazon, which was clear evidence of a running battle with an enemy that had since disappeared into the jungle. The trail leading to the deep tributary that led to that dark and beautiful lagoon was never found. As for the men of Padilla's brave band, the Spaniards never found a trace of them or the gold they had sought. Pizarro, in what little time remained to him, would continue to lust for El Dorado. But in the end another generation of explorers and adventurers would have to do the searching.

Rumors of the lost expedition of Captain Padilla filtered down through the years, and even a few old artifacts turned up from time to time as the jungle begrudgingly gave up her digested secrets. Whatever lived in that forgotten lagoon would wait patiently for men to come into its realm once again.